DARK ROOMS

Lynda La Plante was born in Liverpool. She trained for the stage at RADA and worked with the National Theatre and RSC before becoming a television actress. She then turned to writing and made her breakthrough with the phenomenally successful TV series *Widows*. She has written over thirty international novels, all of which have been bestsellers, and is the creator of the Anna Travis, Lorraine Page and *Trial and Retribution* series. Her original script for the much-acclaimed *Prime Suspect* won awards from BAFTA, Emmy, British Broadcasting and Royal Television Society, as well as the 1993 Edgar Allan Poe Award.

Lynda is one of only three screenwriters to have been made an honorary fellow of the British Film Institute and was awarded the BAFTA Dennis Potter Best Writer Award in 2000. In 2008, she was awarded a CBE in the Queen's Birthday Honours List for services to Literature, Drama and Charity.

Join the Lynda La Plante Readers' Club at
www.bit.ly/LyndaLaPlanteClub
www.lyndalaplante.com
Facebook @LyndaLaPlanteCBE
Twitter @LaPlanteLynda

Lynda La Plante

DARK ROOMS

ZAFFRE

This is a work of fiction. Names, places, events and incidents are
either the products of the
author's imagination or used fictitiously. Any resemblance
to actual persons, living or dead,
or actual events is purely coincidental.

First published in Great Britain by Zaffre in 2022
This edition published in the United States of America in 2022 by
Zaffre
Zaffre is an imprint of Bonnier Books UK
4th Floor, Victoria House, Bloomsbury Square, London WC1B 4DA

Paperback ISBN: 978-1-83877-951-1
Ebook ISBN: 978-1-83877-953-5

For information, contact
251 Park Avenue South, Floor 12, New York, New York 10010
www.bonnierbooks.co.uk

For Noel Fitzpatrick and his wonderful team at Fitzpatrick Referrals, who helped save Hugo, you have mine and Hugo's sincere thanks and gratitude.

CHAPTER ONE

'Detective Inspector Jane Tennison.' Jane had repeated it out loud four times, looking at herself in the mirror. She couldn't help admiring her reflection, enjoying the reality of her new promotion. It hadn't been easy to get to where she was.

She hadn't shared the news with her family yet, deciding that she would go and see them, taking a bottle of celebratory champagne. Her parents had been somewhat confused by the fact that Jane had had to spend almost a year in uniform as part of the promotion process. Although she had tried to explain the reasons, her mother seemed to think she had been demoted, so Jane felt that the less said about it the better.

Due to her work schedule, she had spent very little time at her new home recently. Moving into the two-bedroom terraced house had been a major step up for her on the property ladder, but the responsibility attached to owning a much larger property was only just beginning to dawn on her. There were a lot of repairs that needed doing, including a persistent electrical fault in the kitchen. She decided that she would make a list of what needed doing. Until she was given the location of the station that she would be working from, she could spend more time focusing on redecorating and organising her new home. She had already made two purchases for the kitchen, a new fridge freezer and a washing machine. After passing the exams, she had been back on shift work and busy running a uniform team. Now, with her promotion and on a higher wage, she was determined to get all the home improvements necessary.

Jane glanced in the bathroom mirror again before leaving for her parents'. 'Good evening, I am Detective Inspector Jane Tennison.' She was secretly bursting with pride and was eager to impart the news.

* * *

Although Jane had a front door key to her parents' flat in Maida Vale, she rarely used it as she didn't like to invade their privacy. Before tonight, she'd always called her mother to arrange a visit and had never just turned up. She rang the doorbell and her father pulled open the front door, looking at his daughter with delight.

'This is a surprise!' He ushered Jane into the hall.

Through the sitting-room door, Jane could see her parents' neighbours sitting on the sofa. On the coffee table in front of them was a tray of sherry glasses and neatly cut sandwiches, while the radio had the volume turned up loud.

'Guess who's here?' her father called out.

Rather embarrassed, Jane held up the bottle of Moët & Chandon. Her mother clapped her hands.

'This is wonderful, darling! You know Mr and Mrs Murphy, from the flat above? And the Silvermans from the basement flat are going to be joining us any minute. Why didn't you call and tell me you were coming over? It's going to be the most fantastic evening.'

Jane was feeling distinctly nonplussed. She hadn't expected her mother to be hosting a gathering. It was clearly neither the time nor the place to announce her promotion.

'Good God!' her father said as he took the bottle out of Jane's hand. 'This is very expensive. I'll put it in the fridge.'

'Actually, Dad, it's really for a celebration . . .'

'I quite agree. I've never known your mother so enthusiastic about hosting, but she seems to be enjoying herself. Pam and Tony are coming along with the grandchildren as well. Come into the kitchen.'

As her mother returned to her guests, Jane followed her father into the kitchen as he put her champagne bottle into the fridge.

'Is everything all right, Jane?' he asked.

'Yes, everything's fine. I was just stopping by for a few minutes to tell you the good news. I've been promoted. I'm now Detective Inspector. I wanted to tell you both personally . . .' She hesitated, then lied. 'But I was actually just on my way to meet a friend for dinner.'

'Well, that *is* good news,' he said, rather unconvincingly.

'I'm waiting to find out which station I'll be working from. I just wanted you and Mum to know. But I won't take up any more of your time.'

'Are you sure? You know we have the Silvermans coming up soon? They have a lovely daughter, although I believe their son is in a bit of trouble. Why don't you just stay for a glass of sherry?'

'No, Dad, I'll just slip off. I don't want to intrude any further.'

He gave a resigned smile. 'I understand. I think your mother is getting her second wind in life! How is everything at the new house?'

'Fine, thanks. There are a few electrical problems, and I'm having some new kitchen appliances fitted, but I'm just going to take it one step at a time.'

He nodded. 'That's sensible. Just make sure you get a proper professional to do the electrics. Don't just go for the cheapest. We've had a problem with a light switch in the hall for six months. When one of the light bulbs pops, it trips all the lights in the hall. We've had two "more than my job's worth" electricians in organised by the caretaker but neither of them could fix it.'

'I'll take your good advice, Dad,' Jane replied, eager to leave.

By the time she reached her car, she felt a bit foolish for not staying. But the truth was her parents' friends interrogating her about her work had always made her feel uncomfortable. At least her parents hadn't asked if she was seeing anyone, as they usually did. The fact was that she had been focusing all her attention on getting promoted and hadn't had time for a relationship. She was now looking forward to finding out which station she would be attached to and what she'd be working on. As a detective inspector, she was really hoping that she might be assigned to an important case.

* * *

Mrs Tennison couldn't believe that Jane had left without saying goodbye. Even her husband telling her that she'd only popped round to tell them that she had been promoted didn't satisfy her.

'I mean, how long has it been since we had one evening with her? I know she's been very busy, and all this going back into uniform doesn't really seem to make sense if she's supposed to have been promoted now.'

'I think she was on her way out to a celebration dinner. She just wanted us to be the first to know her good news,' Mr Tennison said, trying to appease her.

He was saved from any further discussion by the doorbell, heralding the arrival of the Silvermans.

* * *

When Jane returned home, she felt depressed. It was a Saturday night, and there were no friends eager to go for a celebratory drink with her. She had been so intent on her work, she had not kept up the friendship with her next-door neighbours, Gerry and Vi, even though to begin with Gerry had been very helpful, offering to do any small jobs she needed. Actually, she had felt he was a bit too nosy. She knew his dog (who had liked to use her gate post to urinate on) had died a few months ago, and she was a bit relieved that this meant his day and evening walks past her house were no longer so frequent. As for the young couple in the house on the other side, she hadn't met them yet as they appeared to leave very early in the morning and return before she had got home.

She walked into her kitchen where the new fridge freezer was still in its wrapping, next to the washing machine. She had purchased it so that she would no longer have to go to the launderette, but had no notion of how to plumb it in.

She put the kettle on the hob and, feeling peckish, decided she'd make some cheese on toast. But the bread was mouldy, and the sliced cheese looked unappetising. She would have to go to Bickley's Best, the small local corner shop a five-minute walk away.

Jane was already on good terms with the Caribbean owner who ran the shop with his wife and nephews. Winston greeted her warmly as she entered.

'Good evening, Jane.'

She gathered a sliced loaf, a block of cheddar cheese and a tin of baked beans and put them down on the checkout counter.

'Having a party, are we?' he said, with a mischievous grin. Jane turned and took down a bottle of vodka from the shelf next to her.

'I wasn't, but I will now. Do you have any tonic water?'

'It's on the opposite side, with the soft drinks.'

As she picked up a large bottle of Indian tonic water, she noticed the board with advertisements for flats to rent, along with numerous cards for interior decorators and plumbers, including one very professional-looking flyer for Fraser & Son.

She turned to Winston. 'These electricians ... can you recommend them?'

He nodded enthusiastically. 'I most certainly can. They fixed up my nephew's garage with strip lights. He also had a lot of problems with his garage doors, but they sorted it really good. And if you want any decorating done, Dwight – the card next to theirs – is very professional.'

Jane jotted the number down. She paid for her groceries and by the time she got home, felt in need of a vodka and tonic, only to discover the ice box in the old fridge would need a hammer and chisel to get any ice out.

Although it was now early evening, she put in a call to Fraser & Son, noting that their address was local, in Bromley. The answerphone clicked on and she listened to the message.

'You have called Fraser & Son electrical engineers. Our office hours are Monday to Friday 9 a.m. to 5 p.m. Please leave your

name and number and we will return your call as soon as possible. Let us know if you need urgent assistance.'

Jane left a message saying that she could wait until Monday. Hopefully by then she would know which station she was going to be working from.

At half past seven, having consumed two large vodka and tonics, Jane got a call back from the electrician to arrange an appointment for nine o'clock on Sunday morning. Mr Fraser said that he would give her an estimate for checking her wiring and suggested that the washing machine might require a plumber, but his son would be able to recommend someone.

Jane thought about getting a second estimate from another electrician but decided to wait until she had met Mr Fraser. In the meantime, she began re-organising the kitchen to make room for the new appliances.

* * *

At half past six on Sunday morning the foreman, John Bishop, was the first to arrive at the building site in Stockwell. The site was surrounded by high corrugated-iron fences and Bishop began removing the chains from the corrugated gate. He was expecting three skips to be delivered for clearing the large garden of the five-storey house that was being demolished, after a series of delays caused by the council.

It still amazed him that the huge Victorian house, with its neglected half-acre garden, was still standing in the middle of this redeveloped area. It was going to take considerable time to clear the dense overgrowth and ancient trees, as well as the large rotting greenhouse which was only being held up by the overgrown plants and weeds growing inside. If there had ever been a path from the back of the house, it could no longer be seen. Also on his schedule was the demolition of an old air-raid shelter situated, according to the council plans, almost in the centre of the large overgrown garden.

The demolition team began arriving at seven, and the large digging equipment to clear the garden was due to be arriving on a heavy loading lorry at eight. It was an exceedingly costly project, and they were under pressure to get the land cleared as soon as possible so the new owners could begin building a block of flats on the site.

Bishop had given the men orders that as soon as the skips were full, they were to be taken away immediately and replaced with empty ones, knowing it would take several loads to clear that volume of debris. But if they could complete the garden clearance by the afternoon, then use the same team to demolish the air-raid shelter, they should be on schedule. When he had been overseeing the demolition of the house itself, he had been astonished at the size of the basement which, according to the council, had been off-limits to the tenants, along with the garden. No wonder it was such a jungle, he thought.

* * *

As soon as Edward Fraser, the son in the electrical firm Fraser & Son, walked into Jane's kitchen he had told her that she would require a plumber, as her new washing machine would need to be plumbed in by drilling through the wall to connect the water pipe to the mains. On the other hand, connecting her new fridge freezer was a very simple matter. His main concern, though, was that the kitchen's electrical circuits had probably been installed when the house had been built in the 1930s.

Jane stood in the kitchen doorway. 'Are you saying I can't just plug it in?'

'Usually you can do that, but I think with your electrics you might have some major problems. I need more time to check all the wiring. I noticed that there was a dimmer switch in your hallway.'

Jane nodded. 'Yes. It doesn't work, though. How long would it take to rewire everything in the kitchen?'

Edward Fraser had never come across anyone quite like Jane Tennison. She seemed to be absolutely clueless, and when he showed her some of the damaged wires she became quite agitated.

'I haven't been living here very long. Are you saying that I could have been electrocuted?'

He smiled reassuringly. 'No, I'm just saying that it would be wise for you to have your kitchen rewired. I need to take up the floorboards and check underneath, but you've got considerable damp around your sink unit. If you're going to have a washing machine installed you really need to check the existing plumbing too.'

Jane was beginning to get annoyed. She knew she had got the house at a very good price, even though she had been told by her solicitor that the property needed some renovation. Now she was in a quandary as to how much trust she could put in this electrician, Edward Fraser, or whether should she get a second opinion.

'Can you give me an estimate for the works?' she asked.

He shrugged his shoulders. 'What estimate do you want? For rewiring? For checking the damp as well? And as I said, I think you should get a professional plumber in for the washing machine.'

'Do you think you could give me an estimate for the whole thing, and if you know a good plumber then perhaps he could come to the house to quote. At the moment I have a kitchen that I'm rather afraid to use.'

Edward looked pointedly at his watch and said that he had another job to go to, but he would be able to fax her his estimate and would make inquiries with a friend of his who was a professional plumber.

Jane sighed. 'I don't have a fax machine here.' And she could have added that at the moment she didn't even know where she would be working from.

They eventually agreed that he would come back later in the afternoon with his friend, and together they would give her the estimate to complete all the necessary work.

* * *

Eight skips had now been filled with the debris from the garden in Stockwell, but the work was continuing, with a digger trying to break down the roots that had once belonged to an enormous oak tree. The tree itself had taken considerable time to cut down, and Bishop had now assigned six men to the clearing process as he was concerned they were falling behind schedule – not to mention the numerous complaints about the traffic disruption the work was causing. The police had been called out every time the full skips had been removed because they blocked most of the main road.

His hard hat on, Bishop was now talking to the representative of the new owners of the property, who told him that many of the old Victorian bricks should be put in storage as they were quite valuable. Holding his clipboard in his left hand, Bishop said they would need scaffolding to be erected on the standing walls, but he could make sure the bricks were salvaged.

Bishop heard a shout and turned to see one of the men working on the gardens clearly in a distressed state. 'There's almost been a fatal accident,' he explained breathlessly. Bishop, keen to end the conversation, followed his worker back to the garden.

The ten-foot-high corrugated fencing which had been erected around the half-acre site had been pulled down to allow the diggers to enter. Bishop stood in shock as he was told that a large crater had appeared in the ground, and the digger had almost tipped into it. When the machine backed away, it had clipped the side of the now partially visible air-raid shelter. Bishop made his way around the crater as the men gathered, all looking down. It appeared that at one time it had been some kind of tunnel as they could see part of a concrete wall. He instructed the men to stop working as he checked through the plans on his clipboard. He was surprised at the size of the air-raid shelter as the measurements didn't correspond with his plans, and there was certainly no reference to any kind of tunnel.

Bishop was joined by Tom, the worker who had been overseeing the clearance of the garden, a huge man also wearing a hard hat. 'I reckon we need to take a look inside the shelter,' he told

Bishop. 'I'm worried more craters could appear, and my team can't work safely.'

The shelter had what looked like a heavy garden door, with iron studs and hinges, secured by a large chain. Another worker appeared with a jack to break open the chain and the three of them heaved open the door, releasing a dreadful stench of mould and sewage. Wincing, Bishop stepped gingerly into the first chamber and was again surprised at the size of it. There were old tables, chairs, cupboards storing tinned food, lamps and candles. Shining a powerful torch beam, Bishop made his way to an archway.

'None of this is on the bloody plans I've got,' he muttered, shaking his head. 'This place is twice the size that's indicated.'

There were four steps down to the second chamber where there was an array of old iron bedsteads stacked with blankets and pillows, all of them green with mildew. He shone the torch towards another door and could see the debris from where the digger had struck the outer corner. From the first chamber Tom called out that they needed to be careful that the shelter didn't collapse. Bishop moved cautiously further in and then almost dropped the torch in shock. There was a corpse lying on the mattress of a small cot bed.

He gasped. 'Jesus, God! Tom, you better get the police here. There's a bloody dead body. I'm coming out.'

Bishop had not stayed long enough to note that the grotesquely shrivelled victim was female, what remained of her long blonde hair spread like a halo around her skull. Nor did he notice the worst horror. The dead woman was chained to the bed.

CHAPTER TWO

Jane tried to keep her expression neutral as she scanned the detailed estimates from Edward Fraser and the plumber, Archie. Although at first the size of the estimates was a bit of a shock, with her promotion she would be earning around £12,000 to £13,000 a year, and she began to think that it would be sensible to agree to both of them. The fact that Archie was much older than Edward – known as Eddie – and had brought with him a number of letters of recommendation made him seem trustworthy.

She also decided that she would like Archie to look at her upstairs bathroom and toilet as she was thinking about having an en-suite in her bedroom. Eddie accompanied Archie upstairs and they spent a good fifteen minutes checking everything out. Jane stood by the open door as Archie examined a number of tiles and at the same time removed the side panel of the bath, pointing out that the carpet was badly stained so at some point there had been considerable flooding. They all then went back downstairs, and Jane made a pot of tea, whilst Archie discussed with Eddie what he felt the estimate would come to.

The phone rang in the hall and Jane hurried to pick up, instantly recognising the voice of her superintendent. 'You're going to be part of a team working out of Stockwell police station, Jane. Sorry for not contacting you earlier, but you need to be there first thing in the morning. The case you'll be working on has only just been brought to my attention, so I'm afraid I can't give you a lot of detail. All I know is that a body has been discovered by a demolition team on a building site. The DCI heading up the investigation is Detective Chief Inspector Wayne Carter. He's very experienced, and I'm certain it's going to be a very good fit. Any questions?'

'No, sir,' Jane replied, already feeling excited by the prospect of joining the investigation. 'Thank you, sir.'

When Jane returned to the kitchen, Archie had already left to complete another project he was working on.

Eddie pointed to the back door. 'I locked it after him.'

Jane smiled, impressed by the fact they had washed their mugs and left them on the draining board. Eddie leaned against the sink.

'Archie's a bit strait-laced, but he's a good guy. He thinks the job up in the bathroom will need more consideration, so he'd like to provide an estimate which includes that. He feels it's important that your plumbing upstairs is closely examined and reckons you may also require a new boiler.'

Jane sat down at the table and gathered all the estimates together, eager to get Eddie to begin work as soon as possible.

'Do you mind if I ask you a couple of personal questions?' she said.

'Sure, go ahead,' Eddie said.

'I'm sorry to have to ask this, but I need to know if either of you have had any criminal convictions of any sort?'

'Convictions? You mean prison time? No, I haven't and I'm damned sure Archie hasn't either. He's a straight-as-a-die kind of bloke.'

'Yes, I'm sure he is.' Jane nodded. 'I hope you understand why I need to ask these questions. You'll be having my house keys, so I need to know that you're trustworthy and reliable.'

'Well, you can trust and rely on me,' Eddie smiled. 'But you should ask Archie for yourself. Whilst I'm here, can I suggest you get some sort of security light in your porch? If you're coming home late at night it's quite dark out there, and there isn't much overhead lighting in the street.'

Jane nodded. 'Yes, I agree . . . When do you think you'll be able to start? I'm starting a new position over in Stockwell, so I'll be leaving first thing in the morning, and I'll be out all day. I often work very long hours, sometimes into the night if needed.'

Eddie hesitated. 'I can start immediately. Like I told you earlier, your wiring is pretty dangerous. Are you a nurse?'

'No, I'm actually a detective with the Metropolitan Police.'

Eddie gave a quick laugh. 'Well, I didn't see that one coming. I'd better do a good job, then!'

Jane fetched her spare keys and handed them to Eddie. 'Thank you,' she said, shaking his hand enthusiastically. 'If you need anything, I should be able to give you a work phone and fax number soon.' She paused. 'Do you work at weekends?'

Shrugging into his leather jacket he gave her a cheeky smile: 'If I want to get a job finished fast I do, yes.'

* * *

John Bishop was at his wit's end. The police had cordoned off the garden and the partly demolished house, as they examined the body that was still in the shelter. His team had been released and he had had to inform the owners that work had been stopped until further notice. Police patrol cars were parked at the opening of the corrugated-iron fence that had been used by the diggers and dumpers, and yellow-and-black crime scene tape was stretched across the opening. Bishop's men had placed long planks of wood across the large cavity that had appeared, but there were concerns that the tunnel might collapse. It had been confirmed that there was a locked door in the basement which presumably led into it.

Bishop insisted that none of this was marked on the council plans, and he could not be held responsible. But that didn't alter the fact that the cost of the delays to the demolition would be astronomical. And the fact that Detective Carter was arrogant and even abusive didn't help. Bishop had been repeatedly questioned about what he had touched inside the shelter, even though he had made it clear that he had only entered, seen the horrendous sight of the corpse by torchlight, then left.

Three SOCOs were now down in the shelter and Emra Saddell, a forensic scientist, was examining the corpse. She looked up as DCI Carter, being over six feet tall and of athletic build, stooped to enter the second chamber. He was a snazzy dresser who prided himself on his designer jackets and was known to wear rather overpowering cologne. He also had quite a reputation as a ladies' man, but Emra did not exactly find her heart racing as he joined her.

When Carter had first met her, he had presumed she was a clerk and told her he needed a white coffee with two sugars, as it was obvious the pathologist was going to keep him waiting! And he hadn't even apologised when she'd explained that she was, in fact, the pathologist.

As Carter approached, she pulled off her face mask – she had worn it into the bunker, having been tipped off that the stench in there was sickening.

'I would estimate she has been down here maybe eight or nine years,' she said, anticipating his first question. 'But I won't be able to confirm that until I have examined her more closely. As you can see, the ankle chain bolted to the ground would have become looser as she starved, but it was still tightly attached to her boot with her foot inside. I am not removing it here. Her clothes are modern, quite good quality, and I would estimate her age to be early twenties. She is wearing some gold bangles, which you can see from their position on the ground may have slipped from her wrist.'

Carter rubbed his nose. The stench was overpowering.

'When is she going to be removed? I've got the foreman pestering me about how long this is going to take. You found anything to identify her?' he said brusquely.

'I will take dental imprints as soon as she's in the lab and get onto a dental forensic odontologist, so that should help you. I would suggest you get on to missing persons. As I said, she's wearing rather good fashionable clothes and when her hair was attached to her skull it was in reasonable condition and well cut. She's been down here for a considerable time, so even though it must have been quite airtight, the decomposition is pretty advanced; I can only give you more specific details when I have her on my table. Hopefully that'll be first thing tomorrow morning.'

Carter nodded and turned to the SOCO. 'Found anything to tell us who she was, or why she was down here? A handbag or coat or anything?'

The SOCO shook his head. 'No, nothing in either chamber.'

Carter frowned, while the photographer continued taking shots of the chamber as well as close-up pictures of the corpse, focusing on the ankle chain and bolts.

Carter checked his watch. It was already after seven and he was concerned the generator for the big lamps would soon be running out. But he was also keen to get home and remove the hideous stench from his usually immaculate clothes.

* * *

Jane was dressed in one of her best suits, over a clerical-collared shirt, with her camel overcoat. She had washed and blow-dried her hair and was wearing it in a fashionable pageboy style. She had even applied some makeup and lipstick.

She arrived at Stockwell station just before a quarter past eight, driving through the open station yard gates. She noted the number of spaces already allocated to officers, with the majority of the space for patrol cars. Parking as unobtrusively as possible, she went to the rear door of the station. There was a keypad for entry, but she had no idea what the code was, so she walked round to the front.

The façade was reminiscent of her days at Hackney, even down to the old blue lamp above the station door. There was a rather overweight, balding duty sergeant on reception, who seemed to take great pleasure in asking for her identification before giving her directions to the main incident room.

As she climbed the worn stone stairs, a girl with bouncing curly blonde hair appeared and looked at Jane with surprise.

'Can I help you?'

'I'm sure you can,' Jane said, affably. 'I'm Detective Inspector Jane Tennison.'

'Oh, I'm Barbara. I'm the CID clerk. If you turn to the right, there is a ladies' toilet which we have only just been allocated – before that any women working here had to go to the top floor. If you continue down that corridor you'll see the double doors which lead into the main offices.'

Barbara turned to continue down the stairs and then looked back. 'Are they expecting you?'

Jane found her tone rather over-familiar and replied curtly, 'I certainly hope they are. I'm joining DCI Carter's team.'

Barbara didn't seem to react as Jane proceeded down the corridor and entered the main room where all the DCs' and DSs' desks were lined up. There didn't appear to be anyone there expecting her, but just then the double doors banged open, almost hitting her, as people started streaming in. A couple of young officers muttered 'Excuse me', but otherwise they just ignored her. Jane was wondering what to do when a suave-looking man emerged from one of the doors leading off the main office and strode towards her. He was wearing a chequered jacket, pristine pressed trousers and highly polished shoes.

'You must be Jane Tennison,' he said, looking her over. 'I'm DCI Carter. Glad you could join the team. We've had rather a night of it and haven't yet had time to get the incident board up and rolling.'

She followed him as he made quick introductions to various officers, before gesturing towards a door next to his office. It had clearly once been the corner of the main room and was now partitioned off to make a very small office, but at least it had a window.

'Park yourself in there, then come in and I'll give you an update. Not that there's much to tell, and it's quite an unpleasant case.'

Jane didn't even have time to thank him as she stepped into her 'cubby hole' of an office. She hung her coat on a hook on the back of the door and looked at the small worn desk. It had three drawers on either side, an empty in-tray, a telephone and a desk chair that had seen better days. The wall had faded markings where previously, pictures had hung. She placed her briefcase down on the desk, took out her notebook, then ran a brush through her hair and checked her watch. It was nine o'clock.

Her office door opened, and the bubbly blonde Barbara popped her head round. 'Fancy a coffee?'

'No, thank you,' Jane said.

Barbara shrugged. 'The canteen's two floors up if you change your mind.' She turned without shutting the door. Jane was already finding her irritating.

She straightened her jacket and with her notepad and pencil ready went out into the main room and knocked on DCI Carter's door. He was sitting behind a modern desk and his office was at least twice the size of hers, with a reasonable carpet and two armchairs. There were several rows of bookcases which were crammed with files and Met Police manuals.

'Right, are you settled in, then?' he asked, waving his hand for her to sit without looking at her. She was about to reply when he looked up.

'The superintendent reckoned you would be a great asset on this case as you did some good work on the corpse of that old nun.'

Jane sat down in one of the armchairs, unsure whether she should thank him, but Carter didn't appear to expect her to answer.

'Well, you've got another old corpse case here. We don't actually know how long the body's been in the shelter . . . we'll only find out after forensics and pathology have done their work. But Emra estimated eight or nine years.'

Jane had no notion of what shelter he was talking about and before she could ask him there was a knock on the door and Barbara appeared, carrying a mug of coffee.

'They're putting the photographs up, sir,' she said, placing the mug on his desk.

Carter gestured to Jane. 'Barbara, this is Detective Inspector Jane Tennison.'

'Yes, we met on the stairs.' She flounced out as Carter took a beer mat and placed it under his coffee.

'Obviously our priority will be identifying the victim, but I think you'd best go and familiarise yourself with the details first. When Emra Saddell is ready, we should go over to the lab for the PM.'

Jane felt she'd been dismissed. 'Yes, sir.' She left Carter's office and went and stood in front of the large noticeboard, trying to work out what the case was all about. The photographs from the scene at the shelter were certainly shocking, but Jane couldn't help feeling deflated. She was acutely aware of how much work it would entail to uncover the victim's identity, and also that of the perpetrator. She had worked for weeks on her last investigation into the thirty-year-old corpse of a nun. The thought of having to do another similarly laborious investigation made her feel as if her new rank had hardly been respected.

Putting her disappointment aside, she quickly learned that a foreman had opened the shelter in a garden in Stockwell and had discovered the body, which was now being examined at the Fulham mortuary. There had been no other information from SOCO: all they knew was that the victim had been chained up and possibly starved to death in a shelter resembling a hideous mausoleum.

Jane went back into her cubby hole office and decided that, rather than wait for further information to come in, she would go and look at the shelter herself. She left a memo with a young detective, who she heard complaining bitterly that he had been given the job of listing all the tenants who had once occupied the house in Stockwell. She didn't wait to find out his name and returned to her car.

The crime scene was easy to find from the black-and-yellow tape that was fluttering around the open corrugated-iron fence. A uniformed officer was standing talking to an irate-looking man with a clipboard. Jane parked her car and soon learned that the man with the clipboard was the foreman, John Bishop, and he was desperate to find out when his workmen could continue with the demolition as the delay was costing a fortune.

Jane introduced herself and asked the uniformed officer to take her to the shelter, quickly wishing she had not worn her good shoes and best coat as she made her way over the muddy, uneven ground. It was clear how unsafe the site had become as even more of the tunnel had now collapsed. Bishop went ahead of her, bemoaning what had occurred and stressing that the plans from the council had not shown any of this. He stopped to gesture towards the digger.

'That is costing me by the hour, and we can't do anything with it.' He pointed to the shelter. 'That is twice the size it should be according to the plans I have, plus one corner is already down. It's a hazard.'

Jane found it strange that he had not even mentioned the horror of the chained corpse. However, she was glad that he was there to guide her through the main door into the shelter. Using a high-powered torch, he shone the beam around the first chamber, then led her into the second chamber and shone the torch on the area where the body had been found. The chain, which had been hammered into the floor, had been removed as evidence. Even now Bishop still seemed to lack any kind of empathy.

'I don't know how long she'd been down here, but it has nothing to do with my demolition. They told me they haven't found anything and don't know who she is. All I want is permission to get my men back to work.'

Jane let him continue talking as she looked around. The overpowering smell was quite sickening. Bishop was becoming increasingly agitated as he said that the owner of the property was giving him earache, demanding that he get back on schedule. He made a wide, expansive gesture with his arms.

'How can I get back on schedule? Nobody is telling me anything. I mean, surely I can continue the demolition of the house. And they only want me to save the fucking bricks – excuse my language.'

Jane tapped him on the arm. 'Can you shine the torch over to the area where the corner has come down?'

Bishop turned. 'That's the other thing . . . this place could collapse. The digger hit it, and—'

Jane moved closer and pointed. 'What's that?'

Bishop moved to her side as they both peered towards some large blocks. They were thick with dust, and appeared to be two pieces of cement, twelve to fourteen inches long, tied together with a black leather strap. Jane moved closer still.

'What do you think that is?' she asked Bishop.

'I have no idea, but it can't be anything important because they had those special officers in here looking for anything connected to the body.'

'Can you just move the bricks apart?'

Bishop sighed. He bent down and pushed the bricks aside then, with his foot, he nudged away a large piece of cement.

'Can you bring that section out?' she asked.

Bishop wasn't happy as he was now covered in cement dust. He handed Jane his prized clipboard and asked her to hold the torch. He crouched down and eased forward the blocks tied with the leather strap. Jane leaned forward and shone the torch directly onto them.

'I think it might have been two blocks for a pipe to run through . . . like a drainage pipe,' Bishop said.

'But why would you tie them together with a belt?'

He shook his head. 'Beats me.'

Jane crouched down. Her coat was getting covered in cement dust. The buckle of the belt was tarnished, and she was unsure if she should try to ease it open.

'Can you open it for me?' she asked.

'If you don't mind me saying so, detective, if you want to have a look at it, why don't we take it outside? The stench in here is sickening.'

* * *

Jane had to carry his clipboard and use his torch as he lifted the two concrete slabs in his arms. She followed him out of the shelter and, once outside, took a deep breath. The smell seemed to cling to her nostrils and her clothes as she handed Bishop his clipboard and torch.

'You're never going to unhook that buckle,' he said, taking a Stanley knife from his pocket. It didn't take him long because the leather strap was only an inch and a half wide and was quite worn. The top block came away easily but neither of them knew exactly what they were now looking at. It appeared to be a tightly wrapped bundle in some kind of black waterproof material, maybe part of a tarpaulin.

As much as she wanted to examine it further, she knew that police protocol would mean she would need permission, or someone from the station, to document all findings before they were removed from the murder site. Somebody had taken great trouble to hide whatever it was between the cement blocks. Even so, Jane decided that it was probably something not connected to their victim, and rather than waste everyone's time, she would open the bundle.

She was about to ask Bishop for his Stanley knife when the officer on guard at the opening to the site called him to tell him he had a visitor. Jane lifted the package, which was surprisingly light. Placing it down beside the belt she was able to ease open the waterproof wrapping. Inside there appeared to be soft pale blue material with yellowish stains, wrapped tightly around the almost feather-weight bundle. Jane used the tips of her fingers to draw the blanket aside. At first it looked as though it was covering a doll, but inching the blanket down further, she quickly realised it was the skull of a baby.

* * *

Jane drove to the mortuary and parked in one of the registered bays for the pathologists, hurrying inside to make a phone call. She used the reception phone and dialled the station, asking to speak to DCI Carter. He was not available so she immediately called Emra Saddell, who was working at the mortuary with the pathologist. Jane spoke to her briefly, explaining that she had brought something in from the crime scene that she needed her to look at. 'Is there a mortician available to carry it in from the car park?'

Five minutes later, inside the mortuary, Emra greeted Jane warmly before stepping back. 'Good heavens, you smell awful.'

'I've just come from the shelter. As I mentioned, what I've brought in was found there. I have no idea if it is connected, but it was very carefully wrapped and placed between two cement blocks that were then tied together.'

Emra turned as a young mortician wheeled in a trolley with the two blocks and the leather belt folded on top, along with the waterproof bundle.

'Well, this is intriguing,' Emra said, as the young man lifted it onto a table.

'We are about ready for the female body to be taken to Lambeth. The pathologist reckons she had no visible external scars from knife wounds or bullets, no fractures or broken bones. He would estimate her age to be around twenty to twenty-five. We have taken dental X-rays and he thinks that she had possibly starved to death. Death occurred probably five years ago.'

As she spoke, Jane watched her unroll a sheet of white paper across the table and carefully place the bundle on it. Emra leaned forward and smelled the waterproof material then very carefully, with a fine wooden spatula, eased it aside. The blanket was more difficult to ease off as it had been tightly wrapped around many times. But Emra eased the material away inch by inch, until they were confronted by the tiny, perfectly mummified body of a baby.

Jane watched as Emra gently placed protective material over the fragile body which looked as if it might crumble if touched.

'Does DCI Carter know about this?' she asked, looking up at Jane.

'He wasn't at the station when I rang to tell him.'

'He's probably on his way here. He does put the pressure on. We've been working all morning on the victim, and I've got old Johnson leading the pathology report. But, as you well know, he is not a man to be hurried. He's going to be taken aback when I present him with this little one.'

Jane knew that she was probably losing valuable time and decided she would return to the station. Just as she was leaving she asked Emra if she had any idea how long the baby had been in the shelter. Emra shook her head.

'To be honest, I don't. It's mummified but it has been tightly wrapped which has protected it. I don't think it is connected to the woman who was chained up as on examination we found she had not given birth. Besides, I would say it's been there for many more years than she has.'

Whilst Jane was driving back to the station, Emra called DCI Carter. He listened intently, taking note of the new information, but asked her to repeat how Jane Tennison had brought in the mummified baby. He was furious as he replaced the receiver.

'Jesus Christ!' he said to himself. 'She's only been here ten minutes and she's found another fucking body.'

He took a deep breath to calm himself, then walked into the incident room.

'OK, attention everyone. This girl has probably been missing for a shorter time than initially estimated. Check with mispers, any blonde twenty-to-twenty-five-year-olds who went missing about five years ago. We obviously don't know yet if she was held there as a prisoner before she died or how long she was in the bunker.'

He turned to one of the officers. 'When Detective Inspector Jane Tennison makes an appearance, get her into my office ASAP.'

He walked off, slamming the door behind him.

CHAPTER THREE

Jane arrived at the station and was impressed to see how much the team had already accomplished in tracking down the former residents of the house in Stockwell. One name was underlined, Brian Forgham, and Jane turned to the eager-looking young DC who was writing up the details.

'Why is this name underlined?' she asked. DC Tim Taylor, a probationary DC, checked his notebook.

'We were told that he was not a resident but was employed by the previous owners as a sort of maintenance and security man. We haven't traced him yet, but we think that he could have a lot of information for us.'

Jane nodded. 'Who gave you his name?'

'That was a man from the one family we have traced, Rachit Agarwal. He lived in one of the middle flats. He's married with two children and has a small grocery shop he now lives above. He said he recalled there was another family still living there when he left.'

'Did you interview him?' Jane asked.

'No, it was one of the others who's gone off trying to trace Forgham at Companies House. We don't have an address for him. Apparently, according to Rachit, the basement was always out of bounds and no tenant was allowed in the garden. He also described Forgham as being a rather unpleasant bloke, ex-army.'

Jane took off her coat and was heading for her office when she turned and suggested to DC Taylor that they make it a priority to find the whereabouts of Mr Forgham. As she opened her office door, Barbara looked over from her desk in the corner of the incident room and waved at her.

'The governor asked for you to go in and see him as soon as you returned,' she said.

Jane nodded her thanks and went into her office. After she had hung up her coat and run a brush through her hair, she went next door to see Carter. She would have liked to go up to the canteen to grab a sandwich first as she hadn't eaten since very early that morning, but thought it was probably unwise to keep Carter waiting.

She tapped on the door and entered Carter's office. He was finishing what looked like a toasted ham and cheese sandwich, which made Jane's stomach rumble, and had a large mug of coffee in front of him. He gestured to Jane to sit down.

'Now, what is this new bloody development, Tennison?'

Jane found his tone annoying, but replied calmly. 'I went to the site where the body was found, as there was no real action at the station, and I felt it might be informative.'

'Informative?' he snapped.

'Yes, sir. As it turned out, it was more than that. I spotted two concrete slabs tied together with a leather belt and thought I should examine them. Actually, sir, I think perhaps someone should have a word with SOCO as they must have overlooked them.'

'Don't you start having a go at any of those lads,' Carter said firmly. 'They were working under tremendous difficulty and the bloody shelter was unsafe. Getting the arc lights in was quite a business, along with the generator. Anyway, so, you found these blocks, did you? Near the wall that was damaged by the digger?'

'Yes, that's right, sir. I was assisted by the foreman who carried them out of the shelter. He cut the leather belt as it was tied securely around the two blocks. When I examined the contents, I discovered it was an infant wrapped very tightly in a blanket and some kind of waterproof material. The material had mummified the baby.'

Carter sighed as he wiped his mouth with a paper napkin and threw it in the waste bin.

'Right now, Tennison, we are waiting for as much information as we can get from old Professor Johnson who, as I am sure you know, is very diligent . . . but he likes to take his time. All we have to date is that our victim is between twenty to twenty-five years old, and she possibly starved to death. Our priority now is that we get her identified because Johnson estimates she has been down in that shelter for five years at least. This is also reinforced by the cinema ticket they found in a pocket, but it might have been there for God knows how long.'

'Well, hopefully mispers will have some information on a missing woman,' Jane suggested. 'The pathologist hasn't had time to estimate how long the baby has been in the shelter, but Emra, who was at the lab when I went there, felt that it could have been put there many years earlier. She also said there was no visible signs that the woman had ever been pregnant or had a child.'

Carter sighed again. 'Many years earlier . . . well, there's nothing we can do about any identification. As I said before, our priority is getting information on the adult female. I'd like you to focus on that until we have any further information regarding the second body.'

He dismissed Jane by returning to his typewriter. Frustrated by Carter's lack of interest in what she'd discovered in the bunker and feeling that her first day at Stockwell station was going swiftly downhill, Jane went up to the canteen to grab something to eat. Whilst she was there, DC Taylor came over to her table.

'The sarge has just checked on Mr Forgham's whereabouts. It's not good news. He was murdered five years ago. We're getting the details up, along with some press reports.'

'You would have thought the tenant who was questioned would have mentioned it,' she said, the news not improving her mood. But anyway, get me the criminal reports and case file that'll be at the general registry archives on the murder and find out if Mr Forgham was married and if he had a family.'

'Yes, ma'am,' Taylor said, leaving Jane to eat a tasteless tuna salad.

* * *

It was after six and Jane was closeted in her office catching up on the information about Brian Forgham. He had no criminal record and had been married with one daughter. On his release from the army he had worked at various different security positions. Eight years ago he was employed full time by the owner of the Stockwell property as a maintenance man, and to make sure there were no subletters or squatters using the empty basement. The previous owner was listed as a Jason Thorpe, who lived in Australia and had sold the property when all tenants had left eighteen months ago. Jane also now had the name of Jason Thorpe's lawyer, a Mr Arnold Hadley, of Hadley & March. It had been Hadley who had given the team the information regarding Jason Thorpe.

Jane typed up her notes and then, checking the time, decided she should go home. There was a brisk knock on her door and DCI Carter, wearing a fashionable Burberry raincoat, looked in.

'I'm off. We're still waiting for Johnson's report and until there's any development from missing persons, it's just a lot of tedious interviews.'

'I'd like to see if I can trace the widow of someone called Brian Forgham,' Jane said. 'He took care of all the flats and tenants and—'

'Well, he's no use,' Carter interrupted. 'He's been dead five years. Didn't you get the information from records? He was killed outside a pub in Stockwell by a drug dealer called Simon Root who is still serving time in Wandsworth. Two witnesses saw the attack, so it was done and dusted pretty quickly.'

He shrugged his shoulders.

'I have a nasty feeling that this is going to be one of those bloody cases that takes up hours of time tracking down Christ knows how many people who lived in that house. And I've got the new owners calling me up all the time asking when they can finish the demolition.' He gave a strained laugh. 'I don't want you going back there and digging up any more bodies. Just crack on with the paperwork and I'll see you in the morning.' He walked out.

Jane gathered up her notes and put on her coat, which still smelled of the shelter. She was heading into the incident room as the night officers were all coming in and she really didn't feel like either introducing herself or checking for updates. She logged her report and was about to leave when Barbara, wearing a cherry red coat with a wide velvet trim, waved a sheet of notepaper towards her.

'Detective Tennison, apparently you wanted to question Brian Forgham's widow? We have an address for her, but no phone number. Would you like me to try and get you a phone number for tomorrow?'

'That would be very useful, Barbara, thank you. I'll take the address, though.'

She was feeling guilty about being irritated by Barbara for no good reason. The truth was she was feeling frustrated that her hopes of making a good first impression seemed to have failed.

* * *

When Jane arrived home, it was dark. As she walked up the path to her front door a security light came on and she was able to see clearly to put the key in the lock. She smiled, deciding that this Eddie Fraser was a good find. But when she walked into the hall she quickly changed her mind as the carpets had been pulled up and some floorboards had been lifted, forcing her to step gingerly around them.

She hung her coat up and went into the kitchen. It was in an appalling state. The sink had been pulled out from the wall, and tiles had been removed. On the bright side, a note by the washing machine said that it had been plumbed in, and she could see there were new pipes and a recently cemented wall section for the flue.

Pinned to the back door was a note from the plumber saying that he had completed the installation of the washing machine but needed to find new pipes for behind her sink unit. He would be back the following day.

Jane looked in the fridge and checked the sell-by date on a quiche, then opened a bottle of wine. She had just finished a glass when the doorbell rang. Jane made her way through the obstacle course to the front door. When she opened it there stood Eddie, holding a large cardboard box.

'Sorry to disturb you so late,' he said with a smile, 'but I've brought the piping that Archie needs, and some tiles for you to approve.'

Jane swallowed her annoyance at the state of the house and returned his smile. 'That's all right. I've only just got in from work.'

'I'm really sorry to have left this in such a mess,' he said as he followed her into the kitchen. 'The thing is, I have major concerns about the wiring through to your hallway. That dimmer switch had been put in incorrectly and kept tripping the hall electrics. I had to go out and get a modern dimmer and delay working in the kitchen so Archie could get your washing machine plumbed in. I think most of the problems with the wiring in the kitchen are due to leakage behind your sink unit, which has probably been going on for years.'

Jane felt she needed another glass of wine and offered one to Eddie.

'Thanks, but I've got to get back home to finish a little job.'

'You work long hours,' Jane said.

'Yeah, I do now I've taken on your job. The other few bits and pieces I've put on the backburner, but I still need to complete them. It will take me a few days here, if that's all right with you. If you pick the tiles you want to put up behind the sink, Archie and I will work on that in the morning.'

Jane watched as he put the large box down by the back door. 'If it's easier for you, I don't mind you working in the evening to get things done as soon as possible.'

'OK,' Eddie said. 'Let me see how I get on tomorrow.' He paused. 'Did you have a good day?' he asked, surprising her with the change of subject.

'Not really,' Jane admitted. 'It's definitely been a long one. A woman's body was found in an old air-raid shelter. It was a bit shocking because she had been chained to the bed, and now we have to try and find out who did it and why.'

'Blimey,' Eddie said. 'Rather you than me. I can't imagine finding something like that.'

Jane didn't add that she had also found the dried-up body of a baby. She followed him to the front door. 'Thank you for today, Eddie. Perhaps I'll see you tomorrow.'

He gave her a big grin. 'Yeah, I hope to see you tomorrow night, with not so much damage left behind us!'

Jane shut the door after him and pulled the chain across. There had been no work in her bathroom, so she was able to have a long soak in her bath, the frustrations of the day gradually fading away as she was finally able to relax. But when she got out she saw that there was a stream of water seeping out beneath it and her good mood was instantly gone. With a sigh she decided she would leave a note for Archie asking him to look at the bathroom and give her an estimate for a replacement bath, wash basin and tiling.

* * *

Jane was up and out by eight the following morning. She had already looked up Sharon Forgham's address in the *A-to-Z*, a flat in a high-rise council estate called Hightower, almost walking distance from where the demolition was taking place. Trusting to luck that Sharon would be in, Jane parked her car and headed into the run-down entrance area. There wasn't any kind of reception desk, just a stained, dank-smelling carpet, a lift and a fire door to the ground-floor flats.

Sharon Forgham lived at number 312 and Jane was relieved it was only three floors up as the lift was out of order. She felt sorry for the residents who lived on the sixth floor.

Flat 312 looked as if someone had at one time taken good care of it. The front door was well painted and there was a good quality door mat outside. The surround of the doorbell was brass, but it had not been polished for a considerable time. Jane pressed it, then waited half a minute and pressed it again. She heard shuffling footsteps approaching on the other side of the door.

'Who is it?' a woman asked.

'Good morning, I'm Detective Tennison and I'd like to speak to Sharon Forgham.'

'If you're here about an appeal, then you've come to the wrong place. You can piss off.'

Jane was momentarily confused. 'It's not about an appeal. I need to talk to you about the property where your husband worked.'

'He's dead.'

'I know that. Am I talking to Mrs Forgham?'

There was an irritated sigh from behind the door and Jane heard the bolt being pulled back then the door opened. Sharon Forgham was wearing a pale blue satin quilted dressing gown, with greying furry slippers that must have once been blue as well.

'If that bastard is trying to appeal, I've already told the probation department it'll be over my dead body. He knifed my husband in cold blood, leaving him to die in the street like a dog.'

'Could I please come in and talk to you?' Jane persisted. 'We have a situation which we need some help with.'

'What help do you want? He pleaded guilty. He did it. It's not just him in prison, you know. I'm in prison here. I'm on my own. My husband took good care of me. I never wanted for nothing, and now the bloody council are trying to get me out because I have a two-bedroomed flat. They've offered me a piece of crap so-called studio apartment. I'm not fucking moving an inch.'

Jane let Mrs Forgham vent her anger as she followed her into a small kitchen. Sitting down at the kitchen table, Sharon pulled a packet of Benson & Hedges from her pocket and lit one, inhaling deeply. After a couple of drags, she seemed to calm down and Jane explained that she was working at Stockwell police station and there was a situation at the house where her husband had worked up until the time of his death, which was now being demolished. Jane could see that Sharon had aged beyond her years and there was a bitter tiredness about her as she said that she knew little about her husband's work, but he had always felt that he was doing more than he should and not being paid enough.

'It was steady work, but some of those tenants were shocking, the way the flats were full of their relatives. And there were always problems with the plumbing, but the owner lived in Australia, so whenever poor Brian needed anything he had to go through a lawyer. He wasn't allowed to spend a penny on repairs without permission.'

Jane was eager to get to the point of her visit and brought up the fact that the basement was never rented. Sharon nodded and said that she and Brian had talked about it.

'It was strange, this big old basement all empty . . . and God forbid anyone dared go into the garden, that was out of bounds too. It was just left to rot. There had been an orchard at one time. Brian said it was disgusting, all the fruit just left to rot.'

'So, your husband used the garden?'

'I wouldn't say he used it, but he had access to it. There was a fox that got in which he couldn't get out. And sometimes there were dead birds in the greenhouse.'

'Did he ever mention a tunnel to you?'

'Where from?'

'It probably led from the basement, under the garden, to an old air-raid shelter.'

'No, he never mentioned anything like that.'

'Do you have a daughter, Mrs Forgham?'

Sharon sucked at her cigarette. 'I *had* a daughter. Samantha . . . a right little bitch. She was given everything she wanted. Her dad spoiled her rotten. She'd go off to that shop in the posh part of London, Biba. The clothes that girl had.'

'Do you know where she is?'

'No, I don't. And I don't want to know. She lied and stole from us. She broke my husband's heart, then she ran off with that no-good piece of shit. No matter how much he begged her to come home, she wouldn't leave that disgusting junkie.'

Jane put her hand up. 'Mrs Forgham, you're saying your daughter was involved with a drug addict?'

Sharon nodded. 'She had the audacity to bring him here once, the no-good creep. I told her that if she wanted to keep going out with him then she wasn't getting a penny from me or her dad. She lost her job at Boots . . . just didn't turn up for work.'

'Would this be Simon Root?'

Sharon pursed her lips then nodded.

'I can't stand to even hear his name after what he done. That piece of shit even tried to claim it was self-defence, but it was his flippin' knife. He was a dirty liar.'

'When was the last time you saw Samantha?'

'Just before Brian died . . . about a month before. She came begging for money, same as always. I shoved her out of the door.'

'Do you still keep in touch with her?'

Sharon's mouth turned down. 'I wouldn't let her cross this doorstep because it's all her fault. Brian would still be alive if it wasn't for her.'

'Did your husband keep in touch with her?'

Sharon fished in the pocket of her dressing gown and took out a tissue, blowing her nose.

'He was broken . . . he came to me and was crying. A neighbour had seen her prostituting herself outside Stockwell Tube station. He got her on the game, that so-called boyfriend. She was twenty-two years old and beautiful, and she was doing that for money. Brian went to find her. What upset him more than anything was that she looked in a shocking state because that bastard had got her on heroin. Anyway, Brian told me he'd sort it and make sure that he'd get her off the junk, but he confronted the no-good boyfriend outside the pub and the bastard pulled out a knife and killed him. That's what happened to Brian . . . my daughter's drug-addict boyfriend killed her father.'

'Was Samantha ever in court for Mr Root's trial?' Jane asked.

'No, she didn't dare show her face. Coppers came here asking about her, but I said I didn't even know where she lived. I still don't, and I don't want to know where she is. It was all her fault. My poor husband was just trying to help her and gets murdered for it.'

Jane took a furtive look at her watch and picked up her bag.

'Mrs Forgham, I can't thank you enough for your time. There are one or two other things I need from you. One is a photograph of your daughter.'

'What do you want that for?' Sharon asked, screwing up her eyes.

'I'm unable to give you any details right now, Mrs Forgham, but it would be for elimination purposes. Added to that, could you possibly give me the name of her dentist?'

Sharon blew her nose. 'Have you found her? I'm not stupid, love, I've seen enough detective programmes. You don't ask for dental records unless you've found someone dead. And let me tell you something, love, for what she done to this family, if she is dead, I'm glad. She's been dead to me since I buried her father anyway.'

Sharon stubbed out her cigarette and left Jane in the kitchen for a few moments. Jane could hear her opening and closing drawers in another room before she came back.

'Here's one, when Samantha was at a Christmas party. She'd be about twenty, but I don't have no others. I burned them. I've written her dentist's name on the back, but I don't know if he's still in practice.'

Jane took the photograph and put it in her bag. 'Thank you so much, Mrs Forgham. I promise I'll be in touch if we have any more information about your daughter.'

Sharon crossed her arms, shaking her head. 'Don't bother. We gave her everything we had, and she threw it all back in our faces. I'll never forgive her, and I don't want you back here whatever it is you find out.'

Jane left, deeply saddened that Sharon was living in such pain and bitterness and hoping that she wouldn't have to go back and talk to her about her daughter again. But she knew that the date Samantha was last seen by her father matched the pathologist's estimate of when the young woman in the bunker had died, and she was afraid that could only mean one thing.

CHAPTER FOUR

Even after the detour to interview Mrs Forgham, Jane was still at the station by nine. And again the incident room was eerily empty as the detective sergeant had detailed many of the officers to interview the previous residents of the house in Stockwell. But DCI Carter was in his office and looked up tetchily as Jane knocked to enter.

'I think we might have a breakthrough, sir. I met with Brian Forgham's widow.'

Carter frowned, obviously trying to work out who she was talking about.

'He was the man who looked after the property when the flats were occupied, but he was murdered five years ago.'

Carter gave her a quizzical look. 'Well, I don't know what you call a breakthrough, but that doesn't seem to be a very positive lead.'

Jane tried to ignore his sarcasm. 'It is, sir. They had a daughter, aged twenty-two, and according to the widow, she has not been seen for the same period of time the pathologist estimates our victim to have been dead . . . five years.' Jane opened her briefcase. 'I have a photograph of her and, although it was taken when she was about twenty, she has long blonde hair. Her mother described her as being well dressed, spending money on fashionable clothes.'

Carter squinted at the photo. 'Well, we can't tell what the hell the dead girl used to look like, so you need to find her dental records and see if they match the teeth on our girl.'

Jane nodded. 'If you turn the photo over you'll find the name of her dentist. The girl's name's Samantha. I'd also like to go and talk to her boyfriend. He's currently in Wandsworth prison for the murder of Brian Forgham. After the murder, the officers tried to trace Samantha but I think they assumed she'd done a runner when he was arrested.'

Carter rocked back in his chair. 'My, my, my, you really are a one-woman force – although I'm not sure what you hope to get from Forgham's killer. Your main priority is to see if the teeth match. Also, I'm not putting much focus on the dead baby at the moment. If we can clear up the main case, that's probably the best we can do.'

It sounded to Jane as if Carter resented her even discovering the baby. 'Thank you very much, sir,' she said, trying to keep her tone neutral as she closed the door behind her.

Carter drummed his fingers on his desk. He had been tipped off that Jane Tennison was not exactly a 'team player', but he had to admit that if she was proved right, and they had identified their victim, it was an impressively fast turnaround.

Jane allocated DC Tim Taylor to check out the dentist and find out if he'd had a patient called Samantha Forgham, and if so to get the X-rays checked to see if there was a match with their victim.

Jane went to have a quick breakfast in the canteen before asking the duty sergeant to contact Wandsworth prison to arrange a formal meeting with Simon Root. The message quickly came back that Root was in a rehabilitation group in the morning, but she could have a meeting with him at noon. Jane decided that, rather than returning to the incident room and the official monitoring by Carter, she would go and see if they had any update for her at the forensic lab. In particular, she wanted to see if Emra Saddell could give her access to the clothes worn by their victim.

* * *

Emra was her usual pleasant self, complaining only briefly about the length of time the pathologist was taking. They had already sent samples of the victim's hair for a toxicology report, but Detective Sergeant Lloyd Johnson was a stickler for going by the rule book and he wouldn't even estimate how long he would need to examine the mummified baby. Emra led Jane over to trestle tables covered in white paper where the victim's clothes and footwear were laid out. The boots were size five, well worn, and from the shoe shop Saxone. The tights the victim had worn were frayed and Emra pointed out the period stains on the crotch. The victim's skirt was very short and made of PVC, and the sweater, which had once been white, was stained with sweat discolouration under the armpits.

'Not a very hygienic young lady, but nevertheless a tragic one,' Emra said. 'To have been chained up and starved to death is horrific.'

Lastly, Jane looked at the jacket and the items that had been removed from the pockets: bus tickets, cinema tickets and some lip gloss. Emra then showed Jane a transparent plastic container full of bangles worn by the victim.

'They're actually rather good quality,' Emra said. 'One's eighteen carat gold and three are solid silver. You can see inscribed on the gold bangle *Happy 21st birthday. Daddy.*'

Jane wrote this down in her notebook. 'Thanks, Emra. I think we may have identified her, and if we're right she was working as a prostitute and was possibly a heroin addict.'

'Well, we will know if she was using drugs when they do the toxicology report on her hair,' Emra said. 'Anything on the baby?' she added.

Jane raised an eyebrow. 'If you ask me, I reckon DCI Carter wishes I'd never found it. I think he'll try to do as little as possible with it.'

Emra gave Jane a half smile. 'Don't worry. I won't let this get sidelined. Whoever hid that baby will be hiding a terrible secret.'

* * *

Simon Root appeared younger than Jane had expected from his mug shot, which had been taken five years ago. He was around five feet ten inches, with very dark, straight, collar-length hair and dark brown eyes, and was actually quite good-looking. Like most of the other prisoners, he was clutching a packet of cigarettes as he sat nervously in front of Jane.

'Is this about my appeal?' he asked.

'No, I'm not here in relation to your appeal. I need to ask you some questions about your relationship with Samantha Forgham.'

He raised his eyes to the ceiling. 'Well, I can't tell you much. I haven't spoken to her or seen her since the night I got arrested, so I don't know where she is. She never wrote once. Probably her bitch of a mother has been stopping her.' He gave a strange snort of a laugh.

Jane had read the reports about the night of the murder. It appeared that Brian Forgham had gone into the pub looking for Simon and witnesses had claimed he had shouted at him across the bar. On seeing him, Simon had attempted to run. There had been some kind of confrontation inside the pub, but then it continued on the pavement outside.

Simon lit a cigarette, seeming tense and angry.

'I don't know what Samantha has been saying, but after all this time she should be ashamed of herself. She should have come forward because I never wanted to hurt her father. It was him coming after me. He threatened me. All I did was defend myself.'

'At the time of your arrest, were you and Samantha living together?' Jane asked.

'Yeah, we had a room in a squat, but she often took off for days. I was trying to come off the junk . . . I was on methadone, but she was always trying to score. The other guys there were getting fed up with us not contributing cash for the food and stuff.'

Jane asked for the address of the squat, and he gave the same details that were on record from when he was arrested.

'Did you see Samantha on the night her father approached you?'

'Yeah, earlier in the evening. She was strung out, needing a fix. She told me she might catch up with me later. I never saw her again.'

The cigarette smoke was making Jane's eyes water. 'Can you tell me exactly what happened that night?'

'I've told everybody a hundred times. I was defending myself. I didn't set out to murder him. He came after me.'

'Simon, can you remember exactly what Mr Forgham said to you?'

'Yes, of course I can. I can remember every fucking word. He said, "I've got Samantha and she is never going to see you again. I'm getting her off drugs and if you try to see her, I'll have the coppers on to you."'

Jane quickly jotted it all down. 'Simon, do you know if Mr Forgham had seen Samantha that night?'

He shrugged. 'I don't know, I presume he must have, 'cos he also said something about me turning his daughter into a whore, which wasn't fucking true. She just wanted to make money. That's all it was.'

'When Mr Forgham said he had got Samantha, did you presume he had been with her before he came looking for you?'

'I don't know, but he threw this punch at me. It was a full right hand, right in my face, and he was a big man. So, I did what I did to protect myself, then I ran off.'

Jane tapped her notebook with her pen, turned back a page and then forward again. 'Simon, do you think Mr Forgham could have taken Samantha somewhere?'

He shrugged. 'I don't know. All I remember him saying was that she was somewhere safe, away from me.'

* * *

At three that afternoon Mr Kenneth Patterson, dental surgeon, confirmed that he had a patient called Samantha Forgham, but she had not been to his surgery for five years. He had taken a dental X-ray of Samantha when she was aged twenty and had a trouble-some wisdom tooth extracted. He said they were fortunate because, in most cases, after that length of time they would have destroyed the X-rays, but because it had been such a complicated extraction, he had retained them for future reference.

* * *

Jane was in her office typing up a report of her meeting with Sharon Forgham and the interview with Simon Root. From what Simon had said, she thought there was a possibility that Brian Forgham had taken his daughter back to the Stockwell property.

Jane's suspicion was that, determined to get her off the streets and off the drugs, he had locked her in the shelter, intending to return. But instead, Samantha's boyfriend had killed him. She spent some time checking through all the files. After Root's arrest, the officers had tried to contact Samantha but had been unable to trace her. There were references to conversations with Mrs Forgham, who also said she had no idea where her daughter was and that she had not lived at home for some considerable time.

Officers had visited the squat and it was determined that Samantha had gone off with a drug dealer she was known to score heroin from. The search for Samantha was not continued, as her mother had never reported her missing.

Despite being sure she was right, Jane decided to wait for the confirmed evidence of the X-rays before running her scenario by anyone. There was still a number of questions she wanted answers to. She needed to establish how many of the tenants were in residence on the night of 16 September 1980, the night Samantha's father was murdered. She was aware, from the work the team had done, that some of the residents had not been traced but she felt that five years was a long time for the body to have remained in the shelter without anybody knowing.

Jane now wanted to find out who had replaced Brian Forgham as the maintenance manager of the property, and if she could find any witnesses to validate her theory.

Her desk phone rang. It was one of the clerical staff saying that there was a Mr Arnold Hadley on the line, from Hadley, McKenzie & March. He had been asked to call into the station as his client, Jason Thorpe, had owned the property in Stockwell before it was sold to the development company.

Jane took the call, introducing herself and thanking Mr Hadley for contacting them.

'That's quite all right,' he said before explaining his client's involvement with the property. Mr Hadley appeared to be a pleasant and accommodating man, who seemed appalled at what had been discovered. He was able to clarify that Jason Thorpe had arranged for the house to be divided into six flats, and at that time it had seemed to be a good investment. The actual owner was a Miss Helena Lanark, Jason Thorpe's aunt, who had inherited the property from her father. She had allowed her nephew to lease the flats until it had become unprofitable as the house now required extensive repairs and there were several problematic tenants.

'I'm sorry to interrupt you, Mr Hadley, but what did you mean by problematic?'

'I believe some were subletting, and some were not paying the rent. Miss Lanark's nephew lives in Australia, but he had hired a very good managing agent to oversee the tenants and the maintenance.'

'Was that Brian Forgham?' Jane asked.

'Yes, that is correct. Mr Thorpe had hired him personally.' Mr Hadley hesitated. 'I don't know if you are aware, but Mr Forgham met with a very tragic end.'

'Yes, we know,' Jane replied. 'Was a new managing agent appointed after that?'

Mr Hadley paused before admitting that, due to Jason Thorpe being in Australia, it had become difficult to find the right person. He hesitated again, then continued.

'By this time, it was obvious that the situation at the house was more than problematic. I think Mr Forgham had already succeeded in persuading a number of tenants to leave, but we eventually had to evict two families as the house was no longer heated and the electricity was cut off.'

'When was this exactly?' Jane asked.

'Well, detective, I am going back quite a while . . . I would estimate that it was five and a half or six years ago.'

Jane jotted down the details. The time frame was exactly what had been concerning her.

'Mr Hadley, could you tell me who was still living at the house after Mr Forgham died?'

'No one. It was boarded up and fell into even greater disrepair. Then, eighteen months ago, Jason was given permission by his aunt to sell the property to a developer.'

'Why is Jason Thorpe registered as the previous owner and not Helena Lanark?' Jane asked.

'Jason had lasting power of attorney and was dealing with all her affairs, so it was easier for him to be registered as the owner and deal with the sale of the property.'

'Excuse my ignorance,' Jane said, 'but what does lasting power of attorney mean exactly?'

'Essentially it gave Jason the legal authority to make financial decisions on Helena Lanark's behalf.'

Jane thanked Mr Hadley again for his assistance, then asked him to repeat the timings for her, particularly regarding when the last tenant had left the property. She also asked if Mr Forgham had retained the keys after the tenants had left. Mr Hadley was unable to confirm if he had returned the keys, but he said he would fax Mr Thorpe with any further queries Jane had.

By the end of the call with Mr Hadley, Jane was certain that she was right. She needed to have a conversation with Rachit Agarwal: according to the incident board he was one of the last tenants to remain at the property.

Jane put on her coat, which still held the faint smell of the shelter, and made a mental note to have it dry-cleaned.

As she went into the main incident room, she could see that a lot of new information had been added to the board and decided to ask DCI Carter for a full team briefing as soon as she returned from meeting with Mr Agarwal.

She was just passing through the station reception when DS Derek Hunt gestured to her. 'Could I have a quick word?' Although Jane knew who he was she had only had a brief conversation with him since her arrival. Derek was an 'old school' copper, square-jawed with pockmarked skin, and a First World War haircut. Even though he was approaching retirement, he looked fit and had a strong presence about him.

'I'm just heading out, Derek, but I need to ask DCI Carter for a full team briefing. I shouldn't be more than an hour.'

She was surprised when Hunt took her elbow.

'Do you mind if I have a few words in your shell – like now, love? It's just that, we all know you're new here, but if you'll excuse me giving you a bit of advice, you need to get to know your team. Some of them have done a hell of a lot of leg work tracing some of the tenants, going through all the misper files to try and identify the victim. And there's been no encouragement from you. As the DI on the team, you need to have your finger on the pulse and speak with the team regularly, so we all know what everyone's doing.'

Jane was taken aback but instantly knew he was right. 'Thank you for the advice,' she said, her cheeks flushing. 'You can be sure I'll act on it as soon as I get back to the station.'

* * *

It took Jane ten minutes to get to Rachit Agarwal's small grocery shop on a corner of Stockwell High Street. He and his wife were at the counter, and as soon as Jane introduced herself he became agitated, explaining that he had already been spoken to by a uniformed officer regarding when he had been a tenant at the Stockwell property.

'If it's about the rent owing, I don't know if you are aware, madam, but we were left with no central heating and then they cut off the electricity. I have four children, and to find replacement accommodation was exceedingly difficult.'

'This is not about the rent,' Jane quickly explained. 'Is there somewhere private we can talk? I just have a few questions but it's nothing to worry about.'

Rachit instantly relaxed, leading Jane to the back room of the shop. 'We had many problems at this property,' he began explaining. 'Mr Forgham could at times be very rude, and aggressive. Of course, I was greatly saddened by what happened to him, but he was really quite unpleasant at times.'

Jane took out her notebook and asked if Rachit could clarify the exact dates he and his family left the property. He said it was very clear in his mind because he had left a week before Mr Forgham was murdered. He was also able to tell Jane that Mr Forgham used to drive a small white Ford Transit van, and he repeated what he had said in his first statement, that no tenant had been allowed down in the basement. As far as he knew there was only one other couple still living at the house when he left.

When asked if he had ever met Jason Thorpe, Rachit said he had met him on a few occasions, as he had visited the house with various builders. He had been told that he was the owner but was instructed that any problems they had concerning their rent should be addressed to Mr Forgham, as Mr Thorpe lived in Australia.

'If you want my honest opinion, madam, they just wanted to let the house deteriorate and sell it to the highest bidder. You see, it's a corner property with a large acreage of garden.'

'But you were never allowed to use the garden?'

Rachit shook his head. 'There was no gate from the garden to the road, and the access to the garden from the basement was always locked. From our bedroom window it looked like an overgrown mess of weeds and rotting trees. The company had erected a high corrugated-iron fence around the perimeter, so even if you wanted to, nobody could ever get in.'

Jane thanked him for his time and hurried back to the station. She did not even have a moment to unbutton her coat or go into her office as DCI Carter was standing next to the incident board holding up the photograph of Samantha Forgham.

'Everyone, our victim has been identified. She was the twenty-two-year-old daughter of Brian Forgham.'

Jane folded her coat over her arm and stood at the back of the room. Carter glanced over at her, and was clearly enjoying the fact that he had stolen her thunder, explaining how they had identified their victim through her dental records. He then added, gesturing towards Jane, that with no witness, they could only speculate on what had occurred.

'We are waiting for a toxicology report on the hair from the victim. This will confirm if she was, as her mother has stated, a heroin addict. As Samantha disappeared on the night of her father's death, we have to assume that Mr Forgham intended to protect his daughter from her drug dealer boyfriend by holding her captive in the shelter.'

There was a murmur around the room as he finished with a grin, saying that a lot had been accomplished in a very short time and thanking them for all their hard work.

'We just need to find the last tenant who had occupied the property, inform Brian Forgham's widow, and then I think it'll be "case closed".'

DS Hunt raised his hand. 'Guv, what are we doing about the second body in the shelter – the little baby? We're getting our ears burned from all the calls coming in from the demolition company, wanting clearance so they can get on and finish their job.'

Carter shrugged. 'I'll have a conversation with forensic, but I think we can give the green light for the demolition work to start up again.'

He hesitated a moment before gesturing to the incident board and the photographs of the mummified baby.

'We're at a standstill with this until we have information from the pathologist, but he's already estimated that the mummified baby is twenty-five to thirty-five years old. So, in all honesty, I doubt that we will be able to spare a full team working on that.'

Jane took a deep breath, trying not to show her humiliation on her face. She'd hardly begun her new job, but already Carter had made her position untenable. She kept her coat over her arm and walked out of the station.

CHAPTER FIVE

Arriving home, Jane was about to put her key into the lock when the door opened.

'Hi, I was just leaving, but I'm glad to be able to have a chat as we've made a lot of progress today.'

Eddie stepped aside for her to come in. Jane could see that the floorboards were in place again, but the carpet was still rolled back.

'You actually have pretty good floorboards,' Eddie went on, 'and your carpet is worn and stained. You might think about having the floorboards in the hallway sanded as it would give a much more modern feel and make it look a bit larger, especially if you continue it into the kitchen.'

Jane was taken aback. 'Gosh, I'm sure you're right, but I can't really even think about that right now.' She hung up her coat on the coat stand.

Eddie led her into the kitchen where there had been a great improvement. Tiles had been put up behind her sink unit, everything was plumbed in, her fridge freezer was installed, and Eddie pointed out the new plug sockets.

Jane put her briefcase down on the table and smiled. 'It looks terrific . . . thank you.'

Eddie smiled. 'I have a few new estimates from Archie regarding the bathroom and he's left a lot of leaflets for you to look over and decide what you would like him to do.'

Jane sighed and pulled out a chair.

'Do you want me to take a look over the electrics upstairs? Also, Archie reckoned you could do with a new boiler?'

Jane sighed. 'Oh goodness, I've not had time to even think about that. Maybe I should just settle up with you both for the work done to date and then have a meeting about the other stuff – though I did leave a note to say that my bath leaked last night.'

'Yes, I know. Archie took a look and replaced a pipe that was the obvious cause, but you do have a very damp area beneath the bath, and he reckoned you would be better to get the carpet out and have some tiles or hard flooring put down.'

Jane nodded as she sifted through the invoices, then opened her briefcase and took out her cheque book.

'Please, sit down,' she said, as she began to make out the cheques.

Eddie sat down opposite her. 'I have a few jobs lined up, as I said to you yesterday, but I can make time late afternoon or early evening if you want me to check upstairs. I think Archie is available in a couple of weeks, but he's gone over to do a new build for a couple expecting their first baby.'

Jane passed Eddie his cheque and then put Archie's into an envelope. 'Shall I post this, or can you give it to him?'

'Post it – I might not see him for a few days.'

Jane added the address from the invoice and slipped it into her briefcase to post in the morning.

'Well, thank you for staying. I promise I will give all your suggestions a lot of thought.'

'Good, but you won't want to be sanding floorboards if you're redecorating. It's best to get them done first 'cos the sanding creates a lot of dust.'

'Oh right, yes, of course.'

'What you do is rent the sanding machine . . .'

Jane frowned. 'What? Oh, yes . . . I'm sorry, I can't really think about it right now. I've had one of those days at work and I haven't quite got the energy to focus on anything else.'

She was annoyed with herself for losing control in front of Eddie, as she felt close to tears. Eddie stood as if to leave, but hesitated.

'Do you want to talk about it?'

'What?'

'Sometimes it's good to get stuff off your chest . . . means it doesn't get on top of you.'

'Well, I think it's already got on top of me,' Jane admitted. 'And on literally my second day I think I have already rubbed my boss up the wrong way. I was given a bit of a lecture . . . it sounds stupid, but I felt that I had made great headway only to feel humiliated by him. It's just hard for me to get my head around it. I mean, I didn't want any praise, but I had succeeded in making major steps forwards. But you have to go by the rule book and God forbid you use your own initiative . . . you're considered not to be a team player.'

Eddie just nodded sympathetically, having no idea what she was talking about, but when she suggested they have a vodka tonic he accepted, allowing him to demonstrate the new ice box in her fridge. She fetched the bottle of vodka, and he opened the bottle of tonic.

'You need to do a grocery shop,' he said, closing the door of the empty fridge.

'I know, I know . . . it's just something else I can't think about at the moment. This case I'm working on has really taken precedence over everything else. In all honesty, it's the last thing I wanted to have to deal with after my previous investigation.'

Eddie poured two large vodka tonics and sat down opposite Jane. She let out a long sigh.

'Thank you . . . this is just what I needed. Cheers!'

'I find it easy working alongside my dad,' Eddie said. 'Although he can be a pain in the arse sometimes. But being my own boss is what I like best. When I was starting out at my first job with a big company I used to get run ragged, but Dad insisted I get the best training and qualifications because in a few years he'll be retiring. Then I'll have my own company – and I'm planning on getting a good team of blokes – people like Archie, plus maybe a carpenter . . . make it a tight little business.'

Jane took another long sip of her drink. It was always the same. When people asked if you want to talk about something that's bothering you, they ended up doing all the talking themselves. But maybe that was what she needed.

'Are you married?' she asked Eddie, abruptly changing the subject.

'Me? No way! I've only just bought my flat and I want a few quid in the bank before I commit myself.'

'Play the field, do you?' Jane asked.

He laughed, sounding embarrassed.

They had both almost finished their drinks and Eddie pushed his chair back as if to leave.

'Let's have another one,' she said, already feeling less anxious and rather enjoying his company. He was not like any of the officers she knew, or any of her previous lovers. There was an innocence to him, or perhaps it was just honesty.

'I shouldn't really 'cos I'm driving. But let me fix you one and I'll just have a tonic.'

He stood at the fridge extracting some more ice cubes and asked about her last investigation. Jane dismissed it, saying that it was a long, tedious inquiry into the discovery of a nun's body that had been found when a convent had been converted into luxury flats.

'Been there a long time, had it?' he asked, handing her the replenished glass.

'Yes, three decades. So I was brought onto this new case because I'm now the expert. Only this time the victim's only been dead for five years. Anyway, we think we've identified her.'

Eddie seemed genuinely interested, asking how they went about the process of identification. Jane explained about dental records and then how their inquiries had led them to the conclusion that the victim had been chained and left in an old air-raid shelter. Jane had not intended going into such lengthy details or bringing up the tragic discovery of the mummified baby, but Eddie listened so attentively that it all just seemed to come out.

'Blimey – no wonder you were feeling a bit down when you got home,' Eddie said finally. 'Me, I finish the job, go home and sleep like a baby. But people like you dealing with all this terrible stuff every day must have a hard time putting it out of your mind at the end of the day.'

'Yes, sometimes it is hard, Eddie,' Jane agreed.

'Well, I'd better be getting home,' he said, putting on his leather jacket.

'OK, thanks for listening,' Jane said. 'I'll be in touch very soon to discuss the rewiring upstairs. And I'll also contact Archie after I've made a decision about the bathroom.'

'OK . . . I'll wait to hear from you. Thanks for the drink.'

Jane remained sitting at the table as he let himself out, having left the spare key she had given him on the kitchen draining board. She poured the last of the tonic water into her glass and topped it up with vodka. She walked slightly unsteadily up the stairs to her bedroom before flopping down onto her bed. She wasn't thinking about Samantha Forgham or the mummified baby anymore, but how soon she could get Eddie to begin work.

* * *

The following morning Jane needed two strong black coffees and a couple of Paracetamol before she could function, but she still managed to get herself to the station by a quarter past eight, as the rest of the team began to come on duty. She was relieved to discover that DCI Carter was due in court on an existing case, so wouldn't be in his office.

Jane asked Detective Sergeant Hunt to make sure the team was ready for a briefing and by nine o'clock the room was filled with all the officers connected to the investigation. Jane stood waiting, trying not to show her nervousness as they all waited expectantly. She gave a slight cough and licked her lips.

'I feel I should properly introduce myself to you all, perhaps rather belatedly. I am Detective Inspector Jane Tennison. Although we've been working towards the same result, we've all been allocated various assignments meaning that I've not had time to get to know you. I want to congratulate everyone on what we have accomplished so far, particularly given the difficulty in tracing all the previous tenants of the property and everything to do with the demolition. I know we've been able to have a conversation with Rachit Agrawal and through him we've learned that he believed the eviction of nearly all the tenants had been accomplished by mid-August 1980. There was a married couple that had occupied the middle-floor flat, Mr and Mrs Abdul and their two children, but he thought that maybe they weren't evicted until after Brian Forgham's murder. That would mean this couple was in residence and might possibly have information regarding Samantha Forgham. I'm aware that we have so far been unable to trace the Abdul family and the search is ongoing, so please, make this a priority. Brian Forgham was hired by Jason Thorpe who was registered as the previous owner of the property. However, I have subsequently discovered that Mr Thorpe had been granted power of attorney by his aunt Miss Helena Lanark, and that in reality she owned the property, though Mr Thorpe dealt with the sale.'

Jane waited as the team took notes. DS Hunt raised his hand and asked if Mrs Forgham had been formally told that they now had a match for the dental records of their victim, confirming it was her daughter. Jane looked at the investigation board showing Mrs Forgham's details from her interview. She felt that Hunt should be the one to relay this news.

'Detective Sergeant, I'd like you to go and see Mrs Forgham accompanied by a female officer. Ask her about the white Transit van owned by her husband, which I believe was sold four years ago.'

There was a murmur around the room and Jane waited for it to go silent.

'We need to ascertain if there is any evidence still contained in the Transit van. I also think we should ask Mrs Forgham if we can search her property.'

Jane pointed to the photographs taken at the site, showing the iron chain and leg cuff bolted to the floor.

'This is not standard issue or sold in hardware stores, so it would be good if we had some clue as to where it came from. It is still just a supposition that Brian Forgham was the only person who knew where his daughter was.'

Again, Hunt raised his hand. 'Ma'am, do we know if the demolition company are back at work? I believe DCI Carter was getting ready to give them permission.'

Jane nodded. 'I've received a memo from DCI Carter stating that he had given permission for work to continue on the house itself, but they were to cordon off the shelter until forensics and everyone else were satisfied no further evidence would be forthcoming.'

Jane then smiled broadly and said she had brought in a large box of pastries that she hoped they would all enjoy with their coffee.

As Jane stepped into her office, feeling that she had now at least made them all aware of her presence, her desk phone rang. It was the duty sergeant calling to say that Rachit Agrawal was in reception and was asking to speak to her. Jane immediately went to the front desk and as soon as Rachit saw her, he got to his feet.

'You must excuse me coming here because it is possible I am wasting your time, but this morning my eldest daughter told me there is a new girl in her class who she remembered, because they had lived in the flat above them. Her name is Renata Singh.'

Jane looked puzzled. 'I thought the tenant's surname was Abdul.'

He shrugged. 'All I am saying is my daughter remembers her. If they changed their name, I don't know. I thought as a good citizen I should inform you.'

Jane thanked him and took down the name and address of the school, then hurried back to the incident room. DC Taylor was at his desk typing when she asked him to contact St Mary's Secondary School and ask about a pupil called Renata Singh. She was a new pupil and they needed to confirm her family's name and address.

Overhearing, Barbara got up from her desk. 'That school is literally five minutes away.'

Jane glanced at her. She was eating a jam puff pastry. 'Thank you, Barbara. Perhaps, Tim, to avoid delay, you should just take yourself there. We need to verify that this young girl, Renata Singh, lived at the property and had a previous surname of Abdul.'

* * *

Jane was now on her way to another high-rise estate. Tim Taylor had quickly been able to confirm that Renata Singh was the youngest daughter of Mrs Omala Singh, and she had two siblings aged fifteen and sixteen.

The headmistress had no information regarding whether Renata and her family had previously been in residence at the Stockwell property, but she was able to tell Tim that they had only moved into their present council flat two months earlier. She could not supply a contact number and Jane had no option but to go and visit Mrs Singh in person.

The high-rise estate was in surprisingly good condition and looked to Jane as if it had been built in the sixties. Even the lift was working, which was a blessing given that Mrs Singh occupied a flat on the eighth floor. Jane was impressed at the cleanliness of the communal corridor and flat 862 appeared to have a freshly painted front door and a new door mat. The doorbell also looked as if it had been recently installed and after ringing it Jane only had to wait a moment before the door was opened by an Asian woman.

'I'm DI Tennison,' Jane said, showing her identification. 'Are you Mrs Singh?'

The woman nodded nervously.

'I'm working out of Stockwell police station and need to ask you a few questions regarding a property I believe you previously lived in which is now being demolished.'

Mrs Singh ushered Jane into the flat. She was very attractive and wore her long dark hair in a braid reaching to her waist. It was hard to determine her age, but there were grey strands intertwined with her black hair. She was wearing Western clothes and had heavy makeup with a dark eye liner.

'I assure you it's nothing to worry about,' Jane reassured her, 'and nothing to do with your children. I just want to ask a few questions about your tenancy at the property, and to confirm whether your surname was previously Abdul.'

The mention of the name seemed to make Mrs Singh shudder.

'He was my husband,' Mrs Singh said, coldly.

'Is there somewhere we can sit down?' Jane asked.

Mrs Singh led her into a small but brightly decorated living room with a sofa and a single armchair. Jane sat on the sofa and waited for Mrs Singh to take the armchair.

'I have nothing to say about that man,' Mrs Singh said. 'My life has changed, and whatever criminal act he has been involved with . . . I no longer have any association with him and have not seen him for over four years.'

Mrs Singh pursed her lips and looked as if she had nothing more to say, but with patient encouragement from Jane she gradually opened up, explaining that her husband had been unable to pay the rent for many months and had been equally unable to provide for his family. At that time she had had three young children, but any benefits they received had been frittered away by her husband on gambling and drink. Mrs Singh was almost in tears as she explained there was often little food for her children.

Mrs Singh seemed relieved when Jane steered the conversation around to Brian Forgham. In contrast to what Rachit Agrawal had said, Mrs Singh described Forgham as being very kind. Even though they had major rent arrears he was always polite, and at one time he had even bought them some bread and cheese. He had also been exceedingly helpful with repairs and had appeared to be distressed when the company had turned off the central heating in the building.

'We had no running water or heating for many months, but we had nowhere else to go. My husband was unable to get work . . . and then he simply disappeared. Apparently, he went to Birmingham in the hope of getting work, but I knew he had deserted us.'

Jane remained patient as Mrs Singh became more emotional – and then broke down in tears when Jane mentioned Brian Forgham's murder.

'It was terrible . . . we were so sad. As I've already said, he was a kind man, but he was put in a very difficult position as everyone was being evicted and the house was going to rack and ruin. After Mr Forgham died, there was another man who took over who was terrible. He came and threatened me and the children. We thought he had been hired to replace Mr Forgham, but in the end we found out who he really was. He was the owner of the flats and such an obnoxious young man. He told us that if we didn't leave, he would have our possessions thrown out into the street . . .'

Mrs Singh started sobbing, then plucked a handful of tissues from a box on the table beside her. Once she had composed herself, she went on to explain that the council had rehoused them in a dreadful place for several months, then they had moved from one terrible rental to another until they eventually found this flat.

Jane thanked Mrs Singh profusely, telling her how helpful she had been and reassuring her that she just needed to ask a few more quick questions regarding the time when Brian Forgham had been murdered. Mrs Singh closed her eyes.

'I remember it was a very cold night in September. I think he had been at the house because my daughter remembered the door to the basement was open, and nobody was allowed into the basement. That was where Mr Forgham did repair work, and kept all the paints and maintenance tools, but it was always locked.'

Jane nodded. 'And apparently no one was allowed in the garden either?'

'Yes, that's correct. It was the only time he would become assertive, if anyone even asked to use the garden. I had three young children who would have loved to play there but there was a large, corrugated-iron fence, so you couldn't get in even if you were allowed to.'

'Mrs Singh, after Mr Forgham died, how long did you stay in the flat before you were evicted?'

'I think it must have been early December . . . everyone else had left It was very cold . . . very, very cold.'

'Did you at any time see anyone going into the basement? Or did you see anyone in the garden?' Jane asked.

Mrs Singh shook her head. 'No. We saw no one. But I do remember that we thought an animal might have been trapped in the garden.'

'An animal?' Jane asked.

'Yes, a cat maybe? We thought we heard a cat meowing. It went on for some time. But, as I said, we couldn't go into the garden, and we couldn't get into the basement . . . and then we were evicted.'

'And then?' Jane asked.

Mrs Singh shrugged. 'I got divorced and my cousin introduced me to my present husband.'

* * *

Jane walked into the incident room and stared at all the names and addresses on the board. DS Hunt joined her.

'We found the last tenant in the Stockwell house,' Jane said.

'Anything positive?' Hunt asked.

'Not really, just that they heard what sounded like a cat meowing for days. It could have been Samantha, chained up in the shelter, but that's basically all I got. No one saw Forgham taking her into the basement, just the awful sounds of the crying.'

Sergeant Hunt nodded. 'Well, Samantha's mother did cry, eventually. I have to say that I've never, in all my career, seen a mother show such a lack of emotion when they've received such wretched news; in fact, at one point, she pursed her lips as if she thought it served her daughter right. Anyway, the other good news, if you can call it that, is she allowed us access to her husband's box room where he worked. There were filing cabinets full of old invoices, a few cans of paint, tiles, stuff he used for the maintenance of the property – and an old toolbox containing items he would have used for his work. But we also found two padlocks, various chains and a set of handcuffs. Apparently, our Mr Forgham used them when he was in the army as an MP. I believe we'll be able to match the padlock and even some of the chains to those found at the shelter.'

Jane nodded. 'Good. Good work.'

Hunt sighed. 'Yeah, doesn't feel like it, though. We have no other suspects, so I think as DCI Carter suggested, it's case closed.' He turned and looked at the photographs on the incident board, nodding towards the large black-and-white crime scene photographs of the mummified baby.

'Well, we know for sure that wasn't Samantha's.'

By an awful coincidence, at that very moment Jane received a call from the pathologist examining the mummified child, telling her that he had been able to determine that the child had been buried alive. This was due to the discovery of fine wool fibres in the infant's nasal passages and lungs. Further details would be forwarded.

Jane closed her eyes. She recalled her feelings on her previous case, when the nun's coffin was opened. The scratch marks on the underside of the coffin lid indicated that the poor woman had been buried alive and had been frantically trying to escape.

Jane had persisted in hunting down the nun's killer, even though it had been a long and exhausting process. She had been determined to get justice and she knew now that, no matter what DCI Carter said, she would also get justice for this tiny newborn child.

CHAPTER SIX

Jane had had a sleepless night, but unusually for her, it wasn't because of the case she was working on or the behaviour of her boss. She'd been kept awake by all the decisions she had to make about her house. She got up early, made copious notes about her thoughts and then before she left for the station she called Eddie, leaving a message on his answer machine to ask if he could meet her at seven that evening to discuss things.

When she got to the station, the team were beginning to remove details about Samantha Forgham from the incident board, while DCI Carter was in his office preparing a final report and a briefing to close the case.

The only items now left up on the board were the photographs of the exterior and interior of the shelter, and the images of the mummified baby. The pathologist had forwarded his findings yesterday evening and Carter was looking over the results as he wrote his report.

Jane had breakfast in the canteen before joining Carter in his office.

'Samantha Forgham's case is now officially closed,' he told her, leaning back in his chair with a satisfied smile. 'A fast turnaround and a good outcome, but now . . .' he reached over to pick up a file, 'with regard to this other case, last night we got the report from Mr Johnson, the pathologist. In his estimation the child's body is at least thirty years old. He also found traces of the wool blanket that had been wrapped around the baby in the nasal cavity and lungs.'

He looked at Jane and raised the palms of his hands in an open gesture. 'I have to say that, even with this new information, I'm loath to use my full team. I very much doubt, given the huge time lapse, that we'll ever be able to bring a suspect to the table.'

Jane leaned forward. 'I don't know if you read my report on my conversation with Arnold Hadley, the lawyer for Jason Thorpe who sold the property to the developer?'

Carter closed his eyes. 'Yes, I did glance through it, but I doubt that anything he told you can help us find out what occurred thirty years ago.' He shuffled some papers on his desk.

'When I spoke to Mr Hadley, I did request that Jason Thorpe contact me as he is a relative of the previous owner of the property,' Jane said.

'Until I've had a conversation with him, I'd like you to simply oversee the situation and perhaps pay one more visit to the shelter before we give the demolition company clearance to knock it down.'

Jane was still unsure of what Carter's intentions were.

'Do you want me to investigate the murder of the baby? And try to find some background information about the family who were last in residence at the property? Perhaps they can shed some light on what happened?'

Carter gave a dismissive shrug of his shoulders. 'Let's say we just make the appropriate moves. Right now I have a number of more important cases which require my attention. This dead baby case will probably take up a lot of time and go nowhere, trying to trace possible suspects from thirty years ago. That said, Detective Inspector Tennison, I think with your experience you have some expertise in this area. I'll assign you DC Taylor and if you need extra hands then I'm sure Sergeant Hunt will make the time for you. As you probably know, he's scheduled for retirement shortly.'

Jane had mixed feelings. She wanted to investigate the mummified baby, but it felt as if Carter was deliberately sidelining her to a dead-end case so she wouldn't get in his way.

'Sir, can I just clarify that you want me to take over this investigation and make it my priority, so—'

He interrupted her. 'Yes, exactly.' He thumbed through various documents on his desk before he pulled out a fax from Emra Saddell. He held it up between finger and thumb. 'Miss Saddell has requested that her colleague, Detective Sergeant Paul Lawrence from the forensic department, take over her work on the dead baby. She has been requested to join a team investigating the brutal murder of a banker. As you can read, she's apologetic but she feels that Paul Lawrence's experience on the last case you both worked on will be beneficial to this one. He is, as you are more than aware, very experienced and will decide what should be examined at the lab in Lambeth.'

Carter didn't hand Jane the fax but tossed it down on his desk. Part of her was pleased that she would be working with Paul Lawrence again, but at the same time she couldn't help feeling that the case was not being taken seriously. She pushed back her chair.

'Thank you very much, sir. I'd like to take DC Taylor with me this morning to have one more look at the shelter. If I'm satisfied, I'll then report back for you to give clearance for it to be demolished.'

'Good . . . fine.' He dismissed her with a wave of his hand.

* * *

Jane arrived at the building site forty-five minutes later, accompanied by the young DC Tim Taylor. She found Mr Bishop, the foreman, whose relief at the news the demolition could soon go ahead was palpable. 'These delays have been costing me a fortune, I can tell you. The developer has even been threatening to withdraw from the deal if they can't proceed with plans for building the apartments soon.'

Duckboards had been placed over the area that looked like a bomb crater, and more duckboards led to the shelter, which had yellow-and-black police tape securing the perimeter. Bishop gestured towards the partly cleared garden.

'The tunnel led straight into the basement. Someone must have taken a lot of time and effort during the war because it was very professionally built. Must have cost quite a bit. They somehow managed to get around council planning regulations too. Also – and, again, not shown on my plans – there was a basement in the shelter itself.'

By the time Bishop had finished talking, they had reached the perimeter of the shelter. Jane could clearly see where the digger had struck the corner as it was partly exposed.

'Mr Bishop, is the shelter safe to go in now?'

'Yes, detective. We had to make sure of that. But I wouldn't go too close to the area which was hit by the digger. And you'll need these.' He handed Jane and DC Taylor a couple of hard hats. 'Do you want me to come with you?'

'No thanks, we'll be fine,' Jane said.

Jane and DC Taylor stood in front of the heavy door. This time she was able to ease it back far enough for them to slip through the gap. Taylor had brought a high-powered torch and he was using it to walk carefully through the main living area, shining the strong beam in front of him.

'As you can see, it was stocked with tinned food and blankets,' Jane told him, 'but the bodies were found at the lower level.'

'There's a terrible stink in here,' Taylor muttered.

Jane ignored him and asked him to shine the torch on the stairs so they could see where they were going as they made their way down.

Jane examined the area where the baby had been found. 'Would whoever placed the baby between those two cement blocks have just left it in full view? Or was it somehow hidden behind the other cement blocks which had fallen?' she wondered aloud.

She stepped back and then looked at a sign warning not to enter the tunnel. 'I think I've seen enough,' she said.

'Are you telling me, ma'am, that some bloke built this tunnel from the house during the war?'

She sighed. 'Yes.'

'I just don't understand how no one came down here and found the young woman, or those tied-up cement blocks.'

'No one came down here, Tim, because no one was allowed to use the garden or access the basement.'

'In that case, whoever made those rules must have known what was down here.'

She took the torch from him. 'You're probably right, Tim. Samantha's father made sure no one entered the garden, and no one else accessed the basement – that was his job, But I doubt very much he knew what else was hidden down here.'

She shone the torch over to the iron bedstead. The mattress had been removed and taken to the lab. She could still see the marks on the floor where the chain which had held Samantha had been attached.

'That's where she was chained up,' she said. 'The last people living in the house thought a stray cat had been trapped in the garden because they could hear it meowing. That poor girl must have screamed for days and nights on end . . . what an appalling death.'

DC Taylor remained silent as he followed Jane out, handing his hard hat to the waiting Bishop.

'Do I have clearance to demolish the shelter now?' he asked eagerly.

'I need to report back,' Jane said. 'Then DCI Carter should be in touch later this afternoon.'

Bishop led them out across the duckboards. 'I've heard Jason Thorpe's flown over and he's been in talks with the developer, so hopefully everything can get back on track now.'

Jane thought it odd that Thorpe would be involved with the developer if he had already sold the property. 'Do you know why Mr Thorpe contacted the developer?'

Bishop shook his head

'Did you see Mr Thorpe?' she asked.

'No, I've never met him. I was only told here was here this morning. He usually stays at a posh hotel, Claridge's, I believe. He's a very wealthy young man, apparently, a wine importer. He must have got a fair bundle for selling this monstrosity, too, what with it being five storeys and having this much land attached.'

Jane thanked Bishop for his time, eager to get back to the station to see if Jason Thorpe had contacted DCI Carter.

While Taylor drove, Jane flipped through her notebook back to her conversation with Mr Hadley. She was keen to clarify what he had actually said about the ownership of the property. It had originally been owned by Helena Lanark, but Jason Thorpe had power of attorney and could therefore sell it on her behalf. Jane underlined Helena Lanark's name in the hope she could arrange an interview with her.

* * *

As they arrived at the front of the station, Tim dropped her off and went to park her car. As Jane climbed the steps, she heard her name being called and turned to see Sharon Forgham behind her, clearly in a very anxious state.

'I want to speak to you,' she snapped, 'I just want to tell you that I'm not going to accept my daughter's remains. I don't care what the law says.' She paused to get her breath. 'After you came to see me, I've had my flat searched. I didn't think there could be anything worse than having your husband murdered – but now you're telling me he's responsible for Samantha's death. You have no idea the pain you've caused me. If it wasn't bad enough to lose Brian, to now find out what he did to Samantha . . . you've left me nothing to live for.'

Jane wanted to find words of comfort, but Brian Forgham's widow was so angry and upset, Jane felt it was more respectful to say nothing. Sharon Forgham gave her one last furious look, then turned on her heel. Jane watched her walk away, then went into the station and headed to her office.

Barbara knocked lightly on her door and walked straight in as Jane was hanging up her coat.

'Barbara, would you mind knocking and waiting for me to tell you to come in?' Jane said tetchily.

'Oh, sorry. It's just that I've got a message for you from DCI Carter. He had to go to Shoreditch and there is a Mr . . .' she screwed up her face trying to remember, 'a Mr Thorpe coming into the station this morning. DCI Carter told me to tell you to speak to him and then report back.'

'Thank you, Barbara,' Jane said without looking at her.

She flounced out as DC Taylor walked in without knocking. Jane sighed in exasperation.

'Your car keys, ma'am. I couldn't find anywhere to park in the street near the station, so as I was told DCI Carter's out, I put it in his allocated space.'

'I don't think that's a very good idea,' Jane said.

'I asked Barbara when he would be back, and she said he'd gone to Shoreditch and would be some time.'

She sat down at her desk. 'Tell me, Tim, Barbara seems to have a rather over-confident manner, wouldn't you say? Or perhaps I'm not quite used to a station secretary being privy to her DCI's diary.'

He shrugged his shoulders. 'She is a bit over-familiar, but then gossip has it that she sees a lot of the DCI privately.'

Jane nodded to herself. 'Thank you, Tim, that'll be all. I might ask you to come back into my office in a while. Apparently, Jason Thorpe is coming to the station. Can you bring him up to me when he arrives?'

'Yes, ma'am.' DC Taylor scurried out, looking a bit shamefaced. Jane thought he was probably chastising himself for repeating station gossip.

Her desk phone rang, it was DS Paul Lawrence. She was, as always, pleased to hear from him and as she knew that he had been assigned to examine the body of the baby she was eager to hear his results. They had worked extensively together in the past, and she admired his skill and dedication.

'Just thought I'd give you a quick heads-up, Jane. I'm going over to the mortuary as the mummified baby has been taken back there. To be honest, I don't think the lab quite knew what to do with it after old boy Johnson had finished doing his post-mortem.'

'I haven't actually read the post-mortem report,' Jane said, 'but it was a bit of a shock to find out the baby had been buried alive.'

'Yes, I'm afraid if he found fibres in the airways and stomach that would prove that the infant was still breathing when it was buried,' Paul said.

'I'm really glad you're on this case, Paul. Much as I like Emra Saddell, I don't think there is anyone better than you, or anyone I can trust more to give me accurate information. I know it's going to be challenging, given how long ago the baby was buried in that shelter – Johnson's estimation was that it happened about thirty years ago. I'll keep you updated with anything I uncover, and I look forward to seeing you soon.'

As she replaced the receiver, there was a loud knock on the door. Jane closed her eyes as she knew it would be Barbara. '*Yes!*' Jane said, loudly.

'The duty sergeant has called to say there is a Mr . . . I forgot . . . um, oh yes, a Mr Thorpe at reception. DC Taylor's gone to get him.'

'Thank you, Barbara. Would you be so kind as to bring us two teas from the canteen?'

Barbara pursed her lips. 'Yes, of course. Milk and sugar?'

'That would be perfect, thank you,' Jane said with a brittle smile.

CHAPTER SEVEN

Jane opened her handbag and took out her compact, dabbing her nose and cheeks with powder, then combing her hair. She had just closed her handbag again when DC Taylor walked in, accompanied by a very handsome and exceedingly well-dressed man. He was wearing a pinstripe suit, and his tanned face and sun-bleached blond hair made it obvious that this must be Jason Thorpe. Before DC Taylor could introduce them, Jane stood up.

'I'm Detective Inspector Jane Tennison, and you must be Jason Thorpe?'

'Yes. How very nice to meet you. Just sad it's under such distressing circumstances.'

'Do sit down,' Jane said, nodding at Tim to leave the room.

Jason opened his wallet and handed Jane his business card, showing he was head of a wine import company in New South Wales.

'I would have come in earlier this morning, but I had a meeting to attend,' he said.

'Yes, the site foreman said you were with the developer,' Jane said, eager to gauge his reaction.

He looked surprised. 'Although I no longer own the property, having sold it to the developer, I was concerned that I might in some way be held accountable for what had been discovered and be presented with costs over the delays. I was relieved to hear they had permission to continue work at the site.'

Jane smiled, wondering if he was hiding something from her. 'Yes, I believe today they were given clearance to demolish the shelter, where we made our tragic discoveries.'

Without asking permission, Jason opened a silver case from his suit pocket, pulled out a cigarette and tapped it on the closed case.

He then took out what appeared to be a solid gold lighter and lit the cigarette.

'Although I'm not privy to all the facts, what I've been told via my lawyer, Mr Hadley, is that the victim had been imprisoned inside the shelter by her own father.' He exhaled a plume of cigarette smoke. 'But I really have no further information to give you. I was just overseeing the eviction of the tenants with Mr Forgham when this horrific incident must have occurred.'

Jane couldn't help feeling there was a rehearsed quality to what Mr Thorpe was telling her. She opened her notebook.

'Yes, we know about the eviction of the tenants. The reason the poor girl was not discovered was because after Mr Forgham's murder, and the final eviction, the house was boarded up and left empty.'

'Yes, I suppose that's correct.' By now the ash on his cigarette was almost an inch long and Jason peered around the room as if looking for an ashtray. Jane, who rarely smoked, opened a drawer and took one out, putting it on the desk in front of him.

'Mr Thorpe, could I ask the reason for the long delay between the final eviction and you selling the property eighteen months ago?'

Jason tapped the ash from his cigarette into the ashtray. 'My aunt, who actually owned the house, had always refused for it to be sold. I was able to persuade her that it would be financially beneficial to divide the house into flats, with the income from the rents sufficient to keep it in a reasonable condition. As it transpired, because it had been left empty for many years, it was not in the end that cost effective. Once the house had been divided up there was still considerable maintenance and repairs to be done. When these became too costly, I suggested to my aunt and her lawyer that it would be financially better to sell.'

'So, it was your aunt who had always owned the property?'

'Yes, she had been left it by her father.'

'And it was your aunt who agreed for you to convert it into flats?'

'Yes. I was obviously paid a certain amount to manage it and to hire a reliable maintenance man who would deal with all the problems.'

Jane noticed his hesitancy as he stubbed out his cigarette.

'So after leaving the house empty, when did your aunt agree that it should be sold?'

'My aunt became ill, and gave me power of attorney, so I acted in her best interests. By that time the house was in a bad state of disrepair; in fact, it was becoming quite dangerous.'

Jane made some notes as Jason Thorpe sat back in his chair. He was wearing strong aftershave which she was beginning to find rather overpowering.

'Do you need me for anything further?' he said. 'I'm only here for a fleeting visit and I've got lots of meetings scheduled. Plus, I still need to see Mr Hadley.'

'I won't keep you much longer,' Jane said, 'but I do have a couple more important questions.'

Jason frowned. 'I assure you that Mr Hadley can verify everything I have just told you. He has been my aunt's lawyer for many years.'

Jane ignored him. 'Mr Thorpe, did you insist that the basement should never be rented out?'

He blinked rapidly. 'That was my aunt's decision.'

'Were you aware of a tunnel which led from the basement to the old shelter?'

He shook his head. 'No, I had absolutely no idea about that. To be perfectly honest, I was only ever at the property for short periods of time, and I can't really recall ever even seeing the shelter. My aunt was rather obsessive about her refusal to allow the basement to be used, as well as no tenant being allowed into the garden.' He smiled. 'As her nephew, I just did as I was told.'

Jane lowered her eyes as if concentrating on her notes. She was fully aware that Mr Thorpe had to have known there was a shelter in the garden as it was on all the council plans. However, she decided not to press the matter and was relieved when Barbara knocked and brought in two cups of tea, along with a bowl of sugar cubes and a teaspoon.

'I'm sorry it's taken so long, ma'am, but it's lunchtime in the canteen.'

Jane didn't thank her as she took the tray, placing it on her desk. Barbara gave Jason Thorpe a very obvious once-over.

'If you need anything else, ma'am, just call.'

'I will,' Jane snapped, as Barbara left.

'Mr Thorpe, I now have to tell you about a very distressing detail which you may not yet be privy to.'

She handed him his teacup and he waved his hand as she offered him sugar. He sipped the rather milky liquid with a look of distaste and Jane suspected that it was already tepid.

'In the shelter we also discovered two slabs of concrete tied together with a leather strap. The slabs may have, at one time, surrounded some kind of water pipe,' she stated.

Mr Thorpe appeared not to pay much attention as he put his teacup back down on the tray. Jane continued.

'Mr Thorpe, wrapped in a blanket and a waterproof cloth, we discovered the mummified corpse of a baby.'

Jason's jaw dropped open. 'What?'

'It has been estimated to have been in the shelter for possibly twenty-five to thirty years.'

'Dear God! I don't believe this . . .'

'We have further disturbing information, I'm afraid. Apparently, the baby, possibly a newborn, had been buried alive.'

Jason seemed to be genuinely shocked. He leaned forward.

'Surely you don't think that any member of my family could have had anything to do with this dreadful thing?'

'You must understand our situation, Mr Thorpe. We need to question your aunt as soon as possible in order to eliminate that possibility. We will also need your help in listing which family members lived at the property twenty to thirty years ago. But the first person I will need to talk to is your aunt, Helena Lanark.'

Jason stood up abruptly. 'You'll have to excuse me, but I really need to talk to my lawyer. I'm perfectly willing to assist you in every possible way, but my aunt is in a fragile state, not only physically but mentally, and I am deeply concerned about how this might affect her.'

Jane made a note and looked up. 'I do understand your concerns, of course, Mr Thorpe. How long has your aunt been in a fragile state?'

'For some considerable time.'

'Is this when she gave you power of attorney over her property and finances?' Jane asked.

It was as if she had hit a sore point. Jason Thorpe's mouth turned down and he suddenly looked tense.

'Detective, I really don't like what you're inferring. As I've just said, I'm perfectly willing to have a further discussion with you, but it is imperative that I now pass on to my lawyer all you have just told me.'

Jane stood up. There was no way she could actually stop Jason Thorpe from leaving the station. He wasn't under suspicion, or even assisting police inquiries. However, his reaction had indicated to Jane that perhaps this wealthy young man had not acted entirely in his aunt's best interests regarding the disposal of the house.

* * *

DS Hunt and DC Tim Taylor had already spent over an hour working through the Lanarks' family tree. Jane had also requested that they contact births, deaths and marriages, and if needs be they should go in person to double check the facts. Meanwhile, Jane had contacted Mr Hadley and had been told that he was 'unavoidably detained', but that he would return her call as soon as possible.

DS Lawrence was becoming exceedingly irritated by the mortuary assistant's attitude. The young man claimed that the two concrete slabs the infant's corpse had been wedged between were no longer at the mortuary, and told Lawrence that he thought they had been removed a few days ago.

'Are you serious?' Lawrence said incredulously. 'Have you checked with SOCO to see if they have retrieved them?'

'I don't know,' the assistant said dismissively. 'They were just two concrete slabs!'

Lawrence sighed, asking if he could be given access to the infant's remains, which he knew had been delivered back to the mortuary from the pathology lab. They were held in a fridge in a very large plastic container that had been taped down to make it airtight. Lawrence looked down at his list.

'Apparently there was a leather belt, as well. Do you know where this is now?'

The assistant shrugged. 'No, I've got no idea. It may have been left over at the mortuary. I think you should ask the pathologist or the forensic expert, Miss Saddell. They would have arranged for it to be taken over there when it came in.'

Lawrence shook his head in frustration, surprised that Jane had not made sure the leather belt was retained for examination, given its potential forensic significance.

Lawrence signed out the large plastic container and carried it to his car, placing it carefully in the boot. He had not yet examined a mummified corpse, and if necessary, he was prepared to spend his own free time doing so and bringing in an anthropologist to help with his findings.

* * *

At the station Jane was perched on the edge of her desk whilst Sergeant Hunt went over what he had been able to discover about the Lanark family. The property had been inherited by a Charles Henry Lanark in 1923 from his father, also named Charles. Along with the property was a substantial fortune made from very successful printing companies. At the age of twenty-nine he had married Muriel Petrukhin, aged nineteen, and they had three children: Helena, Beatrice and Marjorie.

'I've been over at the general registry office at St Catherine's House, but it's really complicated going that far back and I'm not that certain I have the correct dates.'

Jane was making notes and held up her pen. 'How old are the three daughters now?'

'Helena sixty-one, Beatrice is fifty-six, and Marjorie died aged twenty-two.'

'Do we have the date of her death?' Jane asked.

'April 1955.'

Jane flicked through her notebook. 'What about cause of death?'

He shook his head. 'But the time frame means that the child could have been Marjorie's.' He frowned. 'It could also have been either of the other daughters. We have the mother deceased aged fifty-five, and the father five years after that. She was very young when they married . . .'

Jane pursed her lips. 'Well, we'll have to check all this out. So, when Charles Henry Lanark died, do we have any information on his heirs?'

'All we have been able to come up with so far is that his eldest daughter Helena was the main beneficiary. As you know, she retained ownership of the Stockwell property until it was sold by her nephew.'

'What about the printing works that all the money came from?'

'I believe they've long gone. But we really need more time to clarify everything . . . and this has taken up hours already.'

'I'm aware of that,' Jane said. 'And I think you've done a good job. My next thing will be a visit to Helena Lanark. I've been waiting on a return call from her lawyer, Mr Hadley. Thank you for all this. I'll let you know what else I'd like you to work on.'

Detective Sergeant Hunt raised an eyebrow and headed for the door. 'I think DCI Carter is back. Do you want me to run this by him?'

Jane frowned. 'I'll have a conversation with DCI Carter when I'm ready,' she said curtly.

* * *

DS Lawrence had carefully removed the mummified infant, who remained encased in the blanket and waterproof wrapping. He placed the remains on the table, which had been covered with white paper, alongside an instrument tray. He checked through the pathologist's notes, stating where he had cut the waterproof wrap and the time he had done so. The material was still pliable and reminded Lawrence of an old Burberry rainproof coat his father had worn. It even had the same almost greenish hue to the material.

The second note Johnson had made was regarding the blue blanket, which he judged to be fine cashmere. To Lawrence's irritation, the blanket had been partly unfolded and cut away from the remains of the infant. Lawrence now paid more attention to the second page of notes. Johnson had identified the remains of the umbilical cord, which therefore indicated that the infant was a newborn. He also estimated that the baby had probably weighed six to seven pounds at birth and appeared to have no physical deformities or injuries. An underlined note stated that by opening the rib cage, thus losing the outer level of mummification, he had discovered minute fibres of the blue blanket. He had also discovered similar fibres at the back of the infant's throat and nasal passages, indicating that the baby had been alive when it had been wrapped in the blue blanket.

Lawrence physically jumped when Emra Saddell tapped him on the shoulder.

'So, you've got it now? I did a bit of a sidestep, to be honest, because I really didn't fancy having to work on this little soul. I doubt that there can be any firm conclusion due to its age . . . and I believe Professor Johnson was of the same opinion.'

Lawrence gave her a small smile. 'I've heard you're working on that banker's murder case. I always find it invigorating to be working on a fresh murder, but I'm really keen to find out just how much more information I can come up with on this old case. For example, someone cut this waterproof square to wrap around the child. Someone also must have owned this fine cashmere blanket which was wrapped around the baby so tightly shortly after the birth.'

'Rather you than me,' Emra said. 'As sad as it is, it could all be a waste of time.'

Lawrence really wished Saddell would just leave him in peace if she was not going to say anything more positive. He then remembered the missing belt. 'Did you ever see a belt, or whatever it was that was tied around the two blocks of cement?'

She nodded. 'I did see it somewhere, but I don't recall where it went. I believe Detective Inspector Tennison was with the foreman when he cut the leather strap at the building site, but I've got no idea if it's still at the mortuary, or perhaps it was brought into the lab here.'

Lawrence shook his head. 'I find this totally unacceptable. All exhibits seized by the police should be recorded in an exhibits book, with a reference number so the items can be tracked.'

'OK, well, I'll make some inquiries,' Saddell said with a shrug. 'I'll leave you to it.'

* * *

The incident room was a hive of activity. There had been a spate of burglaries and a shop keeper had been held at gunpoint; in addition, a local man had been found hanged and a woman had been reported as missing from a nearby nursing home. Samantha Forgham and the dead baby seemed to have been long forgotten as officers busily worked the phones and updated the incident board.

Jane knocked on DCI Carter's door, but before she could even announce herself, the door swung open and Carter was standing in the doorway, rolling up his shirt sleeves.

'I don't believe this! I go out to have a meeting with the super and all hell breaks loose.'

Jane stepped aside. 'I just wanted to run a few things by you, sir.'

'Listen to me, Jane, I've had more things running by me in the past half hour than in the past six months. Do you know about these burglaries?'

'I don't have any of the facts yet, sir . . . but I just wanted to give you an update on the infant found in the shelter.'

He stopped in his tracks. 'What about it?'

'We've been tracing who owned the property thirty years ago. There were three women living there, and one of them may have given birth. In particular, I want to question Helena Lanark, who inherited the Stockwell property after her father's death.'

Carter frowned. 'What?'

'It seems to me that a member of the family had to have been aware of the child in the shelter because the house had been deliberately left empty for many years. Then this Helena Lanark's nephew gets power of attorney and had the house is turned into flats.'

'Yes, yes, I read that. It was on the incident board,' he said tersely.

'My main concern is that no one was allowed to use the basement, and no tenant was allowed to use the garden. This is obviously rather suspicious . . .'

'Suspicious? I tell you what, Jane, I wish to God whoever killed that baby had taken it out and buried it somewhere else.' He put his hands on his hips. 'So, what do you want to do about it?'

'I would like to proceed by interviewing Helena Lanark. And there is a possibility that there could even be a fraud involved.'

'What?'

'Nothing really adds up, sir. The owner's nephew, Jason Thorpe, had power of attorney which allowed him to convert the house into flats, and when that was no longer financially viable, the tenants were evicted before Mr Thorpe sold it for a very high figure. It's possible that Mr Thorpe may have filtered some of the money into his own account.'

DCI Carter folded his arms and leaned against the wall by his office door.

'Tennison, you've gone from suspecting the women who lived at the house to now bringing in some nephew and adding in fraud. To be honest, it's getting fucking out of control.'

The entire incident room went quiet as Carter raised his voice. Jane glanced at the officers, all trying to look as if they weren't listening. She turned back to Carter.

'I really don't like the way you're talking to me, sir. I am just doing my job, attempting to investigate the murder of that infant. To me, it seems quite obvious that the family must have known what was in that shelter. Just as they knew there was a tunnel from the house leading to it. That's why no one was allowed in the basement or garden.'

Carter blew air out through his lips.

'All right, all right . . . I apologise. I spoke out of turn, but I've got a lot of new cases to deal with and, as you are well aware, we work to a budget. This situation with the dead child has already been too costly. Do what you have to and get closure as quickly as possible. Right now, I could really use you on at least one of the other new cases that we're trying to deal with.' He walked off and banged through the double doors of the incident room.

Jane returned to her office. She didn't hear exactly what anyone was saying but it was obvious that Carter's lack of respect for her was now public knowledge.

As she closed her office door, her desk phone rang. It was Arnold Hadley, who apologised for taking such a long time to return her call. Jane tried to keep her voice under control, although she was still seething about the way Carter had spoken to her. She asked Mr Hadley if he could arrange for her to meet with Helena Lanark as soon as possible.

His reply was hesitant. 'Well . . . she's not in good health, to be honest. She's in a care home in Hove.'

'Can you give me the address, please?' Jane said curtly. 'And I'd like a meeting with you at your office tomorrow morning if that would be convenient.'

While she was on the phone, she calculated how long it would take for her to drive to Hove. She wanted to be back at home by seven to meet Eddie, and it was already two o'clock. Almost as an afterthought she asked Hadley about Beatrice Lanark. He told her that she was living in Australia with her son.

'In fact, her son, Mr Thorpe, is here in London. I informed him about what had occurred in the shelter. I believe he's discussing the situation at the Stockwell property with the developer.'

Jane's suspicions concerning Jason Thorpe and the sale of the house were reignited. She made an effort to soften her tone. 'Where does his mother, Beatrice, live?' she asked.

'Just outside Sydney . . . and Jason lives there with her.'

'Thank you so much, Mr Hadley. Could I also just ask you about their younger sister, Marjorie? As far as we have been able to establish, she died very young? But we have no information on the cause of death.'

Mr Hadley paused, then spoke quietly.

'I was obviously not representing the family in those days, but I believe that, very sadly, Marjorie took her own life . . . although I have no further details about the tragedy.'

'Could I ask you how you knew about the suicide, Mr Hadley?'

'My client, Helena Lanark, told me. She said that it had been a tragic and traumatic time in her life, but I know very little about the actual suicide.'

Jane thanked him for his time and ended the call. She realised that it was possible that Marjorie Lanark had given birth to the infant they had found and had then committed suicide. However, to date they had found no reference to the suicide, just a date of her death, and no details of an inquest. There was still a lot she needed to find out.

CHAPTER EIGHT

The residential home in Hove was a large, pleasant, double-fronted house with a small wooden sign saying HILLCREST – PRIVATE RESIDENTIAL CARE HOME. The pathway was immaculate, with beds of flowers either side. At the large glass double-door entrance was a wheelchair ramp and a tub of brilliant red geraniums.

Jane entered through the first set of glass doors into a small, tidy porch area. There was a printed notice stuck to the glass: PLEASE REMOVE ANY SANDY SHOES. Jane opened the door from the porch into a large reception area that had a thick floral carpet, two wingback chairs and a small carved wooden desk. The walls were adorned with beach prints and there were vases of fresh flowers on various side tables. There were further glass doors the other side of the desk leading into a corridor.

Jane approached the desk, which had telephones and a large leather diary on top, with a couple of filing cabinets behind. She was wondering if there was a bell for her to ring, when a smiling, rather plump woman appeared, wearing smart overalls with 'Hillcrest' embroidered on the breast pocket.

'You must be Detective Inspector Tennison?' she said, offering her hand.

'Yes, that's right. And you are?' Jane shook her hand.

'I'm Emily Thompson. Unfortunately, Miss Simmons, who is the main proprietor, has had to attend a staff meeting. But she asked me to be of every assistance to you. I believe that you've come to see Helena Lanark?'

Jane smiled. 'Yes, that's right. I do hope this isn't an inconvenient time?'

'Not at all. We have actually just finished serving afternoon tea, so I can take you straight through to her suite. If you'd like a cup of tea, I can ask one of the girls to bring it to you.'

'No, thank you very much,' Jane replied. 'Miss Thompson, could I just ask you if Miss Lanark has many visitors?'

'No, the only visitor she has on a regular basis is her lawyer, Mr Hadley, who is the most charming man and very protective of her. Her nephew occasionally comes to see her. Also, she has regular visits from a hairdresser and manicurist. I don't know if you've been told that Helena is incommunicative.'

'Incommunicative? Is she ill?'

'It is an illness, yes . . . she has severe early onset dementia. But she is a very sweet-natured woman. We are very fortunate to have her,' Miss Thompson replied.

Jane was led through the glass doors into a long, carpeted corridor. Everything about the place was immaculate. More seaside prints lined the walls and each of the freshly painted cream doors had a discreet nameplate at eye level.

Miss Thompson gestured to the doors as they walked past. 'These are all private residents' rooms, and now we are going into the area of private suites. These comprise a bedroom, an en-suite bathroom and a sitting room.'

Jane could only guess at how much this kind of residential home cost, but she was certain it would not be cheap. They turned right at the end of the corridor, into a thickly carpeted bay with French doors leading out onto manicured gardens.

'We have a very good cook,' Miss Thompson continued, 'and three kitchen staff. We also have four nursing staff. And Miss Simmons is a highly qualified matron. She is very security conscious, and we have a security officer who watches the grounds. At Hillcrest, we are proud to be able to say that no resident has ever lost any personal item of clothing or jewellery.'

Jane was beginning to find Miss Thompson's glowing recommendation of the care home a bit tedious. But it made her wonder exactly how much it cost and whether the proceeds from the sale of the Stockwell property were being used to pay for Miss Lanark's care. She made a mental note to ask Mr Hadley.

Miss Thompson tapped on a door with number 12 on it. There was no answer, but Miss Thompson ushered Jane in ahead of her anyway. Jane was instantly impressed by the beautifully decorated and comfortably appointed room. It had a thick woven carpet, a chaise longue, a glass-topped coffee table and two elegant velvet-covered armchairs.

A bay window was on the opposite side of the room, with a modern desk displaying a spread of glossy magazines. On top of the pile was a large leather photograph album.

'You asked if Miss Lanark had any photographs, so I believe this was put out for you,' Miss Thompson explained.

She then gestured for Jane to sit down and opened a door to a bedroom.

'Your visitor is here, Miss Lanark. Would you like your shawl around your shoulders? I see you finished all your tea . . . and you look lovely . . . I think your hairdresser does a really good job.'

Jane felt even more irritated by Miss Thompson's manner, which made it sound as if she was talking to a child. Then a few moments later, Helena Lanark was wheeled into the room. Miss Thompson stopped beside the desk and applied the brake on the wheelchair. Over her arm hung a pale blue cashmere shawl.

'I'm just going to put this on you, Miss Lanark.' She deftly wrapped it around the frail woman's shoulders, then hurried to close the bedroom door, smiling at Jane.

'She does love her pale blue cashmere shawl,' she said in a conspiratorial tone. 'In fact, when she first came here we found out that she can only wear the purest cashmere, because wool irritates her skin. I believe these come from France. Are you sure I can't get you a cup of tea?'

Jane shook her head, eager for the woman to leave. She drew a chair up to the desk. As the door closed behind Miss Thompson, Jane took the opportunity to have a really good look at Helena Lanark.

It was hard to determine how tall she was, as she was hunched over in her chair and seemed swamped by her quilted satin dressing gown. Her ankles were swollen, and she was wearing very expensive-looking fur-lined suede slippers. Her slender hands were folded in her lap, and she had beautifully manicured shell-pink nails. She was also wearing a gorgeous-looking string of pearls.

Helena Lanark had made no movement whatsoever whilst Jane scrutinised her, which Jane found rather unsettling. She inched her chair forwards to have a full view of the woman's face. Her hair had been cut in a 1920s style, with a parting on her right side giving a thick wave of silver hair. Her thin-lipped mouth was tightly closed, but there was a small blob of saliva at the corner. She had a prominent nose, but nothing really prepared Jane for the astonishing colour of her eyes. They were an almost translucent blue, giving the impression that she could be blind.

Jane leaned further forward. 'Miss Lanark, my name is Jane Tennison, and I am a detective inspector with the Metropolitan Police. I am making inquiries about a property in Stockwell that I believe you inherited from your father.'

There was absolutely no reaction. Helena appeared to be completely unaware that Jane was there beside her. Jane reached over to touch one of the pale white hands and it was only then that Helena recoiled. She moved her hand very slowly away, as if she didn't like to be touched.

'Did you understand what I just said, Miss Lanark?' Jane asked. The only other indication that this woman was even alive was a little puff of air coming from her mouth that made the saliva bubble.

Jane glanced at her watch. This was about as unproductive as it could be, and it was looking as if she'd made a very long journey for no result. She could easily imagine how DCI Carter would react when she reported to him. She eased her chair back.

'Miss Lanark, would you mind if I used your bathroom?' As expected, there was no reaction to her request.

Jane walked through the door that led into the bedroom and the en-suite bathroom. The same thick patterned wool carpet continued throughout. The room was not exactly bare, but there was a feeling of emptiness. There was a neat chest of drawers with a mirror, but no cosmetics or brushes and combs. There was a matching wardrobe, and the single bed had a very expensive-looking pale green satin bedspread with a matching silk drape beneath.

The only indication that this bedroom was used by an invalid was the large orthopaedic pillow which had a pristine white cloth over it. There were two small cabinets either side of the bed and a jug of water with a glass beside it. There were no photographs, just two prints on the walls similar to the ones Jane had seen along the corridors. Jane eased open the wardrobe door. There were numerous silk blouses and pleated skirts, and two pairs of leather court shoes, one in black and one in navy. Jane could see from the inner sole that they were handmade. There was one dark navy coat, which had a protective plastic cover over the shoulders.

On the shelves inside the full-length wardrobe were neatly folded cashmere cardigans, all in various shades of blue. Jane closed the doors, then crept over to the dressing table. She pulled open one drawer after another, finding white linen nightgowns, pristine folded underwear and petticoats. All the items appeared to be hardly worn and were clearly expensive.

The small en-suite bathroom had a special raised step beside the bath and a white handlebar around it. The same handlebar was by the toilet and there was a red alarm cord hanging from the ceiling. Jane flushed the toilet before opening the bathroom cabinet. There was an array of vitamins, sleeping tablets and prescribed medication for arthritis as well as numerous hand creams, all with expensive labels. There was an ornate bottle of

Floris Lily of the Valley perfume and Jane eased open the gold cap to smell it.

On the opposite side of the medicine cabinet was a glass shelf with a silver-backed hairbrush and matching comb, which had probably at one time been part of a set.

Jane went back into the sitting room, unable to tell if Miss Lanark had moved since she'd gone. She remained with her perfectly manicured hands folded in her lap and was gazing vacantly out of the window.

Without asking permission, Jane drew the large leather photograph album towards her.

'Would you mind if I looked through your album, Miss Lanark?'

She responded with the same strange puff from her lips, as more saliva gathered at the corner of her mouth.

The leather-bound album was heavily embossed with gold filigree and there was a brass clasp but no key. Jane opened it up and on the first page was a framed sepia photograph of Charles Henry Lanark, Helena's grandfather, wearing the uniform of a high-ranking army officer. With his clipped moustache and chiselled face, he had the same cold, arrogant stare as his granddaughter. According to the inscription in faded red ink, he had been killed in the First World War in 1918.

On the second page was a smaller photograph of Charles Henry Lanark Jr, dated 1917. He had a hooked nose and like his father he was wearing an army officer's uniform. Over the page was a large sepia picture of the Stockwell property, dated 1923. Standing on the steps at the front door was Charles Henry Lanark Jr. Beside him stood a very pretty young woman in a bridal dress and underneath was written 'Marriage of Charles Henry Lanark Jr and Muriel Petrukhin'. It was obvious that Muriel was very much younger, almost childlike in appearance. Before Jane could begin making notes, there was a knock at the door and one of the young carers stepped in.

'So sorry for interrupting, but it's time for Miss Lanark's medication, and then the night nurse will come prepare her for bed.'

Jane looked at her watch. It was only a quarter past five and it seemed sad that they were preparing this woman for bed at such an early hour. As she was wearing a dressing gown and slippers, she more than likely had slept for most of the day anyway. Jane went to pick up her coat beside the photo album, then made a spur-of-the-moment decision: it was obvious Helena Lanark couldn't tell Jane anything about the people in the album, and she probably wouldn't miss it until Jane returned it. She deftly covered the large photo album with her coat, as she smiled at the young girl.

'Thank you very much . . . I'll be leaving now anyway.' Jane looked at Helena Lanark and said goodbye, but there was no reaction. She didn't see Helena's lips turned down in a grimace as she closed the door.

As Jane was passing through reception, Miss Thompson was sitting at the desk. 'I've had a very pleasant meeting, Miss Thompson, thank you.'

The woman gave her a quizzical look.

'I doubt she would have said much to you . . . she rarely, if ever, speaks to any of us. But we do our best to make her as comfortable as possible, and as I mentioned to you earlier, her lawyer is a frequent visitor. He always expresses his thanks to us for taking such good care of her.'

'How long has Miss Lanark been here?'

Miss Thompson shrugged her shoulders. 'I'm not exactly sure . . . she was here before I came, which was four years ago.'

'Good heavens, that long. Was she previously more alert?'

Miss Thompson frowned, apparently disliking being questioned.

'I'd need to check her medical records, but I would need permission to do so. I'm sure her lawyer could give you more information.'

'I'll contact him,' Jane said. 'Thank you again. I'm certainly very impressed with the facilities you provide.'

Jane hurried out and headed towards her car. She had only just started the engine when she saw Jason Thorpe driving into the parking area in a top-of-the-range BMW. He slammed the driver's door closed and walked briskly into the care home. Jane patted the photo album on the passenger seat, eager to look through it when she got home.

* * *

No sooner had Jane arrived outside her house than Eddie turned up and parked his van behind her car.

'I hope this isn't inconvenient, but I've put together some costings for the work you were interested in . . . I just wanted to run them by you.'

'Please, come on in,' Jane said, pleased to see him. 'I'll make a cup of tea.'

Jane and Eddie sat in her kitchen as they discussed his proposals. She kept on adding more and more work that she wanted done until he leaned back in his chair, laughing.

'Bloody hell! You virtually want the whole house refurbished! I'm going to have to talk to some mates to see if we can do it all.'

'This is exactly what I want, and for it all to be done at the same time – but obviously you'll know which jobs should be prioritised. I'll leave it to you to give me estimates and a time frame of when you think you could start and obviously complete.'

'Right, OK. I'll talk it over with my dad tonight and maybe you should also give it some thought as it'll be a big upheaval – unless you don't intend to be living here when it's all going on?'

'Oh, I'll be here,' Jane said, 'but I'll be out for most of the day, so it won't cause too much disruption. I can sleep in whichever bedroom you aren't redecorating.'

Eddie stood up and reached for his jacket, which he'd left on the counter by the sink. He almost knocked the photo album onto the floor but caught it and grinned.

'Family album, is it?'

Jane crossed over and took it from him. 'No, it belongs to the family I was telling you about. I shouldn't even have it, but I doubt anyone will notice it's missing . . . well, I hope not, as I could get into trouble.'

She carried the album to the table and opened it, leafing through a number of pages, then turned to show Eddie.

'The three sisters, Helena, Beatrice and Marjorie.'

The large black-and-white photograph showed three girls, one sitting on a swing, the other two standing either side of her. They were all wearing beautiful white dresses with white stockings and patent leather shoes, their long hair hanging down to their waists. Eddie leaned forward as Jane spoke.

'They remind me of those old photographs of the daughters of Czar Nicholas . . . you know, the ones that were murdered in Russia?'

'Yes, the Romanovs.' Jane looked at Eddie in surprise.

He smiled. 'I did O Level History, about Lenin and the Russian revolution.' He tapped the photograph. 'It's obviously not quite the same period, though.'

'I think this is Helena standing holding the rope of the swing, and Beatrice on the other side.' Jane pointed to their innocent, unsmiling faces as Eddie peered closer.

'She is very beautiful, isn't she? The one on the swing?'

Jane nodded. 'I think that would be Marjorie . . . You're right, she is very pretty and obviously younger than the other two.'

Jane eased the photograph out of the album corners and turned it over. In very small, neat, handwriting were the words 'Helena – Marjorie seated on swing – Beatrice holding swing rope which Marjorie used to commit suicide'.

Eddie leaned forward as she held it up.

'Wow, that's a bit shocking.'

'Yes, very tragic, isn't it?' Jane slipped the photograph back into the album corners.

Turning another page over there were photographs of the girls as young children, then a full-size photograph of their father wearing a morning suit, standing in a rigid pose beside an exceptionally delicate-looking and pretty bride. Her veil was edged with roses and draped around her tiny satin Cuban-heeled shoes. But what made Jane look more closely was that the bride was wearing a rather elaborate tiara. Eddie noticed it too.

'That looks like an expensive piece,' he said, 'if they're real diamonds and drop pearls. You know the Romanovs had the most incredible jewels, and according to historians the Czarina Alexandra and her daughters sewed millions and millions of pounds' worth of rubies, emeralds and diamonds into their corsets. They were never discovered, but that's about all I can really remember because we then quickly went on to the Tudors. Just ask me anything about Henry VIII and his six wives!' He laughed and then nodded at the photograph. 'He looks twice her age.'

'Yes,' Jane agreed, 'and quite formidable, by the expression on his face. She looks about sixteen, but you can see where her youngest daughter Marjorie inherited her looks from . . . those huge eyes and little cupid lips. Interesting, isn't it? I went to visit Helena in a care home today. She's very frail and suffering from dementia but she had the most vivid icy-blue eyes.'

Jane wanted to talk more but Eddie stepped back and checked his watch.

'I'd better get going. I'll be in touch as soon as I have all the costings done.'

He went to shake Jane's hand, then at the last moment gave her a light kiss on her cheek instead. She was taken aback, and he flushed.

'Anyway, see you tomorrow . . . I'll let myself out, OK?'

Jane put her hand to her cheek as she heard the front door close, wondering what exactly had just happened. But soon the mystery of the Lanark family drew her back to the album and she found herself staring at the photograph of the three privileged young women in their immaculate white summer dresses. She was certain that one of them had given birth to the baby and had then buried it alive – but which one?

CHAPTER NINE

At nine Jane was at her desk typing up her report following her visit to the care home. There was a light knock on her door and DS Hunt walked straight in. He got right to the point.

'We've just had a very unpleasant call from Jason Thorpe. He's concerned that a family photograph album is missing from his aunt's room at the care home. He was told that you visited Miss Lanark there yesterday afternoon, and he's suggesting that you took it without permission. I don't want to go and run this by DCI Carter because you know what a prick he can be.'

Jane pulled out the page from her typewriter and held it up between her finger and thumb.

'I've just finished my report on my visit, stating that I asked permission to take Miss Lanark's photograph album, which she granted.'

DS Hunt leaned against the side of her desk.

'He's saying that she couldn't have given you permission because she has dementia. You, therefore, had "no right to remove the effing album".'

Jane knew she was in the wrong, but she wasn't going to admit it. Instead, she handed him the report to be filed.

'So, you've got the album, have you?' Hunt asked.

Jane sighed. 'Yes . . . all right, I know I shouldn't have, but it was just an impulsive thing and I intended to return it – as I make very clear in my report. Due to the length of time we believe this baby has been buried, it's very difficult for us to work out who could have been involved. Helena Lanark was unhelpful, and I think it is therefore necessary for us to use the photographic information in the album for identification purposes.'

Hunt shrugged his shoulders. 'Yes, ma'am, but you know the boss is getting tetchy about this entire investigation. If you want my humble opinion, he's getting ready to shelve it.'

Jane tensed. 'He can't do that! It's a suspicious death and by law it has to be fully investigated. It's obvious that someone in that family buried that baby when it was alive. I don't care if it was ten, twenty or even thirty years ago. Added to that, I'm beginning to think that some kind of major fraud has been going on concerning Miss Lanark's wealth.'

DS Hunt looked at her quizzically. 'Have you any evidence to support that theory?'

Jane shrugged. 'At the moment it's just a gut feeling . . . but if there is any I'll find it.'

'Well, if you are right, you know Carter will probably tell you to get on to the fraud squad and let them deal with it.'

As Hunt opened the door, he had to step back for DCI Carter to enter.

'I was just leaving, sir,' Hunt said.

'No, you stay,' Carter snapped, giving Jane an icy look.

'I've just had a complaint against my senior officer about removing personal items without permission. We need to sort this out immediately. The complainant wants to take it further.'

Jane stood up, her fists clenched. 'For God's sake! I asked if I could take the family photograph album because I felt it was of evidential value for the investigation. I really don't understand why Mr Thorpe is creating such a fuss . . .'

'Well, he is . . . and I've also had his lawyer, Arnold Hadley, bending my ear about it, and . . .'

Jane interrupted. 'Sir, this is being blown out of all proportion.'

'Be that as it may, Detective Inspector Tennison,' Carter said coldly. 'Hadley's on his way, and I suggest you return their property and apologise. My patience is fast running out and I'm seriously contemplating closing this investigation.'

'Sir, I'm totally against dismissing this case – we still don't have any leads on the murder of the baby,' Jane pleaded.

'Dear God! The only person you can question is a sixty-year-old woman who's suffering from dementia. How far is that going to get you?'

'That's not correct, sir. Helena Lanark's sister Beatrice is still alive and her son, Jason Thorpe, has said that she is in good health. I will obviously return the album, but I'll need to take copies of the photographs before handing it back.'

Carter put his hands on his hips. 'All right, I'll give you a couple of days after the weekend – but sort this out with the lawyer chap. If you think any further expenditure is justifiable on a thirty-year-old case, then you're going to need a lot more than a family photograph album.' He turned and walked out of her office before Jane could respond.

DS Hunt waved her report in his hand. 'I notice you didn't mention that Beatrice Thorpe lives in Australia.'

'Oh, shut up ... just go and file my report,' she said with a half-smile.

Jane also hadn't mentioned that the album was still at her home.

* * *

Arnold Hadley was ushered into Jane's office later that morning. He seemed rather ill at ease but accepted Jane's profuse apology about the photograph album. He was wearing a rather worn grey suit and his tie was skewed.

'I am unsure why Mr Thorpe is so irate, to be honest,' he said. 'I think his mother must have a similar album. Perhaps he was more concerned about what Helena might have revealed verbally ... although sadly I doubt that would have occurred.'

Jane leaned back in her chair, purposely not reacting to his comment about Helena's inability to communicate. It seemed strange that with such a condition both Hadley and Thorpe continued to visit her. As a result of her silence Mr Hadley continued.

'Mr Thorpe arranged the sale of the Lanark property,' Hadley continued, filling the awkward silence. 'And negotiated the subsequent purchase by the development company. Due to the collapse of the previously undisclosed tunnel, and the delays caused by the tragic discoveries, Mr Thorpe is concerned the developer may now take legal action for false representation during the sale of the property.'

Jane glanced at her notebook and frowned. If Thorpe had legitimately sold the property to a developer eighteen months ago, why was he now concerned about any legal action?

Jane leaned forward. 'Mr Hadley, whose idea was it to convert the property into flats?'

'Jason decided that there could be a viable income from doing so, and Miss Lanark agreed.'

'I would appreciate it if you could give me the name of the company that did the conversions.'

'Good heavens, it was such a long time ago. Why could that possibly be relevant now?'

'It would be interesting to know if they were aware of the basement, and obviously the shelter too.'

Jane started writing in her notebook.

'I'm also interested in the time frame. I'm aware that the property was left empty for many years before it was divided into flats. I also know that the basement area was never allowed to be used or rented out, and the large garden attached to the property was out of bounds.'

Hadley began to toy with the crease in his right trouser leg. 'Yes, that is correct.'

'I'm sorry to infer this, Mr Hadley, but it appears to me that your client could have been aware of what was subsequently found in the shelter – at least, the body of the baby.'

Hadley could not meet Jane's eyes.

'I cannot comment on that . . . this was never discussed with me.'

Jane knew she was on to something. She saw him grow tenser as she continued.

'Then Miss Lanark agreed to sell the property, so if she had been aware of what was hidden there, that would be odd. But I know that Miss Lanark has been suffering from dementia for many years.'

Jane saw Hadley clench his fists. He kept his head bowed as he spoke.

'Detective, Jason had power of attorney and as such it was his decision to sell the property. To be perfectly honest, I am uncertain if Miss Lanark is even aware of these transactions.'

'But aren't you her lawyer?' Jane said.

Hadley looked up, unable to contain the anger in his eyes.

'Jason Thorpe's mother is Helena Lanark's sister and she and Jason were financially dependent on my client for many years, so it was entirely her decision to grant him power of attorney.'

Hadley stood up. 'I think I should leave.' He turned, as if eager to get out of her office.

'Mr Hadley . . .' Jane said. He turned back, an almost fearful look in his eyes. 'The family photograph album is not here at the station, but I will make sure it is delivered to your office first thing in the morning.'

He waved his hand dismissively. 'Yes, of course . . . that will be fine. I think you should know that I am retiring today, but I will inform Mr Thorpe of your intention.' He hesitated, apparently unsure of what he was about to say. 'Perhaps I should warn you that it would be unwise to antagonise Mr Thorpe. He is . . . not a man to be crossed.'

Hadley left, closing the door quietly behind him. Jane picked up her pencil and tapped the notes she had made. She was now certain Helena Lanark had known about the buried baby. But she doubted that Helena could have acted alone. Jane was also suspicious about when exactly Jason Thorpe had gained power of attorney. One thing was certain: it was now imperative that she questioned his mother, Beatrice. Hadley had seemed evasive and when she had reminded him that he was Miss Lanark's lawyer, he had been unable to control the look of anger in his eyes. It made Jane wonder if Helena Lanark had ever been aware of the proceeds from the sale of her property, and if Hadley and Jason Thorpe had worked together to defraud her. But then, why would Hadley warn her about Jason?

Jane went over to Sergeant Hunt's desk and told him she was going home. He nodded.

'Are you having a long weekend?' he asked. 'That old boy Hadley, he seemed a bit unnerved when he left. Did you get anything from him?'

Jane raised an eyebrow. 'Can you do me a favour? Could you go to his offices and ask for full access to Helena Lanark's files? He'll know why you're asking for them, but I'll be interested to hear what he says.'

'And if he refuses?'

'I'll ask DCI Carter if we can get a warrant.'

'Did you give him the album?' Hunt asked.

'No, it's still at my house. I'm going to fetch it now.' She walked off as Hunt padded over to young DC Timothy Taylor's desk.

'Come on, son, I need you to drive me. She wants me to do her a favour . . . anything for a change of scenery.'

* * *

That afternoon, Jane spent a considerable amount of time in John Lewis looking at paints and picking up colour charts to take home. She then made her way to the carpet section and requested various samples.

She had missed lunch, so she went into the café on the third floor and bought a pot of tea and a ham sandwich.

Jane didn't arrive home until after four. She put the samples on the table in the kitchen next to the Lanark family photograph album, then opened the album, wondering what could be in it that had made Jason Thorpe so eager to get it back.

As she turned the heavily mounted pages of the album, she was frustrated at how little information was written beneath the sepia photographs. Eddie was right, the numerous images of the three sisters wearing matching white dresses were reminiscent of the Romanovs – but looking at the photographs didn't tell her anything. It was not until she had flicked through to the back of the album that she found several blank mounts where the photographs had obviously been removed. There were also some photographs that had been pasted in, rather than placed in the elegant mounts. One of them showed a boy in a wheelchair, with a woman wearing dark glasses standing behind him. There were three more images of the same woman standing beside a rather good-looking man.

At first Jane wondered if the man was Jason, but then realised that it was perhaps his father. Two more pictures were loosely inserted, one with the same man's face scratched out. The second photograph was even more disturbing as it depicted Marjorie in an open coffin. Jane turned the heavy pages back to some of the sepia photographs and she noticed that the Lanark girls' mother was often wearing elaborate jewellery.

She continued turning the pages back and forth until she found a faded manila envelope that, at one time, appeared to have been stuck down. Opening it, she eased out a folded sheet of almost parchment-like paper. Unfolding it carefully, she saw at the top written in elegant calligraphy the words 'Family Tree'. Jane was afraid of the paper tearing as she carefully flattened a second page. She noted the references to Henry Lanark's parents and grandfather – then her attention was drawn to the marriage between Henry and Muriel. Her parents were listed as Count Antonin

Petrukhin, and his wife Aida and the date of Muriel's birth seemed to suggest that Henry Lanark was marrying a fourteen-year-old.

Jane jumped as the phone suddenly rang. She hurried into the hallway to answer it, carrying the family tree with her. It was Sergeant Hunt.

'We're back at the station . . . it was a bit of a wasted journey.'

He explained that Arnold Hadley had refused to allow them any access to Helena Lanark's files.

'What, he just said no?' Jane asked.

'Yes, he did. He said that he was not allowed to give access to any of his client's files as Helena Lanark's representative had been to see him and warned him that he would take legal action if he divulged any personal information about her.'

Jane sighed. 'I doubt I've got enough evidence for Carter to approve a search warrant. But thank you for trying anyway.'

'I didn't try too hard because I had a gut feeling he was scared. Remember I told you how he anxious he seemed when he left your office?'

'The representative Hadley mentioned – did he say it was Jason Thorpe?' Jane asked.

'He didn't mention him by name. But he said his client's representative, who had power of attorney, had been to see him. Anyway, you have a good weekend, ma'am.'

'Just a minute,' Jane said. 'I need another favour. Can you do a search on the birth and death of Muriel Lanark and reference a Count Antonin Petrukhin? I want both dates.'

'Bloody hell . . . how far back are you going?'

'Just see what you can come up with.'

'Can you just spell it out for me?'

Jane could hear Hunt's heavy breathing as she spelled out the name and he repeated it back to her to be absolutely sure.

'Right, I'll start on that, ma'am. Oh, have you seen the *Evening Standard*?'

'No . . .'

'Apparently, the developers have now been given clearance by DCI Carter, and the headline is, "House of Horrors to be Demolished".'

'Well, that should make Mr Thorpe a happy man,' Jane said, now certain that the threat of legal action by the developer was a fabrication.

'I'll get young Tim to track down as much as we can get on Muriel Lanark,' Hunt said.

Jane thanked him and was just replacing the receiver when the doorbell rang. She put the family tree on the phone table before opening the door, expecting to see Eddie – then stepped back sharply as she found Jason Thorpe on the doorstep.

'Sorry to turn up unannounced,' he began with a smile, 'but I believe you have my aunt's photo album. I want to apologise if I have caused any problem by contacting the detective in charge at the station – it's just that my aunt is very frail, and she was anxious about the album's whereabouts. I'd like to get it back before I leave for Australia.'

Jane opened the door wider. 'Of course, I understand, and I do apologise – but can I ask you how you got my home address?'

'Yes, of course, and I'm sorry again for intruding. I had a chat with old man Hadley, and he gave me your address because you had told him you had the album at home.'

Jane forced a smile but was still hesitant about inviting Jason into her home, as she knew he was lying: she had never given Hadley her home address. However, she kept up the charade and smiled pleasantly at him.

'Yes, of course, Mr Thorpe. If you wait one moment, I'll just get the album for you.' If she was putting on an act, Thorpe was going one better and gave her a dazzling smile. He put his hands in his trouser pockets and leaned casually against the door frame.

'No need to hurry. I'm not going anywhere. Well, I will be soon, as I'm flying back to Oz.'

Jane knew this was a potential opportunity to get the information that she needed, but she was aware she had to be very wary of him. Jason peered into the hall.

'Have you just moved in? We have little terraced houses a lot like this in Sydney and Melbourne, but they all have open verandas at the front.'

'Would you like a cup of tea?' Jane asked.

'I am a bit parched – that'd be very kind. Thank you.'

Jane closed the front door and turned to see Jason pointedly looking at where Eddie had pulled up the carpet.

'I'm thinking of having the floors sanded,' Jane said. 'The kitchen's just on your left.'

Jane followed him into the kitchen and was relieved to see that she must have closed the album in her hurry to answer the phone.

'How do you take your tea?'

'Builder's tea for me. Even though I was brought up in Sydney, my mother used to brew a strong pot for my dad. She joked you could stand a spoon up in it. For her it was delicate Earl Grey in a porcelain cup and saucer. And she makes these little cucumber sandwiches with the crusts cut off.'

Even though he could clearly see that the photograph album was on the table, he made no reference to it.

'Do sit down,' Jane said. He pulled out a chair as he looked around the kitchen.

'This looks like it could do with a makeover,' he commented.

Jane laughed. 'The truth is, I've just had one, with a new fridge and new sink unit. But I picked up some colour charts this afternoon as I can't decide on a colour scheme for in here.'

'White,' Jason said. 'Go with white . . . it always looks fresh. Strong colours tire easily. My mother goes in for flock wallpaper in bright colours and I have to say I think it's a mistake.'

Jane remained standing, leaning against the sink as she sipped her tea.

'I was wondering if it would be possible for me to speak with your mother?'

'Why would you want to do that?' he said, his smile growing brittle.

'Well, the case is still ongoing, Mr Thorpe, and I feel that it would be helpful for me to be able to ask your mother a few pertinent questions. As your aunt, her sister, has dementia, she is obviously unable to assist in giving closure to the investigation.'

Jason had hardly touched his tea and she could tell he didn't like her query.

'I'm afraid, Detective Tennison, I will not encourage my mother to have any conversations regarding this tragic situation. You have to understand she is has not been well. It would be too distressing for her to even contemplate any involvement with your investigation.'

'But perhaps she could help us understand how this baby was found in the shelter?'

He turned his head slowly to look at Jane. Although he had blue eyes, he hadn't inherited the iciness of his Aunt Helena's.

'If you are implying that my mother had anything to do with this, I give you fair warning that I will take legal action for defamation. You have already overstepped your legal rights by taking my aunt's personal photograph album from her care home. When I told my mother you had done so, it made her deeply distressed and she wants me to take the album to her for safekeeping.'

Jane ran her teacup under the tap.

'I'm sorry if I have upset your mother in any way, Mr Thorpe, but the reality is this is a murder investigation and I am legally empowered to ask any question I feel relevant to my inquiry. As you can see, I have your album on the table. Perhaps I should mention that there are a number of mounts without any photographs and there are also numerous loose black-and-white photographs at the back of the album, which were not in any order. But I took great care and did not remove any photos.'

Jason rested his hand on the embossed cover of the album. 'Perhaps, Detective Tennison . . . can I call you Jane?'

She gave a small nod. 'Yes, of course.'

'Jane, the album is of great sentimental value because it shows a part of my mother's childhood which abruptly ended when her beloved sister committed suicide. Their father was exceedingly strict and demanded from his daughters complete obedience. My mother fell in love with my father, but my grandfather refused to allow her to marry him. She had no option but to run away, as far as she possibly could.'

He now appeared more confident, leaning back in the chair and using his hands expressively.

'I think Australia was the furthest possible place from her father she could find. The reason I now have to protect her is that she has had a very hard life. My father became sick and . . .'

Jason turned away as if it was too painful for him to continue. Then he took a deep breath.

'My brother, Matthew, was born severely mentally challenged and my poor mother had to care for him as well as my father. Now, due to my success with my company, she can enjoy her later life.'

He stood up and shook Jane's hand. 'I think it will be beneficial to everyone if this investigation is closed. I will be returning home tomorrow.' He picked up the album. 'I know my mother will appreciate this.'

Jane followed him through the kitchen and couldn't help but notice how beautifully tailored his casual jacket was. In fact, he was exceedingly well dressed from his fawn cord trousers to his silk shirt and heavy gold cufflinks. She kept her tone friendly.

'I must say, that is a very nice jacket,' she said, as they walked through the hall.

'Yes, made for me by my father's tailor in Savile Row. One wouldn't trust any of the outfitters in Sydney.'

Jane smiled. 'Well, I hope you have a safe journey. I understand that everything has now been cleared for the property to be demolished.'

He turned, halfway out of the door. 'Yes, it's a great relief, but I could do without all the sensational press attached to it. Thankfully, I no longer have any association with that house.'

'Do you have a property here in London where you stay when you're here?'

'I have a small flat attached to my offices in Queen's Gate Mews, but I usually stay at Claridge's.'

Jane stood by the front door, watching as Jason Thorpe walked down her path, gingerly stepping over some of the detritus Eddie had left by the door. He had parked his BMW only a short distance from her own car, but she closed the door before he drove off.

She couldn't quite fathom Jason Thorpe out. When he had first arrived he had seemed intent on accentuating his Australian accent. But when he had become defensive about his mother, he had sounded rather aristocratic. She had to concede that he was a very good-looking man, with his tan and his sun-bleached hair. However, there was something unsettling about him. To begin with he had been very pleasant, really laying on the charm, but that quickly evaporated when she mentioned wanting to talk to his mother and he had briefly become quite aggressive. It made her even more determined to find out what Beatrice Lanark knew.

CHAPTER TEN

DS Paul Lawrence was at home checking through his files as he wanted to clear any outstanding matters before he went on a week's leave. He drew out the file labelled 'Infant Mortality' and reread the pathologist's report, alongside his own notes. The words 'belt – query' had been underlined. He recalled his interaction with the mortician at the lab when he had complained about the missing cement slabs and placed a call into the lab to find out if there was an update on the whereabouts of the belt.

He was kept on hold for some time and was eventually told that the belt had been placed in a separate evidence box because there was some confusion about whether it actually belonged to the young female victim who had been discovered in the shelter. Lawrence sighed with frustration. He was aware that items sometimes went missing, but because he had filed a query about the belt, he wanted to follow it up. His request to collect the item was met with a rather disgruntled response and a muttered comment that it was almost five o'clock. But Lawrence remained adamant that he wanted access to the belt that afternoon, reminding the lab technician that due to their lack of professionalism the cement blocks had already been mislaid and he could still make a formal complaint. Eventually it was agreed that he would be met at the lab within half an hour.

* * *

Jane had changed into an old pair of jeans, a T-shirt and a pair of dirty trainers and had begun to take up some of her old carpet. She needed to use a carpet claw as it had been laid on nail strips and the underlay had been stuck to the wooden floor in places. She was using a large flat screwdriver to scrape it off when she heard the doorbell ring.

Eddie stood on the doorstep with an impressive-looking sanding machine.

'I've got this for two days,' he said, hauling it into the hall. 'I've also ordered a skip to be delivered first thing tomorrow morning.'

He looked around, clearly impressed by what Jane had already accomplished and immediately began rolling up the old worn carpet to take it outside. They worked efficiently together and managed to remove all of the stair carpet, the first-floor landing carpet and one of the bedroom carpets. All the waste carpet was dragged down the stairs and into the small front garden. She made Eddie a cup of tea, while they took a breather. As he drank it, he told her they would need to sweep and wash the floorboards in preparation for the sanding.

'But before we do that, I could go and get us some fish and chips,' he said, rinsing his hands in her kitchen sink.

'You know something, I'd really like that. I'll make us another tea.'

Eddie smiled, 'I wouldn't mind some bread and butter, too. There's nothing like a chip buttie!'

Jane agreed, smiling at the sound of him whistling as he left.

* * *

Lawrence opened the small plastic container and read the three different notes attached to the box. Two of the notes had been written when the item had been brought in. The third had no date, just a statement that the belt should be placed with the other items taken from the shelter. Lawrence noted down the names of the officers responsible and went over to one of the lab tables.

The lab technician was pacing up and down as Lawrence checked through the box. 'Are you going to be long?' he asked.

'Are you the only assistant on duty tonight?' Lawrence asked, curtly.

'No, I'm not. But I've been here since half past eight and I was due off at five. I'd like you to know that I had nothing to do with anyone removing those blocks. I've no idea where they went – there are three other guys who work here as well, so I'm not taking the blame. You can see the lab case file: it's got copies of all the police lab submissions plus reports from the scientists who did any work on them. You'll find all the photos taken at the scene. '

Lawrence gloved up and placed the cut belt on a sheet of white paper.

'Hopefully this won't take long . . . though it should have been done already. Please don't think I was born yesterday. I'm fully aware that you guys make a few quid on the side.'

The lab technician stopped his pacing. 'I don't like what you're insinuating. What do you think we can do with two fucking cement blocks? If they were brought in with the instruction to retain, we would've kept them.'

Lawrence glanced at him, then returned to examining the belt buckle. Due to the dampness in the shelter, the buckle was encrusted with mould as well as cement dust. But Lawrence could tell it was very good quality. With a set of fine tweezers, he carefully began removing the clogged-up dirt around the buckle.

* * *

Eddie and Jane finished their fish and chips, accompanied by slices of buttered white bread and mugs of tea. Eddie told her that they would need to cover their mouths and noses and suggested that she find a headscarf or bath hat to put over her hair because as soon as they started sanding the floor it would create a huge amount of dust. He pulled out a well-thumbed notebook.

'I've got four guys who can help me out. I can do all the electrics and I'm going to call a plumber and two decorators. If it's all right with you, we can probably make some major headway this weekend.'

Jane stacked their plates and mugs in the sink.

'It's fine by me, Eddie. To be honest, the sooner we can get it done, the better. By the way, do you remember the photographs in that big album? You said that the photo of the three girls reminded you of the Romanov princesses?'

Eddie nodded but was more intent on making notes in his notebook.

'Well, you won't believe this, but I discovered that their grandfather was actually a Russian count.'

He looked up. 'Wow, really? Now, have you got the paint charts? If I have the lads coming in to do the work, I should get going on ordering the paints. Also, we need to see what colour the floorboards are once we've stripped them . . . you might want them another shade, or just varnished.'

Jane looked around the kitchen and picked up the paint chart.

'I'm going to ask my dad to help us out, is that all right with you?' Eddie asked.

Jane laughed. 'Of course. Why wouldn't it be?'

'He is a bit of a geezer, my dad,' Eddie said. 'He reminds me of that bloke who was in the Disney movie.'

'Which Disney movie?'

'The one where he had a terrible accent?'

'Do you mean Professor Higgins in *My Fair Lady*?' a perplexed Jane asked.

'No, no . . . not that one. He played the chimney sweep.'

'You mean *Mary Poppins*?'

'Not her, who was the bloke who played the chimney sweep? I can't remember his name . . .'

'You mean Dick Van Dyke?' Jane couldn't help laughing.

'Yeah, that's him. Now I've lost track of what I was talking about . . .'

'You were talking about your dad,' Jane said.

'Oh right, yeah . . . like I say, my dad is a real geezer, but I guarantee when I introduce you and tell him you're Old Bill, he's going to start talking to you like he's posh, pronouncing his *h*s and everything. He always does it and thinks no one notices.'

'So do you think he'll be impressed because I'm a detective inspector?'

Eddie nodded. 'He's old East End. I mean, if my mum has to go to the doctor, they get dressed up. It's just the way they are.'

Jane smiled. 'Well, I look forward to meeting your old "geezer"!'

* * *

DS Lawrence arrived at the station in Stockwell just after six. As he went into the incident room, Detective Sergeant Hunt was putting on his overcoat.

'Good evening, sarge,' Lawrence said, affably. 'Is your governor in?'

'No, he's out at some Masonic do.'

Lawrence raised his eyebrows. 'What about DI Tennison?'

'Nah, she's on weekend leave. Anything I can do for you?'

'It's connected to that . . .' Lawrence pointed to a rather crumpled *Evening Standard* with the headline HOUSE OF HORRORS DEMOLISHED. 'Is Jane still handling the investigation?'

Hunt gave a snort. 'Between you, me and the gatehouse, I think it's going to be closed down. The guv gave her two days to come up with a valid reason for continuing the inquiry.' He shook his head and jerked his thumb towards DC Timothy Taylor. 'She's got us on a wild goose chase, looking into some Russian Count who's been dead for twenty-odd years.'

Lawrence held up an evidence bag. 'I think DI Tennison should have access to this. Can I leave it with you to make sure she gets it first thing on Monday morning?'

'Sure, I can do that,' Hunt said.

'Right, I'm off to Tenerife for a week . . . first holiday I've had in years.'

Sergeant Hunt held up the evidence bag containing a large padded envelope with a typed document attached.

'What's this?' Hunt asked.

'It's the leather belt and buckle which was holding the two cement blocks together, with the dead baby inside. It should have been checked over days ago. Sometimes the unprofessionalism at the mortuary is beyond belief. Anyway, I'm satisfied I've done my job.'

'Enjoy your holiday,' Hunt said, taking the evidence bag and envelope over to DC Taylor. 'Put this on Tennison's desk, and then you can get off home.'

The young man nodded. 'This Count Antonin Petrukhin . . .'

'I don't want to know,' Hunt said. 'I need to go home, unlike some who are fucking going to Tenerife. I'll see you on Monday morning.'

DC Taylor went back to sifting through the documents he had sourced from the St Catherine's House archives. He had also been to the British Library to check through old newspaper articles. But, like Detective Sergeant Hunt, he had no real idea what he was looking for.

* * *

Jane and Eddie had taken a while to work out exactly how the sanding machine worked. She hadn't laughed so much in years because you had to retain a firm grip on the handles, otherwise it careered out of control. She had swept and washed down the floors whilst Eddie tried to control the machine. She was wearing a plastic bath hat, a scarf over her nose and mouth and a pair of yellow marigold gloves, and they were now both covered in sawdust from head to toe.

She suddenly felt a sharp pain in her right eye.

'Oh God, my eye.'

'Don't rub it, let me have a look, which eye is it?' Eddie said.

Both of her eyes were streaming, but she pressed the lid of her right eye.

'Take your hand away, let me see.'

Eddie pulled down the bottom lid of her right eye and squinted, his face close, almost touching hers.

'Hang on, I see, it's just a bit of sawdust. Come into the kitchen and try not to touch it.'

She followed him in, her face scrunched up and blinking as he took a section of paper towel and made it into a little cone, then washed his hands, before running the cone under the cold tap.

'OK, now stand right under the light and stay still.'

Jane had her face turned up, as he gently drew down the bottom lid with his left hand, then, using the cold, wet edge of the paper cone, gently removed the bits of sawdust.

He gently tilted her chin up with his hand.

'How is it now?'

'Oh, it's fine now,' Jane said, blinking.

There was a moment between them, while they were still close enough for their lips to meet, but instead he gently pulled her bath hat down a fraction and laughed.

'I've never fallen for a woman in a plastic bath hat before. Now, are you ready to go back to work?'

By midnight they were only halfway through the hall. Jane decided to take a shower and presumed Eddie was getting ready to go home.

She was wrapped in a bath towel, ready to step into the shower, but when she turned the tap on there was no water. She went to the top of the stairs and called down to say that she thought there was something wrong with the boiler, or maybe the tap. Eddie quickly came upstairs to check it out. He stepped into the shower stall and turned the lever.

'You weren't switched to shower,' he said, suddenly getting the full impact of the water that came gushing through the shower-head. Jane couldn't stop laughing as Eddie stood there in his sodden clothes.

Then with a grin, instead of turning off the shower, Eddie started stripping off and grinning, too, Jane quickly dropped her towel to the floor to join him.

CHAPTER ELEVEN

Jane woke up with a start, worried she was late for work – until she realised it was a Saturday. Then she remembered what had taken place the previous night. She sat up and was astonished to smell bacon being cooked. She hurriedly dressed and headed downstairs, pausing when she spotted the clothes hung over the radiator. Eddie was wearing one of her towelling robes and turned to her, grinning. He held up the spatula as the bacon was almost ready. 'Our clothes should be dry soon. You all right about last night?'

She went over and put her arms around his neck. 'I'm *perfectly* all right about last night . . .'

He had two pieces of tissue stuck to his chin. 'That razor in your bathroom is a bit blunt. Want an egg with this?'

'No, just a bacon sandwich is fine. Are you always up this early?'

'Yeah, I'm usually up at a quarter past five . . . and this morning we've got the skip arriving at seven. I'll need to bung all that carpet into it when it comes.'

Jane fetched two mugs and the teapot as Eddie dished out the bacon onto buttered bread. He then crossed to the fridge and took out the tomato ketchup. Jane had never been with a man who had such an ease about him. He certainly had no inhibitions about wearing her robe.

'The lads will be here between half past seven and eight, and my dad at around midday.'

Jane sat down at the kitchen table. 'Do I need to get something for your lads to eat?'

Eddie sat down opposite her. 'No, they'll bring their own sandwiches, but just keep a steady flow of tea coming. I'd like to get all the sanding done today. The tricky part will be doing the stairs, but there's a hand attachment for that. They'll need to move all of the furniture out of your sitting room.' Eddie seemed to be firmly back in work mode.

They finished breakfast and Eddie took their working clothes off the radiator whilst Jane began washing the dirty dishes. As she was drying up she suddenly remembered the envelope containing the Lanark family tree, which she had left on the telephone table. She put down the tea towel and went into the hall. The table had already been taken into the sitting room and the telephone was perched halfway up the stairs. She went in to see if the envelope was in the sitting room, but the small table was stacked on top of an easy chair.

She suddenly wondered if the reason Jason Thorpe had been so eager to get the photo album was actually because of the family tree. Then she remembered the conversation she'd had with Eddie about his father's changing accent. That's what was unsettling about Jason Thorpe, his tendency to switch between an Australian accent and an upper-crust English one. She felt certain that Jason had been acting out a role with her – but she still didn't know why.

The skip arrived and Eddie began heaving the sections of old carpet into it. Jane stood at the open front door and asked him if he had found an envelope on the hall table beside the telephone. Eddie shrugged his shoulders and said he couldn't remember. A short while later, as Jane was finishing cleaning the kitchen, he came in, holding up the envelope.

'Is this what you were looking for?'

She beamed. 'Yes, exactly . . . thank you so much.'

Jane put the envelope into her bag as she heard Eddie's workers arriving. After a brief introduction, the four men finished clearing the carpets and moving the furniture out of the sitting room. Jane asked Eddie what he needed her to do and at first he said that she should just relax and go up to her bedroom to watch some TV. Jane adamantly refused, insisting she needed to help. So she was given instructions to go to a hardware shop, then on to a business associate of Eddie's who ran a paint shop on Brixton High Street. Eddie had made a methodical list of various-sized paint brushes they needed as well as several scrapers to remove the wallpaper. Then on her return she could begin stripping the wallpaper.

At the shop in Brixton, Jane ordered the paint. She had taken Eddie's advice and chosen mostly white matt and gloss, as well as some large cans of gloss finish for the floorboards. Ignoring what Eddie had said about food, she stopped at Tesco and bought packets of ham, bread and salad, plus two bottles of milk.

It was just after midday by the time Jane returned home. She was amazed to see how much rubbish had already been accumulated in the skip. She recalled that she had mentioned to Eddie that a lot of her furniture needed replacing, and he had obviously taken her at her word. However, it looked as though a few other people in the neighbourhood had been dumping their unwanted stuff in the skip as well.

She went into the house via the back door and into the kitchen, having to make numerous trips back and forth to her car to bring in all the supplies. It was now beginning to rain, so she grabbed Eddie's cloth cap and his donkey jacket to fetch the remaining bags. She couldn't have looked less like a detective inspector if she'd tried, but she was also feeling happier than she had for a long time.

Jane was just sorting out the paint brushes in the kitchen when the back door opened and a handsome, grey-haired man walked in, wearing a paint-splattered boiler suit.

'I've just caught the blokes next door filling up my son's skip, so I told them they should effing hire their own!'

Jane smiled. 'You must be Eddie's father?'

'That's right. I would've been here a bit earlier, but I had a complicated plumbing job on. Are you helping the lads out?'

'Yes, as much as I can.'

He moved closer and leaned in. 'I knew Eddie was scraping the barrel a bit for workers, but apparently this woman wants the whole house refurbished. Be a nice earner.'

Jane cocked her head to one side, removing Eddie's cap. 'Actually, I'm that woman.'

'Oh, blimey! Sorry, love, I, er . . .'

Jane extended her hand. 'I'm Jane Tennison.'

Eddie's father, who had big, calloused hands, shook Jane's hand enthusiastically and introduced himself. 'I'm Anthony Fraser . . . Tony. I 'ave to tell you that you are nothin' like what I expected.'

Jane could hardly resist smiling as his son's description of him was perfect.

'I was just going to make some sandwiches and a pot of tea,' Jane said with a smile.

'That is very kind of you . . . thank you. If you'll just excuse me, I am going to let my son know I have arrived.' Tony hurried past Jane, opening the kitchen door to go into the hall, which looked as if a sandstorm had just hit.

* * *

It was after five o'clock and Jane had been scraping wallpaper for hours. Despite having worn out two pairs of yellow marigold gloves and the fact that her right arm was aching, she had still only managed to clear one part of the wall in the hall – so she had finally given up and made herself a large gin and tonic. But Eddie and his team had worked flat out. The only break Eddie had taken was when he had joked about her meeting his father and thanked her for the constant supply of tea and sandwiches.

Jane was impressed at the way the men had prepared and then cleaned up after themselves, neatly covering furniture with dust sheets and sweeping up all the sawdust from the now-finished sanding. As the men left, Eddie came in, covered in sawdust again, saying that he was just going to return the sanding machine as he didn't want to pay for an extra day.

'The floorboards will take a while to settle, then we need to wash everything down, then after that the focus will be on stripping all the wallpaper. The lads can be here again by half past seven tomorrow if that's all right with you.'

'It's fine with me, Eddie . . . they have worked so hard. They're a great bunch of guys.'

He smiled. 'My dad is having a look at your shower head,' he laughed. 'I was wondering if you'd maybe like to meet down the pub later tonight?'

'You know something, Eddie, I think I'm going to have a long bath – unless the shower is working properly – and maybe just make a bowl of pasta.'

He cocked his head to one side. 'Is that a no?'

'To the pub, yes, but if you'd like to have some pasta, it would be lovely to share it with you.'

He grinned. 'I'll bring the wine.'

* * *

Saturday night turned out to be very special. Eddie had returned wearing a pristine white T-shirt and black jeans, with a fashionable leather jacket and the cap that Jane had used earlier. He gave no indication that he expected to stay the night with her – in fact, quite the opposite. When he'd said he would need to go back home to get his work clothes, Jane couldn't hide her disappointment. But then he went over to his leather jacket and took out a new razor from the pocket.

'I suppose I could always leave early in the morning and be back in time for the lads,' he said with a grin.

If the first time they had been together was a blur to Jane, the second night was not. She had never come across anyone quite like

Eddie, although she had mixed with many different types of men at the Met. He somehow always managed to make her laugh, and his physical presence was boyish one moment and very protective the next. In addition, he was a very skilful and considerate lover.

But however good he made her feel, Jane was not contemplating having a relationship with Eddie just now. With everything else she had on her plate, she decided she would just make this a casual affair.

* * *

Eddie woke her up the following morning with a cup of tea and toast. He was already dressed and ready to leave.

'The lads should be here before eight, but hopefully I'll be back in time to get them started . . . and the old geezer is also going to lend a hand.'

Jane sat up and glanced at the alarm clock on her bedside table. It was not quite six.

'You're out of bacon, and you'll need some bread and butter, but I can pick them up from the corner shop on my way back,' Eddie said.

'No, don't worry. I'll do it. This is very good service!' she said, raising her mug of tea.

'I aim to please.' Eddie leaned forward and kissed her briefly on the cheek. She could hear him whistling as he stomped down the stairs, then the front door slammed behind him.

Jane didn't bother to shower but redressed in her scruffy clothes and began dampening down more wallpaper ready to strip it. By the time Eddie's team arrived Jane's right arm was already aching again. She decided this morning she'd try to get to know the four lads better. She knew two of them were Portuguese, and one was Jamaican. The fourth man was an extraordinarily tough-looking Irishman. As soon as they arrived, she brewed up a large pot of tea while they took off their overcoats in her kitchen, and then stayed chatting for a few minutes until they got down to work.

They left a variety of Sunday newspapers on her kitchen table, along with their flasks and Tupperware sandwich boxes. Jane sighed as she washed up the dirty mugs and the blare of their transistor radios began to echo down the hall.

Eddie had returned and was outside piling bags of stripped wallpaper into the now almost overflowing skip. Jane had heard him giving out the orders for the day's work, but he always did it with a laugh and a joke, and it was clear his team were happy to work hard for him. When his father arrived at midday, the repartee between father and son was quite comical and Jane found it hard not to laugh as Tony thumbed through the wallpaper catalogues.

'In my opinion, officer, you would be better off with lining paper, and a couple of your walls will need to be replastered. My son is useless at it himself, but he knows one of the best plasterers in the business. We're also going to check for damp around your front door as there are some dodgy patches.'

As the work continued, the incessant blast of different radio channels began to give Jane a headache. She made herself a cup of coffee to drink whilst she was looking through the wallpaper catalogues. It was only then that she noticed the headline in the partly folded *News of the World*: HOUSE OF HORRORS DEMOLITION GOES AHEAD. The articles had several photographs of the Stockwell property, including one of the half-demolished shelter. There were also photographs of what purported to be the concrete breeze blocks that had encased the body of the baby.

Jane knew they couldn't be the actual ones, and had been mocked up specially. There were also pictures of the dead girl, Samantha Forgham, and a statement from her bereft mother, as well as comments from John Bishop describing the horrors discovered in the old air-raid shelter.

The article noted that the investigation was ongoing, but the police had not disclosed any details regarding arrests or even if they had identified any suspects.

The *Sunday People* ran a similar story, with more photographs of Samantha Forgham. This article also stated that the victim had been chained up and starved to death. The *Sunday Express* had some derogatory remarks about the Metropolitan Police inquiry, and though the article was not front-page news, Jane was upset by the inference that the investigation had been mishandled. It was suggested that the police had not got their priorities right and had given clearance to the development company to recommence the demolition prematurely, no doubt based on John Bishop's statement that the company had been losing money because they had had to retain the large crew without being able to carry out any work.

Jane climbed the stairs and, as she crossed the landing to go into her bedroom, she caught Eddie wearing her police hat. Due to the loud, thudding music nobody had heard her coming up the stairs. Eddie was making some comical reference to *Z Cars*.

'Z Victor 2 to Z Victor 5 . . .'

As soon as he saw her, he quickly removed the hat.

'We were just shifting your wardrobe to one side and one of the doors opened . . .' he began sheepishly.

Jane stood in the bedroom doorway. 'It may be funny to you but let me tell you that I worked long and hard to get that uniform . . . and even longer and harder to get out of it.'

Eddie put his hands up defensively. 'Only joking, darling!'

Jane frowned. 'I've just come up to tell you that I need to go into the station, so could you leave the room while I get changed?'

Eddie carefully replaced the hat in the wardrobe. 'I need to check with my dad how they're doing in the bathroom. I meant to ask: do you want to keep that avocado suite in the bathroom? It's a bit sixties, isn't it?'

'Can we talk about that later, Eddie? And don't worry about the bathroom. I shouldn't be that long.'

Eddie shrugged. 'OK. I'm going to be working late here, and I'll need to go through all the invoices with you. I've agreed that we would pay the lads cash.'

Jane nodded. 'Yes, I know that. I'll go to the bank on Monday.'

Eddie walked past her, then turned back. 'Listen, I didn't in any way mean to insult you, Jane. I don't want you to take it the wrong way.'

'I haven't taken it any way, Eddie. Now, can you just leave me alone?'

'Sure,' he said softly, closing the door behind him.

* * *

Jane was surprised to see how many officers were in the incident room, but there had apparently been a series of break-ins, one resulting in a knife attack.

Sergeant Hunt was standing at the incident board marking up the officers' duties. He turned in surprise when he saw her.

'Have you been brought in, ma'am?'

'No, sergeant, I'm here because I need to speak to DCI Carter.'

'You'll have a hard time. He's been out since the crack of dawn, and . . .' he moved closer Jane and said under his breath, 'Chief Superintendent Bridges is in Carter's office, and he'll be getting ready to oversee . . .' He jerked his thumb towards the incident board, then looked back at Jane. 'He was also asking about the Stockwell case. I don't know if you've read the papers, but he was pissed off.'

Jane nodded. 'I'll just take my coat off then I'll go in and see him. Did you get any information for me about Count Petrukhin?'

Hunt scratched his head. 'Well, I got young DC Tim on that. He was going through the archives, but all this went down, and the guv was bringing in off-duty officers. I think whatever information he got he would've left on your desk.'

Jane nodded curtly and went to her office. She had just hung up her coat when she noticed a stack of notes and photocopies of various newspaper articles on her desk, together with a typed report. It seemed that DC Tim Taylor had actually been very diligent, contrary to what Sergeant Hunt had implied.

Jane down at her desk and drew the DC's findings towards her. She immediately saw that the documents had been placed on top of a large evidence bag. There was a white envelope clipped to it with the words 'Attention DCI Carter and DI Tennison'. Jane pushed DC Taylor's information to one side and opened the envelope. It contained a report from Paul Lawrence, timed and dated Friday night.

> The belt used to secure the two breeze blocks holding the body of the baby had not previously been forensically analysed and had been separated from the other items submitted for testing: 1) Piece of sou'wester, 2) knitted blue cashmere stole/scarf that had been wrapped around the baby's body. I have now examined the belt and note that it had been cut. I felt it was necessary that all the items should be kept together as I am no longer attached to this investigation. The buckle was clogged with cement dust and mould, making it difficult on first sight to ascertain if it was of value to the investigation. I have now done a close examination and part-cleaning and believe this could possibly be of great importance. Sincerely, DS Paul Lawrence.

Because the envelope was jointly addressed to her, Jane broke the seal on the evidence bag. There was an immediate smell of decay as she prised it open. She took a piece of A4 paper, placing it over the blotter on her desk, and tipped out the contents of the bag. She had handled the belt when it was discovered at the Stockwell property and had been with the foreman when it had been cut, but due to the buckle being blackened, the detailed silver filigree had hardly been visible. Now she could clearly see the engraved initials 'HL'.

Jane licked her lips as she felt the adrenaline buzz. She was certain the belt did not belong to Henry Lanark as it was too small, and it therefore had to belong to Helena. If Helena had been the prime suspect even without any evidence, this now suggested very strongly that she had committed infanticide. There was, of course, the possibility that Beatrice or her sister Marjorie had taken and used the belt, but she doubted it.

Jane pushed her chair back. Although this new development strongly implicated Helena Lanark in the baby's death, she still couldn't be sure who the mother was. Jane felt it was now more imperative than ever for her to interview Beatrice Thorpe.

There was a gentle knock on her door and DC Taylor peered in.

'Excuse me, ma'am, Superintendent Bridges would like to talk to you.'

Jane placed the palm of her hand on the documents he had left on her desk.

'I'm really sorry, Tim, I haven't had time to look over the work you've done.'

She stood up, suddenly wishing that she had at least showered or washed her hair before coming into the station.

'It was interesting research,' Tim said. 'But it took hours trying to trace Mrs Lanark's family. Also, there were a number of confusing birth dates. I was told at the archives that around that period it was quite normal for high society ladies to reduce their ages by changing their date of birth.'

Jane frowned. 'Judging from the photographs of Muriel Lanark on her wedding day, surely she would not have done that. She looked very young anyway.'

'That was my problem. She'd added five years *on* to her age.'

Jane was shocked. 'My God! How old was she when she married Henry Lanark?'

'She was only fourteen, but she said she was nineteen. I've also been able to get death certificates for Aida Petrukhin and Count Antonin Petrukhin—'

Jane interrupted. 'This is good work, Tim. Did you find any information on Muriel's her jewellery?'

He hesitated. 'Not too much . . . but there was definitely money in the family and reference to a valuable tiara brought from Russia.'

Jane nodded. 'I'll have a look through everything after my meeting with DCS Bridges. While I'm with him could you do me a favour and contact the Stockwell planning department and the developers? I meant to do it myself but got distracted. I need to know how much Jason Thorpe sold the house for and if he still has any material interest in the development.'

'You think Thorpe might have done something dishonest?' Tim asked.

'Well, let's just say I don't entirely trust him.'

Detective Chief Superintendent Bridges appeared at her open doorway.

'I was just coming to see you, sir . . .' Jane said quickly.

DCI Bridges gestured towards DC Taylor to leave them and closed the door. Bridges had a rather bloated face, and his nose was particularly bulbous. His hair was cut army-style, with short back and sides; in fact, everything about him had a military air. He had quite a reputation as a disciplinarian as well as being known as an officer who had come up through the ranks. Standing with his feet slightly apart, he folded his arms across his substantial chest and looked at Jane with steely eyes.

'Detective Inspector Tennison, I have a lot of questions I need you to answer, specifically about your handling of the Stockwell "House of Horrors" inquiry . . .'

CHAPTER TWELVE

DCS Donald Bridges sat opposite Jane as she carefully went through the details of her investigation. She made no reference to her suspicions regarding possible fraud at the Stockwell property or her interest in the valuable jewellery. Instead, she focused on the possibility that Helena Lanark had buried the baby and the importance of questioning her younger sister, Beatrice.

Bridges began to tap his foot impatiently.

'If Helena Lanark has dementia, even if you were to uncover enough evidence to arrest her, she wouldn't be capable of standing trial.'

'I know, sir, but I do think we need closure on the case by confirming exactly what took place in that shelter.'

Bridges frowned. 'Have you contacted this sister? I mean, if she's of a similar age, is she mentally sound?'

'I have been unable to speak directly to Beatrice Lanark, sir, whose married name is Thorpe. Her son, Jason Thorpe, is extremely protective. He is aware of what was discovered at the Stockwell property, and he also has power of attorney for Helena Lanark's estate.'

DCS Bridges leaned forward.

'Detective Tennison, I have to consider the costs of a trip to Australia to question Beatrice Lanark, and presently there is absolutely no budget for that.'

'I understand, sir, but as I'm sure you are aware from the appalling weekend press, it has been suggested that we have allowed the Stockwell property to be demolished before concluding our investigation. I am not making any accusations about unprofessional conduct, but I have only recently been given a piece of evidence that should have been examined immediately on the discovery of the dead baby.'

Jane had purposefully held her trump card back and now she opened the drawer in her desk to remove the forensic evidence bag delivered by DS Lawrence.

'Sir, Helena Lanark moved from the Stockwell property many years ago. It remained boarded up until about ten years ago when her nephew, Jason Thorpe, was given permission to convert it into flats. The agreement was that no tenant could use the basement of the property or enter the garden. As you know, sir, the shelter was accessed via a tunnel from the basement.'

Bridges started tapping his foot again, impatiently. 'Yes, yes . . . I have read the report.'

'I'm sorry, sir, I just need to make it very clear to you that it is obvious Helena Lanark knew what was in that shelter. But when she was diagnosed with dementia, the Stockwell property was sold to a developer and placed under a demolition order.'

Bridges frowned. 'Are you inferring that this Jason Thorpe is involved?'

'No, not at all . . . I believe he was totally unaware of not only the first victim, Samantha Forgham, but also of the baby.'

Jane carefully opened the evidence envelope and eased out the belt. 'This is the belt that was used to secure the breeze blocks. It had been tied so tightly that we had to cut the leather. As you can see by the size, sir, it is very obviously a woman's belt.' DS Lawrence carefully examined the buckle of the belt and discovered it was a costly-looking silver filigree design with monogrammed initials.

Jane could see that she now had Bridges' total attention. He reached forward and looked carefully at the buckle.

'HL . . . Helena Lanark. I see.'

Jane had been hoping for a bigger reaction. Bridges walked to the door then turned back.

'Fine. I agree with you, Detective Tennison, we do need closure on this, and we also need to quieten the bad press. So find out whether Beatrice Lanark is able to be interviewed.'

As soon as Bridges closed the door, Jane put in a call to Arnold Hadley's law firm, only to be reminded that he had retired and was no longer acting for the company. They would now be looking after his client, Jason Thorpe. But it didn't take much persuasion for them to give her Arnold Hadley's home number and when Jane queried the area code, she was told that it was Brighton.

Jane was just dialling the number when there was a knock on her office door. Barbara, now even blonder, entered in her usual over-casual manner.

'TT asked me to hand this to you,' she said breezily. 'Everyone is caught up out there. I don't know if you've been told, but DCI Carter has got eight arrests for all these break-ins. We've had to bring in two other clerks to cope with all the paperwork, never mind getting solicitors and God knows what, and—'

Jane held up her hand. 'Excuse me, who is TT?'

Barbara waved her notebook. 'Oh, that's DC Tim Taylor . . . he's had to go down to the cells, but he asked me to list some archive material that he felt you would be interested in.' She started to rip out the page from her notebook. Jane held up her hand again.

'Would you please type it out. I don't want it scribbled on a piece of notepaper. In future, if you have anything for me, I'd be most grateful if you would present it to me in a professional manner.'

Barbara pursed her glossy pink lips.

'Yes, ma'am. But I'm actually just doing this as a favour. It is a Sunday, you know, and it's bedlam out there!' With that she flounced out of the room, leaving the door open.

Infuriated, Jane got up to close the door and could immediately hear the commotion coming from the incident room, where it seemed that a jubilant DCI Carter was being congratulated on a successful raid. Jane closed the door and began dialling Arnold Hadley's home number again.

When Hadley answered, Jane quickly explained who she was and got straight to the point.

'I need to ask you a rather important question regarding Beatrice Thorpe, Jason Thorpe's mother.'

'Yes?' he replied, sounding a little taken aback.

'I think it is vital that I interview her, but I am concerned that she may be unwell.'

'Unwell?' he queried.

'Yes, Mr Hadley. When Jason was picking up the photo album, he suggested his mother had been unwell, and that she would find it very difficult to discuss her family.'

'Well, I think that was rather an exaggeration. Although I have not actually seen her physically for quite a few years, I have had communications with her, and she is exceedingly coherent. I think she even assists her son running the wine export company.'

'That's all I wanted to know. Thank you very much for your time, Mr Hadley.' Jane replaced the receiver and resealed the evidence bag which now needed to be taken to the evidence lock-up. She gathered up the documents that Tim had given her earlier and was just placing them in her bag when her office door opened. Thinking it was Barbara again, she looked up with a frown, but it was DCS Bridges.

'I have just had confirmation that Beatrice Thorpe is well enough to be interviewed,' she said.

He gave her a brief nod. 'I need to cost this, but I presume you are eager to interview her face-to-face in Australia rather than have a telephone conversation?'

'I think that would be the right course of action, sir,' Jane nodded.

His eyes narrowed. 'Let's just hope for your sake the interview brings the closure we're looking for, Detective Tennison.'

* * *

Jane arrived home just after seven and as soon as she entered the hallway she could see a great deal of work had been accomplished.

The wooden stair banisters had been sandpapered down ready for painting, and the stripped floorboards looked as though they had been washed thoroughly, ready to be varnished.

One half of the wall on the stairway had been plastered and when she peered into the sitting room she was pleased to see that the furniture had all been piled in the centre of the room and covered with dust sheets. The wall had been half stripped of the old paper, but she felt too tired to begin work that evening.

On the table in the kitchen was a bunch of roses, alongside a note from Eddie:

> *Firstly, I apologise about the hat incident. Secondly, I need to pay the team so would you be able to get some cash tomorrow? Also, I need some additional equipment x*

He had left his contact number and a stack of invoices clipped together. She went to the phone in the hall to call him. There was no reply and no answer machine clicked on. She was feeling hungry but looking through the fridge there was no ham left, the butter dish had been scraped clean and the bread had been finished. She switched on the kettle whilst she continued searching for some food in the cupboards. All she could find was a tin of baked beans, a tin of hot dogs and several cans of tomatoes, none of which were at all enticing.

After making a cup of tea, Jane headed upstairs to her bedroom, where there had been no visible work done apart from the radiator being taken out. She undressed, wrapped herself in a towelling robe and went into her bathroom, only to find it no longer had a bath or a shower and was also missing a radiator. There had been a lot of new white tiles laid, but that didn't help. She was just crossing the landing when the security light came on at her front door. Jane peered down the stairs as the door opened and Eddie appeared.

'Jane?' he called out.

'I'm up here,' she said, coming down a couple of stairs.

'Did you get my note?' he asked.

'Yes, I did . . . and thank you for the flowers. They weren't at all necessary, though.'

'I like to keep my customers happy.' He grinned.

'I'm really impressed by how much work has been done, Eddie.'

He came to the edge of the bottom stair. 'Will you be able to get that cash for me tomorrow?'

'Yes, absolutely. I'll go to the bank before I head into the station.'

'Terrific.'

There was a rather awkward pause between them, but Jane felt no inclination to fill the silence. Eddie pulled off his cap and punched it into a bowl shape before repositioning it on his head.

'Maybe see you in the morning, then . . . I'd like to get cracking around seven-ish. I can bring you the best bacon buttie you've ever tasted if you like.'

'That sounds lovely . . . thank you.'

Again, there was a pause. 'Right, see you in the morning, then.'

He didn't wait to hear Jane's reply and let himself out. Jane felt guilty about being so off-hand with him but she was absolutely exhausted and just wanted to get an early night.

She was already in bed when she remembered she had brought home all the documents from DC Taylor and had left them downstairs in the kitchen. Yawning, she decided she would take a look at them in the morning.

* * *

Jane was used to having a shower every morning, but instead she had to wash her hair in the kitchen sink and give herself a quick wash down with a flannel. She headed back up to her bedroom to blow-dry her hair, making a mental note to call her sister as she really needed her highlights done before her potential trip to Australia. After wearing scruffy clothes into the station the previous day, she made a point of taking out one of her best suits and white blouses.

She was fully dressed by six, giving herself time to check over DC Taylor's documents. She was feeling hungry and was really looking forward to the bacon buttie Eddie had promised. Pouring herself a second cup of tea, she lit a cigarette to stave off the hunger. The young, fresh-faced Tim had actually come up with some rather good information. He had uncovered various magazine and newspaper articles, all providing fascinating background on Muriel Lanark, née Petrukhin. Her mother, Aida, it turned out, had been part of a high-ranking circle of Russian diplomats who were close to the Czar's family, especially the Czarina Alexandra. During the Russian revolution she had left St Petersburg and had gone to America with Count Petrukhin and their young daughter, Muriel Alexandra, who was born in 1909. There were various references to the family living in an affluent Boston neighbourhood, where they frequently entertained. One blurred black-and-white newspaper photograph showed the Countess Aida looking very much like the British Queen Mary, wearing a tiara and an elaborate choker necklace of pearls.

There were also three references to the Russian count's financial ruin in the Wall Street crash of 1929. The last reference to Countess Aida Petrukhin was the presentation of her daughter at a debutante ball in 1921, an elaborate affair attended by members of the English aristocracy.

DC Taylor had attached a handwritten note to this article, stating that perhaps this was when Aida had inflated her daughter's age as debutantes were usually at least seventeen when presented to the royals. Jane made a note to check if Henry Lanark had also been present at the ball, although it was doubtful as his family were not exactly of the nobility. She wanted to find out how Muriel came to be married to him in 1923.

Jane was just checking her latest bank statement, to find out how much she could withdraw to pay Eddie and his team, when the doorbell rang. Jane was disappointed that it was not Eddie bringing her breakfast. Instead, it was his father, Tony, holding up a brown carrier bag.

'Been ordered to deliver breakfast and I brought some invoices I need you to look over. Also, just to tell you Eddie has seen some nice bathroom suites and we can fit in a corner bath and a shower unit.'

True to Eddie's promise, the large bacon buttie was tasty, and Tony was very methodical as he talked her through each of the invoices, insisting she inspect everything that had been done in the house with him, though.

He was not very complimentary about some of the plastering, explaining that it was actually quite an art form.

'If you don't get it absolutely perfect, when it dries out you'll have problems hanging the wallpaper.'

By the time they returned to the kitchen he seemed impatient to leave for another job. He gave Jane a list of payments required and said that because she was paying cash, there would be no VAT. However, if she wanted it to go through his company, she would have to add on the VAT.

Jane agreed she would get payment to Eddie at some point that day.

'You're a police officer, is that right?' Tony asked, as he put on his donkey jacket.

'Yes, I'm actually a detective inspector,' Jane said, smiling.

'Eddie told me you're working on that "House of Horrors" case?'

'Yes, that's right.'

'It was about that junkie, wasn't it, found in the old air-raid shelter? And she gave birth to a baby and put it between some bricks?'

'Well, no . . . that's not exactly what happened . . .' Jane began, but Tony was already walking out.

'Shocking . . . shocking. My wife couldn't even read it,' he muttered, closing the door behind him.

Jane washed up their mugs, then gathered up all the invoices and put them into a cardboard folder. She then went upstairs to finish getting ready and placed all the new information from DC Taylor in her briefcase.

Before leaving she called her sister, Pam, asking if she could have an appointment for her hair to be highlighted early that evening. Pam was in the middle of serving breakfast to her kids and told Jane she would have to be there by five. She was closing the salon early as there was a parents' evening at the school and her youngest had been in some trouble at a school football match.

'I was at Mum and Dad's this weekend . . . they're a bit annoyed that they haven't heard from you or seen you properly in ages, and you haven't had them over to your house,' she said.

'I'm having a lot of decorating done,' Jane replied.

'It's all right for some, isn't it?' Pam continued, ignoring Jane's explanation. 'You should make more of an effort to go and see them. I do, even though going for Sunday lunch is sometimes a bit of a chore.'

Jane sighed. 'Yes, Pam, I'll try and see them as soon as I can, but I've got a lot of work on at the moment.'

'Haven't we all?' Pam retorted.

To Jane's relief, Pam ended the call as she was in a hurry for the school run. The doorbell rang and, once again, Jane was disappointed that it wasn't Eddie, just his team arriving to begin work. She gestured to the kitchen, inviting them to help themselves to tea and coffee and making another mental note to herself that she needed to stock up on milk and tea bags.

* * *

It was a quarter to nine when Jane arrived at the station. She went straight to her office to start typing up the information gleaned from DC Taylor's documents.

The CID room was filling up as, according to the board, there had been numerous magistrate's court appearances after the multiple arrests the previous day. Sergeant Hunt was busy allocating the vehicles for transporting the suspects to court. As soon as he saw Jane enter the room, he gestured to the board.

'A good day, lads. We've recovered a shedload of stolen property and we still have more search warrants to execute on other premises to see what we can uncover from previous burglaries in other areas. In the meantime, DCI Carter's got the teams keeping the properties under surveillance in case any family members start trying to move stolen stuff out.'

Almost as an afterthought, Hunt asked Jane if she still needed Tim, as there was a lot of paperwork they had to wade through. Jane quickly agreed that she could do the necessary herself and returned to her office. She cleared her desk with the intention of seeing what else she could discover about the countess and her daughter.

After half an hour of frustrating telephone calls, as she was passed from one department to another at Somerset House, she was informed that, due to the Blitz between 1940 and 1941 many documents had been destroyed. But at least she managed to discover one fact: Aida, Countess Petrukhin, had died in 1938. She was unable to discover any further information about Muriel, however.

She told the duty sergeant that she would be unavailable for a couple of hours as she needed to go to her bank and run some personal errands. She withdrew £500 from her branch of the National Westminster Bank at the end of Harley Street and was planning to return to the station, but on impulse went to the wallpaper department at John Lewis to choose wallpaper for her sitting room and her bedroom. She then drove back home with some samples to give Eddie the money, hoping that he would also be able to order the wallpaper she had chosen as he had told her he could get it at a trade price.

She arrived to find the team were making impressive progress. Eddie had brought several large tins of white gloss paint and she found him in the kitchen stacking them neatly in the corner. He was wearing jeans and his leather coat rather than his work clothes, and if he felt any awkwardness, he didn't show it. Instead, he smiled brightly, saying that he had just collected his paint order.

'Have you made a decision on whether you want a corner bath?' he asked, passing her a leaflet. 'I think it would be wise to stay with white. I know all these coloured bathroom suites are fashionable at the moment but you're much safer to stick with white, especially if you ever you want to resell the property in the future.'

'I hadn't really thought of that,' Jane said, opening her briefcase. 'I'll go along with whatever you suggest.' She took out the envelope of cash and handed it to him. 'I took out £500. Your dad suggested I should get you enough for next week as well, as he reckoned you wouldn't be finished by then.'

Eddie wrote Jane a receipt as she produced the wallpaper samples.

'They're perfectly all right,' he said, tossing them aside, 'but maybe you should go to Colefax & Fowler . . . they're more expensive but they have a wider range selection, and I think they're better quality.'

'You don't like any of the ones I picked?' Jane asked.

Eddie shrugged. 'You've got quite a big area to cover, especially in the hallway. Come with me and I'll hold up a couple of your choices . . . you'll see what I mean.'

As Eddie held up the samples Jane could tell instantly that she had made the wrong choice.

'I'll go and have another look this afternoon. Do you think I should go to the same place for my bedroom as well?'

'I would. They've got a nice Regency stripe. Are you free for dinner this evening?' he asked, almost in the same breath. 'My mum's cooking a chicken.'

'Tonight?' Jane asked.

'Yeah.'

Jane hesitated. 'Er, yes . . . that would be really nice. I need to see my sister at five, though. What time were you thinking?'

'Around seven thirty to eight. I can pick you up.'

* * *

As Jane drove back to the station, she asked herself why she had agreed to Eddie's invitation. She would be at Pam's salon until at least six, or longer if Pam continued to harangue her with moans about her not going to see her parents.

No one in the squad room seemed to pay any attention to her reappearance as the focus was still on the trips back and forth to the magistrates' courts. DCI Carter caught her as he was leaving his office.

'I heard you didn't think the investigation into the Lanark inquiry had been satisfactory,' he said with a frown.

'I don't know what you heard, sir, but after the weekend's negative news coverage, I just suggested it would be good for us to get some form of positive closure.'

'Really? And in order to get closure, Detective Inspector Tennison, you are planning a trip to Australia? What the fuck kind of budget do you think we have? I doubt very much that the super will give clearance . . . not to mention the fact that I need every officer available to work on other cases.' He turned to walk away, then looked back. 'You're looking very smart.'

'Thank you, sir.' The way he looked her up and down from head to toe made her feel very uncomfortable, especially when he gave her a flirtatious wink.

'I wouldn't mind a long weekend in Australia. It's summertime there, isn't it?'

Jane didn't answer.

As she turned away to go back to her office, he called after her: 'Just joking, Tennison! No need to get your knickers in a twist.'

CHAPTER THIRTEEN

Jason Thorpe held a small bunch of flowers, with the photograph album he had been so eager to have back tucked under his other arm.

'Miss Thompson . . . Emily,' he said, with a smile. 'I'm just about to leave for Australia. I know it's a trifle late in the afternoon, but was wondering if I could just see my aunt for a few moments?'

'Oh, it's perfect timing,' she said, returning his smile. 'We haven't served tea yet. I'm sure your aunt will be delighted to have a visitor.' They shared a complicit look, both perfectly aware that Helena Lanark never showed the slightest reaction to anybody coming to see her.

'Let me sign you in and show you through, Mr Thorpe.'

As they passed through the glass double-doors into the corridor, he touched the small of her back in a familiar way. Emily Thompson knocked gently on Helena's door before opening it.

'Miss Lanark, you have a visitor . . . your nephew. He's brought you some lovely flowers.'

Helena was sitting in her wheelchair, looking out through her bay window into the garden. Jason handed the flowers to Miss Thompson. 'Perhaps you'd be kind enough to find a vase for these?'

'Yes, of course, Mr Thorpe, I'll get one of the girls to do it.'

Jason crossed to his aunt and placed the photograph album on the desk. He leaned forwards and kissed her powdery cheek. She turned, almost in slow motion and looked at him with her icy-blue, vacant eyes. A small glob of spittle formed at the corner of her mouth, as he opened the album at the last page. Before he said anything, there was a light knock at the door and a carer brought in a vase with the flowers.

'Good afternoon, Ms Lanark . . . aren't these pretty?' She placed the vase on the desk next to the album.

'I'll be serving tea soon, sir, so would you like me to bring an extra cup and perhaps a slice of sponge cake?'

'That is most kind of you, but I won't be here for more than a few moments.' The girl smiled sweetly and left the room as quietly as she had entered.

Jason stood up and walked over to the window, loosening the catch.

'Do you not find it stuffy in here?' he asked without looking at his aunt, before pushing the window open. He then began to search the drawers in the desk.

Ten minutes later Jason passed Emily Thompson in the reception as he left.

'She seemed very tired and I can't really stay longer if I'm going to catch my flight.'

'Did the girl bring her flowers?'

'She most certainly did, and my aunt was delighted.' They exchanged the same complicit look as before.

'Have a safe journey,' Miss Thompson said, pleasantly. Jason Thorpe gave her a charming smile and walked out.

* * *

Jane was impressed with the Colefax & Fowler selection of wallpapers, despite their cost. She came away with a glossy catalogue, then drove herself to Pam's salon. There was a CLOSED sign on the salon door, and Jane had to knock several times before a disgruntled Pam unlocked the door and let her in.

'I've had a day from hell,' she said immediately. 'You just can't please some customers. One bloody woman complaining her perm's too curly . . . another one saying it's not curly enough . . . they drive me to distraction. And I've got juniors who are incapable of following the simplest instructions. I asked one of them to sweep up the hair and she just left it in a pile in the middle of the salon.' Pam was on autopilot as she talked, and quickly had Jane sitting down with a plastic cape around her shoulders, whilst she started mixing the bleach and arranging the tin foil pieces on a small wheelie tray.

'How blonde do you want to go?'

'Not too blonde . . . just highlights. And maybe a trim?' Jane looked at herself in the mirror and saw Pam's reflection glaring back at her.

'Do you want one or two inches off? Or shorter? It's up to you, but I think we should cut maybe two inches so it's just below your chin.'

'Fine . . . OK, yes, let's do that.' As Pam got to work, Jane was forced to listen to more complaints about her customers, her husband, her children, and then, inevitably, on to the fact that Jane wasn't pulling her weight in terms of seeing their parents. Jane said nothing until Pam suddenly changed tack, asked if she was working on anything interesting.

Jane told her she had been working on the Stockwell murder investigation. 'Oh my God!' Pam exclaimed. 'I think I read about that at the weekend – all about the girl who was starved to death, isn't it?' By this time Pam had completed a full head of foils and was washing up the plastic pots and brushes. 'Did you find her body?'

'No, but I did have to go in there,' Jane told her. 'It was really tragic, because her father had been trying to get her off drugs and had taken her to the shelter to go cold turkey.'

Pam tutted. 'Drugs! I've got a customer whose daughter has gone all hippy and went to a concert by this group called the Animals and never came home . . . turns out she'd gone off with her boyfriend who was selling marijuana. Right, come on . . . over to the wash basin.'

It never ceased to amaze Jane how her sister could always make any conversation end up being about her and her customers. But on the bright side, it did mean that Jane didn't have to go into details, and two hours later she had to admit that Pam had done a good job with her highlights, and her newly cut and blow-dried hair actually looked very stylish.

They then had the usual battle, with Pam insisting she didn't want to be paid, but eventually accepting Jane's proffered money – even the tip. As she was leaving, Pam asked her if she was seeing anyone.

Jane had a mischievous twinkle in her eye as she told her. 'I am actually . . . he's an interior decorator – he's helping me do up the house.'

Pam looked predictably taken aback. 'What about that architect you were seeing?'

'Oh, that didn't work out,' Jane said breezily.

'So, are you going to introduce this new boyfriend to Mum and Dad?' Pam asked.

'Perhaps . . . it's early days, but I'm having a nice time with him.'

By the time Jane got home it was a quarter to eight and Eddie was waiting for her at the front door. 'I thought you might have stood me up!' he said, smiling. He looked smart in a white linen shirt and jeans, and Jane felt slightly embarrassed that she was still wearing her office clothes.

'Wow! Your hair looks lovely,' Eddie exclaimed.

'Thank you. My sister Pam is a hairdresser. The reason I didn't make it back to change is that she loves the sound of her own voice and tends to go on a bit!'

Eddie nodded. 'I could leave the van here and drive us to my parents' in your car? We should get a move on because Mum will be ready to serve up by five past eight.'

Jane handed him her car keys. 'Well, I haven't eaten since your delicious breakfast was delivered by your dad, so I'm starving.'

Eddie opened the passenger door for her and then had to push back the driver's seat to accommodate his long legs.

'We always try to have dinner together once a week,' he said, starting the car. 'Mum always used to put pressure on me to have

Sunday lunch, but I didn't always fancy it if I'd had a night on the tiles on Saturday. So now we tend to do it on Monday evenings.'

Jane started to feel guilty about not inviting her parents for a meal at her new house, but at least she had the excuse that there was still building work going on.

Eddie drew up into a garage forecourt, then quickly got out and picked up a bunch of flowers from the buckets outside the kiosk. Jane watched through the passenger window, feeling even more guilty that she hadn't thought of getting flowers or a bottle of wine, as Eddie returned with both.

Eddie's parents lived in Bonnington Tower, a 1960s high-rise block in Turpington Lane, near Bromley Common. It was eleven storeys high with fifty-four flats and was in surprisingly good repair, unlike many of the high-rises Jane had been obliged to visit in the course of her work as a police officer. There was a slightly rundown feeling in the large reception area, but the lift was in good working order and didn't have the appalling stench of urine of so many council blocks.

Eddie pressed the bell on number 35, passing the flowers to Jane to give to his mother. Linette Fraser opened the door wearing a floral-print apron and sporting a perm even Pam would be proud of. Eddie gave his mother a huge hug, kissing her on both cheeks and putting his arms around her shoulders as he introduced Jane.

'Mum, this is Jane Tennison, the lady I'm working for. Jane, this is my mum, Linette.'

'He's told me all about you,' Linette said with a nervous smile.

'Thank you so much for having me to dinner,' Jane said as she rather sheepishly handed over the flowers, which had already begun to wilt.

'Everything is ready to be served,' Linette said, ushering them in. 'So, you two sit down and I'll pry Tony away from the TV.' Jane could see the small dining room had been set out with great care, the table laid with cut glasses, lacy white napkins and a white lace tablecloth.

Eddie pulled out a chair for Jane to take a seat and held up the bottle of wine.

'Get Dad to open the wine, would you, Mum?'

'No, you do it, Eddie. You know what he's like . . . he'll either push the cork in too far or break it.'

Eddie crossed over to a sideboard, opened a drawer and took out a corkscrew. Jane looked around the room. There was a large fake coal fire and a pretty, tiled fireplace with a row of framed photographs on the mantelpiece, and a five-bulb modern chandelier lit the room brightly. She couldn't help thinking it was all very neat and uncluttered compared to her parents' house. Jane heard Linette calling out for her husband to come to the table and asked Eddie if she should go and help his mother in the kitchen.

'Good God, no. That's her domain. She'll probably want to show off her new appliances after supper, though, especially her dishwasher.'

'That's me,' Tony said, as he burst into the room with a grin. 'Top bottle washer and dish dryer.'

'Don't be silly,' Linette said, carrying in a tray of covered vegetable dishes. 'Put these out, love.'

Eddie poured the wine, as Linette, now minus her apron, carried in the large roast chicken and sat down as Tony began to carve.

From then on the dinner was easy-going. Tony dominated the conversation with a barrage of funny anecdotes, mostly about when he used to run a market stall – and then became a window cleaner. Then he explained how he got into the home decorating business. By this time, the main course had been removed and Linette brought in a home-cooked apple pie and custard. Tony waved his spoon towards his son.

'He's the first in my family who went to college. Got a degree in electrical engineering.'

'When did you start your business together? Jane asked.

'As soon as he finished his degree, we became business partners.'

There were further amusing stories about their partnership, and it was not until coffee was brought in that the focus turned to Jane. Linette asked how she had got into the Metropolitan Police.

'I read an article, I think it was in *The Times*, about the Met police recruiting more women . . . and I just somehow knew that was what I wanted to do.'

Tony nodded towards Eddie. 'You'll need to watch yourself, son! Better make sure you do a good job or she'll have you in handcuffs!'

'He works hard for everybody,' Linette said, defensively. 'You look around this flat. It's not all down to his father. Eddie has done so much work here.'

Throughout the dinner, Eddie seemed content to let his parents dominate the conversation and was obviously proud of them.

'My mum had it tough growing up,' he said, turning to Jane. 'She came from a really rough area in the East End that was flattened in the Blitz; the whole street she lived on was a bomb site.'

Linette smiled at him. 'Oh, it wasn't all bad, you know. In those days there was more friendliness with your neighbours. We were all in the same boat, and everyone helped everyone else. Nowadays, most people don't even know who their next-door neighbours are – us included.'

'Did you live anywhere near Stockwell?' Jane asked.

'No, we was near the sound of the Bow Bells, darling, but that area got badly hit too. Why do you ask?'

'Oh, it's just a case I've been working on.'

'She's on that murder you was reading about last weekend,' Tony said.

'Oh yes, what a shocking thing. That girl starved and then they found her baby.'

'Actually no, that's not quite true. The girl that was found in the old air-raid shelter had tragically died because we believe her father was trying to get her off drugs . . . but then he was murdered and nobody else knew she was there. Then we found the body of a newborn baby, but the forensic and pathology teams determined that it had been left there possibly thirty years ago.'

There was an uneasy silence around the table, then Linette reached over to take Jane's coffee cup.

'You know, when I was a young girl, there was quite a lot of that. There was such a terrible stigma if you were pregnant and not married. You know, there were these women doing illegal abortions because there wasn't any healthcare like there is today. But families where I come from, if they found out you got yourself up the spout, all hell would break loose. There was a girl my mother knew, and she got herself pregnant by a GI and her dad beat the living daylights out of her. Is that what the father did to the girl you found starving?'

Jane shook her head. 'No, no . . . they are two entirely different cases and there's twenty-five years between them. What I'm trying to do is discover who killed the baby.'

'What's the point after all this time?' Tony said. 'Isn't there enough crime going on right now for you to work on?'

Jane could feel her hackles rising. 'Mr Fraser, I don't think it matters how long ago it was. To extinguish a life is a crime and I believe that it deserves justice.'

Tony carried on regardless. 'I tell you what I believe is justice . . . when you get garbage like Peter Sutcliffe, that Yorkshire Ripper, who killed at least eleven poor women and God knows how many more. Those victims deserve justice. But to me, some poor young woman who had a baby she didn't want and couldn't afford to look after it . . . she's not a criminal. What good's it going to do putting her in jail after all these years?'

Eddie stood up. 'I think it's probably time I took Jane home.'

Linette smiled at Jane, shaking her head. 'Don't mind Tony, dear . . . just don't get him on to hanging. I'm very pleased to have met you, and I hope Eddie brings you to see us again.'

Jane looked over at Tony and gave him a warm smile to show she wasn't upset by his remarks. 'That would be lovely.'

Eddie ushered Jane into the hallway as Linette hurried after them, gently touching Jane's arm. 'Have you found out who did it?'

Jane shook her head. 'Not yet, but I will. Thank you for a lovely dinner.'

In the car, Eddie started apologising for his father.

'It's fine, Eddie,' Jane said. 'Everyone's entitled to their opinion.'

'Well, he's got strong opinions about crime because of his background. He didn't mention why we got out of the East End – it was because all the villains he knew there were beginning to draw him into doing bad stuff. I was surprised he didn't mention how well he knew the Kray brothers.'

Jane laughed. 'Everyone born in the East End seems to have known them.'

Eddie gave her a sidelong glance. 'No, he really did, and I think when he was a youngster a lot of his mates got drawn into a life of crime.'

They pulled up outside Jane's house and, always the gentleman, Eddie opened the passenger door to let her out. He then locked the Mini and gave her the keys.

'Do you want to come in for a coffee?' Jane asked.

'Can I take a raincheck on that?' Eddie said. 'I've got to pick up a couple of the guys early tomorrow to get them to work on time.'

Jane opened the front door as Eddie reached forward and cupped her face in his hands. He gave her a sweet, gentle kiss.

'See you tomorrow.'

Jane closed the door, feeling disappointed to be ending the night alone. She put her briefcase on the stairs by the telephone and went into the kitchen to get a glass of water. She noticed that the folder she had put all the invoices in after her breakfast with Eddie's dad was open and two of them were on the floor. She picked them up and put them back in the cardboard folder, then noticed that the back door was ajar.

She assumed one of Eddie's guys had left it open accidentally, and made a mental note to tell Eddie to remind them to lock it in future, before closing it and pushing the bolt firmly across. By the time she headed upstairs to her bedroom, the warm feeling from dinner with Eddie's parents had gone, replaced by a vague feeling of unease.

CHAPTER FOURTEEN

The following morning Jane got to work early, finding the squad room in a self-congratulatory mood as Sergeant Hunt explained that more stolen property had been retrieved and matched to various thefts over a lengthy period of time. It was as if DCI Carter had captured Al Capone and his mafia mob instead of seven adolescent gang members, and Jane tried not to show her irritation. Everyone seemed to have forgotten about the Stockwell case, so when at twelve o'clock Superintendent Beattie arrived at the station and requested a meeting with her, she was expecting the worst.

She was pleasantly surprised when he told her that closing the case in a satisfactory manner was essential to counteract the bad press the investigation had generated so far. 'So, Detective Inspector Tennison, I am giving you permission to travel to Australia, accompanied by another officer, to question Beatrice Thorpe with reference to the infanticide murder.'

'Thank you very much, sir,' she said, feeling her cheeks flushing. 'I will do my best to get the answers we need.'

'Good,' he said, abruptly, heading to the door. 'I will leave you to run through the itinerary with DCI Carter. You should go as soon as possible, but obviously you need to ensure you have a visa and that your passport is up to date.'

Jane would have liked to let out a yelp of excitement, but instead she took a deep breath to calm herself down. The only downside was having to discuss her trip with DCI Carter.

* * *

Emily Thompson called Arnold Hadley's office, her hand shaking slightly as she dialled.

'This is Miss Thompson from the care home, with regard to Helena Lanark, it is very urgent.'

'I'm afraid Mr Hadley recently retired and is no longer working with the company,' the secretary who answered informed her. 'I'm sorry I can't help you, Miss Thompson, but if he should call here, I will forward your message.'

'Thank you, please do,' Miss Thompson said, her voice catching. 'And please do remember to tell him it's urgent.'

* * *

DCI Carter was having lunch in the canteen when Jane approached his table and asked if she could have five minutes of his time when he was finished. He answered without looking at her.

'Give me half an hour and I'll be down.'

Jane got herself a cup of coffee and a sandwich and went back to her office. It was considerably over half an hour later when Carter entered without knocking.

'I know what this is about,' he said, and with his hands in his pockets walked around her desk and sat on the edge nearest to her. 'So you reckon this woman Beatrice Lanark is going to tell you what exactly happened in that shelter . . .' he cocked his head to one side with a sly smile, 'even though it was thirty years ago?'

Jane knew he was trying to undermine her and found his closeness slightly unnerving. 'I think that the birth of a child is something you would not forget.'

'So, you're suggesting that it could be Beatrice's baby?'

'It's a possibility,' Jane said. 'But I feel it is more likely to have been the very young sister, Marjorie, who subsequently committed suicide. Although we cannot establish the length of time between the birth of the baby and the suicide, DS Lawrence and the pathologist felt they could be close together.'

Carter started swinging his right foot. 'Really? So, you wouldn't say that the belt buckle with the initial HL is enough evidence to accuse Helena Lanark of infanticide?'

'Well, it's obviously evidence implicating Helena but . . .'

Carter reached forward and touched Jane's arm. 'But due to her dementia it would be difficult, if not impossible, to actually determine whether it was her child and if she actually killed it.'

Jane found herself squirming as he leaned over her, disdainfully giving his view of her investigation. Then, to her relief, he uncrossed his legs and folded his arms.

'Helena Lanark didn't actually speak to you at all, did she?'

Jane hesitated. 'No, she did not. In my report I clearly stated that she has been in the care home for a considerable time and is in a completely uncommunicative state.'

Carter nodded. 'So, then you took her photo album?'

'Yes, I did.'

'Without permission or a warrant . . .?'

'I don't quite understand where this is going, sir? I did take the photo album because I felt it would be important to understand the Lanark family—'

Carter interrupted her. 'Then we get the nephew making complaints against you for taking the album, but thanks to me we were able to put the situation to bed.' He reached out and took her hand. Jane wanted to remove her hand, but he held on tightly, and then to her consternation began to stroke it. 'I think I'm going to have quite a time before any of my arrests get to court and I wouldn't mind a nice, relaxing trip away – a couple of nights in a good hotel in Sydney . . . maybe take in a few sights, the Opera House . . .'

Jane could not believe what was happening. With his other hand Carter had moved on to her knee, pushing up her skirt as his fingers inched towards her crotch. He moved even closer and she could see he had an erection pressing against his trousers. 'It would be a good career move, Jane.'

Jane dug her heels into the carpet and pushed her desk chair back on its wheels. She was shaking.

'A good career move?' she repeated, her voice trembling. 'If you lay one hand on me ever again, I will make sure your career is finished.'

Carter had the audacity to laugh as he pushed himself off her desk.

'You thought I wanted to fuck you? You're a stuck-up little bitch. Get your arse off to Australia, then. You can get a flight there and return the following day and you had better get something useful while you're out there. I'm going to make it clear that I think it is an unnecessary expense.'

He walked out of the office as Jane pulled down her skirt. She took a deep breath. It wasn't the first time she had been harassed by a higher-ranking officer, but Carter's clear sexual intention had disgusted her.

Minutes later Sergeant Hunt was at her door. 'You should have seen the look on Tim Taylor's face when they told him he'd be going to Australia with you! He's never been further abroad than Jersey.'

Hunt guffawed.

'I told him not to get too excited, ma'am. You'll be cramped in cattle class on a twenty-four-hour flight from the UK to Perth, refuelling in Bangkok, then a four-hour flight to Sydney . . . and less than a day later, you'll be on your way back again. I doubt you will have any time for sightseeing . . .'

'Thank you, Sergeant Hunt,' she said, cutting him off. 'Can you please ask Tim if he can be ready to leave in about half an hour as we need to go to the Australian Embassy to get a visa?'

'Yes, ma'am,' Hunt said, still smiling as he walked out.

Jane knew the entire incident room would have the same attitude as Hunt, thinking the whole trip was a ridiculous waste of time and money, but she would just have to ignore it. She also knew she had now made a real enemy in Carter and the pressure was on to get a result. If she didn't, he would be waiting to stick the knife in.

Jane had just left when Sergeant Hunt received a call from Arnold Hadley asking to speak to her. He was informed that she was not available and when he requested her home number, Hunt remembered the kerfuffle over Jason Thorpe being given Jane's number, and his request was denied.

Hadley sounded anxious and upset. 'Please tell her it's an urgent matter in connection with Helena Lanark.'

* * *

Jane and DC Tim Taylor were at the Australian Embassy for nearly three hours. When each of them had their interview, they were told that their visa would not be approved for forty-eight hours. Jane was loath to return to the station, so instead she told Tim to ask Sergeant Hunt to contact whoever at Scotland Yard would oversee the tickets and travel arrangements, booking a flight as early as possible to give them as much time in Australia before they had to return the following day.

It was rather challenging trying to explain to Tim that it was probably best to fly out on Thursday night because of the time difference. He couldn't get his head round the fact that they would be eleven hours ahead of the UK. If they arrived early on Saturday, about 6.30 a.m., they would have two full days to speak to Beatrice as their return flight could be on Saturday evening, giving them one night in Sydney. She also instructed him to see if they could get a police car to take them to Beatrice's house in Mosman, and to book a hotel for them both for the one night.

* * *

On returning home, the cacophony of transistor radios in Jane's house was at its usual deafening level. The bathroom suite was just being carried up the stairs as Eddie called out to her from the top landing.

'Your new bathroom has arrived . . . and your bedroom has been stripped. We finished plastering in the bathroom and should be ready to put the tiles up at the end of the week!'

* * *

The station received a second call from Arnold Hadley asking to speak to DCI Tennison. DC Tim Taylor took the call and then went over to Sergeant Hunt.

'He seems to be pretty upset. What do you think I should do, sarge?'

'You can't give him Tennison's number, Tim. Just take his number and then give her a ring, passing on the message.'

* * *

Jane went into the kitchen which was piled with workmen's clothes, stacked Tupperware boxes and flasks. There was a mountain of used tea bags sitting in the sink. Jane decided she would go to the shops to top up supplies. As she went back into the hall, the corner bath was being carefully hauled up the stairs. Eddie was at the top, making sure the boys didn't damage the new plaster.

'I'm going out to do a grocery shop,' Jane called out. Eddie waved to her but was clearly more concerned about the new bathtub.

Still balanced on one of the stairs, Jane's phone rang. The answer-phone had not been reconnected and eventually one of the work-men picked up the receiver. Eddie heard the workman shouting up the stairs.

'It's a call for her!' he said loudly.

'Tell whoever it is that she shouldn't be too long, she's just gone to the shops for some groceries.' Eddie saw the receiver being replaced before he had time to instruct his worker to take the details of who was calling.

Jane went to the local Tesco and bought enough bread to make sandwiches, along with tea, coffee, milk, and some other essentials. By the time she returned home it was almost seven and the lack of blaring radios told her that Eddie's team had left. She staggered into the kitchen with the bags and found Eddie standing at the kitchen sink washing up the mugs.

'Here, let me . . .' He crossed over and took the bags from her.

'I've done a major shop. The boys can make sandwiches if they like . . . and there's more teabags, coffee, milk and sugar.'

Eddie unloaded the shopping smoothly, seeming to know exactly which cupboard to put everything in. He picked up one sliced loaf.

'Shall I put one in the freezer as you've got three?'

She nodded, taking off her coat and throwing it over the back of the chair.

'I'll show you around so you can see what we've done today,' Eddie said.

'I'd like that, but first I need a cup of tea.' Eddie picked up the kettle and filled it as she sat at the kitchen table. 'I've not had a very good day.'

He turned to her. 'What happened?'

She sighed. 'Just something I should have dealt with maybe less forcefully than I did.'

'What do you mean?' he asked.

'One of the officers I work with came on to me. You'd honestly think that by now I'd be used to it, but I just didn't see it coming. I know there will be repercussions and that's what is so shit about this job. Sometimes, I don't know why I do it.'

Eddie nodded sympathetically. 'Do you want sugar?'

'No, thanks.' He put her mug down in front of her.

There was an awkward silence, then Eddie said, 'Do you want to have a look at your bathroom? I think it was a good choice to make it a corner bath – it's going to look very classy.'

Even though she didn't really want to, Jane picked up her mug and followed him up the stairs and into the bathroom. Nothing had been plumbed in but there was a new wash basin, a shower with a glass-fronted sliding door and the most enormous corner bath.

'Wow! It's quite big, isn't it?' she said.

'It'll look better when all the tiles are up. I've decided to tile the whole bathroom white. We should start to get it plumbed in tomorrow and then you need to decide on the floor, because now we've taken up all the carpet.'

'What do you suggest?' Jane asked.

'I think you should tile the floor as well as the walls. You don't want wet wood, and definitely not carpet.'

'OK, that's fine with me,' Jane said, unable to really focus on what he was asking her.

He moved ahead into her bedroom. All the bedroom furniture had been piled into the centre of the room and covered with dust sheets, and the walls had been stripped of wallpaper.

'This room doesn't need plastering so we can hang the new wallpaper sometime this week.'

Jane sipped her tea, wondering where she was going to sleep, as everything in the second bedroom had been piled high with junk.

'I'll need to get some things out of my wardrobe.'

Eddie looked at her. 'You just need to take the dust sheets down. The lads cleared the other bedroom, so you've got somewhere to sleep tonight.'

'I need to get out some summer clothes. I'm going to Australia and it's summer there.' She caught the look of astonishment on Eddie's face.

'You're going to Australia?' Eddie asked, plaintively. Jane nodded, unsure whether he was saddened she was leaving or concerned that he would be out of a job.

She laughed. 'It's only for a couple of days. It's for work.'

He looked relieved. 'Oh, thank God. I thought you might be thinking of selling up and leaving me.'

'No, Eddie, I'm not leaving you,' she said, instantly regretting her choice of words. She hadn't really meant to make it sound so loaded.

She turned back to head down the stairs.

'Actually, Eddie, I have got a bit of a telling-off for you . . . when I got back home last night the back door was ajar. You or one of your team must have left it open. It rather unnerved me.' She walked into the kitchen and put her mug down.

Eddie followed her, frowning. 'Jane, I definitely locked that back door and I guarantee every one of the guys who work for me would double check it before leaving. We are used to working in other people's homes and security is always a priority.'

'I'm sure it is, Eddie, but I'm just telling you the back door was open last night, and I was rather concerned.'

He shrugged. 'I'll check it out with the guys tomorrow. So, you're going to Australia . . .'

'Yes, it's the case I'm working on . . . you know, the one with the baby? I want to question one of the women who used to live at the Stockwell property.'

'OK . . . do you fancy going out for dinner tonight, then?'

'I need to get prepared for my trip,' Jane said. She laughed. 'Actually, what I really need is a long soak in a bath, but that will have to wait. Besides, I'm not leaving until Thursday so . . . yes, I would love to go out for dinner.'

Eddie picked up his jacket. 'I'll pick you up in an hour. I need to scrub up first myself.' He paused. 'You know, if you want, you could come back with me to my place after dinner and have a bath there?'

Jane hesitated. 'OK . . . give me a few minutes to grab a change of clothes.' As Jane went into the hall, her phone rang. She heard her mother's voice as soon as she picked it up.

'So, Pam says you have a new boyfriend? We were just saying to each other that we hadn't seen you properly for such a long time . . .'

'I'm sorry, Mum, I've been really busy at work, and with all the work at the house here. I really wanted to get it all done before getting you and Dad over to show it all off.'

'He's a builder, Pam said.'

Jane sighed. 'Yes, yes, Mum . . . he's fitting a new bathroom and doing some redecoration.'

'Oh, that's nice, dear. Now, we think you should come over to dinner and introduce him to us. Are you free on Friday?'

'Not this Friday,' Jane said. 'But the week after would be lovely.'

Jane closed her eyes and covered the mouthpiece. 'Eddie, would you like to have dinner with my parents a week on Friday?' He was bending down, examining one of the stripped boards in the hall.

'Sure.'

'OK, Mum, Friday it is. What time?'

'Seven thirty – he isn't a vegetarian or anything like that, is he?'

'No, Mum, he's definitely a meat eater.'

'Ho, good. All right, bye bye . . . love you.'

* * *

As Jane and Eddie were about to leave for his house her phone rang again. It was Tim, passing on the message from Arnold Hadley. Jane rang Hadley straightaway, but he wasn't picking up and after a while she gave up. Oh, well, it couldn't have been that urgent, Jane thought.

CHAPTER FIFTEEN

They had dinner at a small Italian restaurant and after a couple of glasses of red wine, Jane began to relax. She liked the fact that Eddie did not probe for more details about what had gone on at the station that day. In fact, he spent most of the time discussing how the work in her house would progress, so she was surprised when he suddenly changed the subject and asked if the photo album that he had looked at with her had proved to be important.

'Actually, that album caused a bit of a problem for me. I'd taken it without permission from the woman I was trying to interview. She has advanced dementia. The station received an unpleasant call from her nephew about it. He spoke to my boss, making threats, and then came round to my house to collect it. He was really suspicious, telling me sweetly that he had a very frail mother – which turned out to be a lie because I've checked, and his mother is in good health. And he said he'd got my address from his lawyer, but that was also a lie because I never gave it to him. But what I really can't understand why he created such a stink about the album.'

'There must be something in the album he didn't want you to find. And he was so desperate to get it, he followed you home from the station.'

'I can't see what that could have been. Unless . . .' She paused, bending down to rummage in her bag.

She held up the old envelope. 'This had been stuck inside the back of the album and it must have fallen loose. I had it in my hand when I answered a call and must have put it on the table. Then he arrived and took the album, and I forgot I still had it.'

'Was that what you were looking for the other morning?' Eddie asked.

She nodded. 'When your lads moved things around in the hall I thought I'd mislaid it.'

She opened the envelope and took out the thick folded pages. 'It's a family tree . . . do you remember when you said the girls in one of the photos reminded you of Czar Nicholas's daughters? And I found out their father was actually a Russian count – Count Antonin Petrukhin?'

Eddie nodded. 'Oh, yeah.'

'Well, we've been checking the dates, and he married their mother when she was about fourteen years of age.'

He tutted. 'He'd be arrested for that now.'

This was the first time Jane had really looked at the rest of the family tree.

'This is interesting,' she said. 'We have Beatrice married to a . . .' She paused and turned the page to show Eddie. 'Beatrice is the middle sister, the one I am going to see in Australia. Then you see beneath her a son, Matthew, and then a second son, Jason. He's the one who came to see me. But look at the arrow and the date of the marriage. She married John Alfred Thorpe. I think he was a bus driver or something. They ran away to be married in Australia.'

'What's odd about that?'

'Well, it looks like she wasn't married to this John Thorpe until after the birth of her children. Then, see the arrow down . . . he died five years after the marriage. But surely this couldn't be what he was so desperate to keep hidden.'

'Sounds odd, but maybe there's money involved?' Eddie suggested.

Jane nodded. 'The house in Stockwell must have sold for a lot of money and the nephew, Jason, had power of attorney for his aunt Helena.'

Eddie shrugged. 'Maybe the brothers had a falling out?'

Jane shook her head. 'No, I remember something else. Jason said his brother was mentally challenged, so I think Jason must inherit everything.'

Eddie looked at his watch. 'It's getting late and if you want to have a long soak in my bath, we should get moving.'

Reluctantly, Jane carefully folded up the pages of the family tree and put them back in her bag. The secrets of the Lanark family would have to wait.

* * *

Eddie's small flat was modern to the point of minimalist. There was one bedroom, a bathroom, and a large living room that led into an open-plan kitchen. Jane remarked how immaculate it was and Eddie laughed, saying he was a bit of an OCD cleaner. His mother couldn't get over it, as she had spent years picking up all his discarded clothes and towels when he'd lived at home. The whole flat reminded Jane of the time she had been with Alan Dexter. In many ways, Eddie had a similar boyish quality to him; only Alan, as a bomb disposal expert, had a more dangerous edge to his personality.

Eddie ran her a bath and poured in some beautiful-smelling oils and bath salts. He gave her time to soak, and Jane lay back for at least three quarters of an hour. But her brain kept revisiting the possibility that Jason Thorpe had not been interested in the photos, but in the family tree – perhaps because, if the dates on the tree were correct, it made him illegitimate at the time of his birth.

Jane wrapped herself in a large white towelling robe of Eddie's. Lying on his low, futon-style bed, she jotted down notes to remind herself that when she arrived in Australia she needed to check the births and marriages records there.

By the time Eddie got into bed beside her, it was after midnight.

* * *

Jane was woken by Eddie's alarm clock at half past five – his usual wake-up time as he needed to sort out the day's itinerary for his team. Jane drove him back to her house so that he could collect his van, and she got ready for work.

Arriving exceedingly early at the station, she grabbed some breakfast in the canteen before checking through the messages in her office. There was a lengthy memo from DC Tim Taylor regarding their travel plans, flight times and hotel bookings, and explaining that they would not be allocated a patrol car in Australia as it would be easier to get to Beatrice Thorpe's property in Mosman by ferry. In addition, their visas should be ready for collection later that afternoon.

Jane almost missed the scrawled message from Sergeant Hunt, saying that Arnold Hadley had called the station twice asking to speak to her. She was suddenly reminded that she still hadn't spoken to him.

It was half past eight and she hoped she would now be able to catch Arnold Hadley at home. The phone rang for only a moment before it was picked up.

'Arnold Hadley speaking . . .'

'Mr Hadley, it's Jane Tennison. I believe you've been trying to contact me?'

'Thank goodness you've called. Yes, I have.' He took a moment to catch his breath. 'I received a call at eleven yesterday morning from Miss Thompson, asking me to go to the care home. Helena Lanark died earlier that morning.'

Jane was shocked, but let him continue without saying anything.

'I eventually got to the care home in the early afternoon. Her body had been laid out, and it was very distressing because her face was badly bruised, appallingly so. When I asked how the injuries had occurred, I was told that the young carer who had taken in her breakfast had found her face down on the floor.'

'Did a doctor attend to examine her body and certify death?' Jane asked.

'Yes. Apparently, he said the injuries were consistent with a fall from her bed, hitting her face hard on the floor.'

'Do you think something else happened?' Jane asked, gently.

'I don't know . . . I'm just repeating what I was told. But I would appreciate it if you could come to the care home this morning. Her body is due to be taken to the mortuary.'

Jane hesitated for a moment. 'Mr Hadley, can I ask if you reported this to any officers you spoke with when trying to contact me?'

'No . . . no, I didn't. I only wanted to talk to you, as you're the one who's been involved in the Stockwell property case.'

Jane glanced at her watch. 'I can be at the care home by ten.'

'Thank you so much, Detective Tennison. I greatly appreciate it.'

Jane quickly picked up her briefcase and coat and left her office. She walked over to Sergeant Hunt's desk where he was nursing a large cup of coffee.

'I just have some business to deal with in connection to Helena Lanark.'

He swivelled around in his chair. 'Was that Arnold Hadley you were talking to? What was it that was so urgent?'

'I'll tell you later,' she said, walking briskly out.

Jane was certain that if DCI Carter found out about Helena Lanark, he would instantly cancel her trip to Australia.

* * *

It was just after ten when Jane pulled into the care home car park. Miss Thompson was sitting at the reception desk with a suitably grief-stricken expression.

'Detective Inspector Tennison,' Jane said.

'Yes, yes . . . I remember you.'

'Mr Hadley informed me that Miss Lanark has died.'

Miss Thompson instantly went on the defensive. 'The doctor who attended confirmed her death was due to a fall but I assure you that no blame can be attached to any of our carers. We are very short of staff at the moment, so the routine of dressing our residents before breakfast did not take place. Instead, it was eight o'clock when one of the kitchen staff took in Miss Lanark's breakfast.'

Jane noticed that she was wringing her hands as she continued.

'She was, as always, checked after she went to bed, and that would have been at about half past ten. We've never had any problems with Miss Lanark being restless or attempting to get out of bed without assistance—'

Jane interrupted. 'Thank you, Miss Thompson. I would like to see her, please.'

Miss Thompson pursed her lips. 'Mr Hadley is in her suite waiting for the undertakers. I can order you a cup of coffee if you want?'

'Thank you. I'll make my own way there.' Jane went through the glass doors into the corridor that eventually led to Helena Lanark's suite.

She knocked once on the door and waited. Hadley opened it.

'Thank you so much for coming, Detective Tennison.'

As Jane walked through the door, she turned back to see Miss Thompson watching from the far end of the corridor. Hadley closed the door quietly behind her.

'Mr Hadley, I was told that they didn't find her until her breakfast was brought in?'

'Yes, that's what they told me. They also said that usually she would have been washed and dressed before breakfast. She often ate out here, in the dining area.'

'Have you spoken to the carer who found her?'

'No, I haven't. I was just told that she was one of the young carers because they're short staffed at the moment.' He gestured for Jane to sit in a chair by the desk. 'I may be being slightly paranoid, but when you see her, I think you will understand my concerns.'

Jane noticed the photograph album lying on the desk. 'I don't understand why this is here. Jason Thorpe was adamant that it had to be taken to his mother in Australia. He even came to my home address to collect it. So what's it doing here?'

Hadley shrugged his shoulders. 'He must have brought it back to her.'

Jane frowned. 'He collected it from me on Friday evening and said that he was catching a flight home that night. I suppose he must have changed his plans.'

There was a knock on the door and Miss Thompson appeared with a small tray. 'I brought your coffee,' she said with an ingratiating smile.

'That's so kind of you,' Hadley said, taking the tray and placing it on a small side table.

'Miss Thompson, do you mind if I ask you a few questions?' Jane said as she turned to go. 'Could you tell me what time Miss Lanark's nephew, Mr Thorpe, last came to see her?'

Miss Thompson turned, looking slightly startled. 'Yes. He came here on Monday evening. I've made a note of it in the visitors' book. He also brought—' she gestured towards a small vase, 'those flowers.'

'And this?' Jane asked, tapping the photograph album.

'Oh, I don't recall seeing that. He arrived at about six, but only stayed a short while because he had a plane to catch to Australia.'

'And Miss Lanark was alive and well after he left?'

'Yes, of course, she was checked in the evening by our carers.'

'Thank you, Miss Thompson.'

'As I said, I made a note in the visitors' book of the time he arrived and the time he left.'

She turned to leave, then stopped to say that Miss Summers would be available if either of them wanted to talk to her. Jane thanked her, impatient for her to leave the room.

'Why would Jason Thorpe lie to me? He created a lot of problems for me at work, accusing me of taking this album without permission. He lied about how he came to have my address, he said that his mother was unwell . . . which was why I contacted you, Mr Hadley, to ask about Beatrice's health.'

Mr Hadley leaned forward, shaking his head as he tore open a packet of sugar for his coffee. 'I have no idea.'

Jane opened the album and turned several of the thick heavy pages. 'There were also a number of photographs missing from their mounts.'

Hadley looked thoughtful. 'Perhaps they were pictures of Beatrice's mother with the young Russian piano teacher? It did create rather a scandal at the time. I believe their father was convinced they were having an affair. That's all I can think of.' He took a sip of his coffee.

'So, you've seen this album before?' Jane asked.

Hadley nodded. 'Oh, yes, on many occasions. It was very precious to Helena.'

Jane closed the album and bent down to open her briefcase. 'I felt a bit guilty about this, but it had been placed in the back of the album and the clips securing the envelope had come loose . . .'

She took out the envelope, the contents of which she and Eddie had been looking at the previous night. 'It's the Lanark family tree. I would guess it had probably been started by their father. Perhaps you'll be able to tell if the later additions were made by Helena?'

Jane handed Hadley the loose pages. She noticed that when he reached out to take them from her, his hand was shaking.

'I believe Miss Lanark did mention this, but I still can't think why her nephew would be so eager to get his hands on it.'

Jane watched as he looked through the pages, running a bony finger down the various births and marriages. 'Poor Matthew, he was born with hydrocephalus and is wheelchair-bound. He's a very sickly man with several long-term complications, both mentally and physically.'

'So, would Matthew not be Beatrice's heir?' Jane asked.

'No, no . . . he's incapable. He requires full-time care and Jason has become the main provider – in a manner of speaking.'

Jane noticed his slight grimace at the mention of Jason's name. She asked Hadley again if he thought the recent additions to the family tree had been written by Helena.

'I believe so . . .' He carefully put the loose pages back into the envelope. 'I think you should see her before the undertakers arrive. I've brought a suitcase to gather all her belongings.'

Jane put the envelope back into her briefcase as Hadley drained his coffee cup and stood up.

Jane had become accustomed to viewing dead bodies, but she felt oddly perturbed when they entered Helena's bedroom. The bed had been stripped of its canopy and pillows, and a white sheet had been laid over Helena's body. Apart from that, the room appeared to be exactly as Jane had previously seen it. Hadley walked over to the side of the bed, his entire body seeming to tremble as he slowly pulled the sheet back from Helena Lanark's head and shoulders. Jane was shocked at the extent of the dark bruises around both her eyes, across the bridge of her nose and on one cheek.

Jane gently touched Hadley's arm. 'Would you excuse me a moment?' She moved him aside and examined Helena's face more closely. 'Do you know if there are bruises on any other parts of her body?'

'I've only been told about the facial injuries . . . and that was all that was on the doctor's report I was shown.'

'If you could leave the room for a moment, I'd like to take a further look . . .'

Hadley bowed his head and hurriedly left the bedroom. Jane eased back the sheet completely to examine the porcelain-white, almost skeletal body. Helena Lanark had clearly been seriously underweight. There were also additional bruises on her right hip and thigh. As Jane replaced the sheet, she noticed two small round discolorations on the side of her neck.

Returning to the sitting room, Jane asked if Hadley had spoken to the doctor, but he explained that the doctor had already left by the time he had arrived at the care home.

There was a light knock on the door and a young female staff member asked shyly if Mr Hadley would like some more coffee. He shook his head, thanking the girl, as Jane stepped forward.

'Excuse me, are you the carer who found Miss Lanark's body?'

'Yes, ma'am.'

'What is your name?'

'I am Maya Lim. Yesterday morning when I brought her breakfast, I found her lying on the floor.'

'We've been told she was lying face down . . . is that correct?'

'Yes, ma'am. She was face down, but on one side. I called matron straightaway.'

'Were you on duty on Monday night?'

'Yes, ma'am, I was.'

'And do you recall if Miss Lanark had a guest?'

'Yes, ma'am. He brought flowers. I was sent to get a vase.'

'And where was Miss Lanark?'

'She was in her wheelchair sitting by the desk. I was then not on duty anymore until yesterday morning.'

'Thank you very much, Maya, you've been very helpful. Just one more thing . . . when you came in yesterday morning, did you notice if anything in the room was different?'

The girl hesitated, at first shaking her head. Then she nodded. 'Oh, yes . . . I notice the window.'

Jane turned to look at the bay window. 'What about it?'

'It was open.'

'Was that unusual?' Jane asked.

Maya frowned. 'Yes, it is not normal. Particularly when our guests are very frail.'

'Did you tell anyone about the window being open?'

'No, I just closed it.'

'I'm sorry, Maya, I just need to go through that with you again – is that all right? You say you brought Miss Lanark her breakfast tray. But then you saw the window was open. Is that right?'

'I carry the tray to the desk because Miss Lanark was usually dressed in her bedroom and in her wheelchair, ready to have breakfast out here. I then notice the window, so I close it before I go into Miss Lanark's bedroom.'

'And she wasn't dressed?'

'No, she was in her nightdress and one of her blue cashmere shawls was over her head.'

'So, what did you do?'

'Well, she was on the floor, and I was very concerned, so I eased the shawl away from her. Then when I saw her face, I ran to get help.'

'Thank you, Maya,' Jane said. The young carer nodded and left.

Jane turned to Hadley.

'Have you checked if there is anything missing, Mr Hadley? Any jewellery, for instance?'

'I'm sure that's very unlikely,' he said. 'This is a very reputable home.'

'Nevertheless, Mr Hadley, I do think you should check.'

Hadley went back into the bedroom. Jane heard him opening drawers before he returned, carrying a velvet jewellery box.

He opened the box. 'I only really recall Helena wearing . . .' He stopped.

'A pearl necklace?' Jane asked.

'Yes, yes . . . a pearl necklace. It had belonged to her mother.' He put the box down. There were some gold chains, an amber brooch, and a few rings, but no pearls.

'I think we need to speak to Miss Summers,' Jane said.

CHAPTER SIXTEEN

Jane was with Mr Hadley for two hours. They had a tense meeting with the head of the care home, Miss Summers, who was adamant that none of her staff would have taken the necklace, but Jane insisted that she would need to question them and might be obliged to file a report of theft because of the pearls' value.

Hadley was becoming increasingly upset, particularly when Jane suggested to him that Jason Thorpe might have taken the pearls when he visited Helena on the Monday night – or perhaps Helena had given them to him.

'Absolutely not! She would never have given them willingly to him,' he insisted, clearly angry.

Jane also noted his reaction as Miss Summers handed her the death certificate, stating that Helena had died as a result of her injuries from a fall.

Jane said she would contact the local Sussex CID as Helena's death had occurred in their jurisdiction. Although it appeared accidental, Jane thought it best that a full post-mortem was carried out and in the meantime the room should be sealed and examined by Sussex scene of crime officers.

Hadley clenched his fists.

'Yes, I think it is of utmost importance,' he said forcefully. He turned to Jane. 'Thank you. I shall take it upon myself to inform her family.'

* * *

Jane returned to the station around three and got straight on the phone to Sussex CID. After a lengthy discussion, they agreed to order a full post-mortem and let her know the results. She knew Carter would go ballistic when he found out, so she was relieved to be told that he was tied up in meetings with the lawyer of one of the young men he had arrested on a burglary charge. She decided to take the window of opportunity that had been presented to her.

'Come on, Tim,' she said, walking over to DCI Taylor's desk, 'let's go to Australia House and pick up our visas.'

On the way out, Jane told the duty sergeant that she would be at home if she was needed, anticipating that she would have a week-end off-duty as she was going to be flying to Australia.

By the time she got home, it was after six. Eddie was there working on his own, hanging wallpaper in the sitting room. He had erected a large pasting table and had already covered one wall.

Jane had stopped off at the local off-licence to buy a bottle of wine, holding it up as she walked into the room.

'Wow! This looks fantastic!' she exclaimed.

'Yeah, I think it's going to be OK,' Eddie said, 'but I'm not sure about doing all four walls in the same paper. Maybe one wall should a lighter shade of the green? Up to you.'

'Listen, I've been happy with everything you've done so far, so it's your choice. Is the bathroom plumbed in?'

'Yup, first thing this morning. The putty should be dry by now, and we'll have the tiles up tomorrow. Go and have a look in your bedroom. I've already papered the walls in there.'

Jane put the bottle of wine down on the kitchen table, took off her coat and hurried up the stairs. The bedroom not only had new paper but also a fresh coat of gloss paint on all the skirting boards and the door. The paint fumes were overwhelming, so she'd probably have to sleep in the spare room, but she was amazed at how fast Eddie and his team worked.

The bathroom was another revelation. Even without the wall tiles or the flooring completed, she felt like a ten-year-old turning on the new taps, and she couldn't wait to test out the elegant glass-fronted shower.

By the time she returned to the kitchen, Eddie was washing his hands in the sink.

'I'm going to call it quits for tonight, Jane. I need to get some more paste for tomorrow when the paper for the hall is being delivered. We're still a long way from being finished, but I'm going to need another £300 to pay the team.'

'I'll go to the bank tomorrow,' she said, taking two wine glasses from the cupboard.

'Did you have a good day?' he asked, drying his hands.

'I'm not sure I would describe it as a good day . . . a bit of a shocker, really.'

'How come?'

'You know this case I'm working on, and the family tree you saw last night? Well, the woman was found dead this morning.'

'Who was?'

'Helena Lanark, the woman in the care home.'

'She was pretty old and suffering from dementia, though, wasn't she?'

Jane poured the wine. 'Yes, she was. And the doctor's report said a fall killed her, but there were a couple of things about the circumstances that made me suspicious, so I got Sussex police involved.'

'What made you suspicious?'

'For one, a window was found open in her suite. Secondly, a valuable pearl necklace appears to be missing.'

Eddie chuckled. 'My God, you really are Miss Marple! My grandmother was about the same age when she snuffed it. What's so suspicious about a window being found open? You were accusing us of leaving your back door open. I don't get why you're so caught up with this? I'd have thought a case about a rich woman in a care home would've been a low priority in comparison to other stuff, like tracking down that railway rapist for instance.'

'What are you talking about?'

'Been in all the newspapers . . . they reckon whoever raped and murdered these girls worked on the railways, so he was moving from station to station . . .'

Jane shook her head. 'I don't believe this . . .'

'It's the truth . . . well, according to the *News of the World* anyway.'

'Thank you for your expertise regarding my career as a police officer,' Jane said tightly, 'but I focus on crimes that occurred in my area, in Stockwell.'

Eddie raised an eyebrow. 'But didn't the old lady fall off her perch in Hove?'

Jane took a deep breath. 'Thank you for reminding me about the back door being left open. Did you mention it to the guys?'

'Er . . . did you ask me to?'

'Never mind, I'll talk to them when I next see them. I just got an uneasy feeling, because I was certain I had left the folder closed on the kitchen table, but it was open and my receipts were all over the floor.'

'Listen, for the next payment, don't worry about receipts as I am getting a good deal from a bloke – you know, back-of-the-lorry kind of stuff.'

'What?'

'Cash in hand.'

Jane frowned. 'I don't really agree with any of that, Eddie.'

'Agree or not, it's a quarter of the price. How do you think I got that bathroom suite so cheap?'

Jane took a deep breath, feeling her anger building.

'How about I go and get us some fish and chips, or a kebab?'

He reached over and drew her into his arms. 'I've just been teasing you, darling. You do get very serious at times, you know.'

Jane gave him a tight smile, not wanting to have row with him before she left for Australia. 'I'll have a kebab, please.'

* * *

Jane made a point of not talking any more about the case that evening. After Eddie had left, she called Arnold Hadley, apologising for the lateness, but saying that she was keen to get an update.

'Helena was taken to the mortuary,' he told her. 'The Sussex police didn't seem that concerned about her death, though. They said there may be some delay with the autopsy as they already have cases allocated for Friday, and then it's the weekend.'

Jane hesitated. 'Have you informed Jason Thorpe, or his mother, yet?'

Hadley hesitated. 'No, due to the time difference I haven't contacted them yet. I will obviously have to let them know as soon as possible as they will probably wish to arrange the funeral.'

Jane chewed her lip. 'Mr Hadley, I will be in Australia to question Beatrice on Saturday, so I could give them the news then, if you prefer?'

She could sense his relief over the phone. 'Under the circumstances I think that would be better.'

'Did the local police make any progress regarding the necklace?'

'No, they questioned all the staff and the young girl who had seen her the previous evening recalled that Helena hadn't been wearing it, which wasn't unusual.'

'What time was that?' Jane asked.

'At half past nine.'

'But the carer didn't notice the window was open?'

'I'm afraid I didn't ask.'

'So, from half past nine until her breakfast was served the following morning, nobody checked on Miss Lanark?'

'Apparently not, as they were short-staffed. But I think this may have been quite usual.'

Jane sighed with annoyance. 'Have you taken all of her personal belongings from the care home?' she asked.

'Yes, I took them in case Beatrice wants any of them.'

'Mr Hadley, is there anything else you can tell me about the pearls?'

'I believe the pearls had belonged to Helena's mother and were part of a rather elaborate set. Each daughter was given a strand, but only Helena's had the gold-and-diamond clasp.'

'Do you know the value of her strand, Mr Hadley?'

'Possibly £2,000 or £3,000 as they were matching-in-size, South Sea pearls.'

'Did you tell the local police?'

'To be honest, they seemed uninterested in the whole thing. They said in any case it would be hard to prove anyone stole them without a witness.'

'Did you take them, Mr Hadley?' Jane said evenly.

'No I did not!' he said, sounding affronted. 'How could you imagine such a thing? There is always the possibility that Helena gave the pearls to Jason when he last visited, I suppose. Or he may have thought it was his right to take them . . . but he'll soon learn how wrong he was.'

He paused as if he had said too much, and then coughed nervously.

'Perhaps when you are in Australia you can ask Jason about the pearls?'

Jane didn't respond to that. Then she said, 'Thank you for your time, Mr Hadley. I'll await the outcome of the post-mortem and will be in touch.'

Jane replaced the receiver. She was surprised that Mr Hadley had even suggested that Helena Lanark could have given Jason Thorpe the necklace, given how vehemently he had previously denied the possibility. She also wondered why he didn't want to contact Jason regarding Helena's death.

Jane made herself a cup of tea and then went upstairs to look over her bedroom. The furniture was still piled in the centre of the room, but it was coming along well

Jane walked back down to the kitchen, and found a pile of dirty cups and mugs in the sink. By the time she had finished cleaning up, she was beginning to feel weary, and decided to make a few notes before heading to bed.

First, she jotted down a reminder to go to the bank to withdraw more money for Eddie. But she quickly found she couldn't really concentrate on anything else to do with the house. She was worried about deliberately not informing DCI Carter of Helena Lanark's death so he couldn't use it as an excuse to cancel her Australia trip, knowing that her decision could have repercussions. But in the end she managed to convince herself that if the post-mortem revealed Helena's death was suspicious, that would make it even more urgent that she go – not so much to talk to Beatrice, but to interview a potential murder suspect – Jason Thorpe.

* * *

The following morning, after a quick breakfast in the canteen, Jane returned to her office and summoned in DC Taylor to discuss their travel arrangements. They agreed to meet at the British Airways check-in desk at 6.30 that evening.

On her way home Jane stopped off at her bank to withdraw £300 for Eddie. She arrived home at lunchtime, and the team were hanging the wallpaper in the hallway, which looked exactly as Eddie had described it. She was told that Eddie had just gone out for a few minutes to collect some more paste.

'Oh, by the way, did he mention to any of you to take more care about checking the back door is locked?' Jane asked. 'The other night when I came home it had been left open.'

There were a few blank looks and shrugs, as Eddie appeared at the kitchen door with the paste, having come in the back way.

'There's no need to worry,' he said. 'From now on I will personally make sure everything is locked up before I leave.'

'Thank you, Eddie. Let me give this to you now.'

She opened her wallet and handed him the envelope, which he stuffed into the back pocket of his jeans.

'That's not what I call very safe,' she said. 'Put it in the folder.'

He shrugged. 'I'll do it later. How come you're home so early?'

'You know I'm leaving for Australia tonight?' she said.

'Crikey, they organise things fast – I didn't realise it was tonight. Where are you leaving from?'

'Heathrow. It's a half past nine flight, so I need to be there by 6.30.'

'OK, I'll get the lads out of here by five so that you can have the house to yourself. Then once you've changed and packed, I can take you to the airport in your car, then bring it back here.'

'Would you do that for me?'

He smiled. 'Come here, you . . . I reckon the sooner you leave, the faster you'll be home and I'll use every minute you're away to get things ship-shape for when you get back.'

Eddie gave her a hug and a kiss, before taking the paste out to the guys. Jane was making herself a sandwich in the kitchen so didn't hear Eddie tell them he had a van load of gear he needed shifting onto a site his dad was working on.

Jane went up to her bedroom to get packed and ready. As Eddie had promised, the guys downed tools at five, giving her plenty of time to use her new shower and pack a small overnight bag. February in Australia would be blisteringly hot, so she packed a light pair of trousers, a couple of T-shirts, a cotton jacket and a pair of slingback shoes.

She washed and blow-dried her hair, then double-checked she had all the toiletries she needed, finally putting on a smart grey suit and white shirt, with comfortable black court shoes to travel in. Eddie whistled when she came down the stairs.

'My, my, you certainly look the business. Is that all the luggage you're taking?'

'I'm only there for a couple of nights, Eddie.'

'Well, I hope they've booked you into Business Class ... it's a hell of a long flight for such a short trip.'

Jane laughed as he took her overnight bag and put it in the boot. 'You must be joking. I'll be in Economy holding the hand of the young DC who is accompanying me. The furthest he's flown before is Jersey.'

Eddie dropped Jane off at Terminal 3 Departures and cupped her face in his hands. 'You stay safe, darling. Let me know when you want me to collect you. Love you.'

Jane smiled and kissed him back. She felt she should have said 'I love you' back, but the moment had gone.

Jane headed into the airport and spotted DC Taylor standing by the check-in counter wearing a thick tweed jacket with cord trousers, obviously unaware that it would be almost peak summer in Australia. Instead of a case he had a rucksack.

'I'm travelling light,' he said, smiling.

'I can see,' Jane replied.

'I made those inquiries with the Stockwell planning department about the sale of the property. I got copies of everything from them and the legal papers that Arnold Hadley drew up.'

Jane nodded. 'Good. I'll have a read of them on the plane.'

Tim's face fell. 'I'm sorry, but I left them in an envelope on my desk. I could ring the station and see if someone can drop them off ...'

'Don't bother,' Jane sighed, 'how much did Jason get for the house?'

'Six hundred thousand pounds, which the planning department reckon was well below the market value.'

'Why would he sell it below value?'

'The planning bloke suggested Thorpe could have got a big cash kickback from the developer because he dropped the price – or even shares in the company. I then checked at Companies House. Jason Thorpe bought £100,000 worth of shares in the development company.'

'Did all the £600,000 from the sale go into Helena Lanark's account?' Jane asked.

Tim nodded. 'On paper it looks above board. Only Thorpe and the developer would know about any backhanders, of course.'

Jane looked thoughtful. 'I wonder if Arnold Hadley knew what Jason was up to and also got a backhander?'

'The planning department said the legal documents were all correct. But obviously Hadley would have been paid by Thorpe for the legal advice.'

'Proving that any fraud took place could be difficult,' Jane said. 'For now I'm more interested in meeting Beatrice and interviewing her about the baby's death. We'll have about two hours after check-in before we have to go through Departures, so if you want to do any duty-free shopping, that's the time.'

He frowned. 'Well, if I go duty-free shopping now, I'll have to carry it with me, right? Wouldn't it be better to do it at the other end when we come back?'

'Whatever works for you, Tim. I'm going to get a bottle of vodka as I'll probably need a few drinks to get over the jet lag. And I suspect they will have a better perfume selection here than in Sydney.'

'I've got no one to buy anything like that for. My mum likes nice soap, but she gets allergies from perfumes and makeup – brings her out in a shocking rash.'

Jane sighed. She reckoned it was going to be a really long flight.

CHAPTER SEVENTEEN

Tim had the window seat and at first had been almost childishly excited, but as he was over six feet tall, he soon began to complain about the lack of leg room.

He perked up when their meal came, though, and when Jane offered him her fruit and jelly dessert, he scoffed it down. After enjoying a couple of glasses of wine, Jane was tempted to settle down with one of the books she'd bought at WH Smith before boarding, but decided she ought to take the opportunity to get to know Tim a little better.

'Do you live with your parents?'

'No just my mother. She's a stenographer – her fingers move like lightning.'

'So she's in court a lot?'

'Oh yes.'

'How did she react when you told her you were going to Australia?'

'She was a bit freaked at first because she thought I was going to emigrate, but then when I told her it was just a few days and part of an investigation she was . . . sort of impressed.'

'Did you mention anything about the reasons we are flying out?'

'You mean the investigation?'

'Yes.'

'No, well . . . not really, just that it was connected to the house in Stockwell. She knew about it because of all the stuff in the papers.'

'So, what did you tell her?'

'Nothing much – just that it was connected to a member of the family. She was more concerned about me not being home to let the cat out.'

Jane was finding it hard work trying to maintain a conversation with him. 'Don't you have a cat flap?'

'No, we live in a flat. He only goes out at night because he has cat litter, which my mum doesn't think is very hygienic. It was my girlfriend's cat – well, it was actually a stray, but she went back to Sheffield, so I was sort of left with it.'

Jane eased her seat back and closed her eyes as Tim began to cross and uncross his legs. Eventually, hunched into the corner of his seat, he fell asleep. Jane, on the contrary, was wide awake. She sat back with her eyes closed and went over her last conversation with Hadley. Something didn't feel right.

Hadley had initially been adamant that Helena Lanark would never have given her nephew her pearls. But during their last conversation he seemed to have changed his mind.

Jane recalled the last thing Hadley said, about Jason learning how 'wrong he would be'. It made her wonder if Hadley knew Jason had used his power of attorney for Helena improperly, and if Hadley had also benefitted from the sale of the Stockwell property.

It all went round and round in her head until she couldn't concentrate anymore and she went to sleep.

* * *

The announcement came across the intercom system that the plane was scheduled to land in Bangkok in forty minutes. DC Taylor woke with a start as Jane gently nudged him. They had two hours to wait for refuelling and were told they couldn't leave the airport but would be allowed into the duty-free area. They were to return to the plane again half an hour prior to take-off.

The airport was stiflingly hot, and most of the shops seemed to be selling cheap tourist gadgets. Jane did find one stall which sold beautiful silk scarves and saris and selected one for her mother and one for her sister. She then went to a small coffee area.

The heat was almost overpowering but after downing an iced coffee Jane continued to stretch her legs as much as possible before returning to the plane. There was no sign of Tim and she waited along with the other passengers at the Departure gate. Eventually their departure was announced, and Jane boarded, returning to her seat. Tim still hadn't appeared and most of the passengers had been re-seated when he hurried on board with numerous packages and carrier bags. Jane stood up from her seat as he opened the overhead luggage compartment and stowed his goods.

'I bought a sari each for both of my sisters,' he said, climbing back into his window seat.

'You never mentioned you had any sisters?'

'Well, stepsisters – they're a lot older, from my father's first marriage. One's an accountant and the other is an estate agent.'

With his purchases safely in the overhead locker, he sat back in his seat, staring excitedly from the window as the plane prepared to take off.

'My dad was a lot older than my mother. He was in the air force – always wanted me to go into the RAF – but he passed when I was only eight, so it's all been down to my mother and she wouldn't hear of it. She's not that keen on me being in the Met, to be honest.'

Jane could tell from the sharp smell of body odour that he had not removed his jacket for some time, and sighed at the prospect of another twelve hours sitting next to him. Tim continued to enthuse about his shopping spree, explaining that he had also bought some candle holders and incense burners for his mother. Jane tried not to get impatient with him; he was just an innocent and rather naïve young man. Instead, she pointedly opened her novel to make it obvious that she didn't want to chat.

When another tray of food was placed in front of her, Jane had lost count of how many meals they had been served. Tim had to make her get up from her seat on numerous occasions to visit the toilet and on his last sojourn she noticed he must have given himself a wash, as his smell was less pungent.

He nudged her arm. 'I'm sure you've checked, but do we know if Jason Thorpe is actually at home?'

Jane pursed her lips. 'It's really Beatrice Thorpe I need to speak to. But Jason told me he was returning to Australia, and I know he lives with his mother, so I certainly hope he'll be there.'

Jane closed her eyes. It was risky for her not to have confirmed that Beatrice was at home, but she hadn't wanted Jason to be forewarned about their arrival. She just hoped she hadn't made a huge mistake by not making the necessary arrangements with the Australian police to confirm if Beatrice was in residence and prepared to be interviewed.

* * *

They spent considerable time going through Customs before they were at last able to get out and into a taxi. The Palm Tree Court Hotel was described by the travel agent as 'a small, exclusive establishment serving breakfasts, with a bar facility in the main reception. Easily accessible to sightseeing and shopping.'

Tim was agog at all the sights as they drove to the hotel. He had taken his thick tweed jacket off but was still sweating profusely. Both had slept for the latter part of the flight so neither felt too exhausted or disorientated by the time difference. Jane had never been to Australia, so she was equally interested in the views. But she started to feel uneasy when they left the affluent suburbs and entered an area which felt quite similar to London's Soho.

Although it was early in the morning, the streets seemed quite busy, full of seedy-looking neon lights and grubby bars. When they arrived at their hotel, Jane was shocked to discover that they had been booked into a very low-grade establishment in the notorious Kings Cross area, rife with drug addiction and prostitution. She was even more disgusted to find there were rooms let on an hourly basis.

'Jesus Christ, this looks like a knocking shop,' she muttered to Tim.

The reception area was dark and there was an unpleasant-looking man behind a grille. Jane asked briskly if they could be shown to their rooms. Hers had a large double bed covered with a cheap cotton throw. The room had a stained carpet, with a wash basin and mirror in the corner beside a wardrobe. Jane checked to make sure that at least the pillows and sheets were clean.

She'd told Tim to unpack quickly and meet her downstairs in the lobby, as she wanted to get to the Thorpes' house as soon as possible.

As she was unpacking her toiletries there was a knock at her door. When Jane opened it, Tim was on the landing holding a towel.

'The bathroom is just down the corridor on the right,' he said, pointing.

Jane decided she would shower later. 'I'll be downstairs in five minutes.'

She changed into her light trousers, shirt and jacket, brushed her hair and dug out her sunglasses from her handbag before descending the three flights of stairs to the lobby.

The same rough-looking man was wiping glasses behind the bar.

'I wonder if you could help. I need a taxi to take me to Circular Quay?'

He completely ignored her.

Jane waited a moment. 'Excuse me, can you possibly order me a taxi, or tell me where I can find the nearest taxi rank, please?'

'Take the first turning right as you leave the hotel,' he grunted.

* * *

They walked out into the sunshine and headed towards the taxi rank. There was one yellow cab waiting and Jane asked the driver to take them to Circular Quay. Then they had a fifteen-minute wait before a ferry going to Mosman arrived. It was eleven in the morning and it was already about seventy-five degrees, but there was a welcome breeze on the ferry.

Tim puffed out his cheeks. 'My God, it's hot.'

'Wait until it gets to the hottest part of the day,' she said, peering at him over the top of her sunglasses.

'You probably should have checked out the weather, as well as whether you were booking us into a flea pit of a hotel.'

'I didn't make the booking, ma'am,' Tim said. 'I think Carter told Sergeant Hunt to do it.'

Jane nodded to herself. 'I bet he did.'

* * *

They were on the ferry for about twenty-five minutes before it slowed down as it arrived at Mosman Bay Wharf, passing several privately owned yachts anchored offshore along the way. Jane instructed Tim to get a ferry timetable as she took in the steep steps leading up to the top of the small cliff beyond the pontoon.

'Bloody hell,' Tim said. 'Do you mind if I keep my jacket off?'

'Not at all,' Jane said. 'I'm going to do the same.' Jane slipped her jacket off as they started the climb, and at the halfway point they both had to pause for breath. After a few minutes they started climbing again, then walked over a small bridge which eventually led them past a small wooden ticket building, with large window boxes full of flowering geraniums.

Jane told Tim to wait as she went inside. 'I'm looking for The Glades. It's a property owned by Mrs Beatrice Thorpe. I was told it was on the waterfront, on Mosman Lane?'

The deeply tanned ticket seller pulled a map out of a drawer and pointed out Mosman Lane.

'If you walk past the bus stop to the left of the ticket box, you'll see this lane here, which I think leads to the property you're asking about.'

Jane sighed. 'How far would you say it is?'

'Oh, only about a fifteen-to-twenty-minute walk. But it is all uphill.'

Jane thanked him profusely and went back to a sweating, red-faced Tim.

'We've got a bit more of a walk, I'm afraid.'

'I wish I'd brought sunglasses . . . this glare really blinds you,' he said.

As they walked, they detected a slight breeze coming up off the water and they began to feel more comfortable. They passed numerous gated properties, many with high white-painted walls.

Jane paused to catch her breath. 'I hope to God we find it soon.' She looked around. 'All the properties on this side of the road must have their rear gardens facing the water. Unsurprisingly, waterfront properties in this area are incredibly pricey.'

Tim wiped the sweat from the top of his lip. 'There's a lot of new-builds high up there on the right-hand side.'

'Yes, I suppose they'd have to go high up to get a good view. Let's keep going.'

They continued walking, passing an abundance of eucalyptus and jacaranda trees. Tim stopped abruptly, and Jane almost bumped into the back of him.

'Look at all the birds! Is that a cockatoo? My God, there's four of them!' Tim was pointing to a large white cockatoo with a yellow crest. It was only when they stopped that they were able to fully take in the sound of the parakeets and lorikeets, who were screeching and cawing.

'I think this is it,' Jane said.

She had stopped beside a high wooden fence and a heavy door with an iron latch. Above it was an iron filigree archway with a hanging glass lamp. Tim puffed out his cheeks.

'Are you sure?'

'Yes, Tim, it says "The Glades", albeit on a very faded plaque.'

Jane paused to put on her jacket.

'Should I put mine on, ma'am?'

'I think so.' She took out a comb, tidied her hair and freshened up her lipstick. She was praying that she hadn't blown it and that Beatrice Thorpe was actually at home. She lifted the heavy door latch and pushed it open.

'Oh, good heavens . . . I didn't expect this from the outside.'

The two-storey house had six shuttered windows at the top level, and on the lower level there were two more shuttered windows either side of a porch, with white stone steps leading to a brightly painted front door. The whole of the house had been painted a fresh cream colour.

There was a short path from the gate, surrounded by grass and flowering shrubs.

'This is old Australian, I think,' Jane said.

When they reached the front door there was a faded notice: PLEASE USE SIDE ENTRANCE. Jane and Tim went back down the white steps to follow the path around to the side of the house, which lead to steps up to a veranda. They then followed the veranda around to the impressive rear of the house.

'Wow!' Jane exclaimed. She walked down the steps onto the lawn and turned to look back at the house. Intricate wrought-iron railings surrounded the top-floor veranda, and one half of the property had an ornate cream stone façade.

Tim stood next to Jane looking out at the bay. 'Well, they've certainly got a view . . .'

The garden was on three tiers, with topiary hedges separating each level. One level had an ornate waterlily-covered pond with a fountain in the centre. The second level had a manicured lawn with neat flower beds. The third level led to a waterside dock.

'They must have a yacht, so there'll probably be a boathouse somewhere down there,' Tim suggested.

'Well, you're not going off to look for it,' Jane replied, but she was equally impressed.

On the veranda there were several white wicker chairs with faded, sun-bleached cushions, as well as a glass-topped table for dining. Jane went up the few white steps to the side entrance, which looked like another front door with a polished brass knocker and old-fashioned bell pull.

She took a deep breath and yanked the bell pull. There was a loud jangle but no response. Jane was unsure if she should pull it again when she heard footsteps and the door was opened by a young housemaid wearing a pale blue cotton dress and white apron.

'Good afternoon. I am Detective Inspector Jane Tennison from the Metropolitan Police in London.' Jane held out her ID. 'This is Detective Constable Timothy Taylor.'

The girl looked rather nonplussed.

'I wish to speak to Mrs Beatrice Thorpe,' Jane added.

The girl nodded. 'Is she expecting you?'

'This is rather an important matter. If you would be so kind as to tell Mrs Thorpe that we are here to see her.'

'One moment, please.' The girl turned, leaving Jane and Tim standing on the doorstep as she disappeared through a wide arch leading onto a staircase. Whilst they waited, a stocky man passed through the hallway, pushing a man in a wheelchair who Jane presumed was Matthew Thorpe.

Although close in age to Jason, Matthew looked to be extremely overweight with a jowly face, sunken eyes and greasy blond hair. Neither acknowledged Jane or Tim as they continued through the opposite arch. Jane then heard the click of high-heeled shoes on the stone floor as a woman walked towards them.

Beatrice Thorpe did not at all resemble her sister Helena, being broad-shouldered and a trifle stout around her waist. She was wearing a floral print dress with frilly sleeves and her grey hair was coiled up into a plait at the back. But it was the string of pearls around her neck that confirmed her identity. She was also wearing pearl drop earrings and was heavily made up, with thick mascara and eye shadow.

'I'm sorry, I'm rather confused . . . the maid said you're from the Metropolitan Police force?'

Jane held up her ID. 'I am Detective Inspector Jane Tennison, and this is Detective Constable Timothy Taylor. We have come from England and are part of a Metropolitan Police inquiry.'

'Oh . . . and you've come to see me?'

'Yes, Mrs Thorpe. We'd also like to talk to your son, Jason.'

'He's not here. He's in Melbourne. But please, do come through.'

She gestured for them to walk through the arch into a sitting room.

'I'll be with you in one moment. I just need to make a call. I was due to be meeting friends for lunch today.' Mrs Thorpe picked up an ivory-coloured phone on the hall table. After dialling, she looked towards Jane and Tim and gestured for them to wait.

'Deidre, my dear, I am so sorry it's such short notice, but I won't be able to join you and the girls for lunch. Something rather important has come up, but I'll call you later.'

She replaced the phone and headed towards her waiting visitors. Jane noticed she was wearing rather elegant, high-heeled sandals.

'I think I may know why you're here. Jason has told me about the situation at the Stockwell property.'

The sitting room had two ceiling fans, and polished pine floors with expensive Persian rugs. There were a few comfortable-looking velvet armchairs and two large sofas in matching covers. On the white marble fireplace was an impressive gold ormolu clock, and either side of the mantelpiece there were framed paintings of floral arrangements. Fine white muslin curtains that billowed slightly from the four open French doors.

'Do please sit down,' Beatrice said, without a trace of an Australian accent; in fact, she sounded rather aristocratic. 'I see you weren't driven here, so you must be thirsty after climbing up all those steps.'

Jane sat down in one of the velvet armchairs. 'Yes, we caught the ferry to Mosman.'

Tim hovered behind her, and Jane turned to indicate that he could sit down. He chose a hard-backed chair positioned next to a polished bureau.

'Would you like some iced tea or lemonade?' Beatrice asked.

'I think lemonade would be perfect,' Jane replied.

Beatrice was wearing a heavy gold charm bracelet which jangled when she moved.

'I didn't actually formally introduce myself, did I?'

She leaned over to Jane with her hand outstretched. 'I am Beatrice Thorpe. Just let me order those cold drinks.' The click of her heels faded as Jane glanced over to Tim. He raised his eyebrows. 'Nice place.'

Jane took a good look around. It was indeed a very nice place. She had read up on Australia's fine houses and exclusive properties and was certain that The Glades was an original old English-style property.

Jane looked to her right and there was another archway into a second drawing room. From where she was sitting, she could see a number of framed family photographs on one wall and there was a grand piano with many more photographs in silver frames displayed on top.

Jane stood up as Beatrice returned, carrying a silver tray. The maid behind her pulled up a small, polished coffee table in front of Jane. Beatrice placed the silver tray down and picked up a large glass of fresh lemonade with ice and handed it to the maid to give to Jane.

Jane sipped gratefully. It really was delicious after their hot, sweaty walk, and she took a few more sips before replacing it on the tray. Beatrice sat down opposite her and crossed her legs, giving Jane an inquiring look.

'I suppose you must be here about that wretchedly sad discovery at my old family home.'

Jane nodded. 'Yes, I am, but I'm afraid that I am also here to inform you of some very sad news that occurred just before I left

London. I'm very sorry, Mrs Thorpe, but I have to tell you that your sister Helena died.'

'Oh my goodness, that is so sad,' Beatrice said. 'But I have to say, we have been expecting her passing for some considerable time now. Please excuse me, but I really should let Jason know. I do hate to be the bearer of bad news to him, particularly as he is currently with his hopefully future in-laws, but I am sure he will want to come home immediately.'

She headed towards the hallway, pausing to look back at Jane. 'Is Mr Hadley aware of her passing? I will obviously need to contact him about arranging a funeral. I don't know whether or not I will be able to make the journey to London; it will depend on what my son feels would be best . . .'

The sound of Beatrice's heels continued as she disappeared into the hallway. She did not appear to be in any way saddened by her sister's death and Jane listened as she made the call to Jason from the phone in the hallway.

'This is Beatrice Thorpe speaking . . . would it be possible to speak to my son? It is rather an important matter. Oh . . .' There was a pause. 'Would you please tell him I rang and ask him to call me as soon as he returns from the stables.'

After a moment, the sound of Beatrice's heels heralded her return to the sitting room.

'He is at the Balfour stables – his girlfriend Arabella has acquired a new Thoroughbred, costing over $25,000 . . . astonishing. They had it shipped all the way from England. Her family have some of the finest racehorses in Melbourne and are very hopeful of winning the Melbourne Cup this year.'

Jane smiled politely, finding it notable that Beatrice seemed more intent on describing the wealth of her hoped-for in-laws than mourning her sister's death. Beatrice paused by an elaborate floral display and frowned before removing a rose and placing it more centrally.

'Flower arranging is one of my favourite pastimes . . . I decorate the church every other Sunday.' She then sat back opposite Jane.

'Your sister Helena apparently fell from her bed at the care home and suffered severe bruising to her face,' Jane told her. 'Sussex Police have asked for an autopsy to be carried out and hopefully that will be completed by the time I return to England.'

'I wouldn't have thought there was a need for that,' Beatrice said. 'My sister was very unwell – I expect you are aware that she had suffered from dementia for many years.' She waved her hand and the bracelets jangled again. 'I know my son found it very distressing.'

'Jason seemed very keen to bring you Helena's family photograph album,' said Jane, changing tack.

'Oh, good heavens! He wouldn't have bothered to bring me that. You will see in the adjoining drawing room an absolute array of family photographs. When he took over the Stockwell property, Jason was able to ship back various items of antique furniture and boxes full of photographs. My father was a very keen photographer; in fact, he was very rarely seen without his camera. Then when he got his cine camera, we were all subjected to his constant filming and were forced to watch endless reels of footage. Besides which, Jason went straight to Arabella's family home in Melbourne when he flew back from London.'

Jane was eager to get to the point of their visit. 'Did Jason make you aware of the tragic discoveries at the air-raid shelter of your old home?'

Beatrice concentrated on her charm bracelet, flicking from one charm to the other.

'There was a girl they found – I believe her father had locked her in? Not that I was privy to any of the details or the salacious news coverage. Jason is very protective of me.'

'Beatrice, I'm here because of the second discovery in that shelter,' Jane said, leaning forward. 'The body of a newborn baby that had been hidden there.'

There was only a short pause, as Beatrice blinked and shook her head.

'I don't know anything about that.'

'Mrs Thorpe,' Jane continued, 'we have discovered that the belt which was wrapped around the concrete blocks which held the child, had a silver buckle engraved with what we believe are your sister's initials, HL. The forensic scientists have also determined that this baby had been buried alive, as fibres from the blanket it was wrapped in were found in its lungs and nasal passages.'

Jane opened her briefcase and removed a large manila envelope. She was keen to put the pressure on Beatrice, who was beginning to show signs of unease.

'May I ask you, Mrs Thorpe, if you knew if your sister owned a monogrammed belt?'

Beatrice shrugged her shoulders. 'I have no idea.'

Jane opened the envelope and pulled out the photograph of the belt and buckle, as well as the scene of crime photographs of the baby. She kept the photographs of the baby face down as she showed Beatrice the pictures of the belt and the close-up photograph of the buckle.

After peering at the photographs, Beatrice shrugged her shoulders again.

'If they are her initials then it obviously belonged to her, but I don't recall ever seeing her wearing it.'

'I do not wish to upset you, Mrs Thorpe, but I need you to look at these photographs of the baby's corpse that was found in the shelter.'

Beatrice was visibly shaking as Jane showed her the photographs.

'I don't think it is necessary for you to show me these horrible pictures. I should have someone representing me, since I feel you are trying to implicate me in some way. I have absolutely nothing to do with this wretched situation and, as I have already told you, I do not have any information about it.'

'But is this your sister's belt? Do you recognise it?'

'I just told you, I don't recognise it.'

'Do you recall if your sister was pregnant?'

'Helena? Are you asking me if Helena was pregnant? No, she was not. And if you knew her when she was a young woman, you would know how preposterous that question is.'

Jane replaced the photographs in the envelope. 'I'm sorry to ask you this, Mrs Thorpe, but could the baby have been yours?'

Beatrice stood up abruptly. 'I refuse to answer any more questions.'

The telephone in the hall rang loudly and Beatrice scuttled out of the room to answer it. Jane could hear sounds of distress and presumed she was talking to Jason. 'There is a policewoman from London here, and I need you to come back . . . but I will talk to you from my bedroom.'

Jane got up from her seat and saw Beatrice hurry up the stairs. She turned to Tim. 'Well, that phone call was bloody inconvenient.'

She stood with her arms folded for a moment, then walked through the archway into the second, larger sitting room containing the grand piano.

She turned back to Tim. 'Come and have a look in here.'

He joined her beside the grand piano. Lined up on top were silver-framed black-and-white photographs, some of which she had already seen in the album.

'Her son threw a wobbler about his mum needing the family album, but if you ask me there are some identical photographs here.' Jane pointed towards the photographs of the three sisters in their white dresses. 'There's Helena, and seated on the swing is Marjorie, then standing on the other side is Beatrice. I believe that Marjorie hanged herself with the rope on that swing.'

Jane also pointed out pictures of the girls' father and some of each of the sisters. Between the historical photographs were numerous pictures of Jason as a child, and of him with a surfboard and one with a motorbike. She noticed there were no pictures of Matthew.

Her eye was then caught by a large sepia-toned photograph in an elaborate gilt frame, hanging on the wall beside the fireplace. Moving towards it, she was certain that this was their mother, Muriel. Around her neck were three strings of pearls, a choker necklace with emeralds and diamonds and she was wearing the ornate pearl and diamond tiara. Jane beckoned Tim over.

'This is their mother, Muriel.'

He stood looking at the image, his hands behind his back.

'My God, she was beautiful.'

'So are those pearls,' Jane said.

There were several gold-edged invitations resting on the mantelpiece, for various social events in Sydney and Melbourne. On the other side of the fireplace was a similar sepia-toned portrait photograph of Henry Lanark, with his bristling moustache, in his army uniform.

'Apparently their grandmother, Aida Petrukhin, was a Russian countess,' she added.

There were more silver-framed photographs on a dresser and Jane was fascinated to see how many of them were of Muriel. She leaned closer, seeing that Henry Lanark's young wife had had an extraordinary collection of jewellery. There was also another sepia photograph of their grandmother Aida in a black, high-necked mourning dress, wearing the large three-stranded pearl necklace.

'Did you see that Beatrice was wearing a strand of large pearls?' she asked.

'No, I didn't notice.' He picked up a photograph. 'Is this her?'

Jane studied it. Beatrice was standing beside a small, dark-haired man who looked uncomfortable in his starched collar. 'That might be her husband.' Jane looked at her wristwatch, impatient for Beatrice to return.

Tim walked over to a bay window with pale green, heavily ruched curtains with gold cord tiebacks. The door was slightly ajar, letting in a pleasant breeze.

'Shall I tell you something?' Tim said quietly.

Jane moved closer, interested if the normally unobservant young man might have anything of value to say.

'If you take a close look around, the first impression of the house is "wow". My stepmother was wealthy – well, she had a very elegant house, lots of antiques, and I went there when I was very young and it really impressed me – and this is just my opinion, but this all looks very old-fashioned and worn. For instance, I noticed the velvet suite in the other room is pretty old and discoloured.'

Jane was impressed by his observations and took a closer look around herself. There was something tired about everything, as if the house was clinging to a past of wealth and style, but it all needed refurbishing. She moved closer to Tim, speaking quietly.

'I need you to do me a big favour. I want you to go and check out their wine export business, and maybe even look into the vineyards.'

'But it's Saturday,' he protested.

'So? There is bound to be someone around you can ask. We can contact the local police here, see if they can help. Jason Thorpe told me he stays in a special suite at Claridge's when he's in London and has a Savile Row tailor make his clothes, just like his father . . .'

Jane nodded to the photo of the man they believed to be Beatrice's husband.

'But I doubt he's ever been to Savile Row. So why the lies? And why his obsession that he had to have Helena's photo album when this room is heaving with family photographs?'

Tim hesitated. 'Do I have to come back here?'

'No, just go and see what you can find out. I'll meet you back at the hotel.'

'OK. And another thing, ma'am, I don't know if you noticed, but there doesn't seem to be a garage, unless it's hidden from view . . . so no valuable cars. If he is an affluent gent and mixing with the super-rich in Melbourne . . .'

'Thank you, Tim,' Jane said, cutting him short.

'See you later, then, ma'am.'

Jane remained standing at the bay window and soon she could see Tim, his jacket slung over his arm, walking up the path. He was stopped by the stocky man they had first seen when they arrived, pushing Matthew in a wheelchair. There was a lot of gesturing and arm waving, as Tim was presumably asking for the location of the export company.

Jane shook her head. He should have waited to ask someone who wasn't connected to the family, in case they reported it back. Jane was distrustful of Beatrice and felt she was going to be a difficult one to break, even more so after a lengthy conversation with Jason.

CHAPTER EIGHTEEN

The sound of Mrs Thorpe's high-heeled sandals alerted Jane to her return.

'My son will be flying out on the next plane,' she announced. 'He was quite distressed, not only because he felt I had been put under unwarranted pressure by your unannounced visit, but also at the news of my sister's death.'

Beatrice turned to look around the room. 'Where is the young man who was with you?'

'We didn't want to inconvenience you unnecessarily, Mrs Thorpe, so he's returned to the hotel. And I won't trouble you much longer.'

Jane knew she had to keep Beatrice calm if she was to glean any more information, but before she could ask her anything, Beatrice picked up a small brass bell, shaped as a figure of a girl in a crinoline, and shook it.

'I hope you don't think it's too early, but with all this shocking news I could really do with something stronger than lemonade.'

The maid who had greeted Jane and Tim at the front door now appeared in the archway.

'Could you bring a bucket of ice, Tina, and my special.' She turned to Jane. 'I make it myself – it's home-made sloe gin. I'm sure you'll find it refreshing.'

'That's very kind of you,' Jane said, gesturing at the photographs. 'You must have some extraordinary family memories.'

'I do, although I don't know if you are aware, but I ran away from home when I was young because my father was very ... domineering.'

Jane didn't say anything but was silently willing Beatrice to continue.

'He always followed the same routine. We would be in the drawing room when he came home from his club . . . we could hear his keys being thrown into the glass bowl in the hall, and there would always be a moment of tension while we waited to see if he was going to come into the drawing room. We were always relieved when we heard him heading down to the basement instead . . . that's where his darkroom was. I think I mentioned earlier that my father was a keen photographer.'

Beatrice walked over to a large corner cabinet with bowed glass-fronted doors. She opened them and pulled out a hidden shelf, taking down two large fluted glasses. With perfect timing, Tina entered carrying a tray containing an ice-bucket and a cocktail shaker which she took over to Beatrice.

'Tina, what are you serving Matthew for lunch today? I hope it's nothing too fattening.'

'No, ma'am . . . we have a tuna salad.'

'I'm sure he'll turn his nose up at that. What dessert is he having?'

'We have sponge and custard with some fresh fruit.'

'Just make sure he doesn't only eat the sponge and custard, Tina.'

The maid nodded, then carried out the empty tray. Beatrice deftly poured the liquid from the large silver cocktail shaker into the glasses, then added two scoops of crushed ice.

'The silly girl didn't bring any cherries . . . never mind. Here you are.'

She held the fluted glass out to Jane and then picked up her own, raising it in a toast.

'To a safe journey back.'

She took a small sip and went to sit on the edge of one of the sofas. Jane was expecting the drink to taste similar to the lemonade, but it was clearly very alcoholic, and she had to stifle a cough. Beatrice, on the other hand, was obviously well used to her cocktail and had already drained half her glass.

'Perhaps I should have ordered a little light lunch for you, dear?'

Jane returned to where she had been sitting and placed her glass on the small side table.

'That's very kind of you, Mrs Thorpe, but I had so many different meals on the flight over that I'm really not the least bit hungry. If it's OK with you, the reason I'm here is to try and get some closure regarding the very unfortunate tragedy that was discovered in the shelter.'

Beatrice shook her head sadly. 'That shelter was a nightmare. My father had become obsessed with it. We were just small children when he hired God knows how many men to dig the tunnel from the basement of the house. We were told that it was because my father suffered from nervous exhaustion during the First World War and that he was invalided home from France. He had nightmares about the house being bombed because his business was destroyed in the air raids. I remember they extracted vast amounts of soil digging the tunnel. The shelter seemed to be very well built, though. They put in large beams – I think you call them RSJs – to hold the roof up . . .'

Jane was about to interrupt, but Beatrice continued.

'I think Father used a lot of the excavated soil to create banks in the garden and then had turf laid down. The orchard also benefitted from the extra soil as we had glorious apples and pears every summer . . .'

'Mrs Thorpe, may I . . .'

'We three girls lived in terror. He forced us to go to the shelter when the sirens sounded. It was always cold and dank, no matter how many gas heaters were lit, and he forced us to sleep in there on many occasions, even when there were no sirens. My mother hated it because she said the heaters were dangerous, but he wouldn't listen to anyone.'

'Please, Mrs Thorpe . . .'

'He insisted that it was to protect our lives and that if the bombing continued, we might have to spend many weeks down there.

He even used a small gas stove to cook on. It amazes me how long it remained standing. Not that I had been anywhere near that dreadful place for years after the war.'

Jane felt that Beatrice was purposefully rambling to avoid any direct questioning about the baby. Beatrice had finished her cocktail and Jane felt that she might be able to encourage Beatrice to talk if she had another. But there was no need for any encouragement as she stood up and returned to the drinks cabinet to replenish her glass. This gave Jane the opportunity to pour the contents of her own glass into the ornate flower arrangement on the table.

'Could I top you up?' Beatrice asked, her back still to Jane.

'That would be very kind. It really is delicious.'

Jane watched Beatrice pour herself a full glass of neat gin, using the crushed ice sparingly. Jane insisted that she would serve herself. Beatrice waved her jangling bracelet.

'Please do.'

'Did your mother also go to the shelter with you?' Jane asked, nonchalantly.

'Good heavens, no! She said we could all die of carbon monoxide poisoning, which enraged my father. He always said that if she was the only woman in the house and it was flattened by a bomb, he would feel no sorrow,' Beatrice chuckled.

'What a terrible thing to say!' Jane exclaimed, ensuring that her glass was mostly filled with crushed ice. 'Your mother was a beautiful woman. I was admiring the photographs of her.'

'Yes, she was extraordinarily beautiful, and she never let us forget it. She was also very temperamental.'

Jane was becoming increasingly frustrated at the lack of progress in her questioning. She regretted bringing up the subject of Beatrice's mother.

With her replenished drink in her hand, Beatrice walked over to the piano.

'You are probably unaware that my mother's family were titled. Her father was Count Antonin Petrukhin and her mother, Aida, was obviously a countess. I met her only once when I was about nine or ten.'

Jane sighed as Beatrice glided from one photograph to another.

'She was a formidable woman. After the death of my grandfather, she set up home in Venice. It was my grandmother's friend who came to London and lived with us, purportedly to teach the piano . . . Mikhail Avilov.'

Beatrice turned towards Jane, sipping her cocktail, but before Jane could interject, she continued yet again.

'He infuriated my father because he and my mother would speak Russian together and it created terrible tension in the house.'

It felt as if Beatrice was bringing up any subject to divert from being questioned about the infanticide. However, it gave Jane the opportunity to mention the jewellery Muriel was wearing in so many of the photographs.

'I couldn't help but notice what sumptuous jewellery your mother wore, especially in this photograph.' Jane pointed to the photograph of Muriel next to the fireplace, wearing not only the three long strands of pearls but a choker necklace and tiara. Beatrice went to stand beside Jane, still holding her glass.

'I have a lovely story of those three strands of pearls. After mother died, Helena inherited the long strand, I was given the second strand and poor Marjorie the smaller strand.' Beatrice lifted the necklace she was wearing. 'I'm actually wearing mine now, because I was due to be having lunch with some of my girlfriends.'

'Her jewellery must have been of great value, especially if they are diamonds and real pearls in the tiara?'

Beatrice nodded. 'My mother was obsessive about every piece. She would delight in calling us into her bedroom and laying them all out on her dressing table. They were part of her trousseau.

I think when they left Russia to go to America, there would have been considerably more, but her family were bankrupted.'

'So, Marjorie had a string of pearls as well?' Jane asked.

Beatrice drained her glass.

'I find this most upsetting . . .' She went back to the cabinet and poured herself another drink. Jane could see that Beatrice was becoming intoxicated, and decided she would just have to be patient and hope that Beatrice would eventually let her guard down and start talking about the baby.

'Father buried Marjorie with her pearls because it was such a dreadful thing that happened,' Beatrice continued, after taking a good sip of her fresh drink. 'The swing was in the garden directly outside my father's study window. He went there in the morning, and it was the first thing he saw. You have no idea how terrible it was, what she did, and the terrible repercussions we had to face.'

'I know she hanged herself on your childhood swing . . .' Jane said.

Beatrice was shaking. 'Oh, you've been told. I know why you are asking me these things and it's awfully distressing. There were always terrible problems between my father and Marjorie.'

'Is that why she did it?' Jane asked.

'My father never believed that she was his daughter. The piano teacher, Mikhail, was sent packing because Father believed he and mother were having an affair, and that Marjorie was actually Mikhail's daughter.'

'So, your mother was in love with Mikhail?' Jane asked.

'We were all very taken with him. He was so young and very handsome, and he would sit very close beside us when we played duets. Mikhail's presence in the house lifted all our spirits because he would make us laugh, and he sometimes would mimic our father, but we knew Mother spent hours alone with him when Father went to his club, and they would speak Russian together. Whether Mikhail was Marjorie's father or not, we never knew . . .

but Father never behaved towards Marjorie as he did with Helena and I.'

'Was he abusive to her?' Jane probed.

Beatrice hesitated. 'She was . . . very wilful and often had to be punished.'

'What about your mother? How did she behave towards Marjorie?' Jane asked.

Beatrice sighed. 'My mother was very selfish and self-absorbed . . . she could be very cruel. I think my mother always felt Father was inferior and was always belittling him. She said she was from aristocracy and that she had been forced to marry him against her will.'

'When I studied the family tree, it appeared that your mother was very young when she married your father . . . only about fourteen?'

Beatrice's eyes narrowed. 'You have been doing your homework, haven't you? My mother behaved like a spoilt brat, delighting in spreading out her precious jewels as if to humiliate us.'

She then gave a strange laugh and Jane could tell that Beatrice was feeling the effects of consuming three glasses of her very potent sloe gin. 'But in the end, I benefitted, and I felt no guilt when I did what I did.'

She poured the last of the gin from the flask into her glass and topped it up with what was left of the crushed ice.

'My father forbade me from seeing my late husband, John, and kept me locked up in my bedroom for weeks on end; he even threatened that he would force me to stay in the shelter.'

'Was this before Marjorie's death?'

'No . . . after . . . after. He said John was a "nothing" and no daughter of his would marry a common bus driver. So, I paid him back. I have no guilt about what I did . . . everyone knew about it eventually. I went into my mother's bedroom, scooped up as much of her jewellery as I could, and left. I had planned my escape . . . had my passport and I had saved what money I could to buy a ticket on the boat. I knew that with mother's jewels I would be able to be together with John, but then . . .' she made a wide gesture with her hands, 'all the best plans can go wrong.'

Tina entered the drawing room.

'Do you require your lunch, Mrs Thorpe?'

'Yes, I do. We'll have it on the veranda?'

'Yes, ma'am.'

'Can you set a place for . . .' She obviously couldn't remember Jane's name.

'Yes, ma'am.'

Jane sighed. The last thing she wanted was to have lunch, but it seemed there was no option if she was to have any hope of getting the information she needed.

CHAPTER NINETEEN

After an exhausting search, Tim Taylor had finally located Jason Thorpe's export offices. Tim had been advised that he should go to the warehouse at the main Sydney docks as Mr Thorpe had a facility there and on a Saturday they would be loading crates of wine for shipment.

In the heat of the midday sun Tim had taken a taxi to the docks and had spent forty-five minutes trying to locate the right warehouse. He had become increasingly disorientated, as there were hundreds of massive warehouses lined up along the dock, with trucks delivering and loading, and he couldn't remember which way it was back to the street. He was also by this time feeling a bit woozy as the jet lag started to creep in on him. He was relieved to spot a pie and drinks stand next to a huge open-doored structure, with lorries driving in and out loaded with crates.

Tim ordered himself a meat pie and two Cokes and sat on a stool at one of the small tables. The man behind the counter suggested he should get a sun hat and as they began to chat, Tim explained that he had been searching vainly for Jason Thorpe's warehouse. Then a heavily tattooed man approached Tim's table.

'What's the name of the company you're looking for, mate?'

'Thorpe's Wine Export.'

'You're not from round here, are you?'

'No, I'm from London.'

'I got an aunt lives in Southport . . . you know Southport?'

'I don't actually. It's up North.'

'I never been to Thorpe's, but I know who might be able to give you directions. He's in one of the loading bays. Lemme get me pie, first.'

A battered old VW pulled up with two equally tattooed men wearing working overalls and string vests. The dashboard was piled with bent lager cans and old newspapers. Tim's new-found friend picked up his pie from the counter and went over to talk to them. As Tim tossed his Coke can and napkin into a rubbish bin, the driver of the VW called him over. He was thick set with spiked black hair and dark stubble, and he put out a big callused hand to shake Tim's.

'Barry Donald, mate. I know the Thorpes' business. My brother-in-law worked for them, but they've been shut for over a couple of weeks now. If you're after any part-time work, I can maybe help you out, though.'

'I'm not actually looking for work . . . but would it be possible to talk to your brother-in-law? I'm here with . . .' Tim fumbled in his jacket pocket to pull out his ID and showed it to Barry. 'I'm from the Metropolitan Police in London . . . just making some inquiries.'

'You're a copper? Jesus, scraping the barrel, aren't they, sending a kid?'

The man behind the counter watched from his food stand as DC Tim Taylor climbed into the back seat of the VW and the car drove off.

* * *

Jane was leaning on the railing of the shaded veranda, enjoying the breeze that was coming off the bay. Tina appeared, carrying a tray of crockery, cutlery and glasses which she laid out on the small round table. The table was covered with a pristine white cloth and four small, gilt-back chairs surrounded it. Jane was about to ask where Beatrice was when she appeared, waving a hand.

'Do sit down. I'm sorry to keep you waiting.' She turned on her heel, calling out for Tina to serve them lunch and to bring a chilled bottle of wine.

Beatrice sat down opposite Jane. 'I hope you enjoy the wine, it's the brand we export, and Jason is very proud of it.' She made a great show of looking at her gold wristwatch. 'Hopefully he should be on his way, as he was catching the next flight from Melbourne.'

Jane was served an avocado salad with white crab meat and delicately sliced brown bread. Tina poured wine for them both and Beatrice lifted her glass.

'Tell me this isn't delicious.'

Jane took a sip of the cold white wine and smiled. 'It most certainly is, Mrs Thorpe. You must be so proud of your son's business acumen, particularly after he sold the Stockwell property. I believe he also has shares in the development company who are building on the site?'

Beatrice shrugged. 'I don't really pay much attention to that side of Jason's business. He enrolled at Roseworthy Agricultural College on his sixteenth birthday, studying three years of agriculture and two years of oenology, until he was twenty-one. He did some winemaking at Seppelt and worked a few vintages at Great Western before he decided that he would be better equipped to export, as financially he could not even contemplate starting his own vineyard.'

Beatrice's charm bracelet jangled as she ate, pausing only to take sips of her wine.

'Jason must have been very successful in his business . . . this is such a substantial property. How long have you lived here?'

Beatrice drained her wine glass, picked up the bottle and poured herself another. 'Considering how my life began in Sydney, I have come a long way. I had only been in Sydney for a few days when I received a cable from John to say he was sick. He had been invalided out of the army and he was often quite poorly.'

Beatrice seemed to gather energy from her bitterness as she angrily pursed her lips.

'You have no idea what I had to suffer. Totally alone and with no financial assistance, I had to fend for myself. I had never worked a day in my life, but I was forced to take any job I could, however demeaning. I had a very small, nasty apartment and in the beginning, I survived by pawning pieces of my mother's precious jewels – though I was deeply shocked to be told that a number of her brooches were fake. I wrote letter after letter to my sister, asking her to help me, but she never replied.'

Tina approached the table to clear the plates. Jane had only eaten half her salad and was astonished that Beatrice had been able to talk non-stop in addition to eating and drinking, even down to wiping her plate clean with the sliced bread.

'We'll have coffee in the main drawing room, Tina, as the sun will be hitting the veranda shortly. Don't take that!' she snapped at Tina, taking back the bottle of wine and refilling her glass. She then waved the bottle towards Jane and indicated for her to follow her inside.

As they walked, Beatrice described her difficult life in Australia, which became even harder when her first son Matthew had been born with severe medical problems. She paused, turning to Jane, and Jane was surprised to see her eyes brimming with tears.

'Do you have children?' she asked.

'No, Mrs Thorpe, I don't.'

'When a mother has a sick child, it is often very difficult for a second healthy boy not to feel slighted. A mother's protective instincts are for the neediest child. We never believed my poor Matthew would live this long . . .'

They entered the drawing room.

'I read that my father had died in an English newspaper . . . can you imagine? Not a word from Helena, even when I was informed that she was my father's sole heir and I had inherited nothing.'

Jane followed Beatrice through one drawing room and into the second.

'It was hard to believe that things could get any worse. I was absolutely poverty-stricken, and then my poor husband, John, died. By then I was writing Helena begging letters . . . but with all her money, and obviously the remainder of my mother's jewellery, as well as what Father must have left her, she boarded up the house for God knows how many years.'

At last Jane had an opportunity to ask Beatrice about why the property in Stockwell had been left empty.

'Did your sister have a reason for not living at the family home?'

Beatrice took another gulp of wine but didn't reply.

'Mrs Thorpe, I'm asking if perhaps Helena had boarded up the property because she was afraid of what might be discovered in the shelter?'

Beatrice shook her head. 'I really don't know . . . I don't want to talk about it.'

'I'm afraid that at some point, Mrs Thorpe, you will have to answer my questions. To me, it doesn't make any sense for your sister to insist on boarding up the property and not allowing anyone to live there.'

'Really? I am certain, my dear, that you have no legal right in a foreign country to make me answer any questions, and I really think I have been exceptionally patient in assisting you so far.'

Beatrice turned away, draining her glass once again.

Jane pressed on. 'Mrs Thorpe, I know that when Jason converted the property into flats, no one was allowed access to the garden or the basement. Don't you find that rather strange?'

Beatrice simply shrugged her shoulders.

'Listen, dear, I've been honest with you about everything and answered your questions. But I really have no notion of how that terrible thing occurred.'

'Why do you think your sister committed suicide?' Jane was desperate to get Beatrice to talk about the baby.

'I have already explained to you that my father was very cruel to her because he didn't think that she was his daughter.'

'Could Marjorie have been pregnant and then, after giving birth—?'

Beatrice slammed her glass down on the table. 'I will not listen to another word. I find this questioning very intrusive ... you're talking about a beloved sister who committed suicide at a horribly young age. If you persist in questioning me further, I'll have to ask you to leave.'

Jane took a deep breath. Questioning Beatrice was going nowhere.

'I'm really so sorry, Mrs Thorpe ... I had absolutely no intention of upsetting you. Please accept my sincere apologies,' Jane said.

Beatrice pulled a tissue from a box by the drinks cabinet and dabbed the corner of her eyes.

'I accept your apology, dear, but you are raking up some very upsetting memories.'

Jane was now beginning to wonder if the baby had actually been Beatrice's. She knew Beatrice's first son, Matthew, had been born before her marriage to John Thorpe. In all probability Jason was also illegitimate. Jane contemplated bringing this up but decided against it.

She was surprised when Beatrice came over and touched her on the shoulder.

'I don't want to talk about any more bad things. My darling son Jason is going to propose to Arabella ... that's why he flew straight to her home in Melbourne. He loves filming Arabella competing in her equestrian events, you know – he takes after his grandfather with photography. He has a darkroom in the boathouse.' She laughed to herself. 'No matter how many times I ask him to tidy up in there, it is still just a mess of old reels of film and boxes and boxes of photographs which he brought back when the Stockwell property was sold.'

Frustratingly, Jane realised that even though Beatrice had consumed a lot of gin and then almost a whole bottle of wine, she wasn't now going to let slip the real family secrets.

'When is Jason due to arrive?' she asked.

Beatrice glanced at her wristwatch. 'Well, it's a less than two-hour flight from Melbourne to Sydney, and he could be an hour or so at the airport, you know how long the queues can be. And another hour at least to get here, so I don't think we will see him until about six tonight.'

Jane had a thumping headache, and the jet lag was definitely kicking in. She decided it would be best if she went back to the hotel to recharge her batteries, rather than wait for Jason's arrival.

'If it's OK with you, Mrs Thorpe, I would like to return to my hotel and come back to meet with you first thing in the morning, before we get our flight back to London.'

Beatrice tightened her lips. 'No, that is not convenient. I feel I have been more than generous with my time, given your unannounced visit, which at times has felt more like an inquisition.'

Jane tried to control her temper. 'It isn't convenient for me either, Mrs Thorpe, but I have to leave tomorrow, and I still have many questions, the answers to which need to be included in my report.'

Beatrice suddenly seemed quite sober as she glared at Jane. 'I would've thought with the death of my sister, any inquiries you had should now be over.'

Jane picked up her jacket. 'No, Mrs Thorpe, they are not over. I will be here tomorrow morning to talk to you – and Jason.'

CHAPTER TWENTY

Jane had been able to have a shower in the rather grotty communal bathroom. Her towel was almost threadbare, but she had at least been able to cool down. She changed into a clean T-shirt and put on her cotton trousers and sandals. She had already checked whether Tim was back, but he was not in his room and no message had been left for her at the so-called reception desk.

It was almost seven and there were a few customers at the bar. The streets outside were starting to fill up, with the neon signs flashing and loud music drifting through the open door. The same barman was on duty, and Jane ordered a lager and lime, picking up a sticky food menu.

Jane was eager to get some sleep and was not very hungry. Her ice-cold lager had no lime, but she picked up a bowl of peanuts from the bar and took them with her drink over to a small table by an air-conditioning unit. She had almost finished her drink when Tim walked in, wearing a worn-looking baseball cap and a pair of cheap sunglasses. His shirt was sweat-soaked, and his arms and neck were sunburned. He was carrying a dirty plastic carrier bag with his jacket sticking out and was about to walk straight past Jane when she called his name.

'I was starting to get worried, Tim. You look terrible.'

'I feel it. My God, have I been on a trip and a half. You wouldn't believe it. And in case you don't know, we're right in the middle of the red-light district here . . . I've been propositioned three times.'

'I'm surprised, looking the way you do.'

'And not a copper in sight,' Tim said, shaking his head.

'You look as if you could do with a drink,' Jane told him.

'Do you mind if I go and have a shower and change my shirt first? I'm drenched.'

'I hope it was all in a good cause and you did better than I did with Beatrice. Meet me in my room as soon as you've changed.'

Jane drained her glass and went back to the bar. It was filling up with unsavoury types, both male and female, and the music had been turned up. She was really going to have a row with Carter when she returned to London. She bought a packet of cigarettes and asked for two cans of lager to take up to her room.

Tim knocked on her door fifteen minutes later. His hair was still wet, and his nose looked as if it was going to peel badly, but he was wearing a fresh shirt. Jane held up the two cans of lager and smiled, gesturing for him to join her on the edge of the bed.

'I think rather than rinsing out the tooth mugs, it'd be better to drink from the can.'

His can opened with a frothy *hiss* and he gulped down a few mouthfuls before slumping down on her bed.

'So, what have you got for me?' Jane asked.

Tim sat up and opened his notebook. He told her that after going to Jason Thorpe's office and finding it shut, and then over to the docks, searching high and low for the warehouse, he had some good fortune when he stopped to have something to eat and drink at a food stand.

Jane turned to look at him. 'Tim, can you get to the point? Are you saying his office and warehouse were closed?'

'Yes, but I got lucky, because I met one of the drivers – name was Barry Donald – and he told me I should talk to his brother-in-law Mitch about Jason Thorpe's export company.'

He licked a finger to turn a page in his notebook.

'That was the good news . . . the bad news was the bloke I needed to talk to lives in Yennora, in the suburbs. He's worked for Jason Thorpe for the past three years but has left under a bit of a cloud. I asked if I could just call him, but Barry said he didn't have a phone.'

Jane sighed, closing her eyes as he flicked over another page of his notebook.

'I had to get a train there and my new friend Barry drove me to the station, then it took me forty-five minutes on the train . . . I was sweating like a stuffed pig by the time I got there. This was around half past one.'

'Yes, Tim, go on,' Jane said, trying to be patient.

He turned another page. 'I got a taxi to Mitch's trailer . . . his wife was a really sweet Asian girl and gave me some chilled lemon juice while I waited for Mitch to get back.'

'Tim, can you get to the point? What did this Mitch have to tell you?'

'Well, first, you need to understand how the export companies work. Jason Thorpe has an office in Adelaide, so he can ship from there . . . but it's just a small place, with one worker checking through the orders. He has a small office here in the city and he leases space at the docks to offload the crates, which are then shipped to wherever he has sold to.'

Jane sighed. 'That's all very interesting, Tim, but did you find out the reason why he parted company with Jason?'

Tim nodded. 'Yes, I did. But he was just part of the chain that had been delivering for Thorpe. He said that he had four big, covered trucks. So, he also had to organise the other drivers. He was a really nice, genuine man . . . much older than his wife, but I would say he was an honest bloke.'

Jane closed her eyes. She could feel the exhaustion flooding through her.

'Tim . . .'

'Sorry.' Tim turned a number of pages in his book. 'OK, it goes back to last year, when Thorpe ordered a large shipment of red wine from one of the major vineyards. There was a real problem for the wine exporters due to a terrible season in the vineyards. The South Australian regions, just north of Adelaide, experienced a hot and dry summer, then they had had a wet March, which apparently put the kibosh on any real chances of producing quality reds.'

Tim studied his notes.

'This is where it gets interesting, because one of the biggest export markets is China. Jason was trying to crack the Chinese market and over-ordered a substantial amount of red. He was basically left with it in his warehouse as it was almost undrinkable. He then made another disastrous purchase of rosé from a vineyard in Victoria. Mitch said the rosé was not really tried or tested, but Jason was convinced it could be really big.'

Jane felt like pulling out her hair. 'You still haven't told me why this guy Mitch left Jason's employment.'

She had to wait yet again as Tim thumbed through his notebook.

'Well, according to Mitch, nine months ago Jason's business was going belly up. He was also getting a bad reputation with the owners of the vineyards for not paying for his goods . . . and he wasn't paying his drivers either. Mitch said Jason was a loudmouthed snob who spent more time mixing with high society than he did trying to salvage his company.' Tim smiled. 'Apparently, our Jason is getting his leg over with one of the richest heiresses in Melbourne. Mitch said that sooner or later her father would find out that his daughter's "suitor" was a lying, two-faced git who left decent men in the lurch, knowing they had families and mortgages to pay, and he would put a stop to the wedding.'

Tim turned yet another page. 'This is interesting . . .'

'Really?' Jane said through gritted teeth.

'Yeah . . . I did a few sums and Mitch told me that Jason had managed to get his hands on a large sum of money which is keeping him afloat. I reckon that money came from the sale of the Stockwell property.'

Jane passed Tim her untouched can of lager. 'Good work, Tim. Very interesting. I would say, with Helena's death the inheritance could save his skin, as Hadley hasn't mentioned any other beneficiaries.'

Tim took a swig of his lager then let out a burp. 'Excuse me, ma'am. I think you're right. I also think, and this is from what Mitch told me, Jason has a very nasty side . . . it even brought them to fisticuffs once.'

'Did this Mitch mention Beatrice?'

'Not really . . . though he would sometimes see her in Jason's Sydney office manning the phone. Jason appeared to go through secretaries like water. He paid them a pittance and treated them badly. According to Mitch, he "fucked them then kicked them out".'

'On that note, Tim, I'm going to have to kick you out because if I don't go to sleep, I'll pass out.'

Tim sprang up and picked up the empty cans. 'I'll just take these back to the bar, then.'

'Thank you. Can you be ready by eight tomorrow? We'll settle the hotel bill and go back to Mosman on the ferry. I want to be there bright and early.'

Tim hovered by the door. 'So, you didn't get much from Beatrice today?'

'No, I didn't. She has an amazing ability to deflect direct questions, but she can talk the hind leg off a donkey. Every time I tried to get her to talk about something important, I failed. I think I made the mistake of being too polite and, in a way, too careful. Tomorrow, I'm going for the jugular.'

'Goodnight, then,' Tim said.

He had barely shut the door behind him before Jane flopped back on the bed and was instantly asleep.

CHAPTER TWENTY-ONE

Jane and Tim checked out of their seedy hotel with their hand luggage and caught the nine o'clock ferry to Mosman. At this hour of the morning the air was refreshing, but Tim's sunburn was making him look like a lobster. He was wearing the cap that Mitch had given to him, and he had put some after sun on his burned nose.

They had noted the schedule of the return ferry, allowing plenty of time to get to the airport for their six thirty flight back to London, and took their time climbing back up the steps to The Glades. They arrived at the house at a quarter to ten, walking around to the back as they had done the previous day. Jane rang the bell and waited. She had to pull it a second time and was just about to pull it again when the door was opened by Tina.

'Detective Inspector Jane Tennison and Detective Constable Tim Taylor. We have come to speak to both Beatrice and Jason Thorpe, please.'

'I am very sorry, but they are not at home,' Tina said.

Jane was taken aback. 'What?'

'They have gone to the ten o'clock service at church.'

'But she knew I was coming.'

Tina looked apologetic. 'I was not told that Mrs Thorpe was expecting visitors.'

Tina started to close the door, but Jane stepped forward, blocking it with her foot.

'How long before they return, Tina?' she asked.

'Perhaps two hours, ma'am. It will depend on if they socialise afterwards with the other parishioners.'

Jane was furious. She gestured for Tim to pick up his rucksack and pushed the front door open with her hip.

'Tina, please look after our bags. We will wait in the shade outside.'

Tina looked dubious, but Jane was so forthright that she eventually picked up the bags and stepped backwards.

'You want coffee or tea?'

'No, thank you. We'll walk down to the waterfront.'

Tina watched them walk away and then closed the door behind them.

Jane was seething.

'That bloody woman . . . I told her I would be here this morning.'

Tim tried to calm her down. 'We've got plenty of time. We don't need to leave until three.'

'If she prattles on like she did yesterday, we'll need a lot longer than that.' Jane sighed.

She walked along the first tier of the garden and down the steps to the second tier, eventually coming to the third tier and the edge of the property with its glorious view of the bay.

'My God, this really is a beautiful place,' she said, calming down.

'It is . . . although I think the sound of those parakeets would drive me round the bend. They never stop screeching,' Tim said.

Jane hesitated for a moment, then walked towards the boathouse.

'Where are you going?' Tim asked.

'The boathouse . . . come on.'

Steep steps led down to a low-roofed building that had once been white, but the paint was now blistered and peeling. From the steps they could see flat boards and iron rails that led down to the actual waterfront and a floating dock. Old iron chains were attached to a big wrought-iron wheel.

Tim was right behind her. 'That must be to lower the boat down to the dock, but it doesn't look as if it's been used for a while.'

Jane stepped onto a rough gravel area and headed towards a large door that was slightly askew on its hinges. She needed Tim's help to drag it open. Conveniently, on a hook just inside the door, was a large torch. They didn't need it, though, because the arched aperture gave enough light to see what must have been, at one time, a very expensive speed boat. The boat was now balanced on blocks, the hull clearly in need of repair and the leather seats torn and stained.

'You know what this is?' Tim said excitedly. 'It's an old cigarette speed boat. I would say this is probably 1920s or '30s. Big, powerful engines. It's shameful that it's been left rotting like this.'

Jane looked at the slatted walls where numerous water skis were tied up, along with a rotting rubber dinghy, oars and, high up on a shelf, a single skiff. Unlike the speed boat, it looked to be in good condition.

'They must lower this down a ramp into the water. I would say from the tufts of grass between the rails, nothing has been lowered into the sea for a long time. I'd give my eye teeth to have something like this,' Tim said.

Jane ignored him, making her way to the rear of the boathouse, past the stacks of old tennis racquets and golf clubs stacked against the wall. Next to them was a door with a notice painted in red: PRIVATE – NO ADMITTANCE.

She looked at the red lightbulb above the door. 'I reckon this could be Jason's darkroom.'

'What?' Tim said, being careful not to trip over the coils of rope left on the uneven floorboards.

'Beatrice told me that Jason took after her father, who was a keen photographer. Apparently, Jason had an expensive movie camera and had been filming his girlfriend, Arabella, at an equestrian event in Melbourne.' She turned and smiled. 'For one godawful moment, I thought she was going to ask me to watch it – that was when I decided I'd had enough yesterday.'

Jane tried the handle of the door. It was locked.

'Can you see if there's a key anywhere, Tim?'

He looked around, then eased past Jane to try the handle himself.

'I think it might just be a bit warped.' He used all his strength to twist the handle and almost fell forwards as the door opened. Jane peered into the room.

'Can you get that torch? We don't want to make a mess.'.

As he went back to fetch it, Jane eased further into the darkroom. Unlike the rest of the boathouse, this was not in a sorry state of repair. There were plywood boards covering the walls, and the ceiling had numerous electric lights, though she was unable to see any switches. There was a long trestle table with neat stacks of plastic developing trays, and bottles of photographic liquids and other developing equipment on the shelves. The only other furniture was two old chests of drawers, and an office swivel chair.

Tim appeared and shone the torch around the room. On one side there was a tied-back black curtain on a rail and behind it were three sinks. Above the sinks were steel hanging lines with pegs.

'Well, she didn't lie about this, did she? Maybe Jason should've spent less time in here and more time at his export company, because this place is obviously used frequently.' Jane pointed towards an electric kettle and a whisky bottle. As the beam of the torch shone on the kettle, Jane spotted the light switches. She made her way over to the old round knobs. They looked fairly antiquated, and she suspected that the electrics could be faulty.

'I'm going to try these switches,' she said, and then was surprised when the darkroom became instantly flooded with light. She could see a number of negatives pinned up behind the black curtain and stacked to one side were four large cardboard boxes. They were thick with dust but she could clearly see written on the lids 'H Lanark, family photographs, 1940'.

'I think Jason must have shipped these over when the house in Stockwell was turned into flats,' Jane said.

Tim folded his arms. 'If you ask me, I think he must have shipped over a lot of that antique furniture in the house as well.'

'Quite possibly. If he's in the export business, he would have the facilities to ship it back easily.' She shook her head, frowning. 'I just can't really get to grips with Helena Lanark. She inherits the house, her mother's jewellery, and money from her father, and what does she do? She boards up the house for maybe ten to fifteen years . . . just boards it up. I can't help thinking she was in some sort of denial about the baby being buried in the shelter . . . maybe even afraid someone would find it?'

'But she couldn't have been that worried, because eventually she let her nephew Jason divide it up into flats,' Tim said.

'I know,' Jane said, 'but he was only allowed to divide the house into flats on the condition that no one was ever allowed into the basement, and no one was ever allowed access into the garden. When I went there after the discovery in the shelter, the garden was like a jungle. The grass had been left to grow about three feet high, and the orchard had just been left to grow wild.'

'But then he sold it, right?' Tim said.

Jane frowned. 'I know, but I think by that time he had got power of attorney because Helena was put into her care home. In reality, she might not even have been aware of what she was signing over to him.'

'What about his mother, Beatrice?'

'I don't know, Tim, I really don't know, but I think she knows what happened in that shelter. God forbid, it might even have been her baby.'

As they had been talking, Tim had carried one of the large boxes over to the trestle table. He found a Stanley knife in one of the drawers and cut through the old hemp string that had been tied around the box.

'I don't think Jason knew anything bad had happened in that house. I think, if he had – given your friend Mitch's description of his behaviour and my own interaction with him – he would have got rid of not only that poor girl who had been chained up in the shelter, but also the baby.'

Jane now carried a second box to the table and instructed Tim to cut the string on it while she eased the lid off the first box.

'Oh my God!' she exclaimed. The box was stacked with hundreds of photographs, some in cardboard cut-out frames, some loose, some with black markings drawn across them.

Jane's hands were now filthy, and Tim had begun to cough. The amount of grime and dust that was coming off the boxes was getting to his chest.

'Are you OK, Tim?'

He nodded.

'OK, let's see if there's anything useful among this lot.'

They started going through the photographs.

'I don't know if this is anyone in the family,' Tim said, holding one up. Jane took it from him.

'Good heavens!' The woman in the photograph was wearing an elaborate embroidered gown with lace and jewelled sleeves. Her hair was coiled in intricate curls on her forehead, the rest of it in a high, plaited bun that reached from the top of her head to the nape of her neck. But it was the necklace that had got Jane's attention.

'Tim – the three strands of pearls.' She turned the photo over and in faded writing read the words 'Dowager Empress Maria Feodorovna of Russia, 1928'.

Jane could see how incredible the large pearls were, each with a beautiful sheen and nearly perfectly spherical.

'You see the third strand, how long it is?' She held the photo up for Tim to see. 'That is the one I saw around Helena's neck when I visited her at the care home.' She pointed to the second strand. 'And I'm certain this is the one that Beatrice was wearing yesterday. She told me that the third strand, the smallest one, was given to Marjorie but was buried with her when she died. Can you imagine what these three strands together are worth?'

'How much do you think?' he asked.

She shook her head. 'I really don't know . . . but I remember a friend of my mother's had an engagement ring with one pearl in the centre and diamonds either side; she told us that even though the diamonds were a good carat, the pearl was worth hundreds, and that was just one, so just think of the value of the three strands – and this photograph has to be proof of provenance.' She put it to one side on the trestle table.

Jane had found nothing else of interest in her box and had begun opening another one when Tim exclaimed, 'Holy shit, you're not going to believe this, ma'am.'

Jane joined Tim at his box. 'He photographed her,' he said in a shocked tone.

Jane looked, and suddenly a chill went through her. Henry Lanark had taken photographs of his daughter hanging from the swing. You could clearly see the young girl's distorted face. They were sickening. But it got worse. In the third battered cardboard box, they uncovered sexually explicit photographs of two of the Lanark daughters, and even cruder photographs of their mother.

Jane selected a number of the photographs, including the ones she considered pornographic, the suicide pictures of Marjorie, and the image of the Dowager Empress's necklace.

'What are you going to do with them?' Tim asked.

'Tim, these are vital evidence, what the hell do you think I am going to do with them? I might not legally be able to take them with us back to London, but that doesn't mean I can't use them to get to the truth by confronting that awful woman and her equally appalling son.'

'Well, I'm just a bit concerned,' Tim said. 'I mean, what if they don't come back before we have to leave?'

'I'll take full responsibility,' Jane replied. 'Now, pass me one of the big envelopes to put these in.'

When they were finished, they switched off the lights and shut the door, making their way gingerly out of the old boathouse. Tim heaved the door closed whilst Jane stood for a moment looking at the view, trying to get the shocking images they'd just seen out of her mind.

She turned as she heard a throaty laugh, and they could see, at the top of the tiered garden, Beatrice, arm in arm with Jason, entering the house.

'Well, we know they're home now. Let's do this,' she said, marching towards them.

CHAPTER TWENTY-TWO

Jane rang the doorbell, and as Tina opened the door, Jane was confronted by Jason Thorpe.

'I'm afraid my mother is not available to speak to you,' he said brusquely. 'She has already given you quite enough of her time and answered all your questions.'

'I do apologise for the inconvenience, Mr Thorpe,' Jane said firmly, 'but your mother hasn't actually answered all of my questions. I would appreciate it if you could encourage her to have a further meeting with me. I would hate to have Mrs Thorpe taken to the police station but will do so if it is necessary.'

His lips tightened. 'That is absolutely preposterous! I'm perfectly aware that you don't have any jurisdiction here. To suggest that you would question my mother at the police station is an empty threat. One call to my lawyers will have you removed from my property immediately.'

Jane stood her ground. 'If I return to London, Mr Thorpe, I will have to report to my senior officer that I believe your mother could be responsible for infanticide.'

'That is fucking ridiculous,' he said angrily.

Jane carried on undaunted. 'I'd like your mother to tell me exactly what happened at the shelter, and whether she did in fact give birth and bury the child. I will treat her with the utmost respect, but I can't guarantee the press won't get hold of the fact that your mother is a suspect in an infanticide case.'

Jane caught a glimpse of Beatrice coming down the stairs behind her son.

'I don't know if you told your mother about the press coverage which we've already had. The papers called it the "House of Horrors". I can guarantee that there will be even more unpleasant headlines.'

Jason stepped forward, as if to grab Jane's arm. His face was distorted with anger as he shouted, 'She has told you the truth! She is not involved whatsoever!'

'Yes, I am, Jason.'

Jane could hardly believe it. Beatrice, wearing a Chanel suit, her famous pearls, and high-heeled black patent leather shoes, appeared at the bottom of the stairs.

'Please tell Tina to bring us a cool drink in the drawing room,' she said.

He curled his hands into fists as if about to argue with her, but she spoke firmly.

'Do it, please.' She then gestured for Jane and Tim to follow her into the drawing room.

Beatrice sat on the sofa. She was wearing the same jangling charm bracelet as yesterday as she indicated for Jane to sit opposite her. This time Tim, without being told, went and sat on the hard-backed chair. The tension in the room was palpable. Jane placed the envelope of photographs on the table beside her. She then opened her bag and took out her notebook.

'I apologise for my son's rudeness,' Beatrice said, tight-lipped. She then gave a small sigh. 'I was not aware of the newspaper stories you just mentioned . . . my son told me that it was not worth reading such garbage. I also chose not to discuss with you the appalling events that he told me had occurred. I obviously feel great compassion for that poor girl they found . . .'

Jane could feel Beatrice was about to go off topic again.

'I'm sure you do, Mrs Thorpe,' she said quickly. 'But that case is closed. What remains unknown is who murdered the newborn baby.'

'There was no murder,' Beatrice said quietly.

'Yes, there was, Mrs Thorpe. The newborn child was suffocated. We have that forensically proven. What we do not have is the identity of the person who wrapped the baby in the blue shawl so tightly that threads of the wool were found in the infant's lungs.'

Jason moved silently into the room.

'Dear God, is this necessary? Are you deliberately trying to shock my mother into some kind of admission when I can guarantee that she was not involved?'

'Shut up, Jason,' Beatrice said.

There was an awkward pause as Tina brought in a tray of iced drinks. Nobody spoke as she handed glasses to Jane and Tim. Jason took a glass from the tray and sat perched on the end of the sofa beside his mother.

'Firstly, I want you to know why I previously declined to be honest with you, Detective Tennison. It was simply to protect my family's reputation.'

Jane could see a strange, frightened look in his eyes as Jason turned towards his mother. But Beatrice took no notice, continuing calmly.

'My sister Marjorie became pregnant. For a considerable time she kept it secret from everyone, but eventually it was too obvious for her to hide, and the poor girl told Helena. She told our parents that Marjorie was ill with flu and had a touch of bronchitis so that she had to wear a quilted dressing gown . . .'

Sensing Beatrice moving off course again, Jane interrupted.

'So Marjorie went to full term?'

'Yes. I lied about the belt, Detective Tennison. I lied about it because I didn't want Helena to get into trouble. But it was her belt, and it was Helena who arranged everything.'

Beatrice had straightened her back and clasped her hands together so that even her charm bracelet was silent.

'She took Marjorie into the shelter through the door in the basement. We knew that Father was not at home. He had gone to the Garrick, his private members' club. Helena took towels with her and there was a gas cooker where she could boil water. Marjorie was to have the baby and as soon as it was born, Helena said she would take care of it.'

'What did you think she meant by that?' Jane asked.

'I don't really know, but I'm sure she didn't intend to harm the baby. I think both Marjorie and I believed she would have the baby taken to a convent.'

'So, what happened?' Jane persisted.

Jason put down his glass and moved from the arm of the sofa to sit closer to his mother, reaching out for her clasped hands.

'You don't have to put yourself through this, Mother, you really don't. Unless Detective Tennison can give you some kind of promise that what you are saying will never be disclosed. I cannot, at this time, afford to have any bad press. As it is, no one here knows that we are even associated with the Lanark family, and we need assurance that this will never be made public.'

Jane gave a small shrug of her shoulders. 'I obviously can't give you one hundred per cent assurance, but if you tell us the truth about what happened, we may simply be able to close the case.'

Beatrice unclasped her hands and patted her son's knee.

'This has been a very long time coming – I cannot tell you for how many years I have been forced into silence. My sister put me in a humiliating position, having to beg her to help me financially here in Australia.'

Beatrice now reached out to clasp her son's hand and gave him a wretchedly sad look. Jane knew instinctively that she was about to begin one of her lengthy sagas.

'Mrs Thorpe, on the night your sister gave birth, could you please tell me exactly what happened?'

Beatrice took a deep breath. 'We were all in the shelter and poor Marjorie was so afraid to cry out, because even our mother didn't know – not that she would have cared. She would have just said "So what?" as she would've been the same age when she gave birth to Helena. You know she locked our father out of their bedroom . . .'

Jane interrupted again. 'Mrs Thorpe, I need to know what happened in the shelter.'

Beatrice glared. 'That is all you care about . . . what happened in the shelter?' Beatrice seemed to be mimicking Jane. 'You never asked me what happened to Marjorie.'

'I know what happened to Marjorie.'

Beatrice was hardly able to contain her rage.

'No, you don't. I even tried to tell you . . . but I just couldn't . . . I was too ashamed.'

Jane frowned, convinced that Beatrice was going to change her story. Beatrice stood up and began to pace the room.

'We would hear him come in – the sound of his keys in the silver bowl in the hall and his footsteps along the corridor terrified us. He wore heavy brown brogue shoes with steel heel caps. We would hear the click-click-click on the marble floor, praying that his footsteps would go down into the basement and to his darkroom.'

Jane interrupted. 'So, were you in the shelter with Helena and Marjorie?'

Beatrice was still pacing up and down behind the sofa, whilst Jason sat straight-backed, his hands clenched.

'I think this has gone far enough. You are clearly distressing my mother.'

Beatrice suddenly shrieked. '*Distressing?* You don't even know the meaning of the word! Yes . . . yes, I was in the shelter. Marjorie had started to feel labour pains and we were trying to calm her . . . but most of all we were desperate to keep her quiet. Helena put a flannel into her mouth and told her to bite on it. She laid towels out on one of the shelf beds in there . . . and then we heard him.' Beatrice was physically shaking. 'Dear God . . . we heard him calling her, he was shouting Marjorie's name . . . and the baby started coming, and Marjorie was moaning in agony and Helena shouted at me to get out of the shelter and into the tunnel. I had to stop Father from finding out what was happening. I was midway through the tunnel and he was shouting so loudly for Marjorie that I thought he was coming to find us. Then I heard the baby crying and I ran into the basement, shutting the door just as my father came out of his darkroom.'

Beatrice started crying.

'I told him that Marjorie was sick in bed and that Helena was concerned she might catch pneumonia, so I had come down in her place.' Beatrice reached into the sleeve of her jacket and took out a small lace handkerchief to wipe her tears. 'That is what happened in the shelter.'

'What happened next . . . after the child was born?' Jane asked.

'Marjorie came back into the house and went up to her room. Helena came in shortly after, as Father was in such a rage, shouting that he needed Helena in the darkroom.'

Jane had been making notes throughout and now closed her notebook. 'Thank you very much for your honesty, Mrs Thorpe. I understand why you have tried to protect your sister. Can I just ask you just a couple more questions?' she asked hesitantly.

Jason stood up abruptly. 'Jesus Christ! Haven't you heard enough? Surely, you've got what you came for? Can't you see the distress you are causing my mother?'

'Actually, Jason, I'm relieved that at long last I've been able to speak about what happened in that bloody, stinking shelter; now I hope to God I will be left in peace.'

Jane knew she had to choose her words very carefully. 'Mrs Thorpe, did you ever confront Helena? From what you just told us, the baby was born alive.'

Beatrice shook her head. 'No, Helena chose not to speak about it again. She just said she had taken care of it. And then, as if it was some kind of sign, my father discovered that part of one of the walls in the tunnel had buckled. Obviously by this time the war was long over, so he bolted the basement door to prevent anyone else from going into the tunnel, or into the shelter, as he said it was dangerous.'

Jane flicked from one page to another in her notebook. 'Did Helena leave the towels in the shelter? They must have been bloodstained. And what about the afterbirth?'

'Oh, she put those things into the furnace that heated the house. We used to have a lorry delivering coal every week, down a shoot into the furnace.'

Jane knew she had to stop Beatrice from going off the subject. 'How long after this happened did Marjorie commit suicide?'

'Maybe a week later?'

Jane was shocked. 'A week?'

Beatrice shrugged her shoulders. 'Yes, something like that, I think. I know it wasn't too long after the birth.'

'Did your father ever wonder why Marjorie would have done such an awful thing?'

Beatrice pursed her lips, then shrugged, as if she didn't want to think about it. Jane concentrated on her notebook, underlining the word 'photographs' and biting her lip. She was certain there would be serious repercussions if she showed Beatrice the photographs they had found in the boat house. She turned back a page.

'Mrs Thorpe, can I just go back to something you said earlier? Your father was calling for Marjorie, then you said you told your father that you had come down in her place, because she was ill. Is that right?'

Beatrice wouldn't meet Jane's eyes. Instead, she stared at the lace handkerchief, twisting it in her hands. 'I made it clear to you that my father was a keen photographer, and we would often be called into his darkroom separately to have our photographs taken. He chose Marjorie more often because she was exceptionally beautiful . . . he really didn't like to photograph Helena as she was not so pretty. He used her to help him pin them up, you know, on a wire with pegs.'

Jane knew very well the kind of photographs their father had been taking of the girls and was in two minds whether or not to let Beatrice know. But then Beatrice gave a strange laugh. 'I was even jealous at one time . . . can you imagine that? Jealous! But when he found out that our mother had been having an affair with the young music teacher, Mikhail, and he suspected that Marjorie was not his child . . .'

Jane leaned forward. 'How long before Marjorie committed suicide had your father started suspecting?'

Beatrice looked up and Jane caught the tightening of her lips again as she gave a sidelong glance at her son. 'A long time before.'

She turned back to Jane and waved her handkerchief.

'The house was consumed with his rage. He physically whipped poor Mikhail and threw him out. My mother was tormented, begging and praying for him to leave Mikhail alone.'

Jane watched, fascinated, as Beatrice stood up and again waved her handkerchief dramatically in the air. 'My mother threatened to throw herself down the stairs, or poison herself. She was a better actress than Sarah Bernhardt. But when father turned on her, she spat and kicked at him like a wild cat. My father was a devious, wicked man. He was able – because of his knowledge of the print business – to alter documents and birth certificates. My mother, for example, was too young to have been married . . .'

'Mother, for God's sake there is no need to go into that,' Jason interjected.

'Go into what? You have no idea what my life was like. You have no idea how my heart was broken.'

It was quite extraordinary to witness the way Beatrice had become so theatrical. It was as though the relief of her confessions had energised her.

'I just have one more question, Mrs Thorpe,' Jane said. 'From what you told me, I'm wondering if inappropriate sexual behaviour occurred in your father's darkroom.' She hesitated before continuing. 'Was Marjorie's baby a result of an incestuous relationship with your father?'

Beatrice's legs buckled under her as she screamed, '*No, no, no!*'

Jason ran to the archway and shouted for Tina, returning quickly to his mother to help her stand. She was sobbing uncontrollably and seemed almost to be having some kind of fit.

Tim stood up, shocked. Jane closed her notebook and also moved towards the panic-stricken Jason, who held on to Beatrice as she thrashed her arms and foamed at the mouth.

Tina, accompanied by the stocky man who had been pushing Matthew in a wheelchair, hurried into the room. They immediately appeared to know what to do, carrying her between them to lay her down on the sofa. Jason pointed a finger at Jane.

'You had better get out of my house now,' he barked. He grabbed hold of Jane's arm just as she was trying to put the envelope with the photos into her bag. Tim stepped forward.

'There is no need for that, sir.'

Jane jerked her arm free. 'Do not touch me, Mr Thorpe. I am very sorry for your mother's distress.' But Jason maintained his tight grip, dragging Jane out of the room and into the hall. He was white with rage.

'Are you satisfied now? I told you my mother was not well, yet you have not stopped interrogating her, even insinuating that she had something to do with the death of that baby.'

As she had been taught to do, Jane took deep breaths to regain her control.

Jason opened the door. 'I hope you now realise this is over!'

'Not quite yet, Mr Thorpe,' Jane said, regaining her composure. 'If you and your mother are planning to be in London for your aunt's funeral, I will require her to make a statement at the station. However, if she is unable to make the journey to London, then I will require written confirmation of what she has told me today.'

Jason pushed his face close to Jane, almost spitting with rage.

'You will get what you want, detective, but I hope to Christ it will then be over.'

Jane stepped back, almost knocking into Tim who was hovering protectively behind her.

'It won't quite be over, Mr Thorpe. I will keep you informed regarding an autopsy on Helena Lanark, and on my return to London I will be making a report detailing my suspicions that your aunt's necklace was stolen.'

Jason stepped back. 'What the fuck are you talking about?'

'You were the last person to see your aunt alive, Mr Thorpe, and her pearl necklace has not been recovered.'

Jane turned to Tim. 'Detective Constable Taylor will bring my bag.' Jane walked out, taking a deep breath to calm herself.

Tim joined her shortly afterwards, carrying their luggage. The front door slammed shut behind him.

'I wouldn't be too concerned about her, ma'am. She was sitting up and asking for a gin and tonic when I left.'

'My God, she can put on a show! But at least I can now confirm exactly what happened in that shelter. And you saw what a nasty piece of work Jason Thorpe is. I am no way finished with him.'

As they walked down towards the ferry, Jane suddenly stopped. 'Damn! I left the photographs. I was just putting them in my bag when he started manhandling me.'

'Don't worry.' Tim grinned. 'When he hauled you away, I snatched them up and snuck them into my rucksack.'

Jane couldn't help laughing. 'Well done, Tim. Still,' she added more seriously, 'best we keep it between ourselves. Hopefully Jason won't be going into the boathouse any time soon, and if he does, we replaced all the boxes where we found them.'

Tim nodded. 'Whatever you say, ma'am.'

CHAPTER TWENTY-THREE

After a long time getting through Customs at Heathrow, Jane and Tim eventually climbed into a black cab to take them back into London. They were both exhausted and Jane suggested that they take what was left of the day off and be at the station fresh on Tuesday morning.

After dropping Tim at a convenient Underground station, Jane got back home just after four and couldn't wait to have a long soak in her new bathtub. Although she hadn't had time to think about Eddie much in Australia, she now found herself looking forward to seeing him again. She had promised to contact him when she landed, so that he could collect her, but she had decided that she just wanted to get home as quickly as possible.

Stepping out of the cab, Jane was dismayed to see her front door was wide open, and to hear the noise of the various different radio channels blasting out into the street. But she forgot her annoyance as soon as she walked into her hallway. The new wallpaper was up, the floorboards had been sanded and varnished and the stair banisters were gleaming with a coat of white gloss.

Eddie hurtled down the stairs. 'I've been waiting for you to call!' he said, taking her in his arms.

'I'm sorry,' Jane said. 'The flight was an hour late taking off and we were delayed in Customs, so we just got into a taxi.' She held him at arm's length. 'I can't believe all this . . . it looks incredible.'

Eddie beamed with delight. 'Wait till you see the sitting room. We've been working around the clock to get as much done as possible. You might want to start looking at getting some new furniture now!'

True to his word, Eddie and his team had done a remarkable job. As he led her from room to room, Jane ran out of compliments.

'Do you feel like going out for dinner?' Eddie asked.

'I would really love that, Eddie, but to be honest we were booked into the most ghastly, seedy hotel and I didn't even have time for a decent shower . . . the communal bathroom was pretty disgusting . . . and I've got a thumping headache from the journey and everything.'

'OK, how about I make you a cup of tea?' he asked.

Jane really just wanted to have that longed-for bath, but he was so eager to please her that she agreed, relieved when he turned off the radio that had been left on in the kitchen.

After Eddie's team left, she told him as much as she thought would interest him about her trip to Australia, but her eyelids were soon drooping with weariness.

'Listen, you go up and have a bath,' Eddie said, seeing the state of her. 'I'll clear up in the kitchen and maybe we can get together tomorrow night instead? The lads and I have a lot of snagging to do, and we still have to finish your second bedroom.'

* * *

Eddie had taken her overnight bag up to her bedroom which, despite the strong smell of fresh paint, was looking amazing. Jane now regretted that she hadn't even considered buying Eddie a bottle of scotch in duty-free.

She didn't bother unpacking her notebook or the envelope containing all the photographs they had taken from the Thorpes' boathouse. She left everything in her bag to take to the station the next morning. Jane was so tired that without any memory of having got into bed, the next thing she knew was being jolted awake out of a deep sleep by her alarm going off at six. She had slept soundly for nine hours.

Sipping a cup of coffee in her kitchen, she made a few notes to remind herself that she still needed to arrange for blinds to be fitted in her bedroom, and to get some curtain fabric for her sitting room. She was just rinsing out her coffee cup when she noticed the overflowing ashtray. She picked it up gingerly, about to tip it into the waste bin when she noticed the charred ends of some rolled-up cigarette papers among the cigarette butts. She sighed, knowing exactly what they were, and placed some of them on a paper towel before tipping the rest into the bin.

Jane knew she would have to confront Eddie with the evidence, and ask if it had been him smoking cannabis or one of his guys. Jane was already concerned about the stuff that had come 'off the back of a lorry' but dope being smoked at her house was even more serious. Did Eddie not understand that she was a police detective? Or perhaps he didn't really take her job seriously.

And on top of all that, Jane she knew she was going to have a confrontation with DCI Wayne Carter that morning. She certainly had a bone to pick with him about his choice of hotel.

She got to the station by eight thirty and began typing up an extensive report on her Australia trip, providing concise details of her conversations with Beatrice, and mentioning that she might be coming to England for the funeral of her sister. She was still typing when her door swung open, and Carter breezed in, neglecting to knock as usual.

'So how was Sydney, Detective Tennison?'

'It would have been a lot better if I had been in a decent hotel. Whoever had the audacity to book me in there . . .'

He laughed, then held up his hands. 'Hey, it wasn't me. Do you really think I've got the time? Check with Barbara . . . I think she was handling it with someone from Scotland Yard.'

Jane pursed her lips. Yes, she thought to herself, it had to have been her. She must have gone out of her way to ensure she could find the worst hotel in Kings Cross.

Carter sat on the edge of her desk, swinging his leg.

'So, our prime suspect, now deceased – actually, she was deceased before you even left – has been fingered by her sister as the baby-killer. Do you have a signed statement?'

Jane knew he must have already spoken with Tim Taylor. 'Not as yet, but . . .'

Carter slapped his palms on his thighs. 'What a waste of a fucking trip . . . especially if she's now going to be coming to England for her sister's funeral. How the hell am I going to justify the expense of you schlepping over to Sydney?'

Jane glared at him. 'I will compile a detailed statement to be sent to Mrs Thorpe's solicitors in Sydney for her to sign and return in the post. If she is here for the funeral, she could possibly come into the station and make a formal statement in person.'

He casually stood up from her desk and glared back. 'Anything else you want to tell me about, Detective Tennison?'

'Not that I can think of, sir,' she said.

'I guess in all the excitement you must have forgotten to tell me about the post-mortem you asked Sussex police to do on Helena Lanark.'

'I didn't get a chance before I left and no firm time was set for it,' Jane said defensively. 'Also, as far as I was concerned, it would be a Sussex investigation.'

'Well, you better hope they don't send us the pathologist's bill . . . as it will be coming out of your pay!'

'What was the result?' Jane asked, trying to keep her voice level.

He pushed the half open door with the toe of his elegant boot. 'The post-mortem is today, as it happens. It seems the death of an sixty-one-year-old woman who resided in a care home for ten years is not exactly a priority.'

'But her pearl necklace was missing from her room, so there's a case for saying her death was suspicious . . .'

'Maybe, Detective Tennison, if you thought her death was so suspicious, you should have made it a priority, instead of wasting your time and my money going all the way to Australia.'

Jane took a deep breath and asked Carter if he had any pressing cases he wanted her to work on.

He turned back to look at her. 'There's a number of domestic situations you can run your lovely blue eyes over, Tennison.'

The door swung closed behind him and Jane sighed. There was no way that she was going to be able to keep working with Carter. She would put in for a transfer and didn't care where to, as long as it was nowhere near him.

Jane made herself focus on completing her report and then filed it. She called Sussex police to find out when the post-mortem was and was told it had been scheduled for that morning and that she should call back after lunch.

Glad of the opportunity to get out of Carter's way, Jane decided she would go to the mortuary in person. On her way out, she passed DC Taylor standing at the incident board, writing up details of a car and driver wanted in a hit and run.

'Shouldn't traffic or uniform be dealing with that?' she said quietly.

He shrugged. 'Carter has got it in for me. I just do what I'm told.'

'Thank you for giving Carter the information regarding our Australian trip,' Jane went on. 'In future, Tim, make sure you've spoken to the senior officer accompanying you before you start giving out details.'

'I'm sorry, ma'am, but he was very insistent . . . and he creased up laughing when he asked me about the hotel. But I never mentioned anything about the photographs, ma'am,' he added.

'And you had better keep it that way,' Jane said. 'I'm going to Helena Lanark's post-mortem if anyone needs to know where I am.'

Before making her way to the mortuary, Jane took several detours to John Lewis, Harrods, Selfridges and Liberty, choosing stair carpets, blinds and curtain fabric, not arriving at the labs until almost three. As she was walking along the corridor she met her old friend, DS Paul Lawrence.

'Hey, how are you doing, Jane?' he asked, affable as always. 'I was hoping to see you. DCI Carter asked me to attend the post-mortem on Helena Lanark. You got the supersleuth pathologist working today so you're in luck, but if you wanted to talk to him, you just missed him.'

'Shit,' Jane said.

'I have all the details if you want. Do you fancy a cup of coffee?'

Jane realised she hadn't even had lunch, so agreed to join Paul at a coffee bar not far from the labs. When they got there she ordered a toasted cheese sandwich and a cappuccino, and he had a BLT with a black coffee.

'I hear you went to Australia?' Paul said.

'Yeah, I was still making inquiries about the deceased's relatives,' Jane said. 'One of her sisters lives out there.'

'Oh, I know, this is all about the baby in the shelter, isn't it?' Paul asked.

Jane nodded. 'I managed to find out what actually happened. It turned out that Helena Lanark's young sister gave birth in the shelter and, even though the baby was born alive, Helena smothered it, intentionally or not we will never know. At least that part of my investigation can be put to rest now. So, what was the outcome of the post-mortem?'

Paul took a bite of his BLT and reached down to his briefcase. He rested it on his knee and opened it as he continued to eat.

'Well, the lady was actually in surprisingly good shape – physically, anyway. The prof said that she must have fallen face forward onto the floor. Her nose was dislocated, both eyes bruised, particularly the right eye, and her eyebrow was cut. She had been lying face down for a considerable time because of the way the lividity showed when she was examined by the doctor at the care home. He reckoned she possibly could've been lying there unconscious for hours before she died. Cause is partly suffocation, plus she suffered a major stroke due to the fall.'

Jane finished her sandwich. 'What about the two bruises around her neck? What did the prof say about them?'

'He said they came from two of her left-hand knuckles. When she fell her hand had been beneath her neck. So, end result is natural causes.'

'But you said suffocated?' Jane asked, draining her cappuccino.

'Yeah, now I think of it, it's a rather grim coincidence, isn't it? She must have been wearing a pale blue cashmere shawl, so when she fell, she had fallen on to the knot of the shawl that must have been round her shoulders.' He cocked his head to one side. 'That little baby had ingested wool fibres, hadn't it?'

Jane pulled a face.

'Not what you wanted to hear?' Paul asked, half smiling.

'Not really. I thought the two bruises on her neck may have come from a pearl necklace being snatched. Are Sussex paying for the post-mortem?'

Paul smiled. 'Although you raised it as a suspicious death, they requested the PM, so the prof said they have to foot the bill.'

'That's a relief,' Jane smiled.

Paul closed his briefcase. 'Listen, I have to go. I have another case over in Islington.'

'Thank you, Paul. I really appreciate your time, and as soon as my house is straight, I'd love you and your partner to come over for dinner.'

'That'd be nice, thank you. Are you seeing anyone at the moment?'

Jane laughed. 'Actually, I am . . . he's my decorator.'

'Well, I look forward to meeting him.'

After Paul had gone Jane sat thinking, wondering if there was any way the professor could be wrong. As it was now almost five,

Jane decided she would go home and call in to the station from there to see if there was anything they needed her for.

Jane was surprised to find that the house was empty. There was a note from Eddie to say he was collecting new paint samples for the spare bedroom, and could she give him a ring at his flat later if she wanted dinner. She had just changed into her dressing gown and was making a cup of tea in the kitchen when her phone rang.

'Good afternoon. Am I speaking to Detective Tennison?' Jane recognised Arnold Hadley's voice.

'Yes, Mr Hadley, it's me. I was actually going to call you about the post-mortem examination that has been completed on Miss Lanark.'

'Yes, I know. I have already been informed. I'm calling to say that I received a message from my chambers that Beatrice Thorpe called to speak to me. I hadn't let her know that I had retired. Apparently, she has asked for them to organise the funeral. It's not something a legal firm is often asked to do, but as her sister had been a client for so many years, they have agreed. I felt I should let you know, in case you wanted to attend.'

'Thank you,' Jane said. 'Mr Hadley, how long had you represented Helena Lanark?'

There was a slight hesitation before he replied. 'I'd known Helena for some years before I started representing her when she was in her early thirties.'

'How did you get to know her?' Jane asked.

'She was a neighbour of my mother's. She was very kind to her when she became ill.'

'I see. Were you aware that Jason Thorpe sold Helena's Stockwell property well below the market price?'

'Yes, I raised it with him at the time. He said it was because he wanted a quick sale and was acting in Helena's best interests. There wasn't much more I could say or do as he had power of attorney.'

'Did you know Jason bought shares in the development company?'

'No. If he did it wasn't with money from the sale as I know it was paid into Helena's bank account.'

'Do you think the developer might have given Jason cash or shares as an incentive to drop the price of the Stockwell property?' Jane asked.

'I suppose that's a possibility. No doubt Jason will say he bought them with his own money or as an investment for Helena's benefit . . . and proving otherwise would be difficult.'

Jane decided not to pursue it further. She was fairly certain now that if there had been any kind of fraud, Hadley wasn't involved.

'When is the funeral going to take place, Mr Hadley?'

'I believe it will be on Monday, at St Martin's Church, with a small reception at the Gore Hotel.'

'Just a thought, Mr Hadley, is Helena due to be buried?'

'Yes, there's a family crypt at Highgate.'

'In that case, I was wondering if you would like me to see about arranging for the baby to be released for burial as well? I've discovered that the youngest Lanark sister, Marjorie, gave birth to the baby and I thought it might be some sort of closure for the family as—'

Hadley quickly interrupted. 'That won't be possible.'

'I'm sorry?' Jane said.

'Marjorie wasn't buried in the family crypt. She was cremated. However, I will forward your suggestion on to Mr Thorpe.'

Jane ended the call. If Marjorie had been cremated, then when Beatrice had said that Marjorie's strand of pearls had been buried with her, that was another lie. Jane wondered how many other lies Beatrice had fed her. She checked her watch and put in a call to the Sussex police, who she presumed would now be investigating the theft of the necklace. The duty officer she spoke to could give her no further details as he wasn't involved in the case but suggested that if she called the station the following morning she could speak to a DS Simpson, who had been at the care home making inquiries.

Jane still felt very jet-lagged, but in the end agreed to dinner with Eddie. They went to the Italian restaurant they had been to previously and Jane perked up as soon as they sat down, even though she didn't have the energy to contribute much to the conversation.

As they were being served coffee, Eddie gave her a quizzical look.

'Can I say something? You seem quite distracted . . . I mean, I'm sure you're probably feeling jet-lagged, but if there is anything wrong with any of my work, I need you to let me know.'

'Oh, Eddie,' Jane exclaimed, 'I can't fault anything you've done for me. In fact, I can't believe how little time it's taken to get the house into such fabulous condition. We must be nearly finished now?'

He nodded. 'Yeah, I would say by early next week. If you've decided on the stair runner, blinds and curtains.'

Jane grinned. 'Fantastic. But I do need to bring something up,' she said, her grin fading. 'I've just been thinking about how to say it.'

He shrugged. 'I'm all ears. Anything that's bothering you, I'm sure I can fix.'

'It's not about your work, Eddie. It's just that I found the remains of some joints in the ashtray.'

He looked aghast. 'You are kidding me.'

'No, I'm not. Now, I don't know who was doing it, but you have to realise how it looks, smoking cannabis in my house. I am a police officer, for God's sake, Eddie.'

He frowned. 'It's not me, but I think I might know who it is and I'll have words with him or fire him if it comes to it.'

'Well, I don't think you need to go that far. Just make sure it never happens again.'

'Done. I won't be using the full load of guys again anyway, unless you want your garden sorted? I won't be doing that, but I know a bloke who does that kind of work.'

Jane yawned. 'Yeah, OK . . . whatever. I need to throw out a lot of the furniture and look at replacing it with some more contemporary stuff. I can wait for the garden to be sorted though.'

'It's up to you.' Eddie signalled for the bill.

Jane hardly said a word on the drive back to the house. When they parked up, Eddie rested his arm along the back of the seat and rubbed her neck.

'You sure everything is OK, Jane? I'll sort this cannabis situation tomorrow first thing.'

'It's nothing to do with that, Eddie, it's just this case. I'm starting to feel there's going to be some serious backlash from my Australia trip. My boss has really got it in for me. Everything in the police is now about budget, budget, budget and he's already suggested I've wasted valuable funds by going. But I just wanted to find the truth about what happened in that shelter.'

'So, did you find it?' Eddie asked.

'In a way. And it was pretty unsavoury.'

Eddie got out of the car and opened the door for her.

'You could do with a couple of days away . . . take a break.'

She laughed. 'I'd like that. But right now, if DCI Carter found me asking for a couple of days' leave when I've only just got back from Australia, he'd blow his top.'

'What about the weekend?' Eddie asked, as he unlocked the front door. They walked into the kitchen and Jane put her handbag down on the kitchen table.

'You know I said it was unsavoury, what had happened? It was actually much worse than that. I discovered their father had more than likely been having an incestuous relationship with his daughter who committed suicide.'

Eddie put the kettle on as Jane opened her briefcase and took out the envelope of photographs.

'He was a keen photographer and had a darkroom in the basement. This is what I found when I was in Australia.' Jane laid out the awful photos of Marjorie hanging from the swing. She then showed Eddie some of the nude pictures of Henry Lanark's daughters. He glanced at them briefly, shaking his head.

'He must have been a monster of a man to do this to his own daughters. I think they were home tutored, and probably very naïve, with a mother who, as far as I can make out, was immature herself, having been married off at a frighteningly young age.'

Eddie placed a mug of tea down on the table in front of her. 'So, what's your point?' he asked, returning to the kettle to fill his own mug.

'What do you mean, what's my point?' she asked, curtly.

'Well, it all happened so long ago . . . aren't two of them dead? Why are you getting so worked up about it?'

'I am not getting worked up,' Jane said.

'Yes, you are. I mean, if you know how the baby died in the air-raid shelter, then isn't that enough?'

Jane pursed her lips, gathered up the photographs and put them back in the envelope.

'Yes, you're right,' she said in a cold voice. 'Sorry if I'm boring you.'

'For Christ's sake, Jane, you aren't boring me. I'm just concerned about you. Maybe you're having trouble with your boss because he thinks, like I do, that there are more pressing crimes out there needing your attention . . .'

'He doesn't think like that. If you must know, the dirtbag even insinuated that he could get into my pants if he accompanied me to Australia. And for your information, I don't care if a crime was committed yesterday or twenty, thirty or forty years ago, it still deserves some kind of justice.'

Eddie held his hands up in a placating gesture. 'You are absolutely right. Look, I'm not going to get into this, but if you want my humble opinion as a lowly decorator-plumber-electrician, you say this lawyer bloke has known the old lady you think was murdered for years. So he must have handled all her legal documents and would know how much money she had and who she left it to and all that.'

Jane looked at him. 'Firstly, you are not a "lowly" anything. Secondly, I wish I'd thought of that. I'm going to call that lawyer right now.'

'Jane, it's half past eleven. I think you'd be better off leaving it till the morning. Plus you've had more than three quarters of a bottle of wine. I'm going to leave you to have a good night's sleep.'

'I'm sorry if I go on about my work too much. I want you to stay, Eddie.'

He put his arm around her as she stood up from the table.

'And showing me those photographs was unprofessional, if not illegal, so I'll have to arrest you,' he said tilting her head back and kissing her. She responded instantly, and even more so when he lifted her up and carried her out of the kitchen. She almost fell and, laughing, they walked up the stairs together.

* * *

Jane woke up, disorientated, then found the warmth of his body beside her and snuggled closer. She could see from her bedside clock that it was a quarter past four. She tried to go back to sleep, but then began to think about what Eddie had said to her in the kitchen. She knew she needed to talk to Hadley first thing, and also to call Sussex police again.

Eddie murmured in his sleep and she slipped her arm around him.

'Is it time to get up?' he muttered.

'No, not yet . . .' she said softly.

He turned towards her as she continued in a half-whisper, 'How about you and I go off together somewhere for a couple of days? I was thinking about a romantic trip to Brighton?'

'Whatever you say,' Eddie replied, tenderly. 'I can get my MG out of storage for the weekend.'

Jane closed her eyes. Brighton ... which just happened to be where Arnold Hadley lived.

CHAPTER TWENTY-FOUR

Eddie left early to go back to his flat and change into his work clothes. He also did a clean-up of his van, taking out the bag of weed and the rollup papers and stashing them under a floorboard in his flat.

When Jane arrived at the station at a quarter past eight, she dealt with the paperwork on her desk and completed filing the report from Australia. She then placed a call to the Sussex police and asked to speak to a DS Simpson, explaining to him that she had spoken to Helena Lanark at her care home in Hove before she died.

'There's a pearl necklace that missing from Miss Lanark's suite . . . I'm just calling for an update to see if you have any further information about that?'

'I don't I'm afraid, Detective Tennison. I did pay a visit, and I spoke to a couple of staff members, but nobody could give me any further details and Miss Thompson denied that any impropriety had occurred. She said it was quite possible that the deceased's nephew had taken it.'

'Well, Sergeant Simpson, a window was left open in Miss Lanark's suite, and some of the drawers looked as if they had been opened and searched.'

Jane hesitated before continuing.

'I think you should perhaps re-interview the staff. The pearl necklace is exceedingly valuable. It might be worth as much as £20,0000.'

Simpson whistled. 'Jesus Christ! Nobody mentioned that to me. In that case, there has to be a formal crime report.'

'I'll let you know as soon as I have a confirmed value,' Jane told him. 'If you wish to contact me in the meantime, I am working out of Stockwell police station, and I'll also give you my home number.'

Jane could sense the sergeant's anxiety as she gave him her contact details, and he said he would definitely return to the care home to make further inquiries.

Jane replaced the receiver and took out her notebook to check for Arnold Hadley's phone number. She had already noted that it was a Brighton dialling code and thought again about his close proximity to Helena Lanark's care home.

The phone rang three times before he answered.

'Mr Hadley, it's Jane Tennison. I know we spoke yesterday, but I have a few more questions I wanted to ask you. It's all a little sensitive so I'd prefer not to talk about it over the phone, but I am happy to come to Brighton.'

Hadley hesitated. 'Um . . .'

'Today, if possible, Mr Hadley.'

She heard him sigh. 'Would four o'clock suit you, Detective Tennison?'

'Yes, thank you, that would be fine. Could you give me your address?'

She could hear him coughing nervously, as if hesitant to give her his home address. After thanking him Jane hung up, tapping her notepad with her pen. Although she didn't know Brighton well, she was aware that Royal Crescent was one of the most affluent areas.

DS Hunt knocked on her door and popped his head in. 'There's a briefing going on about that hit and run.'

Jane glanced at her watch. 'Is it absolutely necessary for me to be there? I have a couple of pressing matters that I need to deal with on the Stockwell case.'

He raised his eyebrows. 'I thought that was all done and dusted after your trip to Australia?'

'Not quite. Tell the duty sergeant that I'll be out of the station. I'm due a couple of days' leave, and I'm still suffering from jet lag from that terrible long-haul flight back . . . but I should be back at my desk on Friday morning. Can you make sure it's put in the diary as well?'

'Will do, ma'am. And talking of Australia, poor old Taylor is being called Rudolph on account of his sunburned nose!'

Jane did her best to smile. 'Thank you, sarge.'

She fetched her coat and dialled her home number. It seemed to ring forever before one of Eddie's team answered.

'Hi, it's Jane. Is Eddie there?'

'Yeah . . . hang on a minute . . .' Jane heard him bellowing for Eddie to come to the phone and tapped her foot impatiently. She wanted to escape from the station before she was caught by Carter.

'Something wrong?' Eddie asked.

'No . . . on the contrary. I was wondering if you could get your MG out of storage sooner than the weekend?'

'What d'you mean?'

'It's just that I struck lucky and they've given me a couple of days leave, starting from today. I thought we might go to Brighton – and, in case you'd forgotten, we've got dinner with my parents on Friday.'

Eddie told Jane to hang on, and she heard him having a conversation with one of his team before he came back on the line.

'What time d'you want to leave?'

'How about lunchtime?' she answered. 'That way we'll miss the commuter traffic. I'll book the hotel.'

'OK. I'll be back here around one. I just need to go home and pack a bag before I pick up the MG but leave it to me to organise the hotel.'

'Fine, see you in a bit. I'm taking your advice, by the way,' Jane said.

'What advice?'

'Never mind . . . I'll tell you later.'

* * *

Jane was impressed when she saw Eddie's highly polished racing green MG, which certainly made a change from his van. She started packing excitedly, and Eddie told her not to forget a swimsuit.

'Are you crazy? The sea will be freezing!'

'Who said anything about going into the sea? There's a spa and pool at the hotel, with a jacuzzi and a hot tub. You can even have a massage if you want.'

Jane grinned, wondering where on earth he had booked for them to stay.

By the time they got to Brighton, it was almost half past two. They decided to stop on the seafront for fish and chips and Jane tentatively mentioned her visit to Hadley.

'I should have guessed you had an ulterior motive,' Eddie said, smiling.

'You were the one who suggested it!' Jane replied. 'I'll only be gone for an hour or so. I said I'd see him at four, then we'll have the entire evening together and the whole of tomorrow.'

They got back in the car, and after a few minutes. Jane was taken aback when Eddie pulled up in front of The Grand hotel.

She laughed. 'Eddie! Are we really staying here?'

He grinned. 'We have an amazing suite with a dining room, bathroom and a canopy bed. I got a good price because it's mid-week. We can order room service tonight and really make the most of it, if you like.'

When she saw their room, with its spectacular sea view, Jane was even more impressed. And Eddie's obvious desire to make their visit special made it even nicer.

They unpacked a few things and Jane said she would take a taxi to meet with Mr Hadley, then come straight back to the hotel. Eddie pulled out his swimming trunks and said he would go for a swim and sauna in the spa.

'We can have a walk on the beach and then a really nice dinner in the suite when you get back,' he said.

When the taxi dropped her off at Hadley's address, Jane was just as impressed at the size of the double-fronted terraced house, situated on the end of the famous crescent. It was facing the sea, with flowering tubs on the porch and neat, well-kept window boxes placed on the ledges. Iron railings led down the basement area which seemed to be part of the same house, unlike many of the houses in that area that had been converted into flats.

When Arnold Hadley opened the door, wearing a fair isle sweater with dark brown cords and a pair of leather slippers, he seemed quite different from the stooping, aged figure she remembered. He still had a greyish pallor to his face, but otherwise he seemed younger and more relaxed.

'Detective Tennison,' he said, affably, gesturing for her to come in as he closed the door behind her.

He gestured down the hallway towards an open double door.

'Please, do make yourself comfortable.'

Jane went into a large, sun-lit room. It was extremely tastefully furnished, albeit rather old-fashioned. On a table was a tray of tea and biscuits, the teapot covered in a knitted tea cosy.

'It's Darjeeling,' he said, gesturing to the teapot. 'But if you prefer Tetley or something like that, I have that in the kitchen.'

Jane smiled. 'No, this will be fine . . . thank you.'

She watched as he deftly poured tea into a gold-rimmed porcelain cup.

'Do you take sugar?' he asked.

'No, thank you . . . just a splash of milk, please.'

'He walked over to the large wing-back chair where Jane was sitting and put her tea down on a small side table. He then returned to pour one for himself, choosing to sit on a Chesterfield sofa opposite her.

Jane glanced at the numerous silver-framed photographs on the mantelpiece, as well as on the various shelves of a floor-to-ceiling bookcase. Jane had no idea if Hadley was married or had children and was about to ask when he got to his feet. Apologising for not offering her a biscuit he proffered the plate.

'Digestive, bourbon or custard cream,' he said. 'Nothing very interesting, I'm afraid.'

She chose a digestive and Hadley returned to the sofa, taking a bourbon for himself.

'Thank you so much for agreeing to see me, Mr Hadley. I just need to ask a few questions that I think might help me fill in some important gaps. When I spoke to you on the phone, I asked how well you had known Miss Lanark. I think you mentioned to me that she was a neighbour of your mother. Did you know her purely on a professional level, or as a personal friend?'

Hadley placed his cup and saucer down on the coffee table in front of him and leaned back into the Chesterfield.

'As I told you, I met Helena many years ago, not in London but in Totnes, where I was brought up. I had left home to study law at Bristol, and had just qualified. I was hoping to find a practice in London, but I was concerned because my mother was becoming exceedingly frail. Helena, who worked in the local library, looked after her when she had a bad fall and they became friends.'

He closed his eyes.

'Helena and I became friends. When I went home, sometimes I clipped Helena's hedges or mowed her lawn. She lived very frugally, although she was always exceedingly well dressed. I found her shyness touching, but I was quite concerned about how cold her house was. It wasn't my place to inquire, but I assumed she had no money apart from her meagre salary as a librarian. Anyway, to cut a long story short, my poor dear mother died. Helena was a great help, because by this time I had moved to London. I wrote a letter to her, thanking her for her kindness, and we began to write regularly to each other over a number of years. I then received a request from her asking for my help and she made an appointment to come in to see me at my London office. As I said, she was always beautifully dressed, and she had the most wonderful blue eyes . . . but I digress. Helena said she had a family situation which she needed my advice about. She was receiving demands for financial help from her sister in Australia.'

Jane had taken out her notebook and was writing as fast as she could. She looked up. 'That would be Beatrice?'

Hadley nodded. 'Yes, Beatrice. Helena wanted me to forward money to her sister as she had been left a widow with two young sons.'

There was a long pause as Hadley sat with his head resting back on the Chesterfield sofa. Jane coughed gently and he opened his eyes.

'It was rather a surprise to discover that Helena Lanark was an exceedingly wealthy woman. She had substantial shares in a variety of companies and numerous bank accounts. She owned her small cottage in Totnes, as well as the substantial property in Stockwell. And yet she lived so frugally. I couldn't understand it.'

Jane raised her hand to interrupt him. 'Could you give me an estimate of her wealth?'

He pursed his lips. 'Oh, it ran into many millions, if you include the property in Stockwell, which she eventually told me had been her family home. She made it clear to me that she did not want to sell it, and it was to remain uninhabited. When I pointed out that this was rather illogical, given the size of the house and the extensive gardens which were all being left unattended, she simply said that was what she wanted.'

Jane took some more notes, then looked back up at Hadley. 'So, these payments to her family in Australia, were they frequent?'

He nodded. 'I have to admit, Detective Tennison, I became concerned because she had apparently been parting with very large amounts of money over a lengthy period, even before she came to see me. Then her nephew, Jason Thorpe, began calling me personally. I had sent them a letter, without Helena's knowledge, saying that I was concerned about the amount of money being forwarded to them. I also informed him that Helena's health was deteriorating. Jason then suggested that he should be given power of attorney. He also had the audacity to suggest that Helena's legal representation should be reviewed.'

There was another long pause before Hadley shrugged his shoulders. 'He had a meeting with Helena and myself and she agreed he should have power of attorney, although there were some legal provisions attached. So there you have it.'

'Mr Hadley, do you believe that there may have been blackmail involved?'

Hadley's response was startling because he gave a rather loud, barking laugh.

'Of course, there was! But Helena never told me what it was about. I suspected something was not right because she always seemed tense and angry when dealing with her family, but I could do nothing. She was adamant they should continue to get the money and, although you saw her in a very frail state, she was an astute businesswoman. She gave large sums of money to her sister and her nephew, but she attached a caveat which gave her the right to oversee her nephew's wine import business. She asked me to take care of her other financial investments and I hoped the payments to Australia were ultimately loans that would be paid back when his business became successful.'

He smiled wryly.

'She found Jason to be very much a showman when it came to his business. The company addresses on his business cards were Wall Street, Mayfair and Hong Kong, even though the only office he actually had was a small rented room above a garage in Queen's Gate Mews.'

'Did you have any inkling at all why she was being blackmailed?'

Hadley shook his head. 'Helena refused to talk about it, saying that it was a family matter and none of my concern. But she clearly felt it necessary to keep her sister happy, and preferably on the other side of the world.'

'How did Helena react when she discovered Jason Thorpe wanted to sell the Stockwell property?'

'Initially he didn't want to sell it; dividing it into four different apartments and renting them out would be more lucrative in the long term. At first Helena said that couldn't happen, but with his persistence, and maybe even my encouragement, she eventually agreed – as long as the basement was not to be occupied and the rear garden never to be used by the tenants.'

'Do you know if Helena ever went to the property?'

He shook his head sadly. 'That would've been rather difficult.'

'I don't understand.'

'By this time Helena was suffering from severe osteoarthritis in both legs and was virtually confined to a wheelchair. Her nephew hired the company that did the renovations, but years later, due to mismanagement and poor maintenance, he had no option but to sell the house to developers who were proposing to demolish it and build a large block of flats in its place.'

'And Helena knew about this?' Jane asked.

'I did inform her of Jason's intentions but I'm afraid that by this time Helena had early onset dementia and often could not recall owning the property, or ever having lived there. At times she didn't even know who I was. I contacted Jason some time later and suggested that Helena needed to go into a care home. Anyway, as you know, there were extensive and costly delays to the demolition work and the development company began to hesitate about the deal going through. Jason was very concerned.'

'That could explain why he eventually sold the property below market value,' Jane surmised.

'Yes, I suppose so . . . he's a sly one, is Jason. He's always got an answer when you challenge his actions. I still find it odd that he never told me about the company shares he acquired.'

'He'd probably say he bought them for Helena's benefit, in an effort to recoup financial losses from the sale, which as her representative with power of attorney is his prerogative.'

Hadley sighed as he nodded in agreement. Jane didn't feel the need to pursue the matter any further and closed her notebook.

'I can't thank you enough, Mr Hadley. You really have been very helpful. As you know, it was the events in the shelter that led me to go and see Helena. Whilst I was in Australia, Beatrice told me that the baby whose body we uncovered had been born to her other sister Marjorie.'

'Yes, I knew Marjorie had taken her own life, but Helena never spoke of it.'

'I believe Marjorie was terrified their father would find out she was pregnant. Helena buried the baby in the shelter, which is probably the reason she would never go back to the house.'

Hadley shrugged his shoulders. 'Surely this is all supposition? Marjorie committed suicide, Helena can't confirm any of these accusations, and Beatrice is clearly untrustworthy. Helena used to say that Beatrice took after their mother. I don't believe that Helena could ever have done such a terrible thing.'

Jane stood up. 'Well, we may never know the whole truth, but there's no doubt Helena was her father's sole heir after Marjorie killed herself. Helena and her father must have been close.'

Hadley nodded. 'I know that she cared for him during his last years, when he was very ill. She adored him, I think. Why she chose to move from London to Devon and live such a frugal life, she never discussed with me, but it was fortunate for me, because that was how we met.'

'And then, it seems, Jason and his mother started blackmailing her. I have to say, I found Jason an extremely unpleasant man.'

'He is an obnoxious creature,' Hadley agreed. 'And Beatrice at times is no better. But I also felt very sympathetic towards her because of her son Matthew's illness.'

Hadley picked up Jane's cup and saucer and put them back on the tray.

'Well, I think I must have answered all your questions now,' he said, suddenly seeming eager for her to leave.

Jane headed towards the double doors, then paused. On a bureau which she had not seen when she had entered the room was a row of silver-framed photographs. In one of them was the same photograph she had seen in Helena's album of the three sisters standing by the swing. She stopped so suddenly that Hadley almost bumped into the back of her.

'I've seen this photograph, and several similar, in Helena's family album.'

Hadley tensed as Jane picked up one photograph after another. She then saw one photograph lying face down and turned it over.

It was a picture of a younger Helena standing beside Arnold Hadley, holding a small bouquet.

Jane looked up. 'Who owns this house, Mr Hadley?'

'Well, as a matter of fact, I do.'

'Is this where Helena lived after she left Devon?'

He shrugged, reaching to take the photograph, but Jane held onto it.

'So, Helena lived here with you, in Brighton?'

Hadley hesitated, then sighed.

'Helena was my wife.' He took the photograph from Jane, carefully putting it back upright.

Jane had not been expecting his revelation.

'May I ask why you never told me you were married until now?'

'She wanted our marriage to be a private affair so, as always, I respected her wishes and we kept it to ourselves. In the end, we only had few years together here in Brighton before she became ill.'

'So did Helena buy this property?'

Hadley seemed slightly embarrassed. 'I also had a substantial legacy from my mother, so we simply bought it together.'

'But the house is in your name?' Jane asked, flatly.

'Yes, it was her wedding gift to me.'

Jane looked at the shelves above the bureau and saw the photograph album belonging to Helena.

'You have the album?' Jane said, moving closer.

'Yes, I brought it back with me from the care home, along with her belongings.'

Jane opened the album and turned to the number of empty spaces.

'I noticed there were missing photographs . . . perhaps they were of you?'

'No, no . . . this album was only for her family. She was obsessive about it. The missing photographs are here.'

Hadley eased open one of the small drawers in the bureau, taking out a creased manila envelope.

Jane watched as he withdrew a number of photographs, browned and tinged with age. He laid them out along the bureau. They were of Helena's mother in a ball gown, standing beside a handsome, young, dark-eyed man. There were two more photographs of the same young man standing next to a grand piano, with Muriel Lanark leaning coquettishly against it.

'Is that the Russian music teacher, Mikhail?' Jane asked.

'I believe so. Helena told me very little about him, just that there was some gossip and unpleasant rumours and he was sent away. Their mother Muriel was so beautiful, and so young when she married. Marjorie inherited her looks. But Beatrice was scathing about her mother . . . she even admitted stealing some of her mother's jewellery when she ran away to Australia.'

Jane nodded. 'Yes, I know about that. I believe Beatrice did try to reclaim some of the items from the pawnbrokers, but it was all so many years ago it was a rather fruitless endeavour.'

Jane turned one page after another in the album before she found a picture of Muriel Lanark wearing not only the three strings of pearls but a high-necked choker of smaller ones with what looked like a sumptuous emerald-and-diamond brooch.

'The pearl necklace . . . Mr Hadley, I was told by Beatrice that each of the Lanark girls was given a strand. Helena received the longest strand, then Beatrice the next longest, and the smallest one went to Marjorie.'

'I am unsure of the details,' Hadley said. 'But I know Helena wore her pearls frequently. I think she did ask Beatrice about the second strand, but I was never told if she had sold them.'

'Do you have any idea of their value?' Jane asked.

Hadley shook his head. Jane went to her bag and took out the photograph of the Russian empress wearing the three strands of pearls. She did not show Hadley any of the other images.

'This photograph is a possible provenance to establish the value. Beatrice mentioned to me that the pearls had been given to her grandmother, the countess, by a Russian aristocrat.'

Hadley peered at the photograph. 'I have never seen this before.'

'Mr Hadley, as you know, Helena's pearls went missing from the care home. I have spoken to the Sussex police who are looking into it and making a formal theft report.'

Hadley frowned. 'Do you really think that's necessary? I mean, they were so caring to Helena for so many years . . .'

'I don't believe any of Helena's carers took them. And Jason Thorpe was the last visitor to see her.'

Hadley pursed his lips and nodded. 'I will search through the insurance, but I had no notion they could be of great value.'

Jane was about to close the album, but then turned to the last page.

'Mr Hadley, you see these small cardboard grips? I found some loose photographs, and pages of what looked like a family tree.'

'Oh yes, that was another obsession of Helena's. Her father had begun to map out the family tree, but I think after Marjorie's tragic death . . .'

He paused, before continuing.

'Helena used to spend hours communicating with births, deaths and marriages, but she told me that after the war so many dates were missing or didn't match up. I think she found it difficult to get the exact date of her sister's death, then her mother died and shortly afterwards Beatrice went running off to Australia. She also inferred that her father was adept at altering documents due to his experience running a printing company, so it was very difficult for her to establish exact dates of births, deaths, marriages, etcetera. Subsequently her father fell ill with cancer, and she looked after him, as I mentioned earlier, until he too died. She also discovered certain discrepancies concerning Beatrice's marriage, as well as the births of her sons.'

He sighed, shaking his head.

'But when the dementia made it impossible for her to concentrate, nothing interested her. I cared for her as best I could, and I believe I was able to make her final years more bearable. Dementia is a wicked illness. She was such a literate woman, but she became so silent. I recall one afternoon I had been for my usual walk along the beach, and she was sitting in here. The radio was turned on and she gave me this extraordinary smile. Her wonderful blue eyes were often vacant but that afternoon they were so expressive. She said, "I think I am dying as Daddy came to see me. He asked if his boy was thinking of him. He always said that I was like the son he had always wanted."'

Hadley blinked.

'She adored her father and would never hear a word against him. She spent years alone with him in that house, tending to his every whim, and in all honesty, although we were content, it sometimes felt as if she had given all the love she had to her father. But that afternoon, she was happy. I knelt down beside her wheelchair, she traced my face with her fingers and then whispered to me that she had completed the puzzle. It was over. Later that evening, after she had retired, I noticed that the phone receiver was placed the wrong way round. I knew it must have been Helena. I was surprised, as she very rarely called anyone.'

He closed the album and replaced it on top of the bureau, slipping the photographs back into their creased envelope. Jane made no mention of the fact that she still had the family tree.

'Mr Hadley, had Helena made a will?'

He hesitated and then nodded.

'Do you have a copy of it, that I could see?'

'The will, Detective Tennison, is kept at my old firm. It required two witnesses and obviously, as her husband, I was unable to be one of the signatories.'

'But even if you could not be a signatory, you must have been privy to the contents, surely?' Jane said.

He shook his head. 'Helena had insisted she should be alone with my partners in the firm.'

Jane had no further questions and thanked Mr Hadley for his time.

On her way out, she noticed an expensive-looking woman's tweed coat hanging on the rack in the hall, with a pair of female walking shoes beneath it. Hadley saw her looking at them as he ushered her towards the front door.

'They belonged to Helena. She wore them when we went for walks along the beach. I was going to take them to a charity shop ages ago, but they are a constant reminder of the happy times we had together when she was well.'

'You must miss her terribly, Mr Hadley, but happy memories hopefully ease the pain.'

After closing the front door he took the tweed coat off its hook, placing it over one arm as he picked up the walking shoes. He remembered he used to love the way she rested against him as she slipped her feet into her brogues, and when he bent down to tie the laces and flip the fringed leather tongue over, she would gently pat his head.

But he had been so very lonely for so long, now it was perhaps time to move forward.

* * *

Back at the hotel, Jane found Eddie freshly showered, saying that he had done a terrific workout. There was an endearing boyishness to him as he excitedly read out the dishes on the room service menu, and Jane found herself more attracted to him than ever. She chose the steak with Béarnaise sauce, chips and a side salad, and Eddie opted for the same. As he called room service to place their order, he covered the mouthpiece and asked if they could make do with what was in the mini-bar, or whether they should order some wine. Jane quickly glanced at the wine list and pointed to a bottle of Merlot.

Whilst Eddie finished ordering their dinner, Jane undressed and wrapped herself in the large white fluffy towelling bathrobe provided by the hotel. On seeing her about to take a shower, Eddie quickly started stripping off.

'Room for two in there?' He grinned.

Jane sensed that this was going to be a positive break away, in more than one way.

* * *

At eight o'clock Jane and Eddie sat perched on the edge of their bed, both wrapped in the hotel towelling robes, patiently watching the waiter wheel in their dinner. He pulled open the leaves of the trolley to transform it into a table. Two large silver domes covered their plates and, after pouring their wine – which Eddie tasted and declared perfect – the waiter pulled off the covers with a flourish before departing.

Eddie frowned, asking Jane if he should have tipped him, but Jane dismissed it, saying that if they had the same waiter for breakfast, they could tip him then. She was now desperate to update Eddie on her visit to Arnold Hadley, and he listened attentively while he ate his steak and dipped his chips into the little bowl of tomato ketchup. Jane waved her knife in the air expressively, telling Eddie that as soon as she got back to the station, she was going to find out when Helena had made her will. She also wanted to look into her marriage to Arnold Hadley, as well as looking into Hadley's finances. She told Eddie that if they took a walk later, she could show him the big house on the crescent.

Eddie poured himself another glass of wine, trying hard to show genuine interest. He was struggling to grasp all the facts as Jane went into more and more detail, explaining her suspicion that Hadley married Helena Lanark for her money. She was certain he'd been lying about being unaware of the extent of her wealth or the contents of her will.

'I want to nail down all these dates because I have a gut feeling that Helena Lanark was being blackmailed over the death of the child. I also want to find out the exact dates when Jason Thorpe gained power of attorney, because surely it would have made more sense if Helena had given it to Hadley before they even married—'

Eddie interrupted. 'Helena's dead! She was probably being blackmailed because she committed a terrible crime. But you told me before she wouldn't have stood trial for the child's murder due to her dementia ... so, what's the point spending so much time finding out all these details? I thought your boss at the station told you it was "case closed" anyway?'

Irritated, Jane poured herself another glass of wine. 'It's my job, Eddie, and all I'm doing is trying to find the truth.'

'But it's not your business, is it?' Eddie said.

'Yes, of course it is!' she snapped.

There was a moment of tense silence, then Eddie picked up the room service menu and asked if she would like to order a dessert, or they could take a walk on the pier and have an ice cream.

Jane begrudgingly agreed to the latter. It was beginning to feel as though she was repeating a relationship pattern and was incapable of finding a partner who was as interested in her work as she was. But at least Eddie hadn't said that discussing her work was boring.

Any awkwardness had dispersed by the time they were walking hand in hand down the sea front, heading towards the pier. There was something very carefree about eating an ice cream under the stars at ten o'clock at night, Jane thought. They had just sat down on a bench to look at the lights when Eddie patted his pocket and turned to her.

'I've got a spliff, just cannabis nothing else.'

'What?'

'I mean, I know how you feel about it and I have given my guy a good ticking off about smoking it in your house.'

'So why have you got a spliff, as you call it?'

'Well, I am being honest with you because I do, very occasionally, have one with him.'

'But why bring it with you?'

'Well, you know, sometimes I get a bit wound up when you start going on about this case of yours, and I don't want to get on the wrong side of you.'

She looked incredulous. 'You are joking?'

Jane shook her head, sighing as he removed from his pocket the small, thin, wrapped spliff, holding it between his thumb and forefinger.

'Are you going to light it up now?'

'I was thinking that you might like to try it with me,' Eddie said.

'Eddie, you must be crazy. I can't believe you are even asking me to. For God's sake, it's illegal and I am a police officer. Someone could walk past, smell it and then the next minute we'd be arrested.'

'Fine, if that's how you feel, but we're out in the open, fresh sea air and there's hardly a soul around. I just thought if you've never done it . . .'

'All right.'

'What?'

'I said, all right.'

Eddie lit up the joint, instructing Jane to take a big lungful, then slowly exhale.

'Like this.' He took a deep drag and handed it to Jane

She gave a cautious look around.

'I can't believe I'm doing this.'

Jane took a drag, then passed it back. Between them they finished the spliff and he carefully stubbed out the end with the toe of his boot.

'Well, I can't feel anything at all,' she said. 'It just tastes worse than a cigarette.'

'Lots of people use this for pain relief, you know. I've been told in the US they get it on prescription.'

'Don't be ridiculous, it's illegal,' Jane said, then suddenly started to giggle.

Then Eddie bent down to pick up the remnant he'd stubbed out, and toppled over.

'Jusht collecting the evidence, shir, to put into the bin.'

They walked back to the hotel arm in arm, both laughing uncontrollably.

* * *

The following morning, after a lazy breakfast in bed, they strolled on the beach for a couple of hours, then had lunch in the hotel restaurant before returning to London. Jane was feeling so relaxed that she actually laughed when he pointed out that they had almost spent an entire day together without her mentioning her case!

When they arrived back at her house, Eddie said he would go and put his beloved MG back under wraps in his garage and that he would see her in the morning before she went to work.

'Don't forget we're having dinner with my parents tomorrow,' Jane said. 'You know, it would be nice to go in the MG.'

'I haven't forgotten. I'll be in my best suit, but I'll need the van tomorrow.'

She waved him off and let herself in, going straight up to her bedroom. The sea air had exhausted her, so she had a long, relaxing bath and was just about to get into bed when her phone rang.

'Inspector Tennison?'

'Speaking . . .' She didn't recognise the voice.

'It's DS Alan Simpson, Sussex police. I just wanted to give you an update. I spent the afternoon at the care home questioning the staff about the missing pearls. I also I had a chat with Miss Thompson and she told me that one of the young carers had broken down in tears and admitted she had taken the necklace. She said it was on the table by the bed, and she made out that she'd just taken it to give to Miss Thompson.'

Simpson explained that the girl was going to be sacked and there were no plans to take the matter any further.

Before finishing the call, Jane gave DC Simpson Arnold Hadley's contact number so that he could arrange to return the necklace to him.

Jane's good mood had gone. She was now annoyed at herself for wasting so much time on her theory that Jason Thorpe took the necklace. She flopped back onto her pillow and closed her eyes, but her mind wouldn't stop spinning. Beatrice had said that the strand which had been given to Marjorie had been buried with her, but Marjorie had been cremated, so had that all been a lie? Jane tossed and turned, thinking about Beatrice's repeated stories of how cruel Helena had been to her, ignoring her letters begging for financial help. Yet according to Hadley, Jane had been paying Beatrice considerable sums for years, enough to enable her to purchase a substantial waterfront property in a sought-after area of Sydney. None of it added up!

Unable to sleep, Jane went down to the kitchen and made herself a cup of tea. Her mind kept going over and over the facts again. Why had Jason come to her house and demanded the photograph album, lying about his mother being frail and needing it, and lying that he was just about to depart for Australia when he had actually visited Helena in the care home? Why did Jason then leave the album there with Helena? Did he leave the window open so he could return later that night, but changed his mind? But if he had intended to steal the pearls, why hadn't he just taken them? Was it Jason who had been searching through Helena's desk and bedroom?

One thing she was certain of was that Jason did not know the truth about the sisters' complicity in burying the baby. And he had clearly been shocked when Beatrice had mentioned her father's abuse.

Back in her bedroom, Jane searched through her dressing table drawers for a packet of cigarettes, smoking one as she finished her tea. She thought about smoking the joint the previous night, and what a stupid risk it had been on her part. She would certainly never do it again.

She could not stop wondering why Jason Thorpe had spun so many lies about the photo album and why he had really been so keen to get hold of it. Jane had found the family tree – could that be what he was searching for? Or was it a copy of Helena's will?

Jane sighed and turned off her bedside light. She would contact Hadley's legal firm in the morning.

CHAPTER TWENTY-FIVE

As Jane was having breakfast with Eddie the following morning, they discussed the stair carpet and curtains. He was going to be at the house all day doing some final touch-ups, so he suggested they spend Saturday measuring up and ordering the last furnishings, as the decoration work was nearly finished.

'I slept like a log after all that sea air, did you?' he said.

Jane smiled. 'I was tired, but my brain kept going over everything Hadley told me. I concluded that Jason Thorpe might have been looking for Helena's will and maybe thought it was kept in her family album.'

Eddie rolled his eyes, smiled and shook his head. 'You're like a dog with a bone!'

Jane arrived at the station by eight and wrote up her report about her visit to Hadley. She waited until ten before calling Hadley, McKenzie & March, the legal firm that Hadley had worked for. When she asked about Helena Lanark's will, she was put through to a man called Kevin McKenzie, who recalled her coming to their offices to execute it. Jane asked what date that would have been, and he responded that it had been some time in the 1970s, but due to client confidentiality he was unable to give any further details, except to say that it was Helena's second will.

When Jane asked when the first will had been written, she was told that it was in 1975. On inquiring whether this was the time Jason Thorpe had been given power of attorney, she was hesitantly informed that it was.

Jane then asked McKenzie if at this time he had known that Arnold Hadley was married to Helena Lanark. At first, he declined to answer the question on grounds of client confidentiality, until Jane informed him Hadley had already told her they were married.

McKenzie replied curtly that Arnold had told him they were married as it would be unethical for him to be a co-signatory on Helena's second will.

'Did Helena Lanark ever call you to make amendments to her new will?' Jane asked.

'She did, but she had become very unwell and required a wheelchair, so I made a private visit to her home in Brighton.'

'Was Arnold Hadley present when the private meetings took place?'

There was an indignant intake of breath. 'Arnold was not present, but here at our offices, as he was still a practicing solicitor.'

'So, he was not necessarily privy to any changes made by Miss Lanark.'

'Certainly not through me. Whether or not Miss Lanark informed him of her wishes would obviously have been her business.'

After ending the call, Jane contacted the Public Registry Office in Devon, who had no record of a marriage between Helena Lanark and Arnold Hadley. However, Deaths and Marriages in Brighton were able to confirm that they held a marriage certificate dated 1971.

Jane took some time in trying to unravel Hadley's finances and was surprised to discover that his mother had left her son £20,000. She then contacted several estate agents in Brighton, finally establishing that the house had been sold for £25,000 in 1971. It appeared that Arnold Hadley had told her the truth. However, Jane was still no closer to discovering the extent of Helena's wealth, or the precise date on which Helena had been admitted to the care home.

After further investigation, she was able to ascertain that Helena had been transferred to the care home in July 1976 so, as Hadley had stated, they had only had a few years living together in Brighton. Finally, she checked with the developers regarding the Stockwell property. The owner of the company informed her that due to various problems prior to the sale, they had intended to withdraw their offer. However, when Jason Thorpe reduced the price they changed their minds, purchased the property and offered him share options in the company, all of which was legally documented. Jane still suspected Jason Thorpe might have benefitted financially but now knew proving it would be a lengthy, if not impossible, task.

Her research had taken virtually all day and Jane's head was aching by the end of it. She called Eddie to ask if he could collect her from the station.

'I think you were right,' she said.

'What about?'

'I've worked all day checking everything out and it appears that Arnold Hadley told me the truth. I still think Beatrice and Jason Thorpe were blackmailing Helena, but I doubt that Hadley had any ulterior motives as he inherited a substantial amount from his mother . . . though it was nothing compared with the fortune I believe Helena inherited.'

'Oh, well . . . actually, I was going to ask you for a couple of grand for a new van,' Eddie joked.

Jane asked if he was being serious, and Eddie became rather embarrassed. Jane insisted that if he needed the money, she was prepared to lend it to him.

'What time will you be home?' he asked, changing the subject.

'That's why I'm calling. I need to sort out a few things that I should have been doing instead of all this research. Would you be able to collect me from the station so that we can go straight to my parents'?'

'Sure. I'll park up outside at about seven.'

* * *

Jane finished her paperwork and went into the incident room to file it, as DC Taylor approached her.

'Is the briefing still going on?' she asked him.

'It's just finishing . . . I was called out to the front desk because Arnold Hadley's here again, asking to speak to you on an urgent matter.'

'Is he still at the desk?'

'No, I took him into interview room one.'

Jane was just about to go and see him when DCI Carter banged into the room, carrying a stack of documents.

'Well, well, DI Tennison. Decided to show your face after taking two days off for travel fatigue, wasn't it? Best excuse I've had to date.'

'I've been catching up on everything I had on my desk, and I've filed a report,' Jane said, not rising to the bait. 'But I've just been told that Mr Hadley is here.'

'Who?'

'He's Helena Lanark's lawyer. Apparently, he needs to speak to me on an urgent matter.'

'Risen from the dead, has she?'

'It may have some connection to her funeral, which I think is taking place on Monday. If you don't need me for anything, I'd like to speak to him.'

'I will be bloody relieved when that entire situation is put to bed. I have to give a final report to Superintendent Beattie tonight, which includes the costs of your trip to Australia and the outcome.'

'I did put a report on your desk, sir.'

'Strange as it may seem, Tennison, I do have other calls on my time. If one of us needs to be present at the funeral, then by all means you go. I am due in court on Monday.'

* * *

Mr Hadley immediately stood up when Jane entered the interview room.

'Thank you for seeing me, Detective Tennison. I am here by way of a warning. Earlier today, Jason Thorpe assaulted me while I was at my old offices.'

Jane couldn't hide her shock. 'I'm so sorry, Mr Hadley, can you tell me what happened?' Jane pulled out a chair to sit down opposite him.

'He flew in from Sydney last night, with his mother,' Hadley began. 'He arrived at the offices this morning, initially saying he was there to discuss the funeral on Monday. While he was there, he demanded that Helena's will be read to him, but my former partner, Kevin McKenzie, told him that since his power of attorney had expired on Helena's death, he could not accede to this request, as Helena had stipulated that her will would be read after the burial.'

Hadley was clearly nervous and had to take out a handkerchief to pat his perspiring brow.

'Jason became enraged and refused to believe Helena and I had been married. When Kevin McKenzie confirmed our marriage was legal, Jason became threatening and abusive, claiming that if Helena had changed her will it must have been while she was suffering from dementia. Kevin told him every legal precaution was taken to ensure Helena's new will was legitimate, and it had been made when she was of sound mind.'

'How did Jason react to that?'

'He now suspected Helena had left him and Beatrice nothing and blamed me. I'd had enough of his behaviour and told him he was right. I then told him Helena left me her share of his wine export company, and unless he repays a percentage of the monies loaned to him, I would become sole proprietor. It was at that point he punched me before leaving.'

Jane gasped. 'Good heavens! Did you call the police?'

'No, I came straight here to inform you of the incident.'

'Do you want to press charges?' Jane asked.

'I suppose I can understand his anger, so the answer is no. I just felt it was necessary to warn you that he is in a volatile state.'

Hadley stood up and removed an envelope from his jacket pocket, handing it to Jane.

'I think you should read this letter. It's a copy as I have retained the original for legal reasons. The letter was only to be read after Helena's death. I think it might help you conclude your investigations. Helena will be buried at St Martin's on Monday at half past ten, but I doubt there will be many mourners. One more thing . . . her beloved pearl necklace. It is as valuable as you suspected. At first, I felt I should donate it to the library where she worked for so many years, but perhaps it would be more fitting for me to give it to Beatrice . . .'

Reaching into his pocket, he took out a large, worn leather wallet and searched through it.

'Kevin McKenzie told me that some years ago Helena had been dealing with Cartier and placed some items of jewellery in their safety deposit box. One item they had details of is a single strand of pearls. They gave me this newspaper cutting and the small photograph.'

Hadley passed the fragile newspaper cutting that had a photograph of the Duchess of Windsor wearing a double-stranded pearl choker.

'If you read the notes – I believe to have been written by Helena – she was seeking to purchase a strand of pearls similar to that worn by the duchess. I suspect she showed them this photograph to ensure they found a match to the length of pearls inherited from her mother.'

She looked up as Hadley next passed her a small cardboard-backed sepia photograph. Written in the same writing underneath was 'Marjorie aged twelve'. She was naked, her hands covering her small breasts and her knees drawn up with her feet crossed. Her thick curls fell to her shoulders, and around her neck was a single strand of perfectly matching pearls.

'Does this mean Helena acquired the necklace after Marjorie died?' Jane asked.

He shook his head. 'Oh, I very much doubt that. I would suspect that Beatrice took it, then sold it when she left England. I think Helena wanted to have a copy made in memory of Marjorie. I certainly know she paid Cartier a vast amount of money for them. I think it would be fitting if Beatrice was allowed to have Helena's and the strand from Cartier so all three strands could be worn together.'

'I think that is very generous of you,' Jane said. 'I noticed she was wearing hers when we met in Australia.'

'I intend to give her as much support as I can,' Hadley continued, 'because whatever the long-standing unpleasantness was between her and Helena, they were still sisters.'

Jane nodded thoughtfully. 'Can I ask you something? I remember you telling me how Helena looked the time you returned from a walk. You said that she told you she had completed the puzzle. What do you think she meant by that?'

Hadley sighed. 'I really don't know. Until I told you about it, I hadn't really given it much thought. The significance for me was that it was the last time she appeared to be coming back, but it was sadly short-lived, the light in her eyes never returned.'

Jane turned the photograph over. Printed on the back were the words 'The Dark Room'. Hadley held his hand out as she passed it to him.

'It's such a disturbing image of a young girl.'

Jane said nothing as he quickly put the photograph in his jacket pocket.

'Thank you for your time, Inspector Tennison. Now, if you will excuse me, I need to catch my train home.'

Jane ushered Mr Hadley out of the interview room, eager to read the letter he'd given her. She went into her office and opened the envelope.

To whom it may concern

You have no comprehension of the horrors I have had to live with. I have never loved anyone in my life, except my father. Arnold Hadley gave me a semblance of what I could have had. I want to show my appreciation for all the years of care and attention Arnold gave to my business, and eventually his kindness in loving me.

I wish to make my sister, Beatrice, and my nephew, Jason, aware of my loathing for them. They have never thanked me or shown me any respect or kindness. All they wanted was my money. Beatrice knew what I had done. She used it against me to ensure her silence and forced me to finance her life in Australia after marrying a man my father detested, and with good reason. Beatrice was not legally married at the time of her first son's birth and there are questions regarding Jason's bloodline and his right to any Lanark inheritance. I have lived with the knowledge of what I did, and I blame myself for Marjorie's suicide, but I could not allow her baby to live. It would have destroyed my father.

I have never asked for forgiveness, and I punished myself my entire life. Now I hope God will embrace me and lay me beside my beloved father.

Helena Lanark

Jane read the letter over twice before making a copy for herself and replacing the original copy back in the envelope. It was now after six and she knew that, as DCI Carter had to update the superintendent on the entire investigation, she should share with him what she had just read.

Jane picked up her coat and bag before going into the incident room. The late shift was just coming on duty, and she exchanged a few nods and smiles before knocking on the door of Carter's office. Impatient to give him what she felt was such a definitive conclusion to the inquiry, she opened the door.

Carter was standing over Barbara, who was sitting on his desk, her legs apart and her skirt rucked up around her buttocks. They both looked at her, shocked, and quickly rearranged themselves.

Jane was hardly able to keep a straight face as she held out the envelope. 'I felt this was important, sir. It's a copy of a letter written by Helena Lanark . . .'.

Carter snatched it from her, removed the letter and quickly read it.

'Where did you get this?'

'Arnold Hadley gave it to me. He has the original.'

'It sounds like the rantings of a bitter old woman . . . but at least the confession means case closed.'

'What about Beatrice Thorpe and her son Jason blackmailing her?'

'Your star witness is dead! She never made a formal complaint of blackmail and the validity of this letter is questionable.'

'The handwriting is the same as I've seen on other documents written by Helena Lanark,' Jane insisted.

'You are not a handwriting expert, Tennison! I'll need to speak with Chief Superintendent Bridges about it, so for now you just sit on it.'

'I have this weekend off, sir, which I hope is still permissible after taking time off for travel. And as you suggested, I will be present at Helena Lanark's funeral on Monday.'

'Yes, yes,' he snapped.

'Thank you, sir, and goodnight. And goodnight to you, Barbara.'

Jane couldn't keep the smile off her face as she left the station, just as Eddie drew up in his MG. He got out to open the passenger door for her.

'You look like the cat that got the cream!' he said, smiling.

'I am! I just caught my boss in a rather compromising position with one of the clerks in his office!' she laughed, as she climbed into the passenger seat.

As Eddie got in beside her, she leaned across to kiss him.

'Once we get through dinner tonight, we have the whole weekend to be together.'

'I can't afford another trip to Brighton!'

'I just want us to be at home together.'

He gave her a warm sidelong smile. 'I'd like that very much.'

CHAPTER TWENTY-SIX

Eddie parked the car in the small back lane at the rear of her parents' block of flats in Maida Vale. They had stopped en route to buy flowers and wine.

Using the block's rear entry door, they walked up the stairs, not bothering to take the lift. Eddie was impressed with the decor, even more so when he saw a uniformed doorman helping an elderly lady out of the lifts on the second floor.

'This is very posh,' he said.

'Not really. They don't own their flat, but it's on a long lease. They've lived here for about twenty years.'

They arrived at flat 210 and rang the doorbell. Her father opened the door almost immediately and gave Jane such a big hug that she had to push him away to prevent him from squashing the flowers.

'Daddy, this is Eddie.'

Mr Tennison shook Eddie's hand warmly and gestured for him to go ahead as he closed the door behind them.

'I see you've got an MG. I was wondering if Jane would park in the back lane, so I was watching out for her. Lovely motor . . . always wanted one when I was your age.'

Mrs Tennison hovered in the hallway, wearing a white blouse and a pleated grey skirt, with a frilly apron.

'Mother, this is Eddie.'

'How nice to meet you . . . please come in. There's sherry in the drawing room, and I hope you're both hungry . . . it's roast lamb . . . and I've made an apple pie for dessert.'

'Sounds great!' Eddie said, passing the wine bottle to Mr Tennison.

Jane was a little embarrassed by her parents' over-enthusiastic welcome. They had set the dining table in the alcove, with all their best crockery, cutlery and cut glasses, but Eddie was quite at ease and within minutes her father had asked him about a hall light that kept tripping.

'Jane said you're an electrician. I have had a go at it myself, but I think it might be a crossed wire on the wall light. As soon as I put the switch up on the fuse box, it blows again.'

Eddie was quickly up on a ladder in the hall examining their wiring with her father beside him holding a torch. Mrs Tennison had poured sherry for everyone and was fussing around in the kitchen putting the flowers into a vase when Jane joined her.

'We are looking forward to seeing all the work you've had done at your house, Jane. We've been waiting for an invitation.'

'Eddie has been brilliant,' Jane said. 'I don't think you'll recognise it when you see it. I just need to organise the curtains and stair carpet, then I'll have you both over for dinner, with Pam and Tony as well.'

Mrs Tennison moved closer. 'So, it's over with you and the architect, then, is it?'

'Yes, Mother, very much so.'

Mrs Tennison lowered her voice and nodded towards the hall. 'He's a bit young, isn't he?'

'For heaven's sake, Mother! To be honest, I've never even thought about it.'

Eddie soon fixed the wiring in the hall, then her father had him checking out the tap in their bathroom. Mr Tennison explained that it always took the building maintenance man weeks to get even the smallest jobs done.

Eddie had completed various jobs around the flat by the time dinner was ready to be served. Everyone agreed it was delicious and Eddie had a double serving of virtually everything. The wine glasses were refilled, and Eddie apologised for passing on a top-up as he was driving. Jane, however, made up for him and had several glasses as she described all the work that had been done at her house. She was on her fourth glass when her father asked about her trip to Australia.

'Considering I probably spent more time on the plane than I did in Sydney, it was actually quite productive. I went out there to get the truth about what happened at the Stockwell property, and to uncover who did what and when.'

'What case is this, dear?' her mother asked.

'It was the same one I told you about last time, Mother . . .'

'Oh, the one where that poor girl was starved to death . . . dreadful! And those awful newspaper reports calling it the "House of Horrors". I'd have thought it would be all over and done with by now.'

Eddie laughed. 'It probably would have been if it hadn't been for Jane. First, she thought a pearl necklace had been stolen from a care home, but then it turned up. And the old lady had died in suspicious circumstances, so Jane insisted on a post-mortem, but it turned out the old lady had died of natural causes. No offence but—'

'Actually, I do take offence, Eddie,' Jane said sharply. 'I was simply doing my job to the best of my ability, and if certain things don't add up then I make it my business to find out why.'

'But I thought they knew who had left that girl to starve to death?' her mother asked.

Jane pursed her lips. 'That was only part of the investigation. The other part was finding out who had buried a newborn baby alive.'

'I didn't read about that; the truth is I couldn't read all those wretched details. Did the girl that was starved do it?'

'No!' Jane snapped.

'When did it happen, then?'

Jane took a deep breath. 'Probably more than thirty years ago, Mother, but the amount of time is immaterial because it's justice that I care about.'

'There were three sisters . . . I saw their photographs in an album Jane brought to the house,' Eddie said.

Jane frowned. 'Eddie, why don't we just drop the subject.'

'Fine by me.' He shrugged. 'You're the one bringing it up at every opportunity. We went for a special overnight break in Brighton, but Jane didn't tell me about this lawyer she suspected of stealing money from the old lady in a care home, and she just happened to know he lived in Brighton! But then he turns out to be a decent old boy . . .'

Jane picked up her plate of half-eaten apple pie and stood up to take it into the kitchen.

'If you must know, I have changed my mind about him as well. I think his behaviour is distinctly odd.'

'If you don't like apple pie, Eddie, I have some nice cheese and biscuits. And can you bring in the coffee tray, Jane? It's all ready.' Mrs Tennison cleared the other dessert plates and followed Jane into the kitchen, just as she opened the dishwasher.

'No, dear, you know I always rinse the plates before putting them into the dishwasher. Just leave it on the side and I'll do them all later. Take the tray in and some extra knives for the cheese, and I'll bring in the coffee.'

Jane returned to the table, relieved to find Eddie and her father were now in deep discussion about maintaining an old sports car.

As the conversation moved on to Jane's childhood, Jane poured the coffee and handed the cups around, while her mother proffered the cheese board and biscuits. It took a while for Jane's feeling of irritation to subside, but eventually she found herself laughing at a story her father was telling Eddie about when her sister Pam had cut all her dolls' hair and then had cut Jane's two plaits off.

'You should have seen the row between them! Pam had always wanted to be a hairdresser, but Jane got her own back when she cut the legs off her sister's favourite jeans.'

Eddie turned to Jane. 'Did you always want to be a policewoman?'

Mrs Tennison answered. 'No, she didn't. But she was always a perfectionist and very competitive. One time we were all doing jigsaw puzzles at Christmas, and there was a prize for whoever finished theirs first. We discovered that Jane had been cutting the pieces of the jigsaw to fit where she wanted them to.'

Jane laughed, remembering. 'It was because the sky pieces were so boring!'

'That's the way you always were, though – you wanted to get things done. You were argumentative, even as a young girl. And she would ask questions about everything . . . it drove me to distraction! In a way, I can understand why she joined the Met because that's all about piecing things together, isn't it?'

Jane smiled. 'In a way, yes, it is. But when the pieces don't fit, I can't use a pair of scissors to make them. So, I don't rest until I have the answers. I'm sorry if you find it tedious, Eddie, but until I am satisfied, I keep on mulling things over. I have had to sift through so many lies on the Stockwell inquiry, and even though we have the answers to most of it, there's something still bugging me.'

'All right, tell us?' Eddie said, cutting a slice of cheese. He reached over and touched her hand. 'I'm serious, go on, what's bugging you?'

Jane sighed. 'Why did Jason Thorpe lie about the family album, saying that his mother wanted it? And why did he leave it in Helena's room?'

'Who's Jason Thorpe?' Mrs Tennison asked.

'He is the deceased woman's nephew. He lives in Australia with his mother, Beatrice, her sister,' Eddie explained.

'How old is Jason?' Mrs Tennison asked.

Jane screwed up her eyes, trying to remain patient.

'What's wrong with asking his age?'

'I don't know how old he is, Mum. He seemed to be about thirty.'

'Is he married?'

'No! Mother, for heaven's sake! My point is, why did he lie to me? He caused me problems at work as well.'

Eddie raised his hand. 'What about this . . . maybe there was something in the album he needed to talk to the old lady about?' He drained his coffee.

'Eddie, she couldn't talk . . . she was suffering from dementia. And there was nothing in the album of significance. I thought at one time it might have been her will . . .'

'So maybe he paid her a visit and took it?' Eddie suggested.

Jane was becoming increasingly tetchy. She had taken the album before Jason's visit, so she knew there was no will.

'It's just the lies. Jason only discovered today that Helena had married Arnold Hadley and made a new will, which her solicitors have. If he knew he was the beneficiary of the first will then I get why he would want a copy of it—'

Eddie interjected. 'Couldn't he just ask the solicitors for a copy?'

'They would never divulge the contents until after a funeral,' Jane replied.

'I'm sorry, dear, I don't get why this Jason would want a copy,' Mrs Tennison remarked with a bemused expression.

'If he was worried that Helena had cut him out of her new will, he might want a copy of the first one to contest the second, perhaps and accusing Hadley of coercing Helena to make a new will while she wasn't of sound mind.'

'So, who gets her inheritance?' Mr Tennison asked, now starting to get interested, despite not knowing who anyone was.

'The bulk of her wealth was left to her husband, Arnold Hadley. She didn't leave Beatrice or Jason a single penny.'

'So, what has that got to do with the murder of the baby?' Eddie asked, glancing at his watch.

Jane sighed, then pushed her chair back.

'I don't suppose it has anything to do with it. Like I said, it's me just wanting to tie up all the loose ends and make the jigsaw pieces fit.'

Eddie stood up and thanked Jane's parents for the fabulous dinner, saying that as he had a very early start in the morning, he thought they should be leaving.

Jane looked at him, puzzled. 'I thought we were going to do some shopping?'

'Yes, but later in the day. I have to do an estimate on a big extension first.'

After kissing her mother, Jane collected her coat and bag as her father shook Eddie's hand and thanked him for helping fix the lights and the tap. As he shut the front door behind them, Mrs Tennison started carrying dirty dishes into the kitchen.

'Well, I doubt that will last,' she said. 'She definitely didn't like the way he cross-questioned her.'.

Mr Tennison sighed. 'Pity. We could do with some decorating.'

* * *

Jane sat in silence as they drove back to her house. Part of her knew that Eddie was right and that she had become obsessed with this case.

'I liked your parents,' he said, trying to ease the tension between them.

'Listen, Eddie, I'm sorry if I got a bit stroppy, but I can't help going over things in my head. I just query everything. I mean, I was certain that Jason was not aware of our discovery in the shelter, but then when I read Helena's confession letter . . .'

'What letter?'

'I told you, her lawyer gave me a copy of it. It was not to be opened until after her death.'

'Oh right, yeah, yeah.'

'But all the years that Helena sent money to her sister . . . and she told me that she had been forced to send begging letters.'

'Who wrote begging letters?'

'Beatrice Thorpe. She was blackmailing her sister and it would seem Jason was also involved. They got a lot of money out of Helena Lanark over many years. He was even able to acquire power of attorney to gain further access to her finances. It's even possible Beatrice blackmailed Helena into making them the beneficiaries in her first will.'

'So what is your point, Jane?'

Jane snapped at him angrily. 'Helena Lanark paid up so she could get away with murder. And if I hadn't gone to Australia no one would ever have found out.'

Eddie pulled up outside Jane's house and got out to open the passenger door for her.

'Sweetheart, the fact is that the old lady never admitted anything until after she died. And she paid the price for most of her life.'

Jane felt near to tears, as he put his arms around her.

'Listen, I'm going to take off home to put the MG in the garage. I'll be over tomorrow about eleven.'

'Why didn't you tell me about the new job?' Jane asked.

'It's not confirmed yet, but as soon as it is, we'll celebrate.' He cupped her face in his hands and kissed her, before getting back into the car.

Jane watched him drive off, taking out her keys to let herself in. She felt bad about how argumentative she had been with Eddie, even more so as she headed up the stairs and could see how nice the house was looking.

She'd been so absorbed in her thoughts that she hadn't seen the car driving past her house, then doing a slow U-turn to park on the opposite side of the road.

CHAPTER TWENTY-SEVEN

Jane was in her pyjamas, her bag open on her bed as she searched for the leaflets on stair carpets. She suddenly thought she remembered leaving them in the kitchen so got out of bed. She was about to put on her slippers but decided to tip the contents of her bag out on the bed first. She put the copy of Helena Lanark's letter to one side, then began to sift through receipts, invoices and paint charts, until she found the old envelope containing the family tree that she had inadvertently kept from the photo album.

She tapped it against her hand, frowning. She had not thought the document was of any importance. The only reason she had not given it to Jason when he came to collect the album was that it had fallen out under the kitchen table.

Jane turned the thick, worn envelope over. Could this be what Jason Thorpe had really wanted? Was this why he went to the care home when he found it was not at the back of the album? She chewed her lips as she carefully opened the envelope. The folds in the documents were almost tearing as she eased each page apart on top of her duvet.

The finely scripted writing in looped black ink named the Lanark grandparents and then documented the marriage between Henry and Muriel. Lines were drawn to show the births of Helena and Beatrice, born within five years of each other, and then a ten-year gap before Marjorie was born. The death of Marjorie had been altered – a date had been written and then carefully adjusted to indicate that she was sixteen years old when she died, not twenty-two.

Jane sighed, aware of the implication of incest between Henry and Marjorie. Even Hadley had remarked on the nude photograph of her being strange. She was certain that if he had seen the poses in the photographs she had found in the boathouse, he would have been even more shocked. Henry Lanark had taken sexually explicit photographs of two of his daughters, but not Helena. She glanced down the page of the neatly written family tree that continued up to the death of Muriel Lanark. Henry Lanark's death was recorded as being five years after his wife and Jane presumed this had been added by Helena.

She carefully put the first page to one side as she picked up the second. It was equally worn, and the creases were splitting. There was the date of Beatrice's marriage to John Thorpe, and the word Australia underlined. The date was five years before the death of Henry Lanark, and other dates were listed and crossed out. John Thorpe's death was dated before Henry Lanark's. There were two further names: Matthew John Thorpe, but there were three different birth dates. The date that was underlined gave his birth date as three years before the marriage of Beatrice and John. This meant that both Beatrice's sons were illegitimate, and that Jason was the eldest.

Jane was trying to understand what she was looking at, remembering that Beatrice had told her she went to Australia alone and waited for her future husband, John Thorpe, to join her. However, judging from the dates on the family tree, Beatrice was already pregnant and gave birth to Matthew before she got married. By this time, according to the dates, Jason was already two years old.

Closing her eyes to concentrate, Jane remembered Beatrice telling her angrily how she had been widowed with two young sons and she had to pawn her mother's jewellery to get by, though oddly she kept the pearls. Jane wondered if this was when the blackmail had started, meaning she didn't need to sell the pearls because she had started receiving money from Helena.

Jane took a deep breath. This had all taken up too much of her time and energy. If there were still unanswered questions, what was she going to gain from answering them? Eddie was right. She had become obsessed and had even put her career in jeopardy.

Jane carefully refolded each page and was about to put them back in the envelope when she noticed, caught in the creases of the last page, a thin folded square of paper. She carefully eased it free and read the faint scrawled writing. John Thorpe, it said, had married Gladys Jones in Lambeth. The date was illegible but not the underlined date of a son born to them and christened David Thorpe. There was a date for the death of Gladys Jones, a year after the marriage, then further underlined dates for John and David Thorpe arriving in Australia.

Jane closed her eyes, recalling Hadley telling her how Helena had reacted when he came back from the walk, whispering to him about the puzzle. She was certain that this had to be it. Jason was not Beatrice's biological son. Beatrice had simply changed his name to Jason. She now understood what Helena had written in her letter, her reservations about Jason's bloodline and his right to any Lanark inheritance.

Jane looked towards her bedroom window. Even with her curtains closed, she could tell the porch security light had just come on. She crossed over to the window and eased back the curtains as the lights went out. Probably a cat, she thought, as she returned to her bed and began to put everything back into her bag – then instantly tensed as she heard a scraping sound inside the house. She quietly moved across to the partly open bedroom door and listened. She heard the same scraping sound again. She stretched out her hand to switch off the bedroom lights, then inched the door open further. She crept silently along the landing to the top of the stairs, half hoping that it was Eddie, but knowing it wasn't.

The hall was in darkness as Jane slowly started to move, step by step, down the stairs. She stopped as she heard a sound coming from the kitchen, as if whoever was in the house had knocked into a chair or the kitchen table. Someone was definitely down there but the phone in the dark hall was too far away for her to be able to use. Trying to determine where would be the safest place for her to hide, she slowly retraced her way back up the stairs and across the landing. She eased open the bathroom door, the only room in the house with a lock. Just as she closed the door, she heard the footsteps on the uncarpeted staircase. Whoever it was was now making no attempt to be quiet. She heard her bedroom door being kicked open, then the click of the light switch and what sounded like heavy breathing.

As she listened to the sound of things being thrown around in her bedroom she tried hard to keep the panic from rising, breathing deeply and hunting for anything in the bathroom that she could use to protect herself – but no tools had been left behind and there was nothing else to hand. Jane could hear the footsteps coming closer and then, terrifyingly, she saw the handle of the bathroom door turning. When it rattled in the lock, the door was kicked hard to force it open.

Jane snatched up a big bath towel and as the door burst open she threw it over the intruder, pushing him backwards with all her strength. He lost his footing and stumbled as she wrapped the towel around his head, but she knew she only had a few seconds to get to the stairs, hoping to run down to the front door and out of the house before he caught up with her. She raced out of the bathroom but as soon as her feet hit the stairs, she felt the ground give way beneath and she hurtled down the stairs, falling head over heels and cracking her head on the newel post at the bottom.

Everything went black, and then Jane, barely conscious, felt herself being lifted. She tried to scream but it was painful even to breathe. She heard the door into her living room being kicked open as she was carried in.

She could smell the dust sheet enveloping her as she was laid down on the sofa, and slowly came to her senses.

For the first time, she heard voices.

'Dear God, what have you done to her?'

'I just wanted to talk to her . . . then she came at me. I didn't touch her! I swear I didn't do anything to her . . . she just fell down the fucking stairs.'

'Get away from her, and get me some wet towels. How could you be so stupid?'

Jane tried to see who was talking but was unable to lift her head.

'You'll be all right, dear, just lie still.'

Jane's eyes fluttered half open and she smelled Beatrice's sickly-sweet perfume as she leaned over and felt for her pulse, the tell-tale jangle of her charm bracelet being the final clue to her identity.

Jason handed his mother a soaking wet tea towel which she rolled up and placed over Jane's forehead. Jane began breathing deeply in an attempt to stem the panic that threatened to overwhelm her.

'See if you can find some brandy.'

'Where do I find that? The place doesn't look lived in.'

'Kitchen . . . go and look in the kitchen.'

Beatrice held Jane's hand, gently patting it and then pressing the cold cloth around Jane's face as she began to try and move.

'Just stay quiet, you'll be all right. It was an accident; he didn't mean to hurt you. Can you hear me, dear?'

'Yes . . . yes,' Jane whispered.

Jason returned with a half-full bottle of whisky and an empty glass.

'There's no brandy,' he said.

'Pour some into the glass and hand it to me.'

Beatrice gently put an arm around Jane's shoulder and eased her up to a sitting position. She opened her eyes, and her head began to clear.

'Just take a sip of this, dear . . . gently does it, just a little sip . . . good girl. I'm going to help you sit up a little bit more.'

Jane could feel the rim of the glass against her teeth as she took small sips, and gradually her breathing calmed.

'I just wanted to talk to her . . . I never meant anything like this to happen. I swear, she just fell.' Jason took a deep swig straight from the bottle. He was shaking badly and sounded near to tears.

'Stay back, Jason. Go and sit down. You could have killed her.'

'But it was an accident . . . you told me to go in and talk to her.'

'Shut up, just shut up!' Beatrice whispered furiously. She gave Jane a few more sips of whisky and helped her to sit up straighter.

'Can you see clearly now, dear?'

Jane was still dazed. 'Yes . . .'

'Have you any pain in your chest?'

Beatrice began to feel Jane's arms, patting gently and then leaning over to feel down her legs.

'Nothing hurts . . . no broken bones. You just banged your head, but you'll feel better in a minute.'

Beatrice threw the tea towel at Jason. 'Go and get some ice and wrap it in that.'

Jane kept her eyes closed. She had a thudding headache, but her main concern was whether she had done something to her neck; it felt painful if she moved her head.

Beatrice stood over her, draining the whisky left in the glass in one swallow. It felt like an age before Jason came back with the ice but Jane felt almost instant relief when it was gently wrapped around her neck. She kept her eyes closed as she tried to figure out what to do. Happily the panic had subsided, mostly because of Beatrice's soothing manner, talking to her as if nothing untoward had happened.

Yet they had broken into her house and Jason had forced his way into the bathroom, terrifying her. Jane tried to think why they were willing to take such risks, intuitively sensing that Jason, despite his protestations to the contrary, was still dangerous. Beatrice took Jane's hand again and felt for her pulse, then stroked her forehead.

'I'm used to looking after my son, Matthew. He often used to fall. I've had to nurse him all his life, so I know what I'm doing, dear. I'll keep on making ice compresses for your neck. Can you sit up now?'

Jane kept her eyes closed, not wanting either of them to know she was fully conscious.

Beatrice got up. 'Stop pacing up and down, Jason. Go and get some more ice, because if she doesn't come round soon, we'll have to call an ambulance.'

'We can't do that,' Jason whined.

'Then what do you think we should do? Can't you get it into your head what you have done? Did you find what we came here for?' she then added in a whisper.

'I think so. These papers were on the bed. They've got names and dates of birth . . .'

Beatrice snatched the sheets from him. 'I knew she had them, I just knew it!'

Jane heard them both walk out of the room and opened her eyes, scanning her surroundings for anything she could use as a weapon. There were numerous work tools on the seat of a straight-backed chair, including a thin-bladed chisel for stripping wallpaper. Leaning over the arm of the sofa, Jane was able to reach out for it, snatch it up and hide it in the fold of the dust sheet. Beatrice and Jason were still in the kitchen talking, the fridge door opening and closing as Beatrice's voice became increasingly shrill.

'Just leave. I mean it . . . just get out and let me talk to her. Go back to the hotel and wait for me. Just give me time to explain everything.'

'No, this is my fault. I'll take the blame. I'll do whatever you tell me to do, but I won't leave you.'

'You will do whatever I say. Now get out. You drain me dry . . . you always have.'

Jane straightened up as she heard what sounded like a scuffle, then something smashed, and Beatrice screamed.

'You ever hit me again and I swear to God, I will leave you here to fend for yourself – and we both know how that will turn out. Just like everything else you have ever touched. All you had to do was talk to her. You could have killed her, you bloody idiot.'

There was another scream, more glass shattering, and the back door slammed hard enough to break the hinges. Jane was sitting upright, the chisel in her hand hidden at her side when Beatrice walked back into the room. She was holding the ice pack meant for Jane to her own nose to stop it bleeding.

'Are you all right?' Jane asked.

Beatrice gave a humourless laugh. 'That's rather ironic, coming from you, wouldn't you say? It's nothing . . . but at the same time it is so very sad.'

She picked up the bottle of whisky and poured the rest of the contents into the now-empty glass.

'I haven't got any copies of Helena's wills, if that's what you're looking for. I don't even know what was in them.'

Beatrice laughed. 'That's not why I'm here. I have a copy of her first will and am prepared to contest the new one if needs be . . . and not necessarily in court.'

Beatrice stood by the fireplace, her back to Jane who could hear the repeated flick of a cigarette lighter followed by the smell of burning.

'What are you burning?' Jane asked

'The family tree.' Beatrice threw the burning papers into the fireplace. 'I haven't been honest about everything for so many years, but I think I have to be now.'

She took a long drink then swilled the remains round in the glass, her charm bracelet jangling.

'My father forbade me to marry John, as he was an illiterate working-class bus driver who had been left a widower with a young child and didn't have a penny to his name. But John was my salvation.' She sipped her drink again, then touched her nose gingerly. It had stopped bleeding. 'I'm sorry, do you need this?' She held up the bloodied compress.

Jane shook her head.

'You know about little Marjorie . . . well, after she died, Father's attention turned to me. The sound of his keys in that silver bowl in the hall, and the clicking of his steel-tipped boots . . . that dread when he called me to go into the basement dark room. There were five steps down and below that was the cellar leading into the tunnel and the shelter.'

Jane gritted her teeth, anticipating that this was going to be a long, drawn-out theatrical explanation, like the one she had been forced to listen to in Australia. She watched as Beatrice sat down in an easy chair opposite her, crossing her legs at the ankles and smoothing down her skirt.

'I didn't think I was pregnant because he used a horrible douche contraption afterwards. Then there I was, all on my own in Sydney. I had to wait for John as he couldn't raise the finances to bring his son with him. By the time he did arrive, poor Matthew had been born.'

'That must have been terrible,' Jane said.

Beatrice looked at her sharply. 'Don't patronise me, dear. You can't begin to know what it was like. I lived in a horrible, damp apartment that smelled like that disgusting cellar. Having a very sickly child, I had to pawn or sell what I could of my mother's jewellery. I was always afraid I might be arrested because I knew my father's enduring hatred and venomous nature. And I had taken my sweet little sister's pearls. I broke them up sold them one or two at a time. We moved to Adelaide so John could try and find work. He cared for Matthew, and poor Jason had to deal with him as well. Then it just got worse. John became sick and died four years later. I was forced to do whatever I could to provide for my sons, one of them sick and utterly helpless. Have you any idea what I had to go through?'

Jane slowly turned, swinging her legs to the floor.

'Mrs Thorpe, I am aware that Helena provided for you . . .'

Beatrice was indignant. 'Provided? How many years did she ignore my pleas before she "provided"? I prostituted myself. My father taught me how to pleasure a man and that's what I ended up doing to survive.'

'Mrs Thorpe, I don't want to . . .'

'You don't want to what? You don't want to hear this, but it's all right for you to dig into my life, delve into private boxes and remove photographs that you had no permission to take? You think I wouldn't find out?'

'I was investigating a child's murder—'

Beatrice interrupted her. 'You broke into my boathouse and stole my property! Let me tell you, I had no notion of what Helena did with that baby, and my son didn't know anything about it either, until you brought it up. For your information, I never threatened or blackmailed Helena about the baby because I didn't know she had left it in the shelter.'

Jane took a deep breath. She knew she shouldn't antagonise Beatrice if she wanted to get her out of the house, but at the same time this was an important new revelation. Beatrice continued, angrily explaining how the medical bills mounted as Matthew needed constant hospital treatment to drain the fluid on his brain. Plus, Jason had begun to go off the rails.

'He grew his hair and started taking drugs . . . staying out on the beaches all day. But then I turned it around.'

She pointed her finger at Jane, standing up and seeming to gloat.

'I threatened to return to England, taking Matthew with me and making sure our monster father's abuse would be splashed all over the papers. I wasn't sure at first, but even with his swollen head you could see he had my father's eyes.'

'Beatrice, are you telling me that Matthew is your father's child?'

'Of course I am – and probably conceived on the night Marjorie was in the tunnel giving birth. He abused sweet Marjorie from an early age, and may God forgive me, I was thankful because if he could have her, it meant he never touched me . . . until that night he came home early, drunk and shouting for Marjorie, and we told him she was ill and he made me take her place.'

She started to run her hands through her hair. 'Helena constantly rejected my pleas for financial help until I threatened to make it public about our father's abuse. Then she sent the money as often as I needed it, but I swear it wasn't because of any threats, but out of guilt for turning a blind eye to our father's disgusting abuse.'

Jane thought Beatrice knew full well her demands amounted to blackmail, but she said nothing, allowing her to continue.

'She paid for Jason to go to college, and when I wanted to move back to Sydney, she even bought a house for us. She helped Jason start various businesses, and he began to get used to a different life. And I spoiled him because I had finally started to live mine.'

Jane held the wallpaper stripper in her right hand and eased forward onto the edge of the sofa.

'What about Helena? Did your father abuse her too?'

Beatrice gave her a twisted smile. 'She was his doting slave, but he wouldn't touch her because she was ugly and thin as a rake. He used to call her his boy. She had to know what was going on because she helped him in his darkroom, developing and pinning up his filthy photographs. She burned Marjorie's blood-soaked nightdress when he raped her and the one she wore when she gave birth. I'll tell you something else about Helena – when Father had terrible fights with our Mama, she would take his side. And she reported back to him like a spy about our lovely music tutor. We hated her, and when I eventually escaped from that house, I was thankful she had him all to herself.'

Beatrice shook her head as if to rid herself of the images she had conjured up and then leaned forwards.

'Helena wrote letters telling me father was gaga, detailing how she washed him and put a diaper on after he shit himself. She fed him and rocked him to sleep, like the baby her skinny body could never conceive. I never wanted to see her again, even when I knew she was in a care home.'

Jane waited, not wanting to interrupt Beatrice's flow.

'Did you ever talk to her?' Beatrice asked.

Jane shook her head. 'No, I only visited the care home shortly before she died.'

Beatrice went on. 'When the call came in the middle of the night I was so surprised to hear her voice. She had strange voice, a very particular way of talking, always very quiet.'

Beatrice cupped her hand up to her ear as if speaking into a phone and mimicked her sister.

'"Hello, Beatrice, I have been working on finishing Daddy's family tree. It has taken me such a long time, but I know your secret now and I will make you pay for it."'

Beatrice raised her hands in a dramatic gesture.

'Knowing she was already suffering from early onset dementia, I asked what on earth was she talking about. Then in that sing-song tone she just repeated the name David and then said Jason's name and I knew she had found out. Then she hung up. I did try to contact her many times after that, but she always put the phone down or Arnold answered and said she was resting.'

Beatrice stood up, shaking her head. 'At first I didn't know what to do. I couldn't tell Jason the truth for fear of what it would do to the poor soul. He never had the acumen to run a business and was always trusting the wrong people. Out of the blue, Arnold wrote to me expressing his concern for Helena's health and questioning the money she was paying us. I made Jason go to London and tell Helena I would no longer keep her secrets, unless she gave him power of attorney and made us beneficiaries in her will.'

'Do you think Arnold Hadley knew about Jason?'

'Not a lot got past him, and dear God, if I'd known they got married and she changed her will I would have done something about it a lot sooner. It's clear now Helena didn't want us to know as I might decide to reveal our father's abuse.'

Jane thought Beatrice was probably right. The two sisters were, in many ways, as devious as each other.

Jane was now desperate for Beatrice to leave. 'Mrs Thorpe, I have a really bad headache. I'm going to call you a taxi . . .'

Beatrice shrugged. 'It's all right, Jason is waiting outside. But you have to understand the depth of his frustration and disappointment. The only successful thing he ever did was taking over the Stockwell property and developing it into flats. Then that became a financial mess, so he had to make the decision to sell . . .'

With Jason waiting outside, Jane knew she couldn't force Beatrice out, especially now she clearly wanted to talk.

'He was so confident and proud of himself, but then came the threat to our inheritance, and the very thing I had hoped would never surface, her threat to reveal his true parentage. He'd always believed me to be his birth mother.'

'He doesn't know you're his stepmother?'

'No . . . and he never will, now I've burned those papers. I told him we needed them to contest Helena's will. Like the fool that he is, he believed me.'

Beatrice sobbed, her bracelet jangling as she wiped her eyes. 'Jason would never be accepted by that girl in Melbourne, or her family, if they found out he was a bankrupt who had lost everything and had no inheritance to look forward to. Looking back, I was foolish to encourage his business ventures, the poor boy is so inept.'

Jane pressed her body back into the sofa as Beatrice moved closer and closer. She decided not to mention Helena's letter of confession and her accusations against Beatrice, fearing it would make matters worse. She also now regretted giving DCI Carter a copy, fearing the contents would become public knowledge.

'I know you could have us arrested, but I am begging you . . . now that you know everything, please, please let him fly back to Australia. I'll get on my knees to you . . . let him go . . . you can arrest me if you want.'

She held her wrists out to Jane in a theatrical gesture, as if waiting to be handcuffed.

'Please, just go now, Mrs Thorpe,' Jane said firmly. 'I want you to leave.'

'What are you going to do? Because you could also be in trouble, you know. You stole my photographs, Helena's album and her family tree. But I'm prepared to do nothing about it. Jason never meant to hurt you . . .'

Jane sighed. 'Tell him to go back to Australia.'

'You won't arrest us or tell anyone what happened tonight?'

Jane shook her head.

'Can you give me your word on that?' Beatrice pleaded.

'You have my word,' Jane replied, knowing that if Beatrice told DCI Carter Jane had stolen the photographs from the boathouse her career, and DC Tim Taylor's, could be seriously damaged, if not over.

She watched as Beatrice walked into the kitchen, appearing moments later in the open doorway with her handbag, wrapping a shawl around her shoulders.

'I will pay for any damages,' she said.

Jane tried to stand up and had to put her hand on the edge of the sofa arm to steady herself. She almost fainted with relief when Beatrice finally left, and the front door closed behind her. She slowly made her way to the window and saw Beatrice caught in the glare of the security light as she walked down the path towards Jason, who had got out of the car to greet her. Beatrice held out her arms and he embraced her as if his life depended on her, as in so many ways it did.

CHAPTER TWENTY-EIGHT

Early the following morning, Eddie let himself into the house carrying a large bunch of flowers and a bottle of champagne. He went into the kitchen to get two glasses, then stopped abruptly at the sight of broken glass and a smashed plate on the floor. Then he saw the open back door, which had been splintered where it had been forced.

He hastily put the flowers and the champagne on the kitchen table and hurried into the hall, pausing at the sight of the dust sheet on the ground, with an empty whisky bottle beside it. From the hall he could see the paint-stripper lying on the floor next to the sofa. Starting up the stairs Eddie stopped to pick up the discarded bath towel, now becoming very concerned. He called out Jane's name, but there was no response. He sprinted up the stairs, two at a time, and when he reached the landing, he saw the broken bathroom door. Panic-stricken, he crossed to Jane's bedroom door and tried to open it. The door appeared to be wedged shut so he pushed hard against it with his shoulder until it opened a fraction, and he was able to put his hand inside. He discovered that a chair had been hooked up under the handle.

'Jane? JANE?' Eddie shouted, managing to dislodge the chair and make his way into the bedroom.

Jane woke up and screamed, then fell back on the bed when she saw who it was.

Eddie raced to her side. 'Dear God! What on earth happened here? Are you all right?'

He had his arms around her as she clung to him, repeating over and over that she was all right. She was so thankful that it was him, and she didn't want to let him go. By the time they had both calmed down Jane said she wanted to get up and get dressed.

Eddie took her dressing gown from the hook on the back of her door, insisting that she was not going to do anything until she told him exactly what had happened. As he gently helped her into it, he told her what he had discovered after letting himself in.

'I was in a right state when I saw that the back door had been broken, almost off its hinges and your bedroom door was wedged shut . . .'

'I'm all right, honestly, Eddie . . . although I could do with a cup of tea.' As she tied the dressing gown cord around her waist, she winced from the pain in her neck.

'Are you hurt? What happened?'

'Please, Eddie, just give me a bit of time.'

He stood with his hands on his hips.

'You go back to bed I'll bring you up a cup of tea.'

As he boiled the kettle, Eddie checked over the sitting room, noticing the charred paper in the grate. Jane came down the stairs, and he could see that she was holding tightly on to the banister.

'I need some Paracetamol,' she said. 'I think they're in the kitchen drawer.'

Eddie put her mug of tea on the kitchen table and found the packet of pills in the drawer. Jane touched the flowers and gave him a smile.

'Champagne too. You've had good news about the job?'

He took the pills out of the box and broke open the foil, handing a couple of tablets to her. Pulling out a chair, he sat down beside her.

'Never mind about the job. Tell me what the hell went on here, Jane. You're freaking me out.'

He watched her swallow the tablets with some tea, then cup the mug in her hands.

'Jason Thorpe and his mother broke in last night. I'm sorry, there is no way I can tell you everything that happened . . . but it was horrendous.'

'Christ! Did he assault you, Jane?'

Jane shook her head. After sipping some more tea, she gradually told him as much as she felt she could, leaving out most of the long conversation with Beatrice.

'You're going to press charges, right? I'd beat the shit out of him if I saw him.'

Eddie couldn't believe it when Jane shook her head again. Then she winced, and he was instantly on his feet.

'Do you have concussion?'

'I don't think so . . . I've just got a headache now.'

He gently touched her neck and then felt the back of her head.

'I'm taking you to A&E right now and I am not going to take no for an answer. Come on, you don't need to get dressed.'

Jane didn't have the energy to argue and then felt herself becoming quite tearful as Eddie went upstairs and reappeared with her slippers and a blanket to keep her warm.

* * *

Jane and Eddie were in the A&E department at Queen Mary's Hospital for three hours. Thankfully, it was a Saturday morning and was not that busy. The young doctor assured them that they had done the right thing in getting Jane checked out. After taking such a bad fall and being unconscious for some time, he recommended an MRI scan.

She was eventually given the all-clear but was told that she should rest in bed until the following day, taking painkillers as necessary.

Back at the house, Eddie made sure she followed the doctor's orders and called his mother to see if she could bring round some soup. Tucking Jane's duvet round her and putting another cup of tea on her bedside table, he told her he would fix the back door to make it safe and would sort out the bathroom door later in the week so as not to disturb her.

Jane took some more pain killers and started to drift off to sleep. She felt safe and realised how lucky she was to have Eddie there.

Whilst Jane slept, Eddie stood looking down on her for a while, curled up beneath the duvet, trying to understand why she had not reported the break-in. It didn't make sense, particularly with her being a police officer. He quietly left the room, closing the door silently behind him. As he went down the stairs, he frowned at the recollection of some of the things she had told him about the family tree and the mistakes she had made.

He then went out to his van and rummaged in his tool kit to find some hinges that would fit the back door.

Eddie worked methodically door, bringing his radio in from the van and switching it on low to help him concentrate. It took longer than he thought it would to refit the hinges, as some of the wood was warped, and the door wouldn't close to his satisfaction.

* * *

Jane wasn't sure if she was awake or still dreaming, as she heard Janice Joplin singing faintly. She recognised the song, which took her back in time and an emotional wave swept over her. 'Piece of My Heart' was the song she had played over and over again when she had been a probationary officer in Hackney. She had been heartbroken when an explosion at the bank had killed DCI Bradford but she had been forced to suppress so much of the pain. Now, all these years later, the memory rose to the surface, and she was unable to stop the floodgates opening. She sobbed uncontrollably.

With all the noise of his hammering and drilling, Eddie didn't hear her crying. He only downed tools when he was completely satisfied that the door was secure. He had taken all his tools back to the van, along with his radio, and was just checking out the Tupperware container of soup and fresh bread his mother had brought round when he heard movement from upstairs.

Jane was standing in the shower, holding her face up to the spray. She tried to understand what had made her return to that fateful day, then bowed her head and let the water soothe her still-painful neck. Not for the first time, she wondered if her feelings about DCI Bradford's death had held her back from committing herself fully in her subsequent relationships. She turned off the shower and wrapped herself in a bath towel, sitting on the edge of the bath to dry her wet hair.

Eddie tapped on the half-open bathroom door, then peered in.

'Did my hammering wake you up?'

Jane smiled. 'No, I had a bad dream and I'm just trying to work out what it meant.'

'No wonder, after what you just went through.'

'It wasn't about that,' Jane said. 'But maybe it surfaced because of it. Anyway, I'm all right now – and I'm starving hungry.'

'I've got Mum's soup here . . . so get back into your pyjamas and I'll bring it up.'

'Why don't we go out, to celebrate your job?' Jane said.

Eddie frowned. 'Have you any idea what time it is? And you've been told you need to rest, so back you go.'

Jane crossed over to him and put her arms around him, resting her head against his chest.

'I do love you . . . I've never had anyone care for me like you do.'

'Feeling's mutual, detective.' He smiled.

'Is it?'

'Yes, Jane. I love you.'

* * *

Jane had an overwhelming sense of release, suddenly feeling happier than she could ever remember. They finished off Eddie's mother's delicious soup, accompanied with crusty fresh bread. Initially, she hadn't really wanted to talk about what had happened the previous night, but now she felt able to calmly explain her decision about not taking the matter any further.

'It's your choice, Jane.' Eddie shrugged. 'Although I don't quite understand it. Does this mean you're having second thoughts about your career?'

'You know, I haven't even thought about that,' Jane said. 'You were right, I did become obsessed, and in some ways what happened was my fault. I have often been reprimanded for not being what they describe in the Met as a "team player". You're always supposed to share your information, never go solo . . . So I guess I need to learn a lesson from what happened.'

Eddie placed their empty soup bowls on a tray and stood up to take them to the kitchen.

'I'll tell you one thing. I'm going to make sure you get an extension phone here in your bedroom. I've fixed your back door securely, with a new lock and hinges, and tomorrow I'll come back and sort out the bathroom door.'

'Are you not going to stay the night?' Jane asked.

'No, you need to get more sleep. Unless you're afraid to be on your own?'

Jane pulled the duvet up around her shoulders.

'I'm not scared, Eddie, I just want you beside me.'

He stood holding the tray and hesitated a moment before putting it down on the side table.

'If you want, we could make it permanent.'

Jane hurled the duvet aside and embraced him, wrapping her arms and legs around him.

'Yes, yes, YES!'

* * *

Sunday was a cold but gloriously sunny. They had brunch together and Jane didn't want to let Eddie go, not even wanting him to go back to his own flat to get some clothes. He kissed her and promised not to be too long.

Jane cleared up the kitchen. When she went into the sitting room, she saw the dust sheet and the wallpaper stripper she had held as a weapon and suddenly doubted her promise to Beatrice. She stood by the fireplace and looked at the charred remains of the family tree, aware of her error in not paying attention to it. But before she could question herself anymore, Eddie walked in holding up one newspaper with more under his arm.

'You're not going to like this, I'm afraid. I bought some of the Sunday papers. A couple of them don't have it on the front page, but . . .'

'What is it?'

'Here you go.'

He passed Jane a copy of the *News of World* and the headline blared out at her.

HOUSE OF HORROR HEIRESS'S CONFESSION.

She started to read the story.

> Detective Chief Inspector Wayne Carter, the lead investigator on the Stockwell baby murder, says 'case closed' after uncovering a letter written by Helena Lanark confessing to killing the child thirty years ago . . .

Eddie was flicking through another paper.

'Didn't you say Helena's letter talked about Beatrice blackmailing her and doubts about Jason's parentage when it came to any inheritance?'

Jane nodded.

'Well, there's no mention of Beatrice wanting money or Jason's parentage in any of these papers. I can't see your name mentioned anywhere either.'

Jane wondered if Carter had discussed the letter with DCS Bridges and a decision had been made not to release its full content. She was somewhat relieved, as Helena's allegations of blackmail and the question of Jason's inheritance might enrage Beatrice and make her decide to lodge a formal complaint of theft.

Eddie continued. 'Carter also gets in that he was recently successful in making a number of arrests after a series of house burglaries and had been congratulated on returning stolen possessions to their rightful owners . . . blimey, talk about blowing his own trumpet.'

'Well, I'm not surprised he left my name out of it,' Jane said. 'Let's just call it another lesson learned. I'm definitely not going to let him or this crap in the papers get to me.'

Eddie continued reading a rather less scurrilous article in *The Sunday Times*, focusing on the fact that the Lanark fortune had been made during the First and Second World Wars, through paper factories and weapons manufacturing. Helena Lanark had been the sole beneficiary, inheriting a vast fortune. 'Christ, she was worth millions!' he exclaimed.

'This is the best place for these.' Jane gathered up the newspapers, then started ripping them up, making them into balls and dropping them in the fireplace. A smile of satisfaction lit up her face as she put a match to them and they burst into flames.

Eddie smiled. He was constantly seeing Jane in so many different lights. Only time would tell if he liked them all, but he certainly admired her now. He had been concerned at how she would react to the stories in the papers, but she seemed to have been energised by them if anything, clapping her hands and laughing.

'It's all over, Eddie, bar the funeral.'

'You aren't going to go, are you?'

'I wouldn't miss it. Now, I want you to give me a proper invoice for the repairs to the kitchen and bathroom doors . . . and make them for as much as you like.'

* * *

The following morning Eddie left before seven, reminding Jane to contact BT to arrange about the telephone extension. With the house to herself Jane took her time carefully choosing her best suit, white high-collared blouse and high heels. She washed and blow-dried her hair and applied subtle makeup with pale lipstick. Instead of the big handbag she used for carrying documents, she chose a small black leather clutch. She stood looking at herself in the wardrobe mirror.

'I am Detective Inspector Jane Tennison,' she said, feeling a surge of pride.

Jane drove herself to St Martin's and went and stood in the entrance vestibule, looking at the list of christenings and funerals taking place that day. She was slightly taken aback to see Helena Lanark's name was given as Mrs Helena Hadley.

Possibly for that reason, there were fewer press photographers than she had expected.

Jane returned to her car and sat inside to wait. She had a clear view of the entrance and at ten to ten a hearse drew up, containing a dark wood coffin and a wreath of white lilies. Behind the hearse was a black Mercedes, with an identical one following.

As the coffin was taken into the church, Arnold Hadley stepped out of the first Mercedes, accompanied, much to Jane's surprise, by Beatrice Thorpe. Hadley appeared poised and almost debonair as he proffered an arm to Beatrice, who was wearing a black figure-hugging suit over a high-necked black silk blouse, tied with a bow at the neck. She had on a small and rather fashionable black feathered hat and wore elegant black leather gloves.

Seeing them together like this, Jane started to wonder about their relationship. She quickly got out of the car and crossed the road, until she was only a few steps behind them. As they entered the church, she stepped closer.

'Good morning, Mr Hadley. You have my sincerest condolences, and those of the Metropolitan Police,' Jane said.

Hadley nodded briefly but seemed uneasy and his expression was cold. Beatrice looked surprised to see Jane. Up close, Jane thought she was wearing too much makeup, with rouged cheeks, bright red lips, heavy blue eye shadow and thick mascara on her lashes.

'My condolences to you as well, Mrs Thorpe. Is your son coming to the funeral?'

'No, he had to return to Australia on business,' she replied with a smug smile.

Hadley took Beatrice's arm and they walked down the aisle together to take a pew at the front. Jane followed, sitting down in a pew a few rows behind.

The service began, and Jane quickly looked around, noticing that there were no other mourners present. It felt like a bleak, cheerless end to a life as the minister gave a lengthy reading then asked the tiny gathering to join him in prayers before ending the service. There weren't even any hymns to raise the spirits.

'Holy Lord, almighty and eternal God, hear our prayers as we entrust to you Helena Hadley, as you summon her from this world. Forgive her sins and grant her a haven of light and peace . . .'

After the bleak service, Hadley stepped to one side to allow Beatrice to move out of the pew. As they walked towards Jane, she noticed Beatrice had unbuttoned her suit jacket, revealing three strands of pearls hanging around her neck. As she passed Jane, she gave her a small, tight smile and drew closer to Hadley. Beatrice's black-gloved hand held him possessively, almost like a claw. Jane suspected she would not be letting him go any time soon.

There was one solitary journalist waiting outside, and as Jane walked out from the church the flash of his camera was directed at Beatrice. She put her hands up in a theatrical gesture and turned away as Hadley tried to shield her. Jane took the opportunity to approach them.

'Excuse me, Mr Hadley. I wonder if I could have a quick word.'

He looked at Beatrice, as if for her approval. She nodded, saying she would wait in the car.

'I wanted to ask you about Helena's letter . . .'

'Well,' he said quickly, 'I have to say I received a rather belligerent phone call from your DCI Carter regarding that.'

Jane was surprised. 'What did he have to say about it?'

'Apparently he wanted the original for evidential purposes,' Hadley explained. But I had already taken the decision to burn it, which, needless to say, did not please him. However, I did assure him that I believed Helena's confession about the death of the baby to be true, thus allowing him to close your investigation.'

'Did he ask about the blackmail allegation?' Jane asked.

Hadley sighed dismissively. 'I assured him Helena had never said anything about it to me and that to my knowledge she had supported Beatrice and Jason financially simply because they were family. I also warned him that any public statement accusing Beatrice of blackmail, or questioning Jason's parentage, would be regarded as libellous and Beatrice would sue.'

Jane now understood why the press reports only referred to Helena's confession. It was clear Hadley had mysteriously changed his previous opinion of Beatrice, making Jane wonder if she was now blackmailing him in some way.

'Is Mrs Thorpe challenging Helena's will?'

'No. We came to an amicable agreement and she agreed not to do so.'

'Would that agreement involve helping her and Jason financially?'

Hadley didn't answer the question. 'I have a great deal of sympathy for Beatrice and her two sons. They have suffered greatly for many years and there comes a time to forgive and forget.'

Jane didn't think he sounded very convincing. 'Do you think Helena would have felt the same way?'

'Helena is no longer with us. I loved her dearly, but I'd like to think she'd agree with my decision . . . as well as yours.' He gave her a pointed look and walked away.

Jane realised Beatrice must have told Hadley what had happened at her house. She recalled Beatrice saying she was prepared to contest the will 'but not necessarily in court'. Helena gave her money to ensure her silence. Had Beatrice used a similar threat with Hadley to reach an 'amicable agreement'? If so, then ironically it had also saved Jane from being investigated for theft.

As Jane walked across the churchyard she noticed the flash of a camera aimed in her direction. The photographer approached her and took out his notebook.

'Are you family?'

'No, I am Detective Inspector Jane Tennison.'

'Then you were involved in the investigation?'

'Yes, I was. But I have nothing more to say.'

'What about that old lady's letter, and her admission about burying the baby?' the journalist asked before she could turn away.

Jane stopped. 'It was a terrible secret she kept for thirty years. However long it took, we were determined to get to the truth and have closure on the case. Thank you, I have no further comment.'

Jane walked back to her car and sat in it for a minute before starting the engine. She had just been given the perfect opportunity to explain how much she had been personally driving the investigation and how without her determination to uncover the truth about the dead child, it would have been quickly shelved. But she had finally realised that it no longer mattered. Helena Lanark had lived in torment and paid a terrible price to protect her father, one sister committing suicide and the other determined for revenge, but now it was over.

She started the engine. Every day was a learning curve, and she was more than ready to handle the other DCI Carters she knew she would come across in her career.

She was happy in her personal life, she had a newly refurbished house, and she had a feeling that the career she had feared was going nowhere was not going to stay that way for long.

ACKNOWLEDGEMENTS

I would like to thank Nigel Stoneman and Tory Macdonald, the team I work with at La Plante Global.

All the forensic scientists and members of the Met Police who help with my research. I could not write without their valuable input.

Cass Sutherland for his valuable advice on police procedures and forensics.

The entire team at my publisher, Bonnier Books UK, who work together to have my books edited, marketed, publicised and sold. A special thank you to Kate Parkin, Ben Willis and Bill Massey for their great editorial advice and guidance.

Blake Brooks, who has introduced me to the world of social media, my Facebook Live sessions have been so much fun. Nikki Mander who manages my PR and makes it so easy and enjoyable.

The audio team, Jon Watt and Laura Makela, for bringing my entire backlist to a new audience in audiobooks. Thanks also for giving me my first podcast series, *Listening to the Dead*, which can be downloaded globally.

Allen and Unwin in Australia and Jonathan Ball in South Africa – thank you for doing such fantastic work with my books.

All the reviewers, journalists, bloggers and broadcasters who interview me, write reviews and promote my books. Thank you for your time and work.

Dear Reader,

Thank you very much for picking up *Dark Rooms*, the eighth book in the Tennison series. I hope you enjoyed reading the book as much as I enjoyed writing it.

At the beginning of the book, Jane Tennison has been promoted to Detective Inspector, so I wanted to present her with a difficult and multi-layered case. When two bodies are found within an underground shelter, she is faced with the challenge of uncovering leads that were buried many years ago – and it soon becomes clear that, even thirty years later, some families will do anything to protect their secrets. With a new boss who certainly has no interest in advancing her career, Jane has to fight for the resources she needs to solve a case that some people would rather she forgot about. For me, this book showcases Jane's determination and her belief that everyone deserves justice. I also enjoyed having the opportunity to send her to Australia in search of answers – and I hope you liked reading about her travels!

If you enjoyed *Dark Rooms*, then please do keep an eye out for news about the next book in the series, which will be coming soon. And in the meantime, early next year sees the publication of the next book in my new series featuring DC Jack Warr, which I'll be sharing more information about very soon . . .

The first three books in the Jack Warr series – *Buried*, *Judas Horse* and *Vanished* – are available now. And if you want to catch up with the Tennison series, the first seven novels – *Tennison*, *Hidden Killers*, *Good Friday*, *Murder Mile*, *The Dirty Dozen*, *Blunt Force* and *Unholy Murder* – are all available to buy in paperback, ebook and audio. I've been so pleased by the response I've had from the many readers who have been curious about the beginnings of Jane's police career. It's been great fun for me to explore how she became the woman we know in middle and later life from the *Prime Suspect* series.

If you would like more information on what I'm working on, about the Jane Tennison thriller series or the new series featuring Jack Warr, you can visit **www.bit.ly/LyndaLaPlanteClub** where you can join my Readers' Club. It only takes a few moments to sign up, there are no catches or costs and new members will automatically receive an exclusive message from me. Zaffre will keep your data private and confidential, and it will never be passed on to a third party. We won't spam you with loads of emails, just get in touch now and again with news about my books, and you can unsubscribe any time you want. And if you would like to get involved in a wider conversation about my books, please do review *Dark Rooms* on Amazon, on GoodReads, on any other e-store, on your own blog and social media accounts, or talk about it with friends, family or reader groups! Sharing your thoughts helps other readers, and I always enjoy hearing about what people experience from my writing.

With many thanks again for reading *Dark Rooms*, and I hope you'll return for the next in the series.

With my very best wishes,

Lynda

TENNISON
from the very beginning

TENNISON

HIDDEN KILLERS

GOOD FRIDAY

MURDER MILE

THE DIRTY DOZEN

BLUNT FORCE

UNHOLY MURDER

and

DARK ROOMS

THE NEW PODCAST

THAT PUTS YOU AT THE

SCENE OF THE CRIME

AVAILABLE NOW